He paused mere inches away from her, and Alexandria was certain he could hear her heart pounding

The knight's gaze dropped to her lips. "I would thank you again for your assistance, Alexandria," he murmured huskily.

With fascination, Alex watched him bend toward her, sighing softly as his firm lips closed leisurely over hers. Alex shut her eyes, losing herself in the tenderness of the knight's caress. His grip tightened briefly on her waist and then he stepped away slowly.

She watched as he swung effortlessly into his saddle, turned his war-horse and rode through the gate.

Alex bit her bottom lip in consternation, realizing with a start that she didn't even know her knight's name....

Dear Reader,

Thanks to the success of our March Madness promotion during 1992 featuring four brand-new authors, we are very pleased to be able to, once again, introduce you to a month's worth of talented newcomers as we celebrate first-time authors with our 1993 March Madness promotion.

Teller of Tales by Laurel Ames. When free-spirited Jenner Page captures the eye of the bored nobleman, Lord Raines, their reckless affair causes a scandal that Regency London is likely never to forget, or forgive.

Riverbend by Mary McBride. Despite their differences, Lee Kincannon and the fiesty Jessamine Dade seem destined to cross paths at every turn, but the jaded gambler still can't believe that fate has finally dealt him a winning hand.

Snow Angel by Susan Amarillas. Katherine Thorn never expected to find herself stranded at the ranch of her unfriendly neighbor during a Wyoming blizzard, and she was even more surprised to discover that Logan McCloud was definitely not the man she thought he was.

Romance of the Rose by Claire Delacroix. Though Armand d'Avigny vowed that he would never again allow the lovely Alexandria de Fontaine to be taken from his side, Alex knew that as long as her enemy remained alive she would never be safe—even in the arms of the powerful knight.

We hope that you enjoy every one of these exciting books, and we look forward to bringing you more titles from these authors in the upcoming year.

Sincerely,

Tracy Farrell
Senior Editor

Romance of the Rose

CLAIRE DELACROIX

Harlequin Books

TORONTO • NEW YORK • LONDON
AMSTERDAM • PARIS • SYDNEY • HAMBURG
STOCKHOLM • ATHENS • TOKYO • MILAN
MADRID • WARSAW • BUDAPEST • AUCKLAND

Harlequin Historicals first edition March 1993

ISBN 0-373-28766-6

ROMANCE OF THE ROSE

CLAIRE DELACROIX

Native Canadian Claire Delacroix has a soft spot in her heart for France, having been fortunate enough to have traveled extensively there. She now makes her home in Toronto, where Claire leads a secret life pursuing graduate studies in history. In her spare time, Claire knits original sweaters, raises herbs and sings along with Freddie Mercury and Patsy Cline much to the disappointment of her neighbors.

Au revoir Viola

Chapter One

September, 1242

Armand glanced up with curiosity as a sudden shaft of sunlight cut into the dusty darkness of his father's stables. No, he corrected himself with a grimace, his *brother's* stables. Never had he understood his father's haste to give Guillaume his inheritance, the past three years having made the old man's decision even more incomprehensible.

The heavy wooden door creaked closed, shutting out the light again, and Armand straightened from brushing down his stallion, wiping the sweat from his brow as he squinted into the darkness. The rustle of fine linen and a coquettishly low laugh identified his sister-in-law's presence, the swing of her hips as she strolled toward him leaving no doubt as to her intentions. Armand gritted his teeth, barely suppressing the vulgarity that rose to his lips.

"What would you have from me, Margrethe?" he demanded sharply as he turned his attention back to his steed. A fool he had been to insist on tending the beast himself and not keeping his squire at hand. Precious little indeed had he learned in three years of staying out of the lusty Margrethe's path.

"Surely there can be little doubt in your mind of that," his brother's wife teased with a throaty chuckle. With a wry smile, Armand noted the mincing pace of her light footsteps progressing hesitantly toward him, suddenly glad that he had chosen to sweep out the stables as the last of his tasks.

The cloying scent of her perfume reached his nostrils, some southern concoction of jasmine presumably chosen to wear down his resistance, and he knew without looking that she had come to stand at the end of the stall. Annoyed at her interruption of his task, he refused to look up and acknowledge her presence, savoring some vain hope that she would take offense at his rudeness.

Margrethe allowed herself the luxury of giving her husband's handsome brother a thorough looking over, her heartbeat accelerating in anticipation. Long she had waited and plotted for this moment and nothing could foil her plans now.

A magnificent animal he was, broad-shouldered and narrow-hipped, years of sword fighting and riding having hardened his body into ripples of muscle. He worked with crisply efficient movements now, bare-chested in only his chausses and boots as he finished with his horse, his auburn hair dark with perspiration. The stall filled with the pungent mingling odors of Armand's sweat and the horse's wet coat.

All man he was, not like Guillaume, Margrethe thought, imagining those strong hands on her breasts, the long fingers curving round her nipples, and almost swooning at the sweet headiness of the thought. No doubt would a woman have that she had been sampled by this man.

Enough, she scolded herself, stepping into the stall to initiate her plan with a racing heart, casually placing her hand on the stallion's nose as she leaned forward to make her play.

Tiberias snorted and recoiled suddenly backward, his great black hip swinging precariously close to Armand, almost flattening him against the wall of the stall.

This time Armand did swear with unrestrained veracity, pressing his hands across his steed's glossy coat, locking his elbows and bracing his legs against the floor. He murmured reassuringly to the big destrier even as his temper boiled, not

doubt in his mind as to what had initiated the stallion's
bolt.

Damn fool woman! How many times had she been told
that Tiberias shied from women?

A quiver rippled down the length of the stallion's flesh as
he settled unsteadily, still stepping nervously. The beast
threw a glance over his shoulder to his master, his dark eyes
wide with an expression that seemed almost apologetic.
Armand patted the horse's rump in mute acceptance and
turned to confront Margrethe's contrived pout.

"*Madame*, many times have I bid you keep your distance from this horse," he spat harshly, his green eyes
snapping in the darkness. "As you have seen before, Tiberias has little affection for the ladies."

"Nonsense." Margrethe tossed her head indignantly and
folded her arms across her chest, pushing the fullness of her
breasts upward. She wore no wimple to conceal her throat,
leaving her lush pearly curves easily visible in the vee at the
neck of her kirtle, a vee coincidentally left unfastened to
gape artfully at her gesture.

There was no denying that his brother's wife was attractive, Armand conceded, narrowing his eyes speculatively as
he tried to guess her game this day. She removed her sheer
veil now with all the languid grace of a dancer in a tavern,
tossing the gossamer garment over the end of the stall in a
cascade of pink softness, shaking her unbraided ebony hair
into a loose fall over her shoulders. She was tall for a
woman, dark-haired and dark-eyed like most Frankish
women, but her features were well made and her figure
lushly curved.

Yet it seemed that Armand alone was aware that the
woman was wed to his brother. Never was she subjected to
an evening of her own company when her husband was
away. And no matter how outrageous her affairs or how
daring her liaisons, Guillaume remained blissfully ignorant
of his wife's activities.

Better a completely uncommitted and uncomplicated
romp with a scullery maid, to Armand's mind, than these
convoluted games of love. Margrethe smiled seductively and

he braced for another onslaught, folding his arms across his broad chest in an unconscious physical echo of his thoughts.

"Many a time have I seen your Tiberias at stud and he is more than enthusiastic at his task," she teased coquettishly, running one fingertip along the edge of the stall. "'Tis merely a prank of his to play the reluctant lover."

Margrethe leaned forward, no doubt deliberately, her dusky nipples visible beneath the gaping kirtle even in the poor light of the stables. Her eyes darkened and she took a tentative step closer to Armand as he stood impassively before her.

"They say knights have much in common with their steeds," she murmured, and advanced purposefully into the stall.

Too late Armand realized that he was cornered, Margrethe deliberately blocking his only exit from the stall. She chuckled, clearly quite pleased with her accomplishment, while Armand reconsidered the small space, calculating whether or not he could vault the wall into the next stall.

"So, you would play the reluctant right to the end," Margrethe mused. "As you wish, dear brother, I have no objection to taking what I desire."

"Noble words," Armand conceded, holding his ground determinedly and meeting her gaze squarely, "but well you know that a man cannot be raped."

Margrethe's gaze flew to his crotch as he had known it would, a frown puckering her brow at the evidence of his complete lack of arousal.

"But the scullery maids whisper of your..." Her words trailed off, her pale skin fading to an unhealthy pallor as she confronted the unwelcome possibility that he did not find her attractive.

"Very particular I am," Armand admitted in a falsely confidential tone, praying that he could maintain his relaxed state long enough to get rid of his sister-in-law. His woolen chausses were tight enough to leave nothing to the imagination and he was uncomfortably aware of Margrethe's gaze fixed there. Just thinking about it was putting his resolution to the test, and he forced himself to conjure up an image of the old woman who tended the pigs in the pasture outside the château gates.

His mind promptly betrayed him by summoning the memory of taking the lovely Roxanne in that pasture one afternoon the previous summer, and his body responded enthusiastically to the thought. He quelled his reaction with an effort, sparing a glance to Margrethe and groaning inwardly at the sparkle that appeared in her eye.

"Never fear," Margrethe purred as she pushed the wide neck of her gown over her shoulders. "I have the skill to convince you to give me what I desire." The fullness of her breasts spilled forth into the shadows, the smooth ivory softness of her skin contrasting sharply with her rough-hewn surroundings. Armand took a slow and deliberate step backward, cursing his recent chastity, knowing that he would be lost if she touched him.

Margrethe unfastened her girdle with slow precision, letting her kirtle fall to the straw in a whisper of pastel linen, a warm drizzle running through her veins at Armand's response to his first sight of her nudity. The rest would proceed exactly as she had planned. Her fingers quivered in anticipation as she reached for the horse's tether, thinking only of letting the troublesome beast out of the stall.

Tiberias went wild at Margrethe's proximity, his eyes rolling desperately as he threw his head back in an attempt to put distance between them, finally rearing up on his hind legs and giving her a dizzying view of his belly. Huge hooves arched in the air over her head and she screamed in terror, the harsh echoes of her response setting those heavy hooves to dancing and the horse himself to violent trembling.

Armand responded instinctively to the stallion's fear, flattening himself against the walls of the stall. He glanced to Margrethe and saw that she stood as motionless as a statue directly below the horse, seemingly incapable of any response other than screaming incessantly.

Immediately he saw her danger and dove toward her, the force of his leap sending them both sprawling into a fresh pile of hay and manure on the far side of the stables just before Tiberias' hooves hit the stone floor.

Armand held his breath while the stallion fought against his tether, tossing his head defiantly, snapping the leather and stamping his feet repeatedly against the stone floor. With Margrethe out of his immediate area, though, the horse was already calming down, his frenzied response slowing imperceptibly as he noisily exhaled.

Armand breathed a sigh of relief and made to stand up, surprised to find Margrethe's arms restraining him. He glanced down into the welcome in her eyes, suddenly aware that 'twas her softness tucked beneath him, not the hay, barely realizing his uncompromising position before the stable doors swung abruptly open again.

Yellow sunlight streamed into the shadowy stables and Armand squinted against the brightness, trying to identify the figure silhouetted in the doorway.

"Humph." The newcomer cleared his throat with evident embarrassment and Armand's heart sank as he recognized his father's voice. Would it be worse to rise and leave the lady's nudity exposed or to remain sprawled casually atop her?

"Now I know for certain that I am getting old," the older man mused thoughtfully after a moment's awkward silence, a thread of laughter in his tone. "I heard Margrethe scream and assumed that something was amiss."

Before the two entangled in the hay could find their voices, the older man turned to leave, pulling the door closed behind him. "Do not let me interrupt you," he concluded even as Armand struggled to his feet.

"Father, 'tis not as you think," he began to explain, and the older man paused in his retreat, turning to run his gaze over his unusually distraught son. He flicked a glance to Margrethe, who barely bothered to cover herself, her interest focused unabashedly on the young knight standing in front of her. Baudouin's heavy silver eyebrows rose thoughtfully, and his still-sharp emerald gaze locked with those eyes so like his own.

"Indeed," he admitted slowly, his voice low. "First impressions oft can lead one astray."

Father and son studied each other silently for a moment before the older man cleared his throat delicately. "The king calls for knights to battle the Normans. Perhaps you had best lead our contingent."

Armand bowed his head slowly, the vise around his chest releasing at his father's unexpected words. Baudouin had believed him.

"As you wish, Father." Armand offered his hand to Margrethe, who accepted his assistance and stumbled to her feet with bad grace.

"*Madame,* my *other* son has been seeking you quite diligently this day," Baudouin added icily. Margrethe's responding blush was visible even in the dusty shadows.

Alex paused in the midst of her toilet as the sound of her uncle's deep voice rumbled sleepily from the adjacent solar. Hastily she washed her face, quelling the temptation to listen to her aunt and uncle, knowing from experience that they were often affectionate early in the morning when they thought the household asleep. With Hugues and Michel departing this morn to answer the king's call, Alex expected that their bed would begin to squeak shortly.

Instead, Sophie's clear voice interjected, followed by more of Hugues' distinctive growl. Arching her brows in surprise, Alex quickly tugged an undyed linen shift over her head and dropped to sit on the corner of the bed while she fastened her stockings with garters below the knee.

"The child has seen her sixteenth summer!" Hugues hissed, his frustrated tones carrying clearly through the common wall between the two rooms.

Alex froze in shock, her deep green kirtle half-pulled over her head. They were talking about her! Sophie muttered an angry rebuttal and Alex found herself straining to hear the words as the finely woven linen slid over her shoulders and down to her hips.

"Hugues de Pontesse." Sophie's normally low voice became clearly audible in her annoyance. "You *promised* me that Alexandria would have the chance to choose her own husband. Would you deny that vow even now?"

"Indeed not, milady, but that was years ago when the child first came to our household. Times are changing and even you cannot deny the new way. No longer can a woman wed at her pleasure." Hugues' voice rose in frustration and Alex easily pictured him shaking one heavy finger to make his point.

"Alliances must be made, contracts sealed with blood. Alexandria's lineage is her greatest asset and I will not have that wasted on some love match with a hapless stable boy."

"Need I remind you that ours was a hapless love match," Sophie retorted coldly, and Alex stifled a giggle, Hugues' embarrassment almost tangible.

"And rare in its success it was," he finally harrumphed, returning immediately to his point. "Surprised I am that you do not flaunt Justine's foolish fancy in my face. For that was a love match, as well, was it not?" Hugues' tone was unusually harsh, bitterness ringing in his voice at the recollection of his younger sister's elopement.

"A commoner and a foreigner both," Hugues continued acidly. "Where did that lead Justine? To a life as a scullery maid when previously she had plied an embroidery needle, and only then in pleasure. Would you have such a match for Alexandria?"

"After all these years, you would take me for a fool," Sophie spat indignantly. "Justine was always an impetuous child and her choices irrelevant to the matter at hand. I only suggest giving Alex her own choice instead of a completed and signed marriage contract."

"Choice?" Hugues demanded in exasperation. "Choice? How many young knights have visited this château these last two years? And not the slightest flicker of interest from the child. Even you must agree that the time for a love match is rapidly passing."

"When you and I pledged our troth, I was three years older than Alex is now," Sophie snapped back, and Alex heard her uncle's rapid footfalls as he paced the solar in agitation.

"What will you say three years hence when Alex has made no choice? When the eyes of the young men follow your serving wenches instead of your niece?'' Hugues demanded finally, and Alex thought she heard Sophie sigh.

"You do not know what will come to pass," Sophie countered, but her voice was softer and carried no real conviction.

"No, I do not," Hugues conceded hotly, "but unlike yourself, milady, I would plan for the worst scenario. I cannot simply trust that the gods will take care of all. A man of action I am, and I will not leave this match to chance."

"I leave it not to chance but to the fates," Sophie corrected, but Hugues snorted indignantly.

"The fates?" he demanded sarcastically. "Be not a fool, Sophie. The fates and gods of old have no place in this world. No longer can you follow the old ways without consequence."

"My beliefs are mine alone," Sophie retorted sharply.

"As were Jean's," Hugues snapped, and Alex's heart leapt in recognition of her father's name, her breath catching in her throat as she strained to make out the muffled words. "A Christian true, but a knight opposed to crusading. Would you bring the misfortune of Fontaine upon Pontesse?"

"What is this you speak? The burning of Fontaine was an accident, no more, no less," Sophie returned, but her voice lacked its usual conviction.

There was a heavy pause before Hugues continued, his voice strained with emotion. "Our noble king has little tolerance for those who oppose him, a trait used to advantage by many who surround him."

Sophie cleared her throat shakily and Alex heard the bed squeak as her aunt got to her feet. "I had always thought the fire an accident," she murmured so softly that Alex barely discerned her words. Fascinated by the rare discussion of the destruction of her family home, so long ago that her escape from the burning keep with Michel remained no more than a hazy childhood memory, Alex crept forward silently, pressing her ear closer to the wall between the two rooms.

"An accident?" Hugues made an attempt to jest, the unsteadiness of his voice revealing his feelings more accurately. "What of your fates, wife, hmm?"

"You knew all along?" Sophie mused thoughtfully.

"I know not the perpetrator but a keep does not ignite alone. Great heat it takes to burn the wood structure beneath the stone." He cleared his throat roughly. "Never have I understood why Jean and Louise did not awaken, light sleepers they were both."

"There are herbs," Sophie said slowly, and Alex could almost see her uncle nod in agreement, her own mouth going dry at the implication of her aunt's and uncle's words.

"And there is gold to smooth the path. An open gate with no gatekeeper? No survivors other than the children? But we shall never know the truth of it, I fear."

Silence filled the two rooms as the three absorbed what had been said, coming to terms with it in their own minds. Had her parents been deliberately murdered? Alex was surprised to find that the idea was not so harsh a revelation as it ought to have been.

Alex easily remembered her father as an unusually articulate man, unafraid to speak his mind openly. Discussion led to informed decisions, he often said, and did not hesitate to criticize even the king and most especially the Crusades. Even as a child, she had noted that he comported himself differently than other men, and now tears rose to her eyes at the price he had paid for his outspokenness.

Jean de Fontaine had made no secret of the fact that he despised the Crusades to the East and everything they stood for, had been harshly critical of the Church for labeling those of another religion as godless infidels. Ignorance, he called it, and when prompted, he would proudly display his collection of Arabian mathematics and astronomy texts, telling evidence of the accomplishments of the race the Church was determined to extinguish.

He had named Alex for what he had called the greatest collection of knowledge of all time. The library at Alexandria, seat of Western culture, repository of ancient wisdom. Knowledge and learning lost to all these last six centuries since the library was ravaged and burned, reduced to ashes for all time.

"I suppose many women learn to love the man chosen for them," Sophie admitted halfheartedly in the next room, and Alex stood quickly, certain that she had heard enough for one day. Regardless of Hugues' plans to the contrary, Alex had no intention of submitting herself to an arranged marriage.

She scooped up her wimple, veil and fillet, resolving to tend to her headgear on the stairs. Pushing her feet into soft-soled leather shoes, she slipped quietly into the ladies' common room, carefully avoiding waking the sleeping women, and trotted down the stairs to the hall.

As she had expected, the hall was bustling with activity, the aging chatelain, Gervais, busily ordering servants this way and that. The air was filled with a mingling of the yeasty aroma of fresh bread rising in the kitchen and the heavy scent of the venison stew that simmered in a cauldron hanging in the great fireplace.

Men at arms sat at the trestle tables, fully dressed for battle, chain mail fitted across their muscled chests, close-cut tunics with short skirts bearing their colors into battle. They sipped beer and ate stew, making lewd jokes and pinching the serving women as they waited for their lord, tearing chunks of bread from day-old loaves that the cook had left out on the tables for them.

Barrels of wine were being rolled noisily into the room from the cellar by two men who joked with each other under der Gervais' frowning scrutiny. Saddlebags lay open by the hearth as women from the kitchen filled them with wineskins, hard cheeses, salted meats, dried fruits and bread.

From the courtyard came the shouts of the saddle boys and the stamping of the great war-horses as they were saddled and caparisoned in Pontesse green, the ringing of the smith's hammer telling Alex that more than one of the horses needed a shoe repaired before riding to battle.

Two more knights joined the company, striding in from the courtyard, their polished mail glinting even in the relative darkness of the hall. One threw Alex an appraising look as he removed his helmet, a twinkle in his handsome gray eyes.

Alex looked away, hoping desperately that she would not blush, uncomfortably aware of the conversation she had just overheard. Every man in the hall suddenly seemed a potential match to her and she was overwhelmingly aware of both the assessing glances they cast in her direction and the relative scarcity of women in Hugues' hall.

"Look not so sad, Alex." Michel's laughing voice came from behind her and Alex turned, her lips curving into a smile at the sight of her brother. "I am not so bad a swordsman as that," he teased, his blue eyes sparkling as he tickled her under the chin. Alex laughed and swatted his hand away playfully.

How tall Michel had grown, she thought, noticing as if for the first time his dark good looks, the broad span of his shoulders, the way he towered over her now in his eighteenth year. She noted the faint shadow of dark stubble on his cheeks and the tiny crinkles from the sun beginning to crease the skin at the corners of his eyes.

His smile alone remained as mischievous as it had been when they were children, that familiar dimple still denting his left cheek. Alex met his gaze, noting the somber expression lurking there despite his bantering tone.

"Indeed I should hope not, else Hugues has gravely erred in knighting you afore this battle," she teased.

Michel waved her worries away good-naturedly, dismissing any concerns with a wave of his hand and a quick smile. "Have you broken your fast yet?"

Alex shook her head. "I have only just risen," she explained and Michel tickled her again.

"Lazy sluggard," he jested.

"Oh, I shall not miss you," Alex taunted, her eyes twinkling as she twisted away from him. "Some woman will regret the day she wed you," she warned, wagging one finger at him in mock admonishment.

"''Tis little to worry about for now," he concluded with a philosophical grin, then offered her his hand. "Shall we break our fast together?"

"Indeed." Alex dipped her head and her brother placed her slim hand securely in the crook of his elbow, the cold steel of the chain mail impressing its rows and rows of pattern against her fingertips.

The armor reminded her more than any words of where Michel would go that day, and her fingers tightened suddenly in a spasm of fear that he would not return. Alex bit her lip, her eyes filling unexpectedly with tears. Instantly, Michel reached to cover her hand with his, his warm palm taking the chill from her fingers.

"Do not fear, Alex," he whispered so that only she could hear. "I will not leave you alone. Long ago did I make that vow and I would keep it even now."

Alex blinked back her tears resolutely, glancing up to find her brother's warm gaze upon her, easily recalling the steadiness in those clear blue eyes when he had solemnly made her that promise, a mere boy of twelve reassuring his sister as the rubble of their home hissed and glowed in the distance. She offered a tremulous smile and he grinned back, his fingers tightening over hers reassuringly.

They had no sooner sat at the head table than the arrival of the lord and lady was announced and all stood in silence. Hugues, still barrel-chested and broad-shouldered despite his advancing years and the silver in his tawny hair, the prancing unicorn of Pontesse richly embroidered on his heavy taffeta tabard and etched on the frontispiece of the helmet he tucked beneath his elbow. His armor made him appear even larger than he was, were such a feat possible, and his wife looked deceptively fragile and petite despite her height.

Sophie smiled warmly as they crossed the room, her fair skin contrasting sharply with the emerald green of her gown, its hem and cuffs finished with heavy gold embroidery. How like a doll she looked, Alex thought, admiring her aunt's willowy grace, the heavily lashed violet eyes and the soft oval of her face.

The lord and his lady advanced to the table, joining their niece and nephew, Hugues waving the company back to their meal as he and Sophie took their places. Hugues took a deep draft of wine, then leaned back with a sigh of satisfaction. Sophie tore into the loaf of dark bread set before them and Hugues cast a glance down the table.

"Good morning to you, Michel and Alexandria," he said, greeting them with a smile as they helped themselves to the morning repast. After they had returned his greeting, Hugues turned a sharp eye on Michel. "Are you well prepared for this day?"

"Indeed I am, sir," Michel responded, squaring his shoulders with pride.

"Hmm." Hugues chewed thoughtfully, his brows pulling together with a speculative frown as he swallowed. "I would think you considerably less than adequately attired."

"Sir?" Confusion clouded Michel's eyes as he looked to his uncle in surprise. Alex glanced down at her folded hands, knowing that if she met Michel's eyes now, she would give away the surprise.

Hugues chuckled softly to himself, turning an indulgent and twinkling eye on his confused nephew as he snapped his fingers to summon Sophie's ladies-in-waiting. The two women giggled and whispered to each other as they stepped forward from the shadows, each carrying a flat bundle of cloth on their outstretched hands.

Alex watched Michel's face, seeing the first flicker of recognition in his eyes as he distinguished the color of the indigo cloth. He flashed a pleased grin at Alex and she smiled back, her heart swelling with pride in her brother.

"'Tis fitting that you wear your own family's colors into battle," Hugues said softly, his voice thick with emotion, and Michel nodded in silent agreement, clearly not trusting himself to speak.

The women reached the head table and Alex slipped from her seat. Stepping forward and lifting one of the bundles, she shook out the velvet cloth and held the tunic aloft for all to see. The three fleurs-de-lis of Fontaine were worked diagonally across the front in white silk, their silhouettes outlined in fine silver thread, a traditional sprig of thyme embroidered in one corner for courage. The armholes, neckline and hem were all edged in a narrow band of white velvet, a row of silver fleurs-de-lis emphasizing the hem. Alex turned to present the tabard to Michel, pride of workmanship in her eyes.

"This you made for me?" her brother demanded, marvel in his voice, and Alex nodded quickly, a flush rising over her cheeks. Without another word, he removed the Pontesse tabard he had worn since his knighting, donning the garment bearing the Fontaine colors to the applause of the assembled company.

Alex reached up and brushed a speck of dust from the garment. Silently, Michel gripped her by the shoulders, pressing a kiss against her forehead in mute gratitude. She flushed crimson and smiled at his attention, slipping past him to return to her seat. Sophie took her place, shaking out the cloak that the other woman had carried to him, her steady gaze squarely meeting Michel's as she stood before him and fastened its silver clasp on his left shoulder.

The cloak was made of tightly woven wool, dyed indigo to match the tabard, its clasp a skillfully wrought silver fleur-de-lis. Michel bowed and kissed the back of his aunt's hand in appreciation, and Sophie reached up to pat him affectionately on the cheek as if he were still a small boy. Alex fancied she saw a shimmer of affectionate tears glaze her eyes before the older woman blinked and abruptly turned away.

Michel turned and faced his uncle, the older man's eyes gleaming with some unidentified emotion. "I thank you for the generosity of your house, milord," he said. Hugues closed his eyes and inclined his head slowly in acknowledgment.

"We shall discuss the passing of your full responsibilities to Fontaine on our return," he said, and Michel nodded before him.

"Arise, my men," Hugues called as he rose to his feet himself. "The time for riding is now upon us."

His words were greeted with rumbles of assent and the men rose noisily, donning their helmets and making their way out to the courtyard.

Alex stood with the rest, intending to see the men off in the courtyard, surprised when Michel took her hand and pulled her to a stop beside him. She glanced up to see his eyes filled with unshed tears and squeezed his fingers reassuringly.

"Thank you again for your gift," he said, his voice thick with emotion. "I cannot tell you what it means to me to wear Father's insignia into my first battle."

"'Twas Hugues' idea," she explained, feeling answering tears well up in her own eyes. "He said the Normans would well remember the house of Fontaine."

Michel smiled. "'Tis my only hope to do the memory justice."

Alex stood on tiptoe and hugged her brother impulsively. "Papa would be proud of you were you struck down this very minute." Michel's arms tightened around her in a bone-crushing hug as words eluded him.

"Godspeed to you, Michel," Alex whispered, and he nodded curtly, releasing her abruptly and striding from the hall. He paused only in the doorway to sip from the stirrup cup that Sophie offered to each man as he departed, sparing not a backward glance in his sister's direction.

"And that is the end of that," Alex stated with finality, her tone reassuring as she made the last stitch and bent over to break the length of tough vine with her teeth. The comfrey spine was sturdy and made neat work of the wound, aiding the healing with its secretions.

Alex glanced up at the young knight's face and noted that he had slipped into unconsciousness again. The flickering candlelight played over his features, curiously childlike for one who swung a blade, prompting her thoughts to return to her brother.

He was even younger than Michel, she marveled, shaking her head at the madness of it all. Alex ran a finger gently over the row of neat stitches she had made in the boy's forearm. The gash had been deep, she reflected, hoping that it would heal without any permanent damage.

"A fine job, Alexandria," Sophie commented in a warm voice beside her, and Alex smiled up at her aunt, noting the blue smudges beneath her eyes and the tiny lines of exhaustion framing her delicate mouth.

Five days had passed since the men had ridden out from Pontesse, yet there was little news of the Lord Pontesse and his party, though by all accounts the battle was said to be going well.

This night was passing in much the same pattern as the two previous evenings had done, occasional small groups of wounded men being brought in by their fellows. Some of the men in the hall now kept vigils beside wounded warriors that Alex and Sophie had already tended. Some talked quietly among themselves, others drank reflectively, the flames in the large stone fireplace casting flickering light over the faces of all.

The air was chilly for this early in the fall, the repeated opening of the door to the courtyard doing little to help the temperature inside the hall. A pot of meat stew hung over the blaze and the men who could served themselves as they arrived, hunkering down near the fire to eat. Alex flicked a glance at her aunt's tired features and touched the older woman's shoulder sympathetically. Sophie closed her fingers around her niece's hand and smiled.

"I can finish here, Sophie," Alex offered, but her aunt shook her head determinedly.

"There will be more wounded before the night is through," she said quietly, and Alex knew she was thinking of Hugues.

A bustle of activity in the doorway heralded the arrival of more men, bringing both Sophie and Alex to their feet, anxiously scanning the men's faces. Hugues and Michel were not among them and the women breathed a sigh of mingled relief and disappointment.

"Perhaps 'tis best they have not returned," Sophie commented philosophically.

"I would much rather they were not among the wounded," Alex agreed, firmly tying the ends of a cloth bandage. She flicked a glance at her aunt from beneath her lashes, catching a fleeting expression of concern on Sophie's features and admiring her strength and determination, trying to recall a single instance when Sophie had not seemed fueled by some inner and undying strength. Alex straightened from her task and Sophie gave her a purposeful smile.

"Come, Alex," she said, inclining her head toward the newly arrived injured. "Let us see what we have here."

The wounds were considerably worse this time and Alex felt the bile rise in her throat at the smell of clotting blood. Two of the six men were already dead, another one too close to death's door for Sophie to help him. She flicked a silent but meaningful glance at Gervais, who nodded quietly, immediately understanding her meaning.

The chatelain crossed himself and spoke to the assembled squires, instructing them to remove the three men, sending one to fetch the priest. Alex refused to imagine the scene behind the stables, where the fallen warriors had been taken throughout the day, and forced herself to concentrate on the men lying wounded before her.

The third man had a deep gash in his thigh and was still conscious, summoning a wan smile as the women approached. Sophie patted his hand, reassuring him that his injury was not severe and that she would be back to stitch the wound. He nodded gratefully and she suggested that he have his squire fetch him some stew.

The remaining two men were more seriously injured, and Sophie pursed her lips anxiously as she examined them. The first knight had apparently been hit in the face with a bludgeon or some similarly horrible instrument and was unconscious. Alex found it difficult to look at the torn mess of flesh that his face had become, watching her aunt's mouth set in a firm line while her gentle fingers probed a cut over the unconscious man's ear. Alex knew that head wounds were notoriously difficult to treat and often indicated internal damage that could not be remedied.

"Will he die?" Alex asked quietly, never having seen such damage to a man who was still alive. Sophie raised her slim shoulders expressively.

"It is far too soon to tell, child. The wound is not deep, so perhaps…" She gestured vaguely with one hand and her voice trailed away in uncertainty. With a sad shake of her head, Sophie got to her feet and looked down at the last man where he lay on the floor. Blood ran freely from a gaping wound in his left shoulder and his arm lay at an odd angle across the stones.

"This looks like something you can handle yourself, Alex," she stated firmly. "Tell me what you will do."

Alex knelt down beside the man and focused her attention on his injuries, lifting the broken chain mail away from his wound and wincing at the depth of the gash.

"The blood runs so freely that there may be something deep in the wound," she said quietly, touching the arm experimentally, relieved to find the flesh still warm. "His shoulder is dislocated, as well." Alex glanced up at her aunt's approving nod.

"I can do this," she asserted firmly, and Sophie smiled.

"Indeed you can, although you may need help with his shoulder," Sophie commented. "This knight is far from small of stature."

At her aunt's words, Alex glanced back at the supine knight, noticing him and not just his injury for the first time.

He would be exceptionally tall when standing, she realized, her gaze skimming the impressive breadth of his shoulders, tall and more than a little imposing. His leather-gloved hand rested on the floor near hers and Alex marveled at the difference in their sizes. Even Hugues would be dwarfed beside this giant of a man and Michel would appear as a child.

The knight's helmet had been removed, and although a mail coif still covered his head and throat, Alex could see that his expression was harshly uncompromising even in sleep. His features were well etched, evidence of a noble bloodline in the aquiline nose and high cheekbones, the square strength of his jaw, the breadth of his forehead. Russet brows and lashes gave a hint of his hair color, his deep golden skin and several tiny scars testament to his profession.

"Is his squire here?" she asked, glancing at the young men clustered at the edge of the room. At her glance, a raven-haired young boy stepped forward, nervously fidgeting with the hem of his red tabard.

Alex noted with relief that his garment sported the same leopard as the fallen knight's and that the squire looked like a strong lad, despite his evident dismay. She smiled encouragingly and the boy hastened his steps toward her.

"I will be fine, Sophie," she assured her aunt with a smile, and Sophie nodded, returning her attention to the knight with the head injury.

"Will milord live?" the boy asked anxiously as he approached, and Alex nodded firmly.

"Indeed, he will. Fully do I expect he will be shouting shortly," she commented wryly, searching her mind for something to say to comfort the boy. "It must have been quite a task for you to bring your lord this far," she added, and the boy's gray eyes flashed with humor.

"A farmer's cart I borrowed," he admitted with an engaging grin, and Alex smiled back encouragingly.

"Trust me not to reveal your means," she murmured conspiratorially, and the boy chuckled.

"Aye, much he would have to say about such undignified travel and little of it good, to be sure," the squire admitted, and Alex chuckled herself, flicking a glance at the tight line of the knight's firm lips. Precious little it took to picture his reaction to the indignity of having been hauled in a farmer's cart.

"Well can I imagine," she agreed. "I will need your help to remove your proud knight's hauberk."

"Yes, milady." The boy knelt over his lord, relief clearly clouding his thinking. Alex laid her hand on his arm to stop him.

"You cannot lift him alone," she chided gently, gesturing to Gervais and pretending not to notice the flush that rose on the boy's neck. Had he lifted this great knight into the farmer's cart alone? Few knights earned such loyalty from their squires that they would even attempt such a feat. A stern master this man might be, but undoubtedly a fair one.

Alex unfastened the knight's red cloak thoughtfully, slipping it from beneath the tall man when he was lifted up. Between Gervais and the squire, the knight was soon divested of his tunic and hauberk, the chain mail falling to the floor with a distinctive clatter. The two lowered the knight gently to his fur-lined cloak and the squire hunkered down expectantly beside Alex.

The man was not much smaller without his armor, Alex noticed, running her eyes over his well-muscled frame with admiration. Even the padded aketon he wore to shield his skin from the chain mail couldn't conceal his majestic build.

His face was turned toward her now and she glanced up at him under her lashes, feeling an undeniable attraction to his handsome features, dirty and wounded as he was. He was probably ten years her senior, she surmised, and he had spent those years living by his sword from the look of him. His auburn curls were tousled from the removal of his clothing and Alex caught herself wondering what color his eyes were.

"Will you need my help for anything else?" the squire asked quietly. Alex nodded, a slight flush rising on her cheeks as she forced her mind to return to the job at hand.

"Indeed I will. His shoulder is out of its socket," she explained, watching the boy blanch at her words and holding his gaze steadily. "It can be repaired but I will need your help to twist it back into place." The boy swallowed with visible effort, then met Alex's eyes with determination.

"Yes, milady," he said quietly, and Alex gave him an encouraging smile.

"I expect we may awaken him with this," she murmured in a confidential tone, and the boy grinned at the prospect. She bade him fetch her a bowl of hot water from the kitchens, pointing out the doorway that led there, then bent to the task of removing the aketon.

With her tiny blade, Alex cut the quilted padding of the garment from around the wound, biting her lip as she saw how the blood had dried, adhering the cotton lining to his flesh. She pulled tentatively on the aketon, wrinkling her nose in sympathy as the skin tore away with it.

There was nothing else to be done, Alex resolved. The garment had to be removed for her to work on his shoulder. She bit her bottom lip and tugged the fabric again, working it back from the wound. As she had suspected, the russet hair on his chest was dried into the blood. Reluctant to hurt him, Alex sighed and bent to her task, tugging the cloth a tiny bit at a time.

Chapter Two

A painfully repetitive tugging on his shoulder brought Armand slowly to his senses. He opened his eyes with difficulty, surprised to find a woman bent over him, biting her lip as she pulled gently on his aketon. The soft scent of roses assaulted his nostrils, and the ends of her blue veil rested lightly against his skin.

Armand flicked a quick glance around, surprised to find himself in the hall of a nameless château. He wondered absently how he had gotten from Saintes to wherever he was now, before returning his attention to the woman working on his shoulder. Finding himself unobserved, he studied her unabashedly, watching the concentration etched on her delicate features as she worked.

Her eyes were thickly lashed and filled with sympathetic concern, a tiny frown etched between her winging dark brows. Her lips were deep red and sweetly curved. The fullness of her bottom lip was pulled gently askew by a row of straight white teeth as she nibbled it in consternation, and Armand barely restrained himself from reaching up to touch the tempting softness.

The wimple that draped around her neck combined with her veil to conceal her hair and throat, leaving only the pretty smooth oval of her face exposed, but he guessed from her coloring that her hair would be dark. Judging from the size of her nimble fingers, she was a small woman, delicately built and petite. The woman pulled the aketon again and he grimaced, determined suddenly to end her torturous removal of the garment.

A shudder rippled through the man's broad frame and his hand suddenly clutched hers, stilling Alex's fingers in his powerful grip. She looked in surprise at the tanned fingers engulfing her tiny hand, her eyes flying to the knight's face. His steady green eyes regarded her calmly, a flicker of humor in their depths.

"Which way?" he demanded tersely, his voice deeply resonant. At her questioning look, he gave her a wry grin. "I would rather the task be done quickly, milady." Alex felt a telltale flush rising on her cheeks, but whether it was caused by the knight's words or his warm scrutiny, she could not have said.

"Milord!" the squire exclaimed from behind Alex with evident pleasure, his words accompanied by the sound of water splashing onto the stone floor. "I thought you dead!"

Grateful of the opportunity to escape the knight's probing gaze, Alex extracted her hand and jumped quickly to her feet, lifting the brimming bowl from the boy's hands and placing it safely on the floor.

"Not yet, Roarke," the knight responded, flicking a glance at the boy, then looking back to Alex, a smile tugging the corner of his mouth. "Although should the lady continue with her torture, I may well wish I was."

" 'Tis your shoulder, milord," the boy rushed to explain, but the man held up one hand to still his words.

"Roarke, little doubt have I that my shoulder sports the wound," he commented in deep tones, and the boy flushed, his eyes moving involuntarily to the gash. Alex cleared her throat, feeling that she had regained at least some of her composure, despite the man's unnervingly steady gaze.

"The aketon must be removed that I may work on the wound," she said quietly, and he nodded at her reasoning.

The knight took the fabric in hand and, inhaling deeply, wrenched it violently toward his waist in one smooth gesture. Alex winced sympathetically.

"''Twas preferable?'' she demanded doubtfully, and he grinned, the display of even white teeth making Alex catch her breath.

"''Twas quick,'' he conceded with a wry grin, and Alex chuckled. Her heart gave an unfamiliar lurch as those fathomless green eyes collided and locked with hers again.

What was wrong with her? Why was she so aware of this man's bare chest in a roomful of men in various stages of undress? Tearing her eyes from his with an effort, Alex dropped to her knees beside him, leaning forward to examine the wound.

"I hope the rest is as quick," she murmured. Out of the corner of her eye, Alex saw him lift one eyebrow inquiringly and she smiled ruefully in response, desperately trying to act as though touching his skin didn't remind her of stroking heavy sun-warmed satin.

"Your shoulder must be put back in its socket." He nodded in mute resignation, frowning to himself as she turned to Roarke and asked him to fetch some brandy from Gervais. Feeling as awkward as if they were alone instead of in the middle of the bustling hall, Alex refused to look down at the knight, letting her gaze run absently over the others in the hall as the silence stretched between them.

Roarke returned with Gervais in tow, the chatelain giving the flask of eau de vie directly to the knight, who took a deep swig of the liquor, wincing as the strong spirit burned its way down his throat. Alex urged him gently onto his right side, annoyingly aware of the taut muscles stretched beneath her fingertips. Ignoring the mischievous twinkle in the warrior's eyes, she firmly told Roarke to hold the wadded bandage against the wound. "''Twill bleed again as soon as I move his arm,'' she explained, instructing the boy to keep pressure on.

For a brief instant, Alex met the knight's gaze and forced her most professional smile, telling herself to concentrate on the task at hand as she knelt behind him and planted one palm firmly against the breadth of his shoulder. She grasped his elbow with the other hand, twisting his arm backward suddenly with a precise expert movement.

He inhaled sharply at her action, his entire body stiffening with the pain, even as Alex swore softly under her breath. The joint had not moved as she had hoped. She cursed her abilities silently, uncomfortably aware that she had caused him unnecessary pain by her own failure to focus on what she was doing.

Much to her surprise, he chuckled, though the sound of his humor was strained. "Such words from a lady," he chided in a hoarse whisper, and Alex flushed crimson to the roots of her hair.

"Would you like another drink?" she asked quietly, and he closed his eyes for a moment at the implication in her words. She watched his jaw tighten as he gritted his teeth before meeting her gaze steadily and shaking his head with a single curt movement.

Alex braced her knee against his back and, taking a deep breath, threw her body weight into twisting his arm once again. The knight grunted, his lips pulling back from his teeth. His eyes squeezed shut, the tendons in his neck stretching as he threw back his head and grimaced in pain.

Feeling the joint move, Alex shoved the palm of her hand hard against his shoulder, smiling with satisfaction at the distinctive sound of the joint popping back into place. She glanced down at the knight, not surprised to see that he had passed out.

Roarke proved to be a great help, fetching hot water for Alex to wash out the wound, holding his unconscious lord still while Alex ran her fingers inside his wound. She retrieved a shard of metal that might have been the tip of a broadsword blade, showing it to an astonished Roarke, who slipped the minute souvenir into his pocket.

The boy washed the dried blood from the knight's skin, a task Alex did not trust herself to do. Never had she been so aware of a man before, never so conscious of the feel of another person's skin beneath her fingers or the weight of their eyes upon her. Truly Sophie and Hugues' conversation had given a different twist to her thinking, she told herself, determined to put no more meaning in her unusual sensitivity than that.

Armand returned to consciousness through a gray mist, smiling as he felt tiny fingers pressing gently against the numbness of his shoulder. She had not yet quit his side and the realization sent a curious swell of pleasure through his frame.

He stirred slightly and at once felt the difference in his shoulder. Although it still ached, he felt the control of his arm again and knew that the joint was back in place. He opened his eyes to watch his benefactress, noticing with a smile that she immediately sensed his scrutiny. She flicked a glance to his face and he watched with fascination as a rosy blush warmed her creamy complexion.

No coquetry or contrivances from this one, he thought, surprising himself with the turn his thoughts were taking. What was he thinking? An innocent she was clearly, the daughter of a lord preserved for cementing some powerful alliance.

Not for him this one. No serving wench eager for a romp was she, and no political union had he to offer to some ambitious father. Armand frowned thoughtfully to himself, disliking his conclusions more than the fact that his heart had prompted romantic thoughts for the first time in years.

Kneeling beside the knight's chest, Alex was carefully stitching the wound closed when she felt suddenly self-conscious. Instantly guessing the reason, she glanced to his face, not surprised to find him steadily watching her once more. Alex flushed slightly under his gaze, once again painfully aware of the vital masculinity that this man exuded. He frowned and looked away, and she frantically searched her mind for something to say, certain that her blush had somehow annoyed him.

"You slept through the best part," she finally accused lightly, deciding to appeal to his sense of humor as she made the last stitch. He snorted and Alex felt his gaze on her again, curiously pleased that she had restored his good humor so easily.

"Your torture is complete?" he teased, giving her another unexpected glimpse of that devastating smile. Alex felt her insides melt, her fingers fumbling unsteadily with the knot in the comfrey spine, which she usually made quickly and easily.

"Indeed I have, sir," she answered brightly, bending out of habit to break the vine with her teeth.

Alex froze with the slim strand trapped between her teeth, her nostrils filled with the musky scent of the knight's skin, her mind drowning in the sudden realization of how close her lips were to his bronzed flesh. She flicked a glance up at his face to find him watching her avidly, a bemused smile curving his lips as he noted her discomfort.

"'Tis quite intimate, this healing," he whispered in a husky undertone that only Alex could hear, his eyes dancing with mischief.

Disappointment flooded her heart at his jest. She was acting the fool, believing this man to be flirting with her. 'Twas clear he thought her no more than a child. Alex reddened in embarrassment at finding herself the brunt of his joke and his lips curved into a self-satisfied grin.

Unaccountably annoyed, Alex bit the vine, giving the end a little tweak with her teeth before releasing it. The knight inhaled sharply, then chuckled softly at her response.

"Roarke, help your lord to rise," she said curtly, pushing away from him and turning her back. No more would she be a target of his jest.

Alex composed herself while she cut a length of clean cloth, then knelt beside the knight again, occupying her attention with the task of binding his shoulder and determinedly ignoring the speculation in his eyes.

The moments stretched between them and it became clear that the woman would not look at Armand, much less continue their conversation. Perhaps he had been too quick to conclude that she had no games to play. His eyes narrowed speculatively as he watched her complete her ministrations.

His expression softened as her nimble fingers made short work of the bandage, his eyes noting the unmarred softness of her complexion. Young she was, and sheltered. Perhaps she was merely unaccustomed to the bluntness of men like himself. Long it had been indeed since he had seen maidenly shyness.

She knotted the ends of the linen bandage and would have moved away but Armand caught her hand in one lightning-quick movement, his fingers closing around hers tightly so that she could not pull away. The open fear that flashed through her eyes at his touch convinced him he'd been right, and the urge to fold her into his arms stunned him. Instead he limited himself to smiling reassuringly into those wide blue eyes, his tired body leaping to life when her full lips parted, unconsciously inviting the caress he suddenly longed to give her.

Alex's hand was lost in the warm expanse of the knight's palm but the sensation was far from unpleasant.

"I would thank you for your assistance, milady," he murmured quietly. Lifting her hand to his mouth, he brushed his lips across the back of her hand, sending a deliciously secretive quiver down Alex's spine.

The knight's eyes darkened and he turned her tiny hand over, pressing a kiss against the sensitive skin inside her wrist. Alex shivered openly in response to his gesture, pulling her hand abruptly from his warm grip.

"'Twas nothing," she said hastily, pushing to her feet and brushing off her kirtle.

"'Twas considerably more than nothing, milady, and I shall not forget it," he assured her quietly, surveying her from the stone floor before he also pushed to his feet.

He did indeed make an imposing figure, Alex admitted as she tipped back her head to hold his gaze. The knight towered easily over the other men assembled there and Alex felt a rush of possessive pride at his stature, immediately scolding herself for the inappropriate turn her thoughts had taken.

As if he sensed the tumult of her emotions, the knight watched her steadily, his eyes filled with that now familiar warm bemusement. Roarke brought him a shirt and he tugged it over his head, his gaze leaving Alex's face for only the briefest moment.

Alex marveled at his strength so shortly after his wound
had been tended. If she had not stitched the cut herself, she
would never have believed him the same man who had lain
unconscious just half an hour earlier.

"Alexandria?"

Armand watched her turn at the sound of another woman's voice, unable to prevent a satisfied smile from stretching across his lips.

Alexandria. Now he knew her Christian name at the very
least.

She was as tiny as he had imagined, he observed with
pleasure. The draping of her purple surcoat and deep blue
kirtle did little to conceal the delicacy of her tiny figure.
Lovely, shapely, innocent, possessed of healing skills and a
gentle sense of humor. A fine wife Alexandria would make
some lucky man.

"You appear to have accomplished quite a healing here,"
the other woman commented with amusement, and Armand watched that enchanting flush rise over Alexandria's
features once again. Her innocence fueled some long-
forgotten protective urge within him, an urge that made him
want to shelter her within his arms from all the evils of the
world. What foolish thoughts were these? he chided himself, surprised to hear such poetry come from his own normally matter-of-fact mind.

"Indeed, *madame,* I feel strong enough to return to
Saintes this very night," he confirmed as the older woman
stepped toward him, an assessing glint in her eye.

"Not so quickly, young man," she chided, craning her
neck to fix him with a reprimanding glance. Tall and slender as a reed, this healer was, willowy and blond. Unless
Armand missed his guess, the two women were not blood.
"I would check my apprentice's work. Let me see your
shoulder."

Armand removed his shirt amiably, wry amusement
curving his lips at the woman's authoritative attitude.

She stood on tiptoe and examined her apprentice's even
stitching with a frown. "Did you clean the wound?" she
demanded sharply.

"There was a shard of metal lodged there, as we suspected," Alexandria responded quietly, examining the toe of her shoe with apparent interest.

The older woman nodded without surprise. "Any infection?"

"None. I rinsed the wound out with witch hazel to prevent any from developing."

"And a fine job you have done, child. Find Lisette and have her prepare more clean linen for bandages."

Alexandria dipped her head obediently and turned away without sparing the knight another glance.

"Would that all should learn the old ways so easily," the woman commented under her breath, tossing her retreating assistant a pleased look over one shoulder. Armand snorted at the familiarity of the sentiment and she fixed him with a sharp glance.

"An avid Christian, are you then?" she asked, but Armand shook his head with a chuckle, his eyes tracking the progress of one slim figure across the room even as he spoke.

"Not with a father who so looks forward to dancing on Winter Eve," Armand admitted under his breath, and the healer grinned as she ran her fingers over the knight's shoulder.

"A joy it is to hear of one who savors the old ways. No *Toussaints* for we old ones," she said, sneering slightly over the new name the Church had given to the old feast day. "Change our holidays into theirs, they do, and call us the uncivilized ones," she continued under her breath as she pressed the joint experimentally, nodding as she noted it back in place.

"Be we so uncivilized, why must they steal our feast days, our holidays, our customs and rituals? Always had I understood mimicry to be flattery in bright clothes," she concluded archly. Armand raised his eyebrows, declining to comment, and the woman sighed with resignation.

"Clever you are indeed to hold your own counsel in these times." She smiled ruefully. "Sadly 'tis not a trait I possess. In my birthplace, the very kings themselves practice the old ways and there is no price to be paid for professing that one follows the traditions of the past."

Sensing that the knight had no intention of joining the conversation, the healer stepped away with a philosophical shrug and raised her voice with authority.

"Lift your arm," she commanded, and Armand did so, moving his fingers as she demanded until the woman tilted her head to one side and fixed him with a steady glare. "You will not return to Saintes this night," she insisted firmly, and Armand grinned openly.

"And you will go to Mass," he retorted as he tugged on his shirt again, drawing a chortle of laughter from the blond woman.

"A fortnight without battle," she decreed, trying for a second time to admonish him, but Armand just threw back his head and laughed in his turn.

"We are at war, milady," he maintained quietly when he sobered, holding up his hand when the healer opened her mouth to protest. "The king has summoned all who can ride to Taillebourg. I would not refuse my liege lord."

The woman closed her mouth with a snap, evidently displeased with his assertion but recognizing that she would not change his mind. "You will doubtless do as you will, milord. Take care lest your wound become infected."

"If perchance it does, I will know exactly where to come for assistance," Armand answered smoothly, flicking a warm glance at Alexandria, where she spoke to a serving woman by the fire.

"Indeed." The woman followed his gaze, and Armand watched her eyes narrow speculatively as the younger woman sensed their scrutiny and her color rose yet again.

"Take care lest you be misunderstood, milady," Armand counseled the healer softly, drawing her attention back to him. "Times change even as we speak." She nodded once in thoughtful acknowledgment of his warning, abruptly fixing that bright gaze upon him once more.

"What would your father's name be?" she demanded sharply.

Armand hesitated for an instant, realizing that he had revealed much of his father's activities, activities frowned upon by both church and state. The woman's eyes were devoid of malice, though, and he found himself trusting her, recalling how his father loved to hear of others still following the old faith.

"Baudouin D'Avigny," he responded, but the woman slowly shook her head with evident regret, the brightness in her eyes fading at his words. 'Twas as he suspected, Armand concluded to himself, wishing his father's name could have brought her some small pleasure.

"I know him not," she admitted, forcing a smile to her lips through her disappointment. "But no matter. My regards to your father and his health."

Armand inclined his head politely, then lifted his eyes to watch Alexandria for a moment while she fidgeted uncomfortably, finally glancing up. He smiled slowly in an attempt to reassure her and she smiled tremulously in return, her hands interlocking tightly before her.

The sounds of more knights arriving in the hall carried from the portal when Armand might have stepped toward Alexandria, and his lips thinned when she tore her eyes away from his. He watched the two women stretch on tiptoe to scan the arriving company with anticipation, noting Alex's avid interest with disappointment. So, she anxiously awaited the return of another man. He had been unrealistic even to consider that such a lovely woman would be without prospects.

Summoning Roarke with a curt gesture, he had the squire help him into his torn aketon and hauberk. Finally pulling the tabard emblazoned with his family coat of arms over his head, he winced as the stitches in his shoulder pulled. He wished an abrupt good-evening to the older woman, who in turn wished him godspeed, and strode purposefully from the hall.

Alex watched the tall knight depart with disappointment welling up in her chest. Why had his manner changed so abruptly? Had she completely misread his interest in her?

"I think I will take a breath of air," she murmured, turning away from her aunt's perceptive gaze and walking toward the door to the courtyard before she could change her mind.

She paused on the step in the doorway, watching as Roarke saddled his master's horse with efficient gestures. The knight buckled on his sword himself, apparently unimpeded by his injury, his broad frame silhouetted against the flickering lamps of the adjacent stables. Alex stood silently in the shadows, wishing she knew what had happened to change his attitude back in the hall.

"Excuse me, milady," a knight said behind her, and Alex stepped aside with an automatic smile, the tingle of awareness at the back of her neck telling her that her knight had looked up and seen her. She glanced toward him to find his eyes on her, his expression inscrutable.

They stood silently regarding each other for a long moment, then he stepped toward her as if he would speak. Alex's heart beat a staccato against her ribs as she watched him approach, her breath catching in her throat as he grew nearer.

He paused mere inches away from her and Alex was certain he would be able to hear her pounding heart, but she did not move away. His gaze dropped to her lips and they parted of their own accord, the night air seeming to heat around the two of them as they stood silently confronting each other.

Alex felt one leather-clad finger fit itself under the palm of her hand and the knight took a step backward, his smoothly encased fingers closing around her own as he led her away from the door. Without a second thought, she followed him until he paused a few steps from the busy portal, instinctively knowing he would not hurt her.

"I would thank you again for your assistance, Alexandria," he murmured huskily, her name on his lips making her heart leap to her throat. With fascination, she watched him bend toward her, her knees trembling as she realized his intent, sighing softly as his firm lips closed leisurely over hers.

Alex closed her eyes with pleasure, losing herself in the tenderness of his caress, leaning against the knight's broad chest as she found herself unwilling to trust her quivering legs. Sensing her unsteadiness, he spread his hands across her narrow waist, his fingers fanning to support her back as she arched to meet him, her body intuitively responding to the steady pressure of his lips moving against hers.

The world tipped and fell away, leaving nothing but the lazy caress of the knight's mouth slanted across hers, the combined scents of his skin, his mail, the wind and horse-flesh in her nostrils, the steady grip of his fingers spanning the back of her waist.

When his tongue meandered between her lips, a warning shiver tripped along her spine, the abrupt sensation recalling Alex to her senses. She pulled away hastily, her breathing ragged, and spared a glance upward. A muscle tensed in the knight's jaw, and his nostrils dilated sharply as he steadied his own breathing. Her heart soared at the realization that he had also been affected by their embrace, and he glanced down at that moment, his eyes warm with some unspoken emotion.

His grip tightened briefly on her waist before he stepped away and offered her his hand. Alex swallowed with difficulty and placed her hand in his, letting him escort her back to the door while she fought to make some sense of her tumultuous response to even the touch of his hand.

"Lady Alexandria?" A knight stepping into the hall caught himself in surprise, recognizing Alex in the shadows as he made to step into the château.

Alex flicked a disinterested glance at the man, recognizing him as one of Hugues' vassals. She responded politely as she climbed the step, her eyes returning to the tall knight, who now stood just to her left in the courtyard below, the expression in his green eyes unfathomable, her fingertips still trapped within his.

"I passed Michel on the road, milady," the man continued, and Alex spun to face him anxiously.

"He is unharmed?" she demanded, her breath caught in her throat, the knight at her side momentarily forgotten in her desire for news of her brother.

The man nodded reassuringly, his lips curving into a tolerant smile. "Indeed, milady. He and Lord Hugues ride together and should arrive shortly."

"I would thank you for this news," Alex stammered, grasping the man's strong hand with gratitude as tears of relief filled her eyes. The knight waved her off with a smile and a bow, ducking into the light of the château.

She turned back to the tall knight again to share her news, surprised to find him gone.

Alex quickly picked out his form across the courtyard as he swung effortlessly into his saddle, turning his war-horse adroitly and riding through the gate, seemingly unaware of her presence once more. Alex bit her bottom lip in consternation, realizing with a start that she didn't even know her knight's name.

Not until dawn two days after the tall knight had left did Hugues and Michel return to Pontesse, Hugues' triumphant shout bringing the entire household out to the courtyard at a run.

Unscathed and high-spirited, the two were filled with enough tales of the victories at Saintes and Taillebourg to entertain the entire company throughout the morning. Large quantities of ale were hauled to the trestle tables in the hall, the sounds of food being prepared hurriedly and the smell of baking bread carrying from the kitchens to the assembled company as they laughed, gasped and held their breath in turn as Hugues' resonant voice echoed through the hall.

Once assured that Michel was safe, Alex found herself unable to concentrate on her uncle's stories, her mind wandering off in idle daydreams. Her thoughts had immediately returned to the tall knight and she found herself praying that he too had left Taillebourg unscathed.

"And now Michel has something to tell you all," Hugues' voice boomed, shaking Alex from her thoughts as her uncle stood and gestured proudly to his nephew. "Tell them, boy."

Michel stood up slowly, more self-conscious than his uncle before the entire company. He flicked a glance to Alex, meeting her eyes for an instant as if in warning before tipping his chin proudly and addressing the crowd. Alex's heart began to pound in trepidation.

"I have sworn my blade to the Crusades," Michel declared, and Hugues' household broke into cheers and applause.

The Crusades! A rejection of everything their father had believed. Foolhardy nonsense, she could still hear Jean's voice booming in the hall at Fontaine as he argued, and truly so many left for the East and so few returned. With an effort, Alex forced herself to admit that her father would have honored Michel's right to his own decision. Fighting back her tears, she forced a confident smile to her lips as Hugues jubilantly passed her the chalice to drink Michel's health.

A welcome sight was Avigny's round keep on the horizon to Armand's exhausted mind and body. He urged his great destrier forward, the beast more than willing to comply as he sensed the proximity of familiar stables. The other knights sworn by Avigny to the king's calling had fallen far behind since they had ridden out of Provins, but being so close to home and the king's own demesne, Armand knew that no harm would come to them.

"Hold up, milord!" Roarke shouted from behind, and Armand grinned at the boy's clattering as he strove to keep close behind.

"To the gate we race," he shouted jubilantly over his shoulder, momentarily forgetting the complications of his father's home in his desire to talk to the old man.

The Lady Alexandria's image had haunted Armand's thoughts these last few nights, the recollection of those wide blue eyes forcing him to question the harshness of his conclusion that evening, demanding that he reexamine the circumstances that left him unable to wed.

The memory of how she had sweetly returned his kiss made him feel more lighthearted than he had in years, impulsive and carefree. No manner was it for a grown knight, but a refreshing change he found it indeed. Armand allowed himself the luxury of optimism for the first time since he could remember, his heart unusually determined that there be some path to the result he desired, however tortuous that path might be. Baudouin might well have an idea or two.

"Hah!" Roarke laughed at his knight's jest. "No match is this poor palfrey to that beast of yours. Ill-advised would I be to take such a wager!"

"No wager," Armand conceded with a wink. "And I will hold this beast of mine back."

"To the gate, then!" Roarke dug his heels into his mount eagerly, his laughter filling the air in his wake as he darted past Tiberias. Armand had no need to urge the great black destrier forward. Sensing a run and the comfort of home, Tiberias was hot on the heels of the smaller gray beast in an instant.

"You urge him forward," Roarke accused laughingly as the bigger horse pulled alongside.

"I do nothing of the kind," Armand denied, shouting over his shoulder as Tiberias galloped to the gates, the reins lying slack on the saddle. Seized by a curious playfulness, he straightened his legs out to either side, demonstrating to his squire that he did not use his spurs on his mount.

Roarke laughed loudly at Armand's antics until he coughed and lolled helplessly in his saddle. Stifling a mischievous grin, Armand pulled Tiberias up short just before the gate, letting his squire catch up before they entered the gates, both beasts and men short of breath from their frivolity.

"High time you managed to find your way home again," Guillaume commented sarcastically, his hands perched on his hips as he awaited his brother in the outer bailey. Armand flicked his elder brother a curious glance as he dismounted, wondering what had stirred his ire this time.

"As doubtless even you can see, we have ridden with haste, Guillaume," he retorted sharply, gesturing to the sweat on the horses' flanks and their accelerated breathing. He paused to stroke his destrier's nose, ignoring his brother's stormy countenance.

Guillaume stepped forward quickly, surprising Armand as he snatched Tiberias' reins from his hands and thrust them toward a groom. Tiberias snorted at the indignity of this abrupt handling but permitted himself to be led away. Armand raised one eyebrow inquiringly at his brother's hostile glare and Guillaume swore vehemently under his breath.

"Care you for nothing other than that faithless beast?" he demanded curtly, and Armand smiled dryly, the object of his earlier thoughts drifting into his mind's eye again.

"A few things," he conceded good-naturedly. "What troubles you, Guillaume?"

"Milord!" Guillaume corrected in an annoyed undertone. "How many times must I remind you to address me as your liege lord."

Armand's face closed in stony withdrawal, his eyes narrowing and his voice dropping to a growl. "Remind me as often as you will, brother, but do not expect to hear the words fall from my lips ere our sire draws breath." He watched the color drain from Guillaume's features with satisfaction, ignoring the gleam that came into the shorter man's eyes.

"My blade is pledged to him and thence our king alone," Armand continued coldly, "and that you would do well to recall."

"You would do well to guard your tongue, brother," Guillaume warned. "The time of which you speak rapidly approaches."

Armand's jaw tightened as he immediately realized the import of his father's absence in the bailey. "Where is he?" he demanded harshly, and Guillaume jerked his head toward the keep.

"In his rooms, where he has remained these eight days."
Guillaume paused and fixed Armand with a coldly assessing look. "The old man insists on speaking only to you."

Without further word, Armand turned and strode quickly to the keep, his desire to see his father redoubled with Guillaume's news.

Baudouin lay propped up among the pillows of his bed, his hair starkly white in the darkness, his pallor scarcely better. When bidden, Armand advanced into the room, his pace slow as he noted suddenly the evidence of his father's age. Always he had thought his father invincible, a great knight victorious in battle, and it was disconcerting now to think of the old man becoming weaker, unthinkable to imagine Avigny without him.

"Old man," the two boys had called him in jest when his auburn hair had transformed to white almost overnight, but Baudouin had swung a mighty broadsword even in those days.

"You are ill, milord?" he asked quietly, and Baudouin turned to watch his son's progress into the room, his eyes bright with interest.

"Not enough that I cannot stand the strength of a man's voice," Baudouin retorted, his words bringing a wry smile to Armand's lips. He perched on the edge of his father's bed, removing his helmet and coif, dropping both to the floor as he ran tired fingers through his hair.

"What ails you, then?" he demanded more sharply, and the older man chuckled in turn.

"Ever a miser for words, you were, boy." He shook his head, pulling himself up to a sitting position without apparent difficulty, his eyes gleaming in the darkness. "How went the battle?"

"Better than expected."

"Hah." Baudouin's eyes glinted and he nodded with satisfaction. "Gave that Henry something to think about. Heartily do I approve of that."

Armand smiled at his father's enthusiasm. "As did Louis, I am certain," he conceded, not missing the older man's sharp look.

"You were hurt?"

"A trifle." Armand tried to dismiss his injury but Baudouin would have none of it, insisting that he be shown the wound.

"Otherwise I have no knowledge that you have had it tended," he maintained while Armand removed his tunic and hauberk, sparing his father a baleful glance. The old man pointed an accusing finger in his direction as he removed the patched aketon. "Or had some useless squire tend to it for you. Well do I remember that incident and the scar you bear from that foolishness. A competent healer could have left your flesh unblemished."

"As this one has?" Armand asked mildly, sitting back on the side of the bed and shaking his head at his father's low whistle of admiration.

"Woman's work, this," he declared, tapping his son's bare shoulder knowledgeably and fixing him with a piercing stare. "Comely she must have been for you to have tolerated her tending."

Armand felt his color rising and he deliberately avoided his father's knowing eyes. "Little choice had I in the matter. Roarke dragged me from the field and pressed me into her care."

The older man's lips twitched at this confession but he wisely did not comment further. "A toilsome burden it is to bear a woman's gentle ministrations," he agreed simply, and Armand glanced at him sharply, sensing his father toyed with him but finding the old man's expression deceptively bland.

Armand frowned at the floor, trying to find the words to ask his father's counsel without actually speaking of this foolishness in his heart and mind. He looked up to find Baudouin fighting to suppress a grin, eyes twinkling as he leaned expectantly back against the pillows.

"Much taken with her, were you?" the older man demanded, and Armand nodded in relieved agreement. "No burdens have you, boy, and a strong warrior, too. With your blade, you could earn enough to support a modest home and a wife. Gladly would I support such a union.''

Armand nodded and turned to face the expanse of the room, dropping his elbows to rest on his knees, considering his hands thoughtfully as he intertwined his fingers. "Of noble birth, she is," he admitted in a low voice, his heart sinking as Baudouin tut-tutted under his tongue.

"Any brethren?"

"I know not."

"A different tale that be, indeed," the older man agreed with a frown, tapping his fingers impatiently on the side of the bed. "Has she a betrothed?"

"I know not," Armand conceded with a sigh, feeling his newfound optimism slip away with his father's unconcealed disappointment. He pushed to his feet and paced the length of the room and back, the sound of his footfalls and Baudouin's tapping fingertips filling the silence between them.

"What ails you so that you spend eight days in bed?" Armand demanded abruptly when he reached the side of the bed again. Baudouin shrugged.

"I tire of the company," he said unexpectedly, and Armand laughed aloud in his surprise, the rich timbre of his voice echoing in the small room.

"Indeed? Have you told Guillaume of this?"

"Bah." Baudouin waved the thought away dismissively. "No care does he give to anything other than his own importance. And that wife." The older man rolled his eyes emphatically. "A sorry day 'twas for the lot of us the day she crossed the threshold. Know you that the woman cannot even candy elecampane," he demanded incredulously, shaking his head as Armand grinned. "So hard she makes it, I fear to break a tooth, and I have precious few to spare these days. 'Tis a sign of inadequate breeding, no doubt."

"To poorly make confections?" his son asked doubtfully, and Baudouin nodded with assurance, drawing a soft chuckle from Armand.

"Most definitely. Take care to avoid that trap yourself, lest you rue the day you slip a ring on some pretty maid's hand."

"I shall remember that," Armand responded, his grin fading as his father's words recalled Alexandria's unavailability to him.

"Bored I am with the lot of them," the old man complained testily, warming to his theme. "And nary a grandchild to be found. Does he not bed the woman?" Baudouin demanded of his younger son in exasperation, while that son stubbornly maintained his silence.

"Not for convenience did I so willingly abandon the lord's solar. Thought I to see my line continued before my very eyes and children to bounce upon my knee in my winter years." The older man sighed with discontent and folded his arms across his chest. "Glad I am that Elise did not live to see this sad day."

Armand pursed his lips and studied his toe. "You miss her?" he asked in a low voice, but the question was more a statement of fact.

Baudouin nodded slowly, the droop of his mouth making him look older than his years. "Blood of my heart, she was," he confessed under his breath, turning to watch the flames dancing on the hearth with apparent interest.

Armand studied his father's averted profile for a long moment, his mind filtering through what precious few memories he had of his mother. He watched Baudouin's gnarled fingers curl against the wool of the coverlet and reflected that it had been long indeed since Elise's laughter graced these halls. A mere boy he had been when she had taken the ague, and sadly his memories of her grew fainter as the years slipped away.

On impulse, he reached and closed his hand over his father's wrinkled one, surprised when the hand beneath turned over and clutched at his strength.

The winter sun had barely managed to tinge the eastern sky when Alex heard the first men arrive in the stables to saddle their steeds. Fearful that she would be discovered, she

held her breath, waiting patiently among the bales of hay as
she had most of the night, biding her time until enough
knights and squires had assembled that she could slip undetected into their midst.

Alex had not needed to ask to know that she would be
forbidden to accompany Michel. Too many horror tales had
she heard of men abandoned to die beneath the desert sun,
their injuries minor but the lack of healers rendering them
fatal. She could not let Michel and these men that she had
known since childhood ride to certain death when she could
so easily make a difference to their survival.

Admittedly, her reasons were not all altruistic. Days of
embroidery, hours of tending Sophie's herbs, the prospect
of an arranged marriage to some wealthy old man; a month
ago this scenario had been enough to look forward to, but
not anymore. Alex's brief encounter with the tall knight had
tantalized her, hinting of an outside world she had not experienced, tempting her to taste adventure instead of settling easily into the security of hearth and home.

So she perched in the last stall of the stable in her pil-
fered boy's clothing, listening to the growing crescendo of
voices, hoping that the pounding of her own heart did not
give her away. Alex knew which horse she would saddle with
which trap, her mind reviewing each motion so that her in-
experience would not draw anyone's attention.

Michel would be furious when he discovered her, of that
much she was certain, but if she could remain undetected for
a day, maybe two, they would have gone too far for him to
turn back. And he would never dare to send her home on the
treacherous road alone.

The day had fully dawned when Alex finally slipped into
her saddle, keeping her head down even within the pack of
young squires. The knights were mounted already, their mail
gleaming in the cold light, their destriers' breath making
white clouds as they pranced restlessly. Alex's heart was
beating a merry staccato, jubilantly proclaiming her success in remaining anonymous. She inhaled deeply and ex-

haled slowly to calm her jangled nerves, resisting the urge to adjust the unfamiliar coif and hat.

"Onward!" shouted Michel from near the gate, and Alex glanced up to see him wave the party forward, two squires at the front hoisting pennants of Fontaine into the breeze. The sun broke out from behind a low cloud, its rays glinting off the silver gleam of polished mail, the points of sharpened lances and winking jewels embedded in lavish scabbards.

As if anticipating his run, Alex's gray tossed his head defiantly, his nostrils flaring as he jostled against the others and moved forward. As she reached the gate, Alex threw one last glance over her shoulder to the portal where Gervais and Hugues stood, her heart stopping dead in her throat when she found Sophie's steady gaze locked upon her.

Alex felt the color drain from her face, but her aunt shook her head imperceptibly in reassurance, mouthing two familiar words of encouragement. Before Alex could respond, her horse was through the gate, the stone wall blocking her view of her aunt more effectively than the unruly tears that had suddenly risen to her eyes.

The horses' hoofbeats echoed hollowly on the cobblestones that extended out the gate, then were muffled on the dirt track that began just outside the château walls. As they reached the road, Michel's warhorse instinctively began to canter, then started to run, the other horses following his lead, the entire party passing through the awakening valley of Pontesse like the summer wind running through the grass.

Blessed be, Alex repeated in her mind, hugging her aunt's words to her heart. Blessed be.

Chapter Three

Jerusalem, August, 1244

Armand wiped the sweat from his brow and surveyed the neat columns of figures he had made. He threw a glance at the arched windows, hating the arid heat that crept in from the outside, the dust that rose from the streets below, his only consolation being that he did not wear his heavy hauberk in the scriptorium.

A fool he had been to dream of glory in the East. A year in the land of the exotics had brought no more than ceaseless heat, endless flies and the yoke of uncompromising boredom. Impulsively indeed had he tossed aside the life he knew, that one spark of youthful vitality that had flickered in his heart swept away by the sobering of his father's face when Armand had mentioned that Alexandria was of noble birth.

He had thought himself frustrated then, uncertain when or even if he would be permitted to marry, not knowing whether he would look forward to a hearth of his own. Margrethe had unwittingly expedited his decision, cornering him in his bath with her provocative nonsense.

'Twas with some embarrassment that he recalled losing his temper now, tipping the tub in his haste to escape her, bellowing for Guillaume and Roarke, losing his footing on the slickly wet stone floor. Indeed he had made a fine spectacle of himself. Perhaps the embarrassment of confronting servants and family alike sprawled on his bare backside had also contributed to his impulsive announcement that he would join the Knights Templar.

Never would Armand forget the look on his father's face as the words fell from his lips, the way the old man's mouth had drawn to a thin line, the brief glimpse he had had of the disappointment clouding Baudouin's eyes. But once uttered, such a vow cannot easily be withdrawn, especially when it has been made in front of so many.

And so, Armand had made his way to Provins the next day, the heady scent of damascus roses reminding him of wide blue eyes as he sought the Temple and requested admission to the Order. A fitting choice, his joining the Order had seemed, taking a vow of chastity when the lady who haunted his dreams could not be his. Shortly thereafter he had donned the white tunic with its distinctive red cross and traveled east to Jerusalem with a party of brother knights.

Never having thought particularly about other people and their society, Armand was surprised to find how much he missed Roarke's hearty laughter, the bite of a robust wine in his throat, the conversational patter surrounding him as he dined among his peers.

But there was none of that here in the Temple. Conversation during meals was against the Rule. As was almost everything else. He for one was heartily sick of the Rule, sick of his twenty-six Paternosters before dinner, sick of being trapped within these four walls and scribbling in a ledger.

For that was the crux of it. He was cursed by his father's ''gift'' of literacy.

Precious few there were indeed among the Templars who were literate, who were capable of knowing or even guessing what this intricate ledger of notes and loans had to say. A poorly educated lot of warriors they were, and here, at the Temple of Solomon, the center for the order's business affairs, Armand had been pressed into service as an accountant.

'Twas not the task he had envisioned for himself when he joined the Order. On better days, he could see the humor in the situation, but of late, those days had been few and far between. Armand's patience was wearing thin.

He had not expected the myriad tales of failure, the treachery, the inability of these supposedly elite knights to complete the most elementary sortie with success. It chafed him that he could not lend his blade to the foray when he heard these tales, infuriated him that as a Templar he was expressly forbidden from contributing to their military might. A waste of his experience it was, his experience and knowledge and expertise.

Still worse, of late he had begun to wonder whether the Templars were truly interested in winning military battles in the Holy Land, and this treacherous thought made him deeply uneasy. If the Templars were here to repossess the Holy Land, as they maintained, why had they spent the last century losing almost every significant battle in which they engaged? Something, somewhere, didn't add up.

Armand ran his fingers through his hair, frowning as he picked up the next contract, surveying the numbers at the bottom with a grimace. Yet another poorly handled transaction by another near illiterate. He cleared his throat and beckoned to the Grand Master of the Temple, who was working nearby.

"I fear we must summon Bertrand of Avignon and settle this debt," Armand explained, indicating the contract with one finger. The Master studied the document over his shoulder, shaking his head with a frown.

"I do not see your point, Brother," he confessed mildly, throwing Armand a vaguely puzzled glance.

"But, sir, the gentleman retrieved less than half the money he entrusted to us for passage to Jerusalem," Armand insisted, his heart sinking when the Master's expression did not change. It was another one of *those* deals, something in the ledgers that didn't add up.

"Certainly, the remainder is our fee," the Master responded sharply, his mouth thinning to a hard line as his tone became reprimanding. "Surely I do not have to explain this to you again, Brother."

"Indeed not, sir, but well you know that I can only list a tenth of the total per annum as a transportation fee," Armand responded coolly, daring to meet the Master's eyes in challenge. "More than that would be usurious and, I believe, against the Rule, not to mention the dictate of Rome."

The Master's eyes narrowed and he deliberately placed his hands flat on Armand's desk, leaning forward menacingly as he bit out his words. "I *know* the Rule, Brother, and you would do well to remember its teachings yourself."

Armand gritted his teeth. It was time he aired his suspicions. "This is a scandalous amount of money," he charged softly, tapping the blunt end of his fingertip against the offending document, "and sadly not the first I have seen."

"Far be it for you to comment on our business transactions. I notice your horse eating well in the stables below and your countenance promptly appearing at the board thrice daily," the older man hissed, and Armand thrust to his feet.

"'Tis an aberration of our oath and well you know it," he spat back, keeping his voice below a shout with an effort. Other brothers at work in the scriptorium flicked surreptitious glances at the heated exchange, maintaining the outward appearance of industriousness while they strained to hear the tersely bit out words.

"Consider it a donation to the cause," the other man responded, and Armand snorted derisively, shoving his ledger aside with open disdain. Another brother gasped at his audacity and the Grand Master shot a quelling look across the room.

"Opportunists you are, one and all," Armand sneered. "This is not a crusade to regain the Holy Land but a campaign to empty the pockets of Europe! Perhaps I should check the Rule to see the Grand Master of the Temple's share of such contributions to the cause. Who pays the Order to lose every battle against the infidels? Or perhaps conquering the infidels would make pilgrimages so much less dangerous that none would entrust their finances to the mighty Templars?"

Armand halted his flow of accusations abruptly, suddenly realizing how much he risked with these rash words.

The Grand Master glared at him angrily and Armand took a deep breath, knowing without a doubt that he had pushed too far.

"I will see you lose your habit for those remarks," the Master hissed, his eyes blazing as he advanced on the younger man. Armand's chin snapped up at the threat, his eyes glinting with anger.

So he was to lose his habit for noting the truth? To be demoted from his knighthood to join the ranks of the common sergeants? Such a fate was unthinkable. Long years had he worked to earn his spurs and he would not lose them over such a trifling matter as the Templars' sordid financial practices. Better to lose the house as well as the habit and become a mercenary to earn his keep. Indeed, he had almost forgotten the welcome weight of a blade in his hand.

"Take it and welcome," Armand spat, pulling the garment in question over his head in one angry movement and tossing it onto the floor with open disgust. "I see no reason to remain in this treacherous den."

"Go then!" the older man shouted, the blood rising in his face. "Go then and find your death among the godless infidels that surround our walls."

Armand faced his former superior, his countenance harsh as he took in the rapt expressions of those he had called his brethren. "Take care lest those godless infidels you condemn decide that this den fits their needs," he shot back, and the other man stiffened proudly.

"They would not dare to storm these halls," the Grand Master sneered in turn, but Armand chuckled under his breath.

"Surely even you do not believe that they have been taught to fear the mighty Templars?" he demanded sarcastically, watching his words hit home before he turned on his heel and strode from the scriptorium.

It was hot in the Holy Land, even this late in the year, hotter than Alex would have believed possible, the brightness of the sun on the sand road forcing her to squint her eyes against its assault, the endless dust compelling her to breathe through the end of her faded and threadbare veil. With a stifled sigh, she reviewed in her mind the string of events that had brought her here almost two years after Michel had sailed east, flicking a glance to her Aunt Justine as the slim woman trudged determinedly along beside her.

Michel's furious cry of discovery still echoed in her ears, somewhat tempering Alex's pride of accomplishment in remaining undetected for four entire days after leaving Pontesse. He had been unwilling to return, as she had anticipated, but Alex had not foreseen his insistence to leave her in Venice in the care of Hugues' sister, Justine, and her husband, Guilio. What fortune to have a healer of one's own when expecting a baby, Justine had said, her belly swelling with the weight of a child, but her pleasure had not reached her eyes.

Barely had Michel found passage on a ship for his men and horses, when Justine began to press Alex for details of Sophie's "pagan heresies." To Mass she had dragged Alex regularly, but this did not visibly distress the younger woman, Alex considering herself merely a guest in another's church. Well she understood the doctrine of the Christians and did not find their faith abhorrent, as they seemed to find her own simple beliefs.

But the baby had been stillborn, as had the next, and the extent of Justine's hatred of pagan ways became abundantly clear. Alex had watched, amazed, when the madness took her aunt's eyes and Justine begged Guilio to grant her permission to pilgrimage to Jerusalem to save Alex's wayward soul and curry favor that she might yet bear him a son. Foolishness 'twas, in Justine's weakened state, and Alex said so, her words convincing the pair confronting her that she feared the power of the Holy City.

Justine had insisted on making a true pilgrimage of the journey, so they had taken a ship only as far as Constantinople, procuring horses there for the remainder of the journey. The unbearable heat had increased as they traveled south along the coast, banding together with one party of pilgrims or another on the road, all huddling together at night or crowding into the courtyard of a Frankish fortress for shelter against the dangers of the darkness.

The journey was torturous, first one horse and then the other dying in the dust under the merciless sun as the two women struggled onward. A brief respite could be gained at each of the European holdings, Antioch, Tortosa, Tyre, Acre, but sooner or later they stumbled forth from the gates, heading farther south under the relentless eye of the sun, successive days blurring together into an endless stream in Alex's mind.

A curious camaraderie had grown between the two women, undoubtedly born of the monumental strain of the pilgrimage past and the unknown travails still ahead. Under the harsh light of the sun, differences of faith seemed as irrelevant as the faded color of a once pretty kirtle, as meaningless as the chests of gold discarded at the side of the road by pilgrims who could no longer carry their weight.

Everywhere Alex searched for Michel, asking other knights if they knew or had seen him, scanning the hostels and barracks for some sign of his insignia, but no news could she find. She refused to acknowledge the possibility that her brother might have fallen in battle until she had been to Jerusalem. If she left that city without finding him, Alex told herself, she would give Michel up for dead.

'Twas August when the two women stumbled through the gates of the Holy City, clutched in a crowd of pilgrims from a dozen foreign lands, the leather soles of their shoes riddled with holes, their cheeks gaunt from lack of food. Justine faltered in her gait and Alex put one arm around her aunt to support her, wondering in some corner of her mind whether either of them would see Venice again.

Shouts echoed with no warning through the narrow streets, the hoarse cries interspersed with screams of terror bringing Alex to a surprised halt. Suddenly, dark-skinned Muslims leapt from rooftops and over stone walls into the street, their blades flashing in the sun as they cut down any unfortunate caught in their path. The exhausted pilgrims panicked, scattering in all directions like leaves before an ill-tempered wind.

Alex grabbed Justine's limp hand and ran blindly. Closing her ears to the uproar surrounding them, she turned and ran down a narrow alleyway, dragging her aunt behind her. They ducked beneath one swinging blade, slipping down one twisted alley and another, their feet sliding on the loose stones as the sounds of fighting grew louder all around them.

The alley wound right then left, then turned sharply right again, the passage terminated by a single broad portal. Footsteps echoed in pursuit as Alex searched for a place to hide, the wheeze of Justine's breathing loud in her ears.

A white flag with a red cross fluttered dejectedly over the pointed archway, limp in the heat, its insignia heartwarmingly familiar to Alex in this foreign and dangerous land. The Order of the Poor Knights of the Temple of Solomon.

The Templars.

Armand tugged his hauberk over his shoulders, savoring the familiar weight of the metal chausses and chain mail coif. The armor felt comfortable after his long break from warfare and he drew his sword experimentally.

Watching the sunlight dance along the blade, Armand permitted himself to wonder about his father for the first time in months, his mind making that easy association to Alexandria. Women, another luxury forbidden by the Rule that no longer bound him. Soundly wed with a babe the lady would be by now, he concluded with a wry grimace, pushing such frivolous thoughts from his mind.

He had a living to make once again with his blade. Tossing his sword easily into the air, he caught it by the hilt and replaced it in his scabbard in one smooth move.

"Perhaps we erred in assigning you to the scriptorium," came a dry voice from the doorway. Armand spun on his heel, surprised to find the Grand Master framed in the doorway, his eyes narrowed against the bright sunlight.

"Perhaps," he agreed noncommittally, wondering what had prompted this unusual visit. The older man threw Armand an assessing glance and stepped into the room.

"Where will you go?" he asked softly, and Armand was so surprised by the question that he answered immediately.

"Home, I suppose. Provins."

The Grand Master nodded slowly, his gaze running over Armand. "I have a package for the Temple in Paris," he began slowly, and Armand noted the slim package he carried and the tunic folded over his arm. "I would ask you to surrender your habit there."

Armand raised one eyebrow silently at this breach of the Rule, unable to quell his surprise completely. No Templar should even be speaking to him right now, let alone the Grand Master. 'Twas clear there was no other way to get the package to Paris and he stifled a childish urge to refuse. Paris. Provins. A day's ride apart at most. Surely he owed the Order that much for almost two years of food and shelter for both himself and Tiberias.

"I will gladly do so," he replied, not missing the flash of relief in the older man's eyes.

"Justine," Alex whispered, staring with horror at the blood flowing freely from the gaping slash across Justine's midsection as the older woman collapsed into a limp pile on the stone floor. She whispered her aunt's name again, unable to believe that one fleeting instant and the swipe of an enemy blade had snatched her life away.

A bellow from the other side of the hall brought Alex's head up with a snap, only to find a dark-skinned man bearing down on her, the glint in his obsidian eyes leaving little doubt in her mind that he intended to repeat his feat. She backed away from Justine's body, her mind busily enumerating her somewhat limited options. Little safety had they found indeed within the walls of the Temple.

Her dagger! She recalled with a sudden burst of inspiration. If only she could get to her garter without arousing the man's suspicion.

Alex began to crouch slowly as she stepped backward, her heel abruptly encountering a stone obstacle. The man grinned at her predicament, and Alex spared a hasty glance over her shoulder. Stairs stretched up into the darkness behind her. For the briefest second, she wondered what or who was at the top of the stairs, then pushed the fear resolutely out of her mind, carefully sliding her foot up onto the first stone step.

As her foot slipped onto the second step, her opponent made his move, diving forward with his menacing blade, but Alex was ready. She snatched the short dagger out of her garter, swinging upward in a sharp arc.

With reflexes like a cat's, the man jumped immediately backward as soon as he sensed her move. Her blade merely nicked his throat, drawing an ineffectual line of blood instead of dropping him to his knees in defeat. Alex gasped and turned to run up the stairs, her assailant lunging forward with a growl, the deadly sweep of his blade barely missing her feet.

Fool! she chided herself. How could she honestly have expected to surprise a battle-hardened warrior?

Alex gathered her skirts above her knees and scampered up the shadowed stone passageway. Her feet found each step in the increasing darkness, the stairs curving endlessly upward, the smooth walls on either side offering no place to hide.

She heard the man's footsteps falling ever more closely at her heels. Fancying that she could feel his hot breath on her back, Alex panicked, darting forward, praying that she would not trip. Her heart pounding in her mouth, she rounded a corner and unceremoniously barreled into a solid wall of muscle.

Vaguely Alex registered the red cross of the Knights Templar as she was shoved abruptly to one side, her breath abandoning her lungs as her back hit the wall. She barely caught a glimpse of a rising blade as it flashed in the darkness, instinctively squeezing her eyes tightly shut and averting her face before the blow fell.

The Muslim dashed around the corner in hot pursuit, his gasp of surprise at the sight of his unexpected opponent the only sound before the Templar's sword swung through the air. A dull thud was followed by a sickening gurgle as the man dropped to a heap on the staircase.

Alex bit her bottom lip in a desperate effort to keep the bile from rising into her mouth, digging her fingers into the reassuring solidity of the cold stone wall as she fought to regain her composure. She felt the weight of the knight's gaze upon her but did not look up to meet his eyes. He swore vehemently and she felt the color drain from her face, all the tales she had heard of the Templars' nefarious exploits rising to haunt her terrified mind.

Armand took a second look at the woman in front of him in stunned disbelief.

What on earth was Alexandria doing here in Jerusalem?

His amazed eyes took in her gaunt cheeks and the shadows beneath her eyes. Her kirtle and surcoat were filthy, the wimple and veil draped over her hair torn and threadbare.

It was beyond comprehension that she should be here and he shook his head in astonishment, letting loose a string of curses when he noted her barren left hand and the fact that she was clearly unescorted. Did her family care so little for her welfare?

The lady clenched and unclenched her fingers against her kirtle, the rapid rise and fall of her breasts telling Armand that she was deeply afraid. And no wonder. The Temple under siege was no place for a lady.

"What are you doing here?" the knight demanded abruptly, the anger in his deep voice carrying clearly to Alex despite his helmet. She forced herself to breathe slowly and remain calm. Only her wits could help her now.

"My brother," she managed after a moment's hesitation and a fearful glance up at the tall knight. "I search for my brother."

"Describe him to me," the knight barked, planting his sword in the fallen Muslim and folding his arms across his chest at her quick look of surprise. "Perhaps I have seen him," he added more gently, and Alex nodded quickly in comprehension.

"His coloring is liken to mine," she began, still suffering from an alarming shortness of breath, "but he is taller, of course." Alex gave the knight facing her a quick appraisal. "Though not as tall as you are, sir."

"His colors?"

"Three white fleurs-de-lis on a dark blue ground," she explained. The knight shook his head, stopping abruptly at the sudden sound of ringing blades carrying from above.

"I know him not," Armand concluded tersely, reclaiming his sword and starting to tug Alexandria back down the stairs.

The boy could be stationed anywhere in the Holy Land, Antioch, Tyre, even as far north as Constantinople, but she had the misfortune to look for him here while the city was under its greatest trial since the first Crusade.

Swords clanged overhead again and Armand's gut tightened at the thought of what the Muslims would do to the lady were she captured, his thoughts prompting him to haul her roughly toward the stables. Somehow he had to get her out of here safely.

Alex's heart sank, and she pulled her hand childishly from the knight's firm grasp. It was too much. She was exhausted, famished, thirsty beyond compare, Justine was dead and still she had not found Michel. She wanted nothing other than to bury her face in her hands and weep. And now the city was under siege. Was there any hope of getting home again?

"The Muslims are down there," she argued, but the knight shook his head and grabbed her hand again.

"As are the horses," he snapped impatiently, giving her hand a tug. "Hurry, milady, there is little time to waste."

The knight took the broad stone stairs three at a time, leaving Alex scampering in his wake as she tried to keep up with him and still not touch the fallen man's body.

Sounds of swordplay carried up the staircase from the stables below as Armand paused in the shadows to survey the sentry room before declaring his presence. Two Arabs were pitted against one Hospitaler knight, who was already dead on his feet. There was nothing Armand could do now to help him. Only those who could walk or run would get out of the city alive today.

Two opponents and a lady to protect. Armand watched the Muslims as they finished the fight, eyeing their stance and swing. If his luck held, he could take one out quickly while they were still surprised. Besting the other was a gamble he would have to take.

Alex peered around the width of the knight's shoulder at the two massive men, grimacing slightly as the last Frenchman in the room joined the pile of carcasses on the floor. The knight in front of her stiffened and Alex tightened her grip on her small blade with determination.

"Stay behind me," the knight murmured so softly that Alex thought she might have imagined it. "Neither the strength nor the blade have you, milady," the Templar argued, the low timbre of his voice oddly reassuring in the midst of all this confusion.

Alex sighed softly, forcing herself to acknowledge the truth in his words as she reevaluated the short dagger and the menacing bulk of the men in the room below. She ran her eyes over the uncompromising line of her knight's shoulders and knew that she could trust him to protect her.

Armand heard the lady's soft sigh of defeat and relaxed slightly, knowing that she had conceded the point. But could he trust her to stay right behind him in the heat of battle? Armand knew that he would not be able to watch his back, protect her and fight decisively, as well. If things went poorly and they had to run, she was too tiny to be able to keep up with him.

Tiny, he thought again, and an idea struck him.

"On my back," he whispered tersely, stretching his left arm out behind himself to support her climbing.

Alex stared at the back of his head as if he were mad. "'Tis improper," she hissed indignantly, catching the sound of something that sounded suspiciously like a chuckle.

"'Tis your best option," he murmured back, forcing Alex to reconsider the array of bodies cast about like carcasses after the slaughter. He was right again, she admitted, studying the broad expanse of his back and wondering how she would ever manage to hang on.

"Grasp my shoulder," he commanded softly as if sensing her predicament, stretching his free arm back toward her again. " 'Tis completely healed, milady."

Alex's head reeled even as her heart leapt in recognition of that deep voice, a thousand tiny details jumbling together in her mind at his words, his height, the feel of his hand closing over hers, the way he inclined his head, that hauntingly familiar trace of his scent, the rumble of his deep voice.

"You *knew*," she whispered accusingly, unable to stop a quiver of excitement from racing through her veins as she climbed onto his back, barely stifling an urge to cuff his ears for teasing her so, "and yet you said nothing to me." The knight's broad shoulders shrugged noncommittally, though whether he was adjusting her weight or dismissing her accusation, she could not tell.

" 'Tis hardly the time for conversation," Armand observed dryly, shoving her feet unceremoniously through his belt and threading her hands under his arms and beneath his tunic so she could grab the fabric from the underside, tucking her heavy cloak between them so that it did not hang loose. He bent his knees and shifted from side to side experimentally, pleased to find that the lady was even lighter than he had thought.

"Keep your head below my shoulders lest I duck and you do not," he warned curtly. Alex nodded automatically, gasping under her breath as his gruesome meaning dawned on her, but he had already stepped out of the shadows and was halfway across the room, the walls echoing with his lusty bellow, his blade swinging before the Muslims were even aware of his presence.

Armand watched the light of surprise dawn in the invaders' dark eyes with satisfaction, slicing the closest one down before he even had time to draw his blade. He stepped over the corpse and swung hard to the right to parry a blow from the other, willing the lady on his back to hold tight.

Alex clutched the knight's back with every fiber of her being, the cold rings of his chain mail imprinting their pattern on her cheek, as she desperately tried to make herself as small as possible.

It seemed the battle had barely started before it was done, fresh blood rushing to cover the already stained flagstones even as the knight broke into a run with Alex on his back. She squeezed her eyes closed as he darted through the endless labyrinth of corridors, turning first this way and then that, his pace never faltering despite the half darkness cast by the flickering torches.

Suddenly he paused, his breathing heavier, and she felt his fingers fumbling with her feet. Alex glanced over her shoulder as she lowered herself to the floor, and he spun quickly around and pulled her protectively into the shadows beside him.

She could smell the horses below them now. The knight pointed down a darkened staircase to their immediate left and touched one gloved finger to her lips in warning. Alex nodded that she understood and unsheathed her tiny blade with resolute fingers.

The knight slipped into the inky shadows ahead of her, his feet silent on the flagstones despite the armor he wore. Alex followed close on his heels, desperately trying to match the silence of his passage. Never before had she tried to walk soundlessly, and even the soft brush of her leather soles on the stone sounded relentlessly loud in her ears. The Templar took the stairs one at a time, cautiously peering into the shadows ahead.

Alex followed him, her shod toe inadvertently striking a loose pebble and sending it skittering down into the darkness below. The knight flattened himself immediately against the wall and Alex followed suit as the reverberations of the stone's passing filtered back to them, the seemingly inconsequential sound magnified a hundred times before the echoes died out somewhere far below.

Alex didn't have to look at her companion to feel the heat of his disapproval, holding her breath as she leaned into the shadows beside him, cursing herself for being seven kinds of careless fool. When the echoes died, the sounds of fighting overhead grew louder and the knight threw a glance over his shoulder, lifting his blade and taking several steps before he paused again to listen with Alex close on his heels.

Alex stared into the shadows of a doorway facing her, certain that her mind was playing tricks on her when the silhouette of a man became clear in the blackness of shadows among shadows. Then the deeper patch of darkness moved, his sword catching a glimmer of light, dispelling all doubt from her mind. As the Muslim stepped forward, a rush of adrenaline pumped through her veins, her fear giving the strength to bury her blade in the middle of his chest. The man groaned as he tumbled and the Templar spun around, his amazement obvious in the way he stared between Alex and the fallen warrior.

"Indeed you learn quickly, milady," he commented softly, but Alex was immune to his humor, the world spinning unsteadily around her, a wave of nausea threatening to steal away her consciousness as she gripped the solid reality of her knight's hand.

"I fear I slow your progress too much, sir," she murmured apologetically, barely seeing the curt shake of his head from the corner of her eye.

"'Tis your progress alone that concerns me, milady," the knight responded, squeezing her hand reassuringly as his voice dropped to a timbre that weakened her knees.

"Pray do not faint now," he murmured. "You are still far from safety." Alex gulped for fresh air, unable to tear her gaze away from the man sprawled across the stone at her feet.

"Never have I killed..." she began unsteadily, her eyes widening with surprise as the supposedly dead man made a lightning-quick grab for the blade that had fallen from his hand.

The knight brought one mailed foot down heavily on the Muslim's jaw and Alex thought she heard something crack before he bent and slit the man's throat with a flawlessly steady hand.

"And still you have not, milady," he concluded tersely, pulling her resolutely down toward the stables. "Hurry now before the Temple is truly lost."

The Templar hurried down the remaining stairs and Alex struggled to match his new pace.

She was barely aware that they had stepped out into the cavernous catacomb of the stables before the knight tugged her back into the shadows once again, his breathing seemingly stopped as he waited motionless and listened. Before she could demand an explanation, the distant sound of galloping hooves echoed through the vaults, the beast's footfalls becoming gradually louder. The Templar pulled her deeper into the shadows and tucked her protectively behind him as the rider approached.

Despite the danger of their position, Alex felt more than a twinge of awareness of the knight's proximity. The horseman grew closer and the knight backed her into the wall, trapping her between the cold stone wall and the solidity of his mail-draped back.

More than adequately protected by the shadows and her knight's lethal blade, Alex stretched her neck to see the rider as he passed, letting out a surprised cry of recognition that startled both men.

"Michel!" she shouted jubilantly, drawing an amazed stare from both her brother and the knight in front of her.

"Alex?" Michel demanded, pulling his horse up short and peering into the darkness of the stall.

Armand stared at the younger man in surprise, his memory conjuring up that long-past evening in the courtyard when the lady had admitted to waiting for a knight named Michel. A knight he had assumed to be her betrothed.

Suddenly Armand felt an overwhelming urge to laugh aloud.

"This is your brother?" the Templar demanded curtly, and Alex nodded happily.

"Indeed, 'tis he," she asserted, pushing him easily out of her way in his surprise.

"Alex!" Michel declared again in amazement when she stepped toward him. He muttered something uncomplimentary under his breath and Alex felt the color rising in her cheeks. She froze in her tracks, embarrassed by the abrupt manner of his greeting.

"What are you doing here?" he demanded, his eyes flashing with annoyance. "Jerusalem in these days is no place for a woman."

"Glad I am to see that you are a man of common sense, Chevalier," the Templar commented dryly, stepping forward and scooping Alex effortlessly up off her feet.

Before she could think to argue or struggle, Alex found herself unceremoniously deposited behind Michel. She looked down at the Templar, who dropped his hands to his hips and leveled an uncompromising glance at Michel.

"Get you to Jaffa," he commanded crisply, but Michel shook his head in emphatic denial.

"No nursemaid will I play when there is a battle to be fought!" Michel shot back, but the older knight shook his head impatiently.

"Be not a fool, there is no battle to be fought." Armand gestured to the halls above them, disliking the battle-hungry gleam he saw in the younger man's eye. Proving his manhood at the expense of his sister's safety would be a poor choice for Michel to make. Could he trust the boy to see his lady safely out of the besieged city?

A persistent voice in the back of Armand's mind suggested that he see to the lady's escape himself, but he pushed the thought aside with an effort. As long as he wore the habit, his fitting place was here, defending the Temple itself, much as he might desire to do otherwise.

"Ride while you may," Armand commanded sternly, hoping the young man would do as he bade. "We are vastly outnumbered and the city will fall before the sun completes its path."

"Surely you jest," Michel snorted indignantly, his derision fueling Armand's fear. "This is just another battle for supremacy. Should they win today, we will retaliate on the morrow."

"Are you so green that you cannot smell the winds of change?" Armand snapped angrily, his tone incredulous as he saw how lightly Michel took his responsibilities. "The ships will begin leaving immediately. Ride forth now and assure your sister's passage."

That said, Armand sheathed his sword smoothly and swept off his helmet and gloves, running his fingers through his hair before reaching for Alex's hand and pressing a kiss onto its back. Her skin was as soft as he remembered, and he once again caught the elusive scent of roses.

Armand glanced up and met the fathomless blue of her eyes, allowing himself just a fragment of a dream. He recalled the taste of her lips and restrained himself from pulling her down beside him with difficulty.

The lady had remembered him, apparently with favor, he marveled, and now they both headed back toward home, his days as a Templar soon to be well and truly ended. What fate awaited her there? A wealthy betrothed? The fact that Alexandria was here, in Jerusalem, and alone seemed to make that possibility unlikely, the welcome in her eyes telling Armand that perhaps she had not yet given her heart. For the briefest second, the idea of dying in the final defense of the Temple lost some of its noble luster.

Alex caught her breath at the knight's tribute, savoring the warm imprint that his lips left on her flesh.

"The score is truly even then, sir," she commented softly, but the knight shook his head, his green eyes glowing with unexpected humor.

"Nay, milady, the Muslim on the stairs leaves me once again in your debt." He smiled gently at her and Alex saw the shadows around his eyes, the faint lines of fatigue bracketing his mouth.

"Travel safely, milady," he added, the rich timbre of his voice striking a resonant chord in her heart. "I would see your fair countenance well within the confines of the King's lands."

"As I would hope to see yours," she responded boldly, feeling Michel's shoulders stiffen at the impropriety of her remark. Despite her brother's evident disapproval, she closed her fingers tightly around the knight's hand and smiled into his eyes.

A futile dream, 'twas no more than that, Armand admitted. The lady was simply appreciative of his efforts. He brushed his lips against her fingertips once more, turning her hand to let his lips linger on the smoothness inside her wrist before he stepped back.

"Ride swiftly," Armand commanded with a sudden frown, his tone authoritative as he replaced his helmet, "lest the ships sail before your arrival."

Chapter Four

Michel urged Sebastien forward as the knight strode away, but Alex pulled on her brother's sleeve, twisting around to call back to her knight.

"Sir! Are you not a Templar?" she cried, her pulse accelerating when he hesitated and turned at her words.

"That I am, milady," he agreed calmly after the barest pause.

"Is it not then your mission to escort pilgrims between Jerusalem and Jaffa?" Alex demanded, her heart beating a staccato at her daring. Ahead of her, Michel hissed her name disapprovingly but otherwise restrained himself from commenting.

"Indeed 'tis our duty, milady, but responsibilities have I here at the Temple," Armand countered smoothly, not requiring a great deal of imagination to see where the lady's argument was headed. But why? he asked himself, unwilling to trust the most simple answer.

"The same Temple you just claimed would fall into enemy hands before this day is ended." Alex took a deep breath before plunging onward, her next words tumbling out in a rush. "Would you stay here to perish like a dog rather than assist two travelers?"

She wished him to escort them to Jaffa! For their own safety, to be sure, Armand rationalized, the rapt expression on the lady's face as she awaited his response telling him otherwise.

Was it possible that this lovely creature was concerned that he live to see another dawn? His hand rose to his chest as he suddenly recalled the Grand Master's package to Paris tucked beneath his hauberk, the recollection of his task throwing further weight behind her proposal.

Armand smiled at the irony in choosing to accompany pilgrims as his last deed as a Templar. 'Twas fitting somehow that he choose that fundamental mission, that oldest part of the Rule, over the defense of a mere building. The lady's idea had merit, to be sure.

For a long moment, he stared back at Alex, weighing the idea in his mind. Finally, Armand turned away and strode to a stall, quickly harnessing the long-ignored Tiberias.

"You speak wisely, milady," he conceded, and caught a glimpse of her pleased smile before she stifled it. "We shall ride to the harbor together."

Armand swung into the high saddle with ease, urging his horse forward, when the rattle of hoofbeats far behind him caught his attention. He turned to see a group of Muslims burst suddenly into the far end of the stables.

"Ride!" he cried, urging Tiberias forward and slapping Michel's horse on the rump as he passed, sending the two stallions galloping out into the harsh sunlight.

Disorder greeted them on every side, the corpses of men, women and horses scattered haphazardly across the cobbled streets, blood running freely between the worn stones. Shouting carried over the hills, mingling with the wailing of women who mourned their newly fallen dead, the clashing of blade against blade as the battle waged. Armand glanced back over his shoulder, his stomach plummeting when he saw the crescent flag fluttering in the breeze over the Temple of Solomon.

"Ride on!" he cried, fearing that they had tarried too long. "Pause for neither man nor beast!" Tiberias settled into a steady gallop with a toss of his head at his master's urging and Michel's steed matched the pace, the two warhorses making quick progress through the crooked streets toward the city gates.

"They hold the gates!" Michel shouted when they rounded the last curve. Armand nodded absently, having already noted the Muslims on the wall, his eyes running assessingly over the flimsily enforced barricade. The horses were strong and fresh, he reasoned. They should be able to barrel through the enforcement.

"Draw your blade and do not slow down," he counseled Michel, knowing that this would not be what the Muslims expected. "Ride as though the way were already clear." When Michel nodded, Armand flicked a glance to his lady to find her clutching her brother resolutely, those blue eyes fixed upon him and wide with fear.

"Milady, 'tis no time for proprieties," he instructed her firmly. "Sit astride if you are able and hold on for your life."

Alex nodded in acknowledgment of his words, clutching Michel's waist as she managed to get astride Sebastien, gripping both steed and brother as tightly as she could. Huddling down against Michel to make herself as small as possible, she squeezed her eyes tightly shut.

The two horses bore down on the gates in a flurry of hooves, the Muslims shouting in surprise and trying to force the two knights to a stop. Blade met blade in a resounding clash of steel, the stallions surging ever forward as they struggled to gain passage.

An instant later, Alex gasped in pained surprise when an Arab grasped a fistful of her hair from behind. Clutching instinctively at the roots, she loosened her grip on Michel as she fought to free her hair.

"Alex!" Michel cried in dismay when he felt the shift in her weight, his free hand locking around her wrist to keep her behind him in the saddle. He twisted around as he sought a way to strike her assailant, unable to swing his blade and remain clear of his sister.

Armand heard the younger knight's call, his head snapping around with fear when he heard his lady's name. She wrestled stubbornly with an Arab who clutched the dark tresses of her hair, as Michel held his blade helplessly aloft. Putting his spurs to his horse, Armand joined the fray. Dispatching the dusky-skinned man with one fell blow, he glanced up to find the two stallions surrounded by angry Muslims.

Exactly where he had not wanted to be.

Armand gritted his teeth in frustration and sized up the encroaching horde. Though they had the advantage of their horses, he and Michel were still vastly outnumbered. Only one of them could hope to break free while the other held the attackers at bay.

He turned sharply to the assailant on his immediate left, eloquently and thoroughly insulting the man's virility. The man showed no response and Armand nodded with slow satisfaction.

"They speak no French," he declared to Michel beside him, speaking beneath his breath just in case there was another among them who did. "We will cut a path directly behind you, and as soon as you are clear, you must ride directly to Jaffa with all haste."

"But what about you?" the lady interjected, and Armand spared a quick glance to the concern reflected in her eyes, wishing that things had worked out differently. His gaze ran over the raven tresses scattered about her shoulders, admiring her beauty in disarray. No child was she now, he realized with admiration, but a woman. With an effort, Armand forced his mind back to the task at hand, knowing that he would give whatever was demanded of him to see her safely away.

"I will be behind you," he lied, fixing Michel with an intense gaze, willing the boy to recognize the lie. "Remember your vows," he added pointedly, hoping the younger knight would understand his meaning.

Michel met Armand's look, straightening suddenly in understanding, and Armand breathed a sigh of relief. The lad understood that he did not expect to follow behind and would not stop once he broke free of the surrounding horde.

"On your command," Michel said determinedly, sending a curt nod the Templar's way as he tightened his grip on the hilt of his sword. Alex looked back and forth between the two men, certain that she had missed something in the silent exchange, something of tremendous importance judging by the silent resolve the two knights now showed.

But she was spared no time to reflect upon it further. The Templar bellowed and buried his spurs in the black stallion's side, charging into the Muslims to one side with Michel close behind him. Battle cries and the sound of clashing blades filled the air, scattering all coherent thought from Alex's mind as she hung on to Michel for dear life.

The Arabs were all around them, pressing against the horses, their vicious blades glinting in the harsh sunlight. One man latched onto Alex's leg and she tried desperately to shake him off as she fumbled with Michel's belt, searching for the quillon dagger she knew must be there.

The man's brown eyes widened in surprise when she suddenly produced the blade, burying it in his upper arm. He loosened his hold momentarily and she jerked the dagger out of his flesh, kicking him solidly in the chest as his blood stained her kirtle, the vehemence of her gesture surprising them both.

Adrenaline rushed frantically through her veins and she brought the blade down in a sharp arc against another attacker, her desire to survive overwhelming any other inhibitions. She caught a glimpse of white out of the corner of her eye and knew that the Templar had swung around to protect their backs as they cut a path through the invading army.

The cool shadow of the tall city gates fell over them and Alex realized that they had almost made it out of Jerusalem. In that same instant, the Muslims saw that the knights' escape was imminent and redoubled their attack, determined to add another three to the count of the fallen.

"Ride now!" The resounding smack of leather impacting horseflesh followed the Templar's shout and Sebastien surged forward, through the gates.

Alex twisted in the saddle, her heart stopping when she saw that the Templar was not behind them.

"Michel, we must return!" she shouted, desperately tugging on her brother's hauberk, but he shook his head determinedly without looking back.

"He will follow when he can," he responded with cold impassivity. "We ride to the harbor."

Alex stood on the deck of the last ship, studying each group of pilgrims and knights as they arrived. The road twisting back to Jerusalem appeared empty in the fading light, no clouds of dust rising to indicate the passage of horses or pilgrims along its length. Michel came and stood beside her, slipping one arm across her shoulders supportively.

"Michel, think you that he..." Alex could not even complete the question. The thought of the Templar dying alone at the gates of the city filled her with despair. Michel's fingers tightened imperceptibly on her shoulder and his voice was low when he spoke.

"This last group did not see him there," he murmured apologetically, and Alex closed her eyes against the intensity of her response.

Previous pilgrims had reported the tall Templar clearing their passage from the city, but now it seemed the inevitable had finally happened. Hot tears scalded her cheeks and Alex buried her face in Michel's chest, her sobs breaking as his arms closed protectively around her.

"We should have stayed," she murmured through her tears, knowing without looking that Michel was shaking his head.

"He bade me ride," he repeated sadly, and she knew that he spoke the truth, that that was the silent message the two men had exchanged. The tall knight had traded his life for hers.

The ropes were cast off and the sails hoisted as the ship stole out of the harbor toward the setting sun.

The ship's sails were barely discernible against the orange smudge on the horizon as Armand rode into Jaffa some hours later. A curious mixture of disappointment and satisfaction welled up in his chest at the thought that his lady was safely headed toward home.

His lady. He shook his head at his foolishness. What would her attitude have been had she known that he had left the Order of the Templars for good? He recalled the warm promise in those azure eyes when he had kissed her hand and his heart contracted.

"Antioch, my boy," he murmured apologetically to Tiberias, knowing the beast was as bone tired as he. "Passage will we find there if the fortress is held." The horse nickered, tossing his proud head, and Armand smiled in spite of himself. "Indeed you know the truth of it, there is always Constantinople should Antioch be lost."

Despite her heartache, Alex felt her spirits lift as the spires of Venice finally appeared. Ages had passed, it seemed, since she had left this bustling port, countless weeks since they had sailed from the East.

People came from throughout Europe, from all around the Mediterranean, from Persia, even from the Orient, to trade in this city. Those diverse origins were reflected in the crowd assembled on the quay to meet the ship, their complexions as varied as the colors and styles of their clothing.

The sails snapped in the wind overhead and Alex glanced up, listening to the creaking of the huge wooden masts. The sky arched above the ship like a great inverted blue bowl and Alex drew a deep breath of crisp autumn air, feeling inexplicably glad to be alive.

"'Twill be good to see home again," Michel commented from her side, and Alex threw him a smile of agreement. Michel's arm stole over her shoulder, drawing Alex into an impulsive hug.

If nothing else, she had found Michel, she reasoned, drawing strength from the familiarity of his strong embrace. She returned his hug fiercely, resolutely blinking back unbidden tears. Men shouted from below, and brother and sister turned to watch as the ship was hauled against the docks, grateful for the distraction from their thoughts.

"I will fetch Sebastien," Michel said, and Alex nodded, turning to join the retinue of relieved pilgrims filing slowly toward the gangway.

* * *

"Fair Alexandria," drawled a hauntingly familiar male voice as Alex awaited Michel in the piazza. A chill of recognition tripped along her spine and her heart sank in dismay.

Pièrre de Villiers. She would have given the very devil himself a more friendly welcome. That she should encounter one of her Uncle Guilio's favorite gambling partners so soon after arriving in Venice was sorry luck indeed.

How long had he stood near her? Alex berated herself for not paying more attention, resolutely refusing to acknowledge the man's unwelcome presence. All she wanted was to collect Michel and Sebastien and head home to Pontesse.

An insistent male hand clasped her shoulder and Alex stifled a groan, refusing to look up and meet Pièrre's eyes. There was something about this man's easy familiarity that made her unnaturally cautious. Of noble blood Pièrre de Villiers might well be, but Alex was not convinced that he personally possessed any noble tendencies.

Alex heard his self-satisfied chuckle beside her and closed her eyes, bracing herself for what would come. She let him pull her shoulder until she was facing him.

He was dressed foppishly, as usual, his tunic of the richest red-and-gold damask, elaborately embroidered at the hem and cuffs in an ivylike design, falling to just above his knees. His dark stockings were crisscrossed with decorative garters in the latest mode, his shoes of the finest dyed leather. His velvet mantle was the shade of the deepest red wine, lined its entire length with a soft gray squirrel fur and fastened at the neck with a large brooch set with polished stones.

"Beautiful Alexandria," Pièrre whispered, and Alex cringed in response, pulling away without a second thought. He touched her hair and she backed against the stone wall that surrounded the piazza, flicking a glance for the first time at his face.

Some women might have found his dark features and neatly trimmed mustache elegant, his stylishly bobbed and curled hair attractive. Every fiber of Alex's soul cried out in revulsion and she flattened herself against the wall, instinctively distrusting the cool Frenchman and his charming ways.

"So long it has been and yet you have no pretty greeting for me, *chérie,*" he scolded softly.

"Indeed it has been some time," she agreed smoothly. "I trust that you have been well."

"Sadly no," Pièrre responded with a wistful smile, leaning closer. "Venice has been empty without the grace of your presence."

"You flatter me with idle compliments, sir," Alex shot back, wondering wildly what was keeping Michel.

"I think not, *chérie,*" he responded smoothly. "Even now your loveliness warms my heart."

Pièrre reached out and touched her cheek and Alex jerked away from him. Something of her feelings must have shown in her expression for his brown eyes instantly narrowed to hostile slits and he leaned menacingly toward her.

"A lady who uncovers her hair like a harlot has no reason to step away from a man's touch," he hissed, curling a wayward strand of her hair around one finger and pulling her face to his.

"Touch me not," she spat, but Pièrre only smiled, leaning ever closer, his breath brushing lightly on her cheek.

"But such a lovely harlot you are, *chérie,* that I cannot resist your charms," he murmured, his gaze running over her loose tresses. Alex's eyes widened in horror as she realized finally what had prompted his words and she clutched at her hood, pulling it quickly over her hair.

"Well you know that I am no harlot," she gritted out, resolutely tucking the ends of her hair under the wool hood. When had it slipped from her hair?

"Indeed?" Pièrre arched a quizzical brow. "Your uncle seems intent on selling you like a common harlot," he commented with dry amusement.

A harlot to be bought and sold! Alex slapped Pièrre across the face, the sharp sound echoing loudly from the force of her blow. How dare the man imply that she was nothing more than a prostitute!

Pièrre's eyes flashed fire and Alex noted a small dribble of blood at the corner of his mouth. She glared at him in anger, not even thinking to fear his response. His eyes blazed in silent fury for an instant before they narrowed to hardened glints, his hand moving like lightning to grasp a fistful of the hair at the base of her neck. She gasped as Pièrre smiled maliciously, lifting his hand so that she was compelled to stand on tiptoe.

"I will enjoy taming you, *chérie*," Pièrre whispered, pulling her toward him relentlessly until their faces almost touched. Alex twisted in his grasp, wincing in pain.

"You cannot run away from me," he continued, his eyes gleaming with intent, and the bile rose in Alex's throat. He gave her a little shake as he towered over her and continued solemnly. "Rest assured, *chérie,* you will be mine."

"Never," Alex retorted defiantly, and Pièrre gave her an impatient little shake. The distinctive sound of metal on metal drew Pièrre's attention, leaving whatever cruel response he would have made unspoken. He glanced enquiringly over his shoulder, the snarl on his features turning quickly to an engaging but tentative smile. Alex flicked a glance over his shoulder, relief coursing through her veins at the sight of Michel, his face set, his sword drawn and at the ready.

Pièrre released her quickly, and backed cautiously away, clearly fearing for his health. Alex realized with a start that he carried no weapon.

A small crowd of people gathered around the group and watched with interest, whispering and giggling among themselves.

"State your business with the lady," Michel growled.

Pièrre stood proudly and lifted his chin. "Our discussion is none of your affair."

"Any business you have with my sister is most certainly my affair." Michel took a step closer to Pièrre and the man flushed in discomfort. He tried to take a step backward but the onlookers did not allow him the space. The crowd chuckled at his discomfiture and Pièrre made a nervous attempt to laugh.

"You must be Chevalier Michel de Fontaine," he began engagingly, and Michel nodded firmly, his eyes still an uncouragingly frosty shade of blue.

"That I am," Michel agreed, refusing to let down his guard.

Pièrre smiled. "I had no idea you were home, milord, or I would surely have introduced myself," he said smoothly. "Your sister and I are to wed."

Alex felt as though a bucket of cold water had been dropped over her, so stunned was she at the man's words. What travesty was this?

Pièrre's earlier words echoed through her mind and her eyes widened in mute horror, her mind erupting in a spasm of denial. Guilio couldn't have. He wouldn't have.

But one look at Pièrre's mocking grin told her otherwise.

"Alex?" Michel demanded in an undertone without looking over his shoulder.

"I should think not," she replied indignantly. A titter of laughter rippled through the crowd and Pièrre flushed with anger.

"There seems to be some dispute about your claim," Michel asserted calmly.

"There is indeed no dispute to be had," Pièrre insisted stubbornly. "Guilio and I have signed the contract. I would suggest you pursue the matter with him."

"Indeed," Michel responded, his disbelief plain in his tone. "It appears my uncle and I have much to discuss."

"The agreement is made," Pièrre reiterated firmly. He looked as though he would say something else, then changed his mind, turning abruptly to stride off into the crowd.

The assembled onlookers dispersed slowly, mumbling in disappointment that there had not been a fight.

"Did he hurt you?" Michel asked, turning to Alex with concern, but she shook her head.

"He thought my loose hair encouraging," she explained quietly, her eyes downcast. Michel reached out and placed a roughened finger under her chin, forcing her to meet the solemn expression in his eyes.

"There is no need for this marriage, Alex," he said softly. "You dislike the man?"

A shudder raced through Alex's slight form. "He frightens me, Michel," she whispered, and Michel nodded slowly.

"I will handle this matter," he assured her solemnly, and gathered her into a tight hug. "Guilio is not an unreasonable man." Alex nodded against the solidity of her brother's chest, the chill gathering around her heart the only sign of her lack of conviction in Michel's faith.

They found Guilio in the tavern he frequented, bent over the gaming table, a pair of dice jingling in his hand. He glanced up as they entered, and for the briefest instant, Alex thought she saw something flicker through her uncle's eyes as he noted Justine's absence, but 'twas gone as quickly as it appeared and he nonchalantly tossed the dice across the table once more.

"Tales I hear that you publicly insulted your betrothed this day," Guilio said by way of greeting, his words confirming what Pièrre had already told them.

"No betrothed have I," Alex insisted hotly, stepping toward her uncle. A wry smile twisted the older man's lips and he raised his eyebrows in surprise as the dice rolled to a stop. His companions hooted victoriously and quickly cleared the table of coin, laughing as they left the family to their reunion.

Guilio fixed Alex with a cold stare, his good humor dissipated by his loss. "Promised is your hand to Pièrre de Villiers, the marriage contract signed."

"I despise the man!" Alex cried in exasperation, her heart sinking at the news of a completed contract.

"Your feelings on the matter are of little import," Guilio countered with a shrug, sitting down heavily and lifting a goblet to his fleshy lips. "'Twas my duty as your guardian to see you duly wed and I have acted accordingly."

"No right had you to settle my marriage contract," Alex insisted, and Guilio's face bloomed an even brighter shade of red at her impertinence.

"Every right had I as your uncle and guardian," he roared, pounding the table as he rose unsteadily to his feet. "The arrangements are made and you will be duly wed to Pièrre de Villiers!"

Uncle and niece stared each other down in outright hostility, the air fairly crackling between them.

Michel cleared his throat diplomatically, his gesture drawing the reluctant attention of his two companions.

"With all respect, uncle," he began in a reasonable and even tone, "Alexandria's marriage contract is my concern and responsibility now that I am safely returned from the East." Michel bestowed a calm smile on his uncle and then his sister, reaching to tuck her hand into the crook of his arm proprietarily as he continued. "Although I do agree that she is well past the age when she should be wed—" Guilio grunted in agreement with this statement "—perhaps 'twould not be misguided to take the lady's own feelings on the matter into account."

"'Tis too late," Guilio shot back, his voice milder than it had been. When he would have continued, a voice hailing him from the dark recesses of the tavern halted his words.

"Guilio! My friend Guilio!" warbled that drunken voice. "Tell me not that this is the fair niece whose hand you wagered two months past! Had I but known of her beauty I would not have let de Villiers away so cheaply!"

Alex's jaw dropped in astonishment and she turned to confront her uncle, his inability to meet her eyes more damning than any other evidence could have been. Guilio shuffled his fingers aimlessly on the tabletop as if he didn't know what to do with them, recoiling instinctively when Michel stepped toward him, his brow as black as thunder, his voice rising in anger and incredulity.

"You bet Alex's hand at dice and lost!"

The midnight tolling of the bell in the piazza brought Alex uneasily awake. She glanced around her darkened room, the shadows lurking in the corners seeming strangely threatening at this late hour. She shivered and tried to shake off the remnant of some ominous dream. Her door was open and Alex frowned to herself, trying to recall whether it had been ajar before. Picking out the silhouette of a man in the shadows of the hall, she told herself firmly it was a trick of the light. Then he moved and she threw back her head and screamed.

Pièrre came alive, the outline of his figure blurring against the shadows as he jumped, diving across the bed and burying the heel of his hand in Alex's mouth to silence her. His weight knocked the breath out of her lungs and Alex bit into his hand as hard as she could.

Pièrre cursed, pulling his hand away, his eyes flashing with fury. He leaned back and cuffed her sharply across the face.

Alex's world spun from the impact and she fell back against the pillows, her mind reeling as it fought to sort nightmare and illusion from reality. Pièrre took advantage of the moment, jumping astride her and grabbing one of her wrists in each hand.

"Do not fight the inevitable, sweet Alexandria," he murmured in a low voice, grinding his hips brutally against her. Alex opened her lips to scream but he dropped his mouth to hers quickly, silencing her protest. Alex recoiled from the intimacy of his gesture, shuddering as he ended his caress.

"In one short week, my love, we will be duly wed," he whispered, his tone as seductive as if they had made a tryst.

"Why are you here?" Alex demanded sharply, using anger to mask her fear.

Pièrre simply grinned engagingly. "Now that I've bought the vintage, I thought to taste the wine."

Before Alex could respond, he bent and pressed his lips brutally to hers, forcing his tongue unceremoniously into her mouth. Alex squirmed in revulsion and he chuckled against her lips. She choked on his invading tongue and he pulled his mouth away, his eyes gleaming in the darkness. Alex spat as soon as his lips left hers, twisting her body in a desperate attempt to free herself.

"Never will I surrender to you," she hissed defiantly, and Pièrre chuckled again.

"Surrender is by no means a requirement," he asserted calmly, and Alex's heart pounded anew. She tried to scream again but Pièrre was too fast for her, releasing one wrist and slamming the heel of his hand abruptly into her mouth. She felt something warm against her tongue and knew that the impact had split her lip.

"No fool was I to guess fire ran in your veins," he said smoothly, gathering both her wrists into one strong hand while she lay there dazed. Alex shivered in his grasp, uncertain what he would do next.

"Your uncle bade me make myself at home," Pièrre commented, and her eyes widened in horror at his words.

"No one will help you, *chérie,*" he rasped. "Tonight you will be mine."

Was it true? Had Guilio betrayed her again?

Abruptly Pièrre sat up, releasing Alex's wrists and ripping her chemise down the front, still keeping his other palm buried between her teeth. Alex beat at him with her hands, determined not to make his conquest an easy one.

Pièrre's hand latched onto one of her breasts, his fingers curling around its mass as he grunted with satisfaction. He pinched the nipple and Alex groaned in pain, twisting desperately beneath him even as she realized with despair that his weight was too firmly settled over her hips.

A helpless tear trickled down her cheek at her predicament. Was there no one who would help her? Panic rose in Alex's throat and her heart pounded in her ears. She had to get away somehow.

Her energy renewed, she squirmed violently, hitting Pièrre with her small fists and biting his hand.

Pièrre cursed her under his breath, and reached purposefully for his belt. Alex caught her breath as the blade of a short dagger flashed in the darkness.

Did he intend to kill her?

Her eyes widened in horror and she immediately stilled as he pressed the sharp metal point against her throat. Alex closed her eyes and said a silent prayer.

"Unfasten my belt," Pièrre growled, and Alex's eyes flew to his in disbelief. Surely he did not expect her to assist him! He pressed the dagger deeper for emphasis, his lips twisting into a wicked grin.

"Now," he insisted.

Alex swallowed with difficulty, her gaze flickering around the room, searching for some way of escape.

She could not struggle free of him, she acknowledged with despair. She could not defend herself and there was no one in the house who would help her. A chill passed through Alex, making her tremble from head to toe. The intent in Pièrre's eyes was easy to read and she knew he would not hesitate to kill her should she fail to do his bidding.

The dagger probed at her throat insistently and Alex reached for his woolen chausses hesitantly. Her fingers trembled as she fumbled with the fastening, her hands seemingly unwilling to complete the simple task. Pièrre's swollen manhood pressed against her fingers, its heat tangible even through the thick cloth.

As his enlarged member sprang forth from its woven prison, a simple truth struck her. No matter what happened this night, Alexandria de Fontaine was not quite ready to die. And she would not likely die from rape, however brutally it was performed. Determined to live through this ordeal, Alex closed her eyes tightly, refusing to look at Pièrre.

"Spread your legs," her assailant insisted, and Alex hesitated for a heartbeat, knowing what would follow. The blade traced a thin line across her jugular and she reluctantly did his bidding, helpless tears coursing down her cheeks. She prayed silently that the act would be completed quickly. Averting her face, Alex opened her eyes and focused her attention on the draperies.

Pièrre dropped his weight between her thighs with a grunt of satisfaction. He tipped his hips, forcing himself upward and into her with one abrupt thrust. Alex gasped at the pain as her maidenhead broke and he invaded her completely, her eyes flying to his in surprise. Pièrre's eyes were closed as he leaned his head back, oblivious to the pain he had caused her, a smile of pleasure curving his lips.

He did not hesitate any longer, jutting his hips against hers insistently three or four times in rapid succession, his breath coming in shorter and shorter gasps with each thrust. The pressure behind the blade against Alex's throat ebbed and flowed with his movements, digging into her soft flesh.

Alex felt a warm trickle on her throat and knew that the blade had finally pierced the skin. Pièrre's harsh movements tore at her virginal softness and Alex bit into the hand that still silenced her screams in anguish. The thought filtered through her mind that perhaps rape could kill her after all.

Pièrre froze suddenly, and arched his back convulsively above her, emitting a low groan of satisfaction as he gained his release. Alex felt his warmth spread within her and her eyes filled with helpless tears. Pièrre sagged against her, his weight falling across her chest, his breathing heavy, his skin damp with perspiration.

Chapter Five

Outside Alex's window, a cold rain began to fall, the drops beating a steady rhythm against the stone. Slowly the thought of countless nights spent beneath Pièrre's weight in similar fashion impressed itself upon Alex's numbed mind, turning her stomach. Even the thought of a single repetition of this act was too much to bear. Taking advantage of Pièrre's relaxed state, she unceremoniously shoved him to one side and leapt from the bed.

By the time Pièrre had grasped her intent and rose to pursue her, Alex was halfway out the door. The oaken door banged against the wall as she gained the hall, her heart pounding, Pièrre's footsteps right behind her.

Racing down the stairs, she glanced up from the landing just in time to see Pièrre launch himself from the top step. She hastened her steps in panic, but to no avail. Pièrre landed squarely atop her, the impact sending the two of them tumbling noisily down the remaining stairs. Dazed from the fall, Alex struggled to her feet, the cold edge of a dagger against her throat bringing her to an abrupt halt.

"So, you would run from me," Pièrre hissed, and Alex twisted away, only to have him grab a fistful of her hair. "Well you know I cannot allow such a thing." He backed her up against the stone wall, stroking under her ear with the point of the dagger. Alex averted her eyes, her breath still coming in short gasps from their tumble on the stairs.

How could anyone have slept through the noise they had made when they fell? Or did Guilio simply not want to interfere?

"Where were you going, *chérie*?" Pièrre whispered insistently, and Alex lifted her chin another notch, refusing to meet his eyes. "Answer me," he insisted, the dagger point digging into her neck. A wave of anger swept through Alex, surprising her with its intensity. Had this man not already abused her enough to satisfy his base desires?

Alex turned slowly to meet Pièrre's gaze, letting him see the anger simmering in her own. She watched the surprise register on his face and felt the hand holding the dagger slacken its grip.

In one smooth movement, she slammed her knee upward into his crotch with all the force she could muster. Pièrre's eyes bulged, as surprise and pain mingled in his features. He doubled over and Alex took the opportunity to duck beneath his arm and dart across the stone floor toward the back door.

Pièrre recovered too quickly for her, leaping to his feet with startling speed, one arm lashing out to fasten around her neck and pull her violently back against his hard chest.

Alex glanced back over her shoulder just in time to see the flash of the descending blade. A scream tore from her lips as Pièrre buried the dagger deep into her left shoulder. Dazed by the sudden pain, Alex collapsed to the floor, her vision clouded.

Pièrre tumbled clumsily behind her, his fingers still locked around the hilt of the dagger. He pulled the knife from the wound and Alex gasped as she felt the pain anew. Blood ran freely from the wound on her shoulder, and the room was fading to a soft gray mist around her.

"Alex!" Michel called, his footsteps echoing on the flagstones in the courtyard, his voice carrying clearly through the house as he returned from an evening at the tavern.

Alex tried to call out a warning but succeeded only in making a low moan. With a herculean effort, she raised her head, feeling consciousness slipping away.

Michel's silhouette in the doorway barely impressed itself on her mind before her cheek fell to rest on the cold floor again as Pièrre moved silently into the shadows.

"Stay away," she murmured, fighting the darkness that rose in her mind, threatening to drag her into its murky depths. "Stay away," she repeated weakly, but her voice faded to a mere whisper in the night air. Her eyes closed and she tried to summon what little strength she had left.

"Alex!" Michel's voice was filled with concern as he spied her prone figure on the floor and rapidly closed the distance between them. "What has happened?" Alex looked up at her brother, her eyes glazed with pain, and shook her head, desperately trying to communicate with him.

Pièrre stepped out of the shadows behind Michel, dagger poised, and Alex reached out, her lips parting to scream, her eyes widening in horror.

Michel glanced over his shoulder just as Pièrre brought down the blade, his eyes widening as the knife neatly slit his throat from one ear to the other.

Alex's mind spun giddily as she watched Michel lift his hand to touch the blood running freely from his throat in disbelief. He fell unsteadily to his knees, his pain-filled eyes seeking out Alex across the narrow room, his once powerful frame crumpling. Alex extended her hand to him, ignoring the pain of her own wounds as she struggled toward her brother, her lungs constricting in a sob of fear. Michel's eyes widened, then they rolled slowly back in his head.

Choking on her tears, Alex strained to reach her brother as he balanced precariously on his knees. The blood flowed freely down his chest as his body wavered, then he crashed face first to the floor.

Tears flowed freely down Alex's cheeks as she grasped Michel's outstretched hand. Her fingers searched for his pulse instinctively, a cold weight settling around her heart when she detected none. She squeezed his hand desperately, unwilling to believe that he was gone, and Michel's fingers curled around hers reflexively. She pressed a kiss to his knuckles, tasting her own salty tears on his flesh, and rested her forehead against the coolness of his hand, still gripping his fingers tightly.

In the piazza, the bell in the campanile chimed the quarter hour, its rich tone resonating through the room as hastening footsteps echoed on the cobblestones outside, and Alexandria knew no more.

The rain had settled to a steady beat when Alex struggled against her stupor, forcing herself to return to consciousness. Nausea rolled over her and she lay motionless for a moment until it passed.

Pièrre was gone, that much was clear, but when would he return? Her mind hazily made the connection between Michel's death and the fact that she had witnessed the crime, the implications bringing her shakily to her knees. Pièrre must have thought her dead, as well, Alex concluded shakily.

If she remained as the only witness to Michel's murder, 'twas not difficult to imagine herself mysteriously disappearing. For who would defend her in this foreign land? Certainly not Guilio.

Alex's heart went cold at the realization that this might be her only chance to save her own life.

Fear gave her the strength to climb the stairs on all fours, stanching the blood flow from her shoulder with a sloppily applied makeshift bandage. Wiping the blood from her face with trembling hands, she struggled into her heavy woolen kirtle and surcoat.

She could not remember coming back downstairs when she found herself kneeling beside Michel again, brushing the curls from his forehead and kissing his brow one last time. Helpless tears streamed down her cheeks as she stumbled out into the courtyard to find Sebastien still saddled and standing silently in the rain, his breath steaming the dank air before his nose.

Alex choked back a sob at having to abandon her brother's body. Praising the patience of the great stallion, she hauled herself into his saddle on the third try from the slippery mounting block. The world spun giddily from her exertions and Alex closed her eyes, the smell of wet horseflesh filling her nostrils as Sebastien stepped out of the darkened courtyard.

The cobbled streets were sleek with rain, the light drops falling steadily on the back of Alex's shoulders as the horse wound his way through the darkened town. Her vision faded in and out, the dampness against her shoulder spreading, and Alex realized groggily that she would not be able to make her way out of Venice alone. She lifted her head and spied a warm golden light flickering ahead, the sound of voices carrying through the night air as she urged Sebastien toward the glowing lamp.

Armand took another draft of wine from his goblet, savoring the almost forgotten pungency as it trickled down the back of his throat. He sighed and leaned back against the wall in relief, enjoying the snug dryness of the tavern, the warm array of smells assaulting his senses, the babble of conversation that rose and fell around him. A fine thing 'twould be indeed to shed this habit from his shoulders at last and become a simple knight again. He praised his luck in finding passage so quickly from Constantinople, knowing that he should reach home before winter.

The game of dice at the next table grew more boisterous, attracting a small group of onlookers, and he watched the play from the corner of his eye with feigned interest, feeling the tension ease from his muscles.

A cry of greeting from the direction of the door heralded the arrival of another customer and Armand did not bother to look up, gesturing to the keeper to fill his goblet yet again. A civilized place this was, much safer than what he had grown accustomed to. Perhaps he would take more than a fair sample of the house wine this night.

When his goblet remained stubbornly empty, Armand looked up with a frown, only to find all eyes fixed on a be-draggled and shivering form huddled just inside the door.

"Please," the figure whispered weakly, the soft intonation of a woman's voice carrying through the silent room before she wavered and crumpled to the floor.

"Poor soul," crooned one old-timer as he bent over her prostrate form sympathetically. "Too drunk she is to earn her keep tonight."

"Give us a look," a ribald voice called from the back. "A shapely wench is just as warm whether she be asleep or not."

A rousing cheer went through the company, followed by a round of toasts and an apparently lewd verse in some Germanic tongue that was met with great approval. The old man who had first gone forth to investigate hefted the unconscious woman onto a nearby table, an appreciative whistle rising collectively when he pulled the hood back from her face.

Armand's fingers tightened their grip on his empty chalice as Alexandria's face was revealed. His mind filled with questions even as he noted the unusual pallor of her complexion and the dark stain on her shoulder beneath the folds of her surcoat.

Injured, not drunk, he corrected, wondering how he could hope to whisk her away from here.

"I say we share," came a suggestion that turned Armand's blood cold.

"Highest bidder," came another.

"Why pay for something we can have for nothing?" questioned a man from the back.

"I say we each take a turn," Armand bellowed as an idea struck him. As he rose to his feet, his towering height immediately drew the awed attention of the others. He noted their recognition of his insignia and the resulting confusion with a skeptical eye.

"Aye, a Templar I've been, denied the companionship of women and the comfort of wine these two years past," he roared, pointing a finger at one man's doubting expression and savoring the fear that flickered through the man's eyes.

"'Tis two years since a wench has warmed my bed," Armand shouted, tearing the tunic from his back. Hurling it down, he ground it into the floor with his heel.

"No longer will I chafe against this unnatural vow of chastity!" he cried, and the crowd roared their approval, pounding their tankards on the tables. "A woman will I have this night, and by God, 'twill be this one!'' Armand bent and scooped Alex up smoothly, tossing her limp form across his shoulder and striding to the back of the hall with determination.

"First rights to the Templar!"

The company parted before Armand like the Red Sea itself, congratulatory smiles and back slaps urging him forward until he kicked open the door to the back room. He threw the crowd a leering grin, much to their delight, pushing the door shut behind him and leaning against it as he let the lady slip from his shoulder and onto her feet.

"It seems we shall even the score after all, milady," Armand murmured softly as he cradled her slight weight against him, his fingers gently pushing aside her kirtle to see her wound.

'Twas a deep and ugly gash, though the blood had stopped flowing. He grimaced, wishing that he possessed the lady's healing skills, momentarily uncertain of what to do.

Alex drifted toward consciousness again, some vague comprehension that a man held her against him impressing itself on her mind. Before she could summon the energy to pull herself away, her senses picked out a particular masculine scent, noted the tenderness in the rough fingers brushing aside her kirtle, recognized a familiar sense of safety that could only mean the presence of one tall knight. The fates had been kind to her this night indeed.

Armand nearly jumped from his skin when the lady's fingers spread tentatively across his chest and she opened her eyes to glance upward. She smiled softly, the warm recognition he saw there making Armand's heart lurch and then swell beyond compare.

"'Tis not so bad as it appears," Alex whispered huskily, seeking to ease the concern from his gaze, her eyes drifting shut despite her efforts to keep them open.

"Milady," Armand muttered, his mind flooding with a thousand questions as he gave her a little shake. Who had stabbed her? Where was she going? Why was she alone? Uncomfortably aware that the rabble in the next room would be patient for only so long, he knew he had to find out what had happened before she passed out again.

"Milady," Armand repeated firmly. He caught a glimpse of hazy blue before her dark lashes fluttered to her cheeks again and gripped her chin firmly, forcing her face up to his.

"Where is Michel?" Armand demanded, hoping to shock her into a response.

Her face crumpled at his question, leaving no doubt in his mind the answer was not good news. He leaned down to her, his low voice compelling in his determination to know the worst.

"Tell me," he commanded softly. The lady shook her head helplessly, her small hand gripping his wrist as she parted her lips with agonizing slowness.

"Dead," Alex whispered flatly, and Armand saw the sparkle of tears on her lashes before she opened her eyes wide, impaling him with that clear sapphire blue.

"I saw him killed," she added unsteadily, her fearful gaze holding his until she saw him grasp the implication of her words.

Murdered! Armand's fingertips fell to the bloodstain on Alex's shoulder of their own volition and she nodded slowly, her eyes swimming out of focus as she collapsed softly against his chest.

Without another thought, Armand bent and scooped up the lady, lifting her small frame into his arms. The back room had another door and he lifted its latch quietly, breathing a sigh of relief when he peeked out and saw the timbers of the stables behind the inn.

He laid Alex carefully in the hay as he saddled Tiberias, tossing a heavy red cloak in his family colors over his shoulders before bending to retrieve his precious burden.

Alex did not stir as he wrapped the warmth of her woolen surcoat snugly around her, lifting her into the saddle before him and tucking his fur-lined cloak around her, as well. Curiously Tiberias did not object to Alex's presence, merely turning an indulgent eye on Armand when her weight settled in the saddle. Alex's chin rested against Armand's shoulder as he held her against his chest with one arm, a protective smile curving his lips as he carefully pulled her hood to shield her from the light drizzle. Satisfied that none had witnessed their departure, he tightened his grip around her waist and urged Tiberias toward the street.

Armand recognized Michel's horse tethered in front of the tavern, remarkably out of place amid the smaller palfreys, his blue-and-white caparisons loudly declaring the identity of his rider's house.

The destrier's head drooped, making him the very picture of dejection, almost as if he instinctively knew of his knight's untimely demise. Without dismounting, Armand untethered the beast, his fingers slipping against the smoothness of the wet leather as he tied the reins to the back of Tiberias' saddle.

When the cobblestone road petered out to hard-packed dirt, Armand glanced back at the dawn breaking through the storm clouds over Venice as the city towers disappeared in the distance behind them. The blue waters of the Adriatic sparkled with orange lights, and the horizon faded into a blue gray mist where he knew Byzantium and the Holy Land itself lay.

His mind filled with unbidden images of the destruction he had witnessed there, the relentless and seemingly endless shedding of blood, the bodies of pilgrims and warriors cast in the dirt like so much carrion.

And he remembered Michel. Perhaps a little young and foolhardy, but surely that did not merit such an early death. He cast a glance down at the woman slumbering in his arms, wishing for an instant that he knew where Michel had fallen.

But there was little he could do about the savagery in the East and no way that he could tend to a dead knight whose location he did not know. Indeed, he did not even have the skill to tend the lady's wound. The only thing he could do for her was escort her home as quickly as possible. His heart filled with resolve, Armand turned his back on the rosy dawn and urged Tiberias forward.

* * *

They did not pause until late afternoon, when Armand left the road and led their horses toward the tinkling waters of a nearby stream. It had not rained, but the sun remained hidden behind clouds, and eerie banks of fog crept across the gently rolling countryside as the damp of night began its descent. The air was disconcertingly still, the slightest sound echoing relentlessly into the distance, making Armand curiously loath to stop even for this brief respite.

Alex stirred as Armand slipped from Tiberias' back, her lashes fluttering open as he reached up and fitted his hands around her waist. He caught the barest glimpse of blue as he lifted her down before she flushed and looked away modestly. Seating her gently on one of the flat stones that bordered the stream, he sat back on his heels and studied her pale face with concern, noting with mingled affection and amusement that she adamantly refused to meet his eyes.

"Will you be able to tend your shoulder alone, milady?" he asked softly, and her eyes darted to his before her gaze scurried away again, her fingers tangling together in her lap.

'Twas the weakness from her blood loss, Alex surmised, uncomfortably aware of her response to the knight's presence. What other reason would she have to feel so awkward under his steady perusal? They had been alone together before, had they not?

As she acknowledged that she had felt the same way each time in the past that she had seen this man, Alex's heart took a leap at the late realization that he had not died in Jerusalem after all. And he no longer wore the colors of the Knights Templar. Why had he left the monastic order?

"Yes, I believe so," she murmured finally in response to his question. Armand nodded, pushing to his feet. The hairs pricked on the back of his neck and he was struck again by his intuitive dislike of this place.

"I would prefer not to light a fire here, milady," Armand cautioned, the timbre of his voice dropping. "Can you manage without one?" Alexandria lifted the edge of her kirtle, peering obliquely at the wound on her shoulder, then nodded slowly, flicking a look up at him.

"Have you a clean cloth that I might use?" she questioned hesitantly, telling herself that she needed to put things in proportion and ignore the false sense of intimacy created by the soft fog.

"Perhaps even a needle and thread," Armand said with a nod, moving to Tiberias' saddlebags. "Well do I remember how you enjoy to ply that tool," he muttered, surprised when the lady chuckled at his comment. He grinned at her over his shoulder and she smiled at him for an instant before looking modestly away.

"The angle is poor for sewing," Alex countered softly, her pulse throbbing insistently in her ears. "I shall have to sear the wound when we have a fire."

"I will build one if you desire," the knight offered anxiously.

"Indeed there is no need to sear it now," she argued, tossing an uncertain glance over her shoulder. "I share your disquiet." She shivered delicately, her gaze running over the thickening barrier of gray fog. " 'Tis something ominous about this mist."

Armand nodded and spared a last look around as he bent to hand her the cloth he had retrieved. "Tend yourself quickly," he murmured. "I would ride before darkness falls."

Alex nodded and took the length of linen from the knight, biting her lip as he strode off. He paused at the edge of the clearing to wink reassuringly before he inclined his head, turned and was swallowed up by the mist.

The sound of his footsteps was muffled by the fallen leaves as they faded from earshot, the scurrying of other small creatures filling the yawning silence. A bullfrog sang out suddenly, from a clump of rushes at Alex's elbow and she jumped in surprise.

Feeling alone and a little nervous, Alex dipped the linen in the clear running water, ignoring the trembling of her fingers as she sought to get on with her task. A splash echoed in the stillness and she started again, breathing a little sigh of relief when she discerned the knight's profile farther down the stream.

She watched covertly as he knelt and splashed the cold water on his face again, running his fingers through his hair, then shaking out the water much like a dog. The mist swirled over the water, partially obscuring his broad shoulders as he dropped against a tree with his back to her.

Reassured by his proximity, Alex shed her mantle and gloves, her fingers expertly probing the cut just above her collarbone. A clean gash but deep, she resolved, pushing the top of her kirtle aside and gently cleaning away the hardened blood and bits of cloth that had stuck there. The wound was closed in a very tenuous manner, she noted with some satisfaction, knowing that if she was careful over the next day or so, it might not need searing. She breathed a sigh of relief, glancing over her shoulder to ensure that the knight still looked away before lifting the hem of her kirtle.

The bile rose in her throat at the blood and semen caked on her thighs, damning evidence of Pièrre's abuse. No dream that, she forced herself to admit, squatting at the edge of the stream and washing away the mess. Whatever the pain she had suffered, she reminded herself sternly, she had lived, and with the kindness of those like the knight who assisted her now, she would continue on despite the cruelty of Pièrre de Villiers.

Suddenly and unexpectedly, her hands blurred before her and Alex squeezed her eyes tightly shut, willing the world to stop spinning. The hem of her kirtle slipped from her fingers and she sat down heavily on the flat stone.

The kitchen floor welled up in her mind's eye, blood running into the crevices between the stones like rainwater after a downpour. Alex gasped as she saw Michel's fingers entwined with her own as if that scene were before her once again. She could feel the tears rising along with the bile as she leaned over the stream on all fours with a sob that shook her to her toes.

There was a crashing in the brush before strong hands closed over her shoulders, supporting her weight as she vomited, bathing her face with blessedly cool water when she finally stopped. Alex kept her eyes shut as the spasms passed, the blackness of despair welling up in her heart and tears running unchecked down her cheeks as she sobbed for her dead brother. Gentle hands brushed the hair back from her face and swept the tears from her cheeks with soothing strokes.

Some minutes later, Alex managed to take a deep shaky breath, her tears spent, her breathing slowing to a more normal cadence. She opened her eyes slowly to find the knight bent over her, his face etched with concern. She gratefully took the wineskin that he offered, rinsing out her mouth and taking a deep swallow of rich red wine. As she lay back at his gesture, her gaze traced the arching branches of the trees above, barely discernible through the soft mist.

The knight leaned over her, his fingertips warm on her shoulder where he worked at cleaning her cut. Alex thought of him waking up at Pontesse, their positions reversed, and smiled softly, relaxing beneath his warm touch. Once again she was struck by how safe she felt in his presence, by his gentleness with her despite his evident strength, by her own conviction that he would never hurt her.

"I do not know your name, Chevalier," she commented quietly, and his eyes flicked to her face, their expression somber, concerned.

"Armand D'Avigny," he responded in a low voice, seemingly unable to tear his eyes away. Alex felt her breath catch in her throat beneath his scrutiny, her gaze flicking to the firmness of his lips as she recalled the sure press of them against her own in the courtyard so long ago.

"I would thank you for your assistance," she managed to say before taking an uncertain breath and plunging on, determined to test his name on her tongue. "Thank you, Armand."

He seemed taken speechless by her gratitude, his mouth opening slowly, then closing again, his eyes darkening to a curious smoky green.

Pounding hoofbeats echoed suddenly through the silence of the glade and Armand's head snapped up, his index finger pressing against Alex's lips as he strained to hear. Alex lay silently, her heart accelerating in fear as she dis-

cerned the riders shouting to each other in French, the
hoofbeats growing louder with frightening speed.

Armand was on his feet in the blink of an eye, lifting Alex
to her feet and pointing into the shelter of the surrounding
forest before giving her an unceremonious shove. Alex
darted toward the trees, throwing a questioning glance over
her shoulder, but Armand simply held up one finger in a
gesture for silence. She nodded mutely, watching helplessly
as he gathered up her cloak, hastily casting a critical eye over
the site for any evidence of their passing.

Alex continued on, expecting the riders to burst into the
clearing at any moment. Who rode with such wanton dis-
regard for his steed on a foul night like this? Alex's heart
clamored with the conviction that it must be Pièrre, seeking the only witness to his crime.

Then Armand was at her side with the animals, his fingers curled into Tiberias' bridle, his hand cupped over the
horse's snout as he led them into the brush. Alex mimicked
his gesture with Sebastien, falling into step behind Armand
as he cut a hasty path through the clutching undergrowth,
the sounds of the approaching riders lending an urgency to
their steps.

Alex struggled to keep up with him, ignoring the bram-
bles clutching at her kirtle, desperately trying to fight the
pain spreading across her shoulder. She felt a warm trickle
of fresh blood mark a new path across her skin and bit her
lip, refusing to let her weakness interfere with their escape.

As the hoofbeats thundered behind them, Armand came
to an abrupt stop, pulling her behind him as he faced back
in the direction of the road, his hand on his sword hilt.

"Hold up!" a man's voice shouted, and the hoofbeats fell
into a jumble of disarray. "This looks a fine place for a
break."

Alex clutched at Sebastien's reins, leaning against his
strong flanks for support, trying to suppress the sound of
her labored breathing. Armand stood absolutely motionless, the war-horses immediately sensing his mood and settling into quiet stances, their ears alone flicking at the
sounds of the new arrivals.

The heavy sound of men dismounting carried to Alex's ears, hauberks and horses' trap jingling, solid footfalls on the earth, chuckles and splashes in the stream. A hauntingly familiar laugh arose over the rest and Alex froze in recognition.

Sure she was that she had made no sound but Armand spun around silently, his searching gaze filled with the inevitable question. Alex nodded slowly and he inclined his head in mute understanding, his gaze dropping to her shoulder. He frowned and Alex glanced down to see a fresh bloodstain spreading on the fabric.

Something white caught the corner of her eye and she saw that Armand offered the still-damp scrap of linen, his expression inscrutable and vaguely forbidding. 'Twas easy enough to perceive his concern, Alex thought with dismay, accepting the cloth with an apologetic smile. She would delay their departure with this troublesome injury. Alex sighed silently and pressed the cool cloth against the cut, willing the bleeding to stop and clinging to her horse's bridle.

"Someone has passed this way," one of the Frenchmen commented. Alex caught her breath, watching with growing trepidation as Armand silently drew the length of his blade from its scabbard and dropped its tip to the leafy mat in front of him.

"What say you, Matthieu?" Pièrre's voice rose, followed closely by a jumble of heavy footfalls. Alex watched Armand adjust his grip on the hilt of his sword, picturing the group of men peering into the murky shadows of the undergrowth.

"Are you mad?" a third man demanded. "Who would go this way?"

"Someone who wished to avoid us," Pièrre shot back coldly, but the third man snorted derisively.

"Only a fool would head into the woods on a night such as this."

"The road curves the other way," pointed out a fourth.

"Fools we are indeed to be riding like madmen in this fog," the third continued sourly.

"And you have yet to tell us whom we pursue, de Villiers," interjected the first man.

"No business is it of yours," Pièrre shot back, but the other men made various sounds of disagreement.

"Risking our lives and our horses are we to ride like this in such foul weather."

"I would know for what end I cast my fate so casually aside."

The men murmured in agreement with one another, their voices fading slightly as they moved away, the apparent path forgotten.

"I seek my betrothed," Pièrre spat, his voice sharp with annoyance. Alex's heart pounded at the reference to herself and she closed her eyes, certain that its beating would be audible to the men even over their argument.

"Oho! The wench you won from Masenti!"

"A fine piece of woman she was."

One of the men chuckled shrewdly. "But not as willing as our friend Pièrre," he observed slyly, drawing hoots of laughter from the others.

"Enough!" Pièrre shouted angrily. "I ride to seek the woman. Follow or not as you will."

A horse's footfalls sounded on the pounded dirt of the road and Alex drew back instinctively as a dark shadow moved through the mists far to one side. The other three men shouted, mounting their horses in a flurry of curses, their outlines barely discernible as they rode off in hot pursuit.

Chapter Six

When the echo of the horses' hooves had faded into the distance, Armand sheathed his blade, turning slowly to face Alex. His lips twisted into a harsh line as he stepped toward her, his gaze fixed on her shoulder. Alex flinched when he raised his hand, bringing his gesture to an abrupt halt.

"Surely, milady, you do not think I intend harm to you?" he demanded softly, his tone incredulous. Alex's face flooded with color, her thoughts falling into a confused jumble as she dropped her eyes and looked away. She felt his warm fingertips easing the neck of her kirtle aside, as he took the cloth from her and wiped away the fresh blood.

"Perhaps your fears are justified," Armand conceded with a sigh of frustration, running his thumb across the again-dry gash. "'Twas my own stupidity that opened the wound once more. I would apologize to you for my thoughtlessness."

Alex's lips parted in surprise, and she was momentarily speechless at the realization that he was angry with himself. "'Twas most important to hide," she whispered, watching with fascination as he smiled down at her.

"'Tis most important to return you safely to France," Armand murmured huskily, his lashes dropping as his gaze fell to her lips. "Did you only mean to clean the cut?" he asked quietly, brushing one warm fingertip across her shoulder.

Alex nodded, clearing her throat with difficulty before she spoke, marveling at how intoxicated she felt in his presence.

"I will sear it closed when we have a fire," she reiterated, darting a glance upward as a thought occurred to her. "If you do not mind my using your dagger."

Armand chuckled, his teeth flashing in the falling darkness, his expression indulgent as he regarded her. "Surely, milady, you know that you are more than welcome to anything I possess or have the ability to give you," he commented, his voice unusually low, and Alex felt a telltale flush rising over her cheeks at his teasing.

"You are too kind," she responded inanely, daring to hope that he did not merely jest with her.

Needing to put some space between them she stepped away, a little unsteady on her feet as she reached for her horse's bridle. Armand must have sensed her discomfort, for he did not touch her.

Armand, for his part, was regretting this lady's ability to loosen his usually reticent tongue and was trying to stifle his impulse to promise this tiny creature every scrap of his body and soul.

He forced himself to focus on the conversation they had overheard, his skin crawling at the recollection of the name Pièrre de Villiers. Know him, Armand did not, but he knew of him and that alone was adequate to fuel his fears.

Was Pièrre de Villiers the one who had killed Michel and wounded Alex? An urge for vengeance rose hot and heavy in his chest, closely followed by another to swear his blade to this lady's defense. Armand quelled both impulses determinedly, knowing that such a gesture would be grossly inappropriate and likely offend the lady's gentle sensibilities.

"How far do we ride this night?" she asked quietly, and he was forced to look at her again, his heart softening at the defiant tilt of her chin despite the pallor of her skin. He cursed himself again for neglecting her wound, determining that he would guard her fragile strength more carefully for the rest of their journey.

Alex watched as Armand pursed his lips and looked away, as if he had been dreading her question.

"Did Pièrre de Villiers murder your brother?" he demanded, his gaze swiveling to meet hers again. Alex swallowed with difficulty, knowing that she would not be able to lie to him.

"I am the betrothed of whom he spoke," she answered obliquely, turning away and missing the flare of emotion in Armand's eyes before he managed to restrain his response.

Betrothed! Armand struggled to recall the remainder of what he had overheard in an attempt to control the maelstrom of emotions in his heart. What had he done to earn such malice from the fates?

"Something was said of winning your hand?" he asked, feeling as though the fog had invaded his very mind, clouding his ability to think clearly. Alex sighed, a frown etching the space between her brows.

"My uncle gambles," she explained in a flat voice, absently readjusting her veil and kirtle. "He lost all his coins while I was in the East and wagered me instead." She threw Armand a wry grin that did not reach her eyes.

"He lost."

Alex watched as Armand frowned, then he turned and paced a distance, his footsteps heavy in the silence of the woods. She heard him exhale, watched him bend his head back and look up at the barren arches of the tree branches overhead.

"I think we should ride steadily until we reach Burgundy," he said finally, his voice calm and curiously distant. Alex opened her mouth in surprise and closed it again, uncertain of what to say.

"Surely that will take days," she managed, and Armand nodded slowly, his back still turned to her.

"At this speed, 'twill more likely take a week," he answered quietly. Alex bent her head and studied the tips of her shoes. Was he then so anxious to be rid of her?

"Why would you ride so hard?" she asked in a quiet voice. Armand sighed with exasperation, stepping quickly

toward her and lifting her chin with one finger. Alex saw the
concern in his eyes and frowned in confusion.

"Milady, you said you knew who had killed Michel."

"Indeed, I do," Alex responded with confusion, "but I
fail to see its relevance."

Armand gritted his teeth in frustration before he responded. "Indeed, 'tis of little matter that this murderer has
already tried to kill you, milady," he growled. "Certain you
are that he knows you witnessed his crime?" he continued.
Alex nodded silently, her mind numbed. "And now you
have deserted an apparently ardent betrothed, as well," he
muttered under his breath. "We shall do well to evade them
both."

She could not correct him, Alex thought wildly to herself, her mind spinning as she stifled the urge to blurt out the
truth. She could not add that burden to Armand's shoulders, as willing as he seemed to be to take up her cause. Already he did too much by assisting her home, not to mention
saving her life in Jerusalem. Tears of self-pity pricked the
backs of her eyelids, that she could not have been paired
with a noble knight such as Armand instead of Pièrre.

"We ride directly toward home," Armand concluded
firmly, watching helplessly as Alex dissolved into silent
tears. To have her hand lost in a gambling match and then
be forced to watch her brother's murder, the lady had been
sorely used indeed. The most he could do for her was to see
her safely home.

Armand bent and scooped Alex up in his arms, lifting her
to sit sideways atop Tiberias. She opened her mouth to protest, but he held up his hand.

"Faster will we ride and you will be able to rest," he said,
his tone brooking no argument. Recognizing the truth in
Armand's words, Alex did not defy him, huddling against
the pommel of the saddle as he swung up behind her. He
wrapped one strong arm around her waist, pulling her back
so that her cheek rested against his chest, and she melted
against him, exhaustion filling her veins and dissolving her
resistance.

"Go to sleep, milady," Armand murmured quietly as the horses picked their way back out to the road in the gathering twilight.

Much to Alex's surprise, she found herself doing exactly that.

When Alex awoke, the night had passed and the fog had cleared. Flat meadows and fields had given way to gently rolling hills, their grasses yellow and gold under the late autumn sun. The scattered trees were barren of leaves and the red-tiled roofs of a town rose between the hills ahead. Alex saw familiar rows of vineyards curving up the hills on either side of the town, the vines now dormant.

"Good morning, milady," Armand's warm voice came from above her, and Alex tipped her head back to give him a smile. The world spun dizzily for a moment and she blinked in surprise as his concerned features swam lazily into focus. Armand's arm tightened around her waist and he leaned toward her.

"Are you well?"

"Hungry no doubt, no more than that," Alex admitted ruefully, refusing to acknowledge a seed of doubt in the back of her mind. Her stomach grumbled loudly right on cue and they both laughed, the brief tightening of Armand's arm around her waist indicating his relief.

"You have not slept," she accused mildly, noticing the russet stubble on his chin and the shadows beneath his eyes.

"Well accustomed am I to this sort of travel," he excused himself simply, drawing an indignant sniff from his tiny companion.

"Even a Templar requires some sleep," she shot back but he made no response.

A ravine carved a deep crevice between two curving hills just ahead and Armand led the horses off the road, following the hill down to the water and stopping under the bridge itself. The horses immediately bent to drink their fill and Armand slipped from his saddle, reaching up to grasp Alex firmly around the waist and lower her to the ground.

She winced fleetingly at the impact, cursing her weakness when Armand immediately sobered.

"Are you well?" he demanded once again, and she threw him a reassuring smile.

"Certainly," she responded firmly. "'Tis just a little tender." Armand studied her for a moment, then nodded in reluctant agreement.

"Surely we could ride the horses into town," Alex commented, wondering why Armand had chosen to stop so close to town.

"We could if you were riding into town," Armand answered calmly as he bent to take a drink from the stream himself.

"You intend to leave me here!" Alex gasped, and Armand chuckled at her response.

"For the twinkling of an eye, no more."

"Where do you ride alone?" she demanded.

"Into that town to fetch something to eat," Armand explained calmly, dunking his face into the stream, apparently not surprised in the least by her reaction.

"I could certainly accompany you," Alex argued.

"You most certainly will not," Armand reiterated firmly, standing up and shaking the water out of his hair.

"And why not?" Alex demanded defiantly, determined not to let the issue go without a fight.

"'Tis unwise for anyone to see you pass this way," Armand answered, dropping his hands to his hips. "We could have passed de Villiers and his men while they slept. Thinking they had missed you, they might retrace their steps and double back." He sighed with exasperation and ran his fingers through his hair, the raggedness of his voice revealing his exhaustion.

"To think nothing of Michel's murderer. I see no reason to leave him an easy trail should he decide to pursue you, as well. We will pass through the town when the sun is high and all are asleep."

"What if he should find me here while you are gone?" Alex demanded, surprised at the flash of anger in Armand's eyes. He stepped toward her and grasped her upper arms in a relentless grip, lifting her to her toes as he glared down at her furiously.

"Find you he will not, for you will hide here silently," he insisted in a low voice. "You will sit with your horse and I will return as quickly as possible." Feeling suddenly vulnerable, Alex bit her lip and tears rose unbidden in her eyes.

Her expression dissolved Armand's determination to keep her at arm's length. Betrothed or not, she spoke straight to his heart with every movement and he was powerless to resist her. He groaned as he gathered Alex close to his chest in a tight hug, his palms cupping her shoulders as he pressed a gentle kiss to her temple.

"I cannot take you with me," he repeated almost as if he were trying to convince himself, and Alex nodded mutely, her face buried in his chest. "Alex, make this not more difficult than 'tis." Alex started at his use of her Christian name, glancing up at him in surprise.

"Certain you are that this is best?" she asked quietly, and Armand nodded ruefully, one hand tracing the curve of her cheek as he gazed down at her.

"No safer way can I imagine to keep you from view," he admitted, his arms tightening protectively around her. "Like as not, I will lose my temper, shout at some sleepy baker and frighten the poor man to death," Armand joked, trying to make light of the matter, wishing that there was some other way to keep her safely tucked out of sight.

Alex chuckled with him, the warmth in Armand's eyes making her very aware of his closeness. He held her tightly, her breasts crushed against his chest, her soft thighs pressed against the hard length of his, every fiber of her being achingly aware of him. She watched in fascination as his eyes darkened the way they had the day before, then he bent and slowly took her lips with his.

Alex opened her mouth, savoring the taste of him as he took advantage of her invitation, his fingers rising beneath her veil and curling in the hair at the nape of her neck as he bent her slightly backward. He ended the kiss slowly, lifting his head and smiling bemusedly down at her when she sighed contentedly.

Armand touched the gentle indent of the dimple in her cheek as she smiled and tapped the end of her nose with one fingertip in a teasing gesture of warning.

"Do not even think of cleaning your wound before I return," he admonished her sternly, waiting for her to nod in agreement before he stepped away.

He swung into his saddle with ease, gave Alex one last glance, then rode out from under the bridge. Alex heard the stallion's hooves on the wooden bridge a moment later and sat resignedly down to wait, her fingertips running over her lips as she replayed Armand's kiss in her mind.

The sound of hoofbeats on the bridge above brought Alex out of her reverie and to her feet, her heart pounding. Sebastien flicked an ear disinterestedly and continued to pull determinedly on the weeds that grew between the foundation stones of the bridge. Alex grasped his halter to silence him as the hoofbeats slowed.

Was it Pièrre? The hoofbeats moved slowly across the wood planks, an accompanying creaking sound indicating that perhaps a donkey or plow horse pulled a cart along the road, and Alex sighed almost audibly with relief. 'Twas no more than a farmer heading into town.

Voices were raised in greeting, the patter of human footsteps echoing across the bridge as someone came from town. Alex huddled against the bridge's stone foundation and held her breath while her horse flicked his tail, chewing calmly, his expression of aloof disdain more than adequately expressing his opinion of her frightened response.

The noises above faded as the travelers continued on their respective ways and Alex exhaled slowly, rubbing the stallion's nose with an apologetic grin and letting him return to his weed pulling.

Alex absently watched him chew, her mind occupied with Armand's earlier comments. Would Pièrre really kill her to remove a witness to his crime? Or would he simply insist on their marriage instead, making it impossible for her to press charges or avenge Michel's murder.

There was no one else to defend her family's honor.

The abrupt realization that she was the last of the once mighty Fontaine house stunned Alex with its unexpectedness. A wave of dizziness washed over Alex again, and she sank down onto the cold earth, feeling curiously alone in the world. 'Twas now her responsibility to rebuild her father's château and there was no one to help her, save the man she took to husband.

Should she marry Pièrre, the Fontaine lands would become his, the mighty heritage of her bloodline tainted with his seed. Jean de Fontaine's legacy would benefit the man who had murdered his only son in cold blood. That would be the cruelest wound of all. Angry tears spilled down Alex's cheeks and she buried her face in her hands, despairing of her ability to affect her own destiny.

Prancing hoofbeats echoed overhead and Alex's chin snapped up, half-certain that her thoughts had summoned Pièrre to her side. The horse flicked his ears in curiosity and she knew he recognized the gait of another knight's charger.

The horse above left the road, and Alex rose to her feet as she heard the muffled sound of his hooves falling on the grass. The stallion beside her listened with interest and stepped toward the edge of the bridge foundation on the side that the other horse approached. Alex grabbed his harness to try to pull him back, but he chose that moment to nicker and Alex's heart stopped in her throat.

"Aye, something I have for you," Armand called quietly, and the beast nickered again, pulling loose of Alex's limp grip and stepping out into the sunlight.

Alex's knees buckled beneath her in relief and she landed on the ground with an ungraceful plop. She tried to return her breathing to a normal rate before Armand came into sight but he was too perceptive as always. He jumped from his saddle with ease and squatted down beside her, tipping up her chin with his index finger.

"Are you well?" he demanded typically, and Alex flushed under his scrutiny.

"A fright you would give anyone like that," she admitted, and he grinned mischievously, the impetuous smile giving him a carefree air that sent Alex's heart racing.

"I shall have to teach Tiberias a distinctive dance so that you can recognize his hoofbeats," Armand teased, and Alex laughed awkwardly, the intimacy of their pose leaving her feeling curiously vulnerable to his charm. So easily had she come to trust him that some part of her could not help but wonder whether her instincts had led her astray.

"Tiberias?" she asked, seizing on a more neutral topic of conversation. "He is named for a city in the East?" At the sound of his name, the dark stallion snorted in apparent indignation. Armand nodded and spared the horse a glance over his shoulder.

"'Twas said he bore fine Arabian blood."

"Certainly has he a noble bearing," Alex commented idly, noting the beast's regal lines as she took a steadying breath. "How sad 'tis that we are all caught in tidings of woe from that part of the world," she mused almost to herself, and Armand looked back at her with surprise.

"You speak the truth, milady. Little do we hear of the fine spices, textiles and horseflesh we have gained from the East, only tales of lost knights in a distant land."

"Always it seems there is battle waging there," she said with a sad shake of her head, her worries about Fontaine giving her thoughts a dismal turn.

"Indeed, milady, the fighting never does cease," Armand agreed heavily, dropping to the ground beside her, the laughter fading from his eyes. "Little do I miss that life." Alex glanced to his profile, watching as he stared out across the pastures, his mind apparently filled with memories of a faraway land.

"Will you return to the Crusades?" Alex asked abruptly, suddenly needing to hear his response.

Armand sat quietly for a moment, studying the ground, a thoughtful frown etched between his brows. "I should think bearing the cross for two years enough of a price for one man," he said finally. "Indeed, were it my choice alone, I would not return."

"The Templars mean to summon you back to the Holy Land?" she asked, her question more a statement of fact than anything else, but Armand shook his head in denial, throwing her a sharp look before he spoke.

"I have left the Order," he admitted, his words bringing a frown to Alex's brow.

"Then I do not understand your meaning," she confessed, and he turned, studying her features. Alex met his gaze unflinchingly, trying to read the expression she saw reflected in the emerald depths of his eyes.

"Well you know that the loss of Jerusalem will not pass unchallenged, milady, and I do not know what my liege lord will ask of me," he said huskily.

Alex looked away and resolutely blinked back her tears, knowing that Armand spoke the truth. A knight pledged to the service of a lord had little choice when that lord dictated his will.

Who could tell what the response had been to the loss of Jerusalem? A Crusade could well be launching to the East even as they sat here. Indeed, anything was possible. Alex stared unseeingly out at the golden pastures, a riot of emotions swirling inside her, the overriding concern she felt for Armand's welfare surprising her with its intensity.

The knight cleared his throat abruptly, then spoke in a light tone. "I had thought you were hungry," he teased in a deliberate attempt to change the subject, opening his bulging saddlebag to show her what he had bought.

The next few days blurred together in Alex's mind, the repetitive rhythm of sleeping and riding, the relentless thudding of the horse's hoofbeats on the earth, the foothills giving way to the snowy peaks of the mountains on either side of the pass, all melding into an incoherent pattern.

She slept throughout the first night, despite her reservations and the increasing cold, and dozed fitfully during the next day, her bouts of dizziness intensifying each time Armand helped her down from the saddle to taste the cool waters of a passing stream.

He asked each time if she was strong enough to continue and she reassured him, her mind fixed on the idea that she could not be safe outside the walls of Château Pontesse, where Sophie's healing hands would undoubtedly do their magic.

Her shoulder began to throb with increasing intensity and she acknowledged the infection somewhere in the back of her mind. Armand offered to make a fire each night but Alex declined, knowing that her wound should not be seared closed in its unclean state.

Clinging determinedly to the belief that they would reach Pontesse in time for Sophie to help, Alex deliberately did not tell Armand of the growing pain or the infection, not wanting to supply him with any reason to slow their flight. The concern she glimpsed in his eyes told her that he suspected something was amiss, but he did not challenge her, trusting in her reassurances and continuing with all speed on the road west.

By noon on the eighth day, Alex was already asleep, her breathing shallow as she leaned against Armand's chest, her hand curled like a child's against his tunic. He glanced down at her with a frown, disconcerted that she had been sleeping more and more. Alex's hood blew across her face and he reached to brush it aside with a gentle finger, his hand freezing in midgesture as he felt the heat emanating from her skin.

Armand's mouth went dry in fear as he touched her brow and found her burning with feverish heat, instantly regretting his belief in her constant reassurances. He had trusted her judgment, never suspecting that she might be less than objective in assessing her own illness. In but a few more days, they would come out of the mountains close to Lyons, and fortunately he knew of an inn where they could take refuge.

Alex tossed in her bed, twisting back and forth, dimly aware of the burning pain in her shoulder. She heard the echo of hoofbeats around her, remembering that Death was said to ride a dark horse. Had he come for her?

Her eyes opened abruptly and she blinked twice at the unexpected brilliance of the room. Everything was pristine, the walls whitewashed, the linen bright and clean.

Bright yellow rays of sunlight came through the open window where a white curtain ruffled gently in the cool breeze. Alex sniffed appreciatively at the crisp air that wafted into the room, carrying the scent of a wood fire.

She sat up to examine her surroundings, the resulting stab of pain in her shoulder bringing her to full awareness. Blinking slowly as the spasm of pain subsided, she braced herself on her elbows and looked around with curiosity.

The room was simply furnished, a table with pitcher and washstand the only fixture other than the rough-hewn bed. Her clothes were neatly folded to one side. The floor was of dark wood and polished to a rich gleam and rough timbers spanned the width of the ceiling, the steep angle indicating the slope of the roof.

Alex's heart contracted when her eyes lit on Armand's sleeping figure. He sat on the floor, his back against the opposite wall, head bowed, knees pulled up to his chest, his arms draped loosely around them. His hauberk and tabard lay on the floor beside him in a heap.

He wore a full-cut white shirt, the open neck revealing a thatch of curly chest hair, his fitted woolen chausses emphasizing the muscular length of his legs. The stubble on his chin, though still short, had filled out into a beard, making Alex wonder how long she had slept.

The call of nature became more insistent and she swung her legs over the side of the bed. Her fingers sought the wound in her shoulder and she breathed a silent sigh of relief when she touched the scar, seared closed and well on its way to healing.

Pulling herself to her feet, she was surprised by the wave of weakness that coursed through her. There was nothing for it—somehow she would have to find the garderobe. She was loathe to awaken Armand so she stood with an effort, steadying herself by clutching the bedpost, inordinately pleased at her accomplishment as she gained her balance.

Glancing down, Alex was surprised to find herself wearing a man's white shirt remarkably similar to the one that Armand wore, its volume dwarfing her small figure as it draped all the way down to her knees. She extended one arm and watched the cuff dangle past her fingertips, unable to suppress a giggle as she pushed up the sleeve.

"In bed should you be, milady," Armand growled goodnaturedly, and she threw him a smile over her shoulder.

"I must seek the garderobe," she explained, helpless to stop the blush that rose over her cheeks. Armand laughed and pushed to his feet, brushing off his chausses and lifting her surcoat down from a hook on the back of the door. He dropped the cloak over her shoulders, his warm fingers brushing her nape and sending a familiar tingle down her spine.

"I will show you the way," he said, offering his arm. Alex hesitated.

"In truth," she said, "I would much rather go alone."

Armand chuckled. "You would think otherwise, did you know the business of this establishment."

Alex frowned. "What do you mean?"

Armand folded his arms across his chest and regarded her indulgently. "You might find yourself accosted in the halls should you go alone, milady."

"In what sort of establishment would a lady find herself accosted..." Alex began indignantly, her voice trailing away as she understood his meaning. "This is a *brothel!*" she gasped, and Armand nodded, his mouth widening into a wicked grin. Forgetting her weakened state, Alex swatted him across the shoulder as hard as she could with her good arm.

"A brothel!" she repeated, unable to believe it. She belted him again and he ducked her blows laughingly. "How dare you do such a thing!"

"'Twas the only place that I knew hereabouts," he admitted, and Alex's eyes flashed in anger.

"You *knew* this place? 'Twas not merely the first place to stop?"

"Once or twice have I visited here in the past," Armand admitted, backing cautiously away from Alex.

"Once or twice?" Alex spat in disbelief, finding herself furiously angry. "And here you bring me to stay? What, pray tell, does that make me?"

"A rose among thorns?" Armand teased.

"Sorry I felt for you having to sleep on the floor," she fumed, waggling a finger at him in accusation. "In truth, you have had a gentleman's holiday!"

"I have done no such thing, Alex," he asserted firmly, his expression suddenly serious.

"Hah!" was her disbelieving response as she cornered him and began to beat on the wall of his chest with her tiny fists.

Swearing good-naturedly under his breath, Armand lifted her up, pinning her elbows to her sides in one smooth gesture, holding her helplessly off the floor. He opened his mouth to speak but Alex would give him no quarter, cutting him off before he even uttered a word.

"How dare you treat me like some piece of baggage!" she spat, aiming a solid kick at his kneecap. Armand winced, a vehement curse erupting from his lips, his eyes flashing as he dropped Alex unceremoniously onto the bed.

Alex stifled an urge to laugh as she bounced on the straw mattress. She scurried to roll across the bed and escape but Armand leapt on top of her with lightning speed, straddling her hips as he planted one knee firmly on either side. Alex tried to twist away but he grasped her shoulders, his eyes gleaming with intent as he leaned over her.

"'Tis likely you expect me to listen to some explanation now," she challenged him, feeling a smile twitch at the corners of her lips in response to his triumphant grin.

"Nay, milady, not yet," Armand responded as he bent with maddening deliberation and took her lips in a sweetly gentle kiss. Alex sighed with contentment and closed her eyes as she relaxed beneath him, savoring the tenderness of his caress.

"Now do I expect you to listen," he murmured against her lips when he finally lifted his head.

"A brothel?" Alex demanded doubtfully, and Armand nodded, albeit a little sheepishly.

"Therese, the woman who owns this inn, owed me a favor," he explained calmly, and Alex laughed aloud, unable to restrain her response. Armand had the grace to grin. " 'Twas not as you are thinking," he insisted.

"Of course not," Alex countered agreeably, watching his discomfort with sparkling eyes.

"I was last here on my way to Constantinople," Armand continued. "A local nobleman was causing difficulties, but several other guests and I managed to convince him to restrain himself."

When Alex simply nodded in understanding and made no comment, Armand rolled easily to his back, closing his eyes in appreciation of the softness of the mattress. "Adamant should I have been on sharing the bed," he pronounced, and Alex swatted him playfully for his impertinence.

"Sleeping in a houseful of light-skirts does not necessarily make me one of their rank," she retorted laughingly, and Armand chuckled along with her, rolling to his side and catching her hand before she could hit him again, the warmth of his strong fingers closing around her narrow wrist like a bracelet.

"Indeed it does not, milady," he answered huskily, his eyes suddenly serious as he pressed a kiss on her palm. Alex swallowed with difficulty, unable to tear her gaze away from the firm outline of his lips.

Armand turned abruptly and got smoothly to his feet, reaching back to offer her his hand. "The garderobe," he reminded her quietly when she looked blank.

"You have yet to tell me why we came here," Alex prompted as she rose.

"Therese, I knew, would hide our presence should I ask her to do so," Armand explained. "She also knows something of healing and had strong words for you for not telling me of your infection."

Alex blushed and examined her toes with interest. "'Twas evidently much worse than I thought," she admitted, and Armand's arm tightened around her waist.

"Do not trifle again with your own life, milady," he chided her gently, giving Alex an affectionate squeeze before leading her into the hall.

Chapter Seven

Therese turned out to be a remarkably pleasant woman despite Alex's reservations, her infectious laugh and bubbly good nature putting Alex immediately at ease as the three of them dined in the cozy hall.

Therese wore her golden red hair loose, the curling mass cascading down her back to her waist and glinting in the firelight. Her turquoise kirtle was exquisitely made, the hems and cuffs etched with delicate embroidery, and her gold girdle was set lavishly with polished stones.

Although Therese was clearly older than Alex, her features were still soft and attractive. She made conversation easily and was cognizant of current matters in the king's court in Paris. In short, she was as distant in manner as possible from any prostitute Alex had ever encountered and considerably better mannered than many ladies of court she had known.

A stable boy rushed into the hall as they sat sipping their wine after dinner and Therese looked up with interest. "Someone arrives?" Therese asked, and the boy nodded eagerly.

"A knight with three men at arms accompanying him."

"What color is his standard?" Alex demanded.

"Black and gold, milady," the boy responded, and Alex got to her feet, her heart pounding in her throat.

"Does his insignia include a lion with a fleur-de-lis in its teeth?" she asked, feeling as though she already knew the answer.

"Indeed it does, milady," the boy responded with surprise, and Alex swayed at the confirmation of her worst fears. Armand stepped behind her, slipping his arm around her waist to steady her.

"'Tis de Villiers' standard," she said hoarsely. "He will surely recognize me, even here, and there is nowhere to hide." She gasped as she remembered Sebastien and lifted her agonized gaze to Armand. "What if he should recognize Michel's horse?"

"It seems we shall have to use your idea, Therese," Armand said quietly, and the other woman nodded, smiling reassuringly at Alex's uncomprehending look.

Therese clapped her hands and the other women in her household gathered around her in curiosity. "There is one more among our numbers this night," she said matter-of-factly, and Alex's eyes widened in surprise. "And her services have been sold for the entire night, should anyone ask you."

The women nodded in understanding and Alex felt her mouth drop open in astonishment. Armand tugged on her hand insistently, making for the stairs, but Alex defiantly froze in her steps.

"I will not do this thing," she blazed indignantly, but Armand shook his head.

"Milady, there is not much time," he insisted, but Alex snatched her fingers from his grip and folded her arms stubbornly across her chest.

"Indeed, sir, there is not enough time," she retorted, and Armand groaned and flicked a warning glance at Therese, who chuckled to herself as she perched on the edge of the table.

"Once again, 'tis not as you think," he muttered to Alex before he scooped her up and bodily tossed her over his shoulder.

Alex squealed at the indignity, pounding her fists against the broad expanse of his back, the sound of Therese's lilting laughter fueling her anger. Armand climbed the stairs quickly, apparently undisturbed by Alex's assault, and made his way purposefully down the hall. He strode into the room they had shared and dumped her unceremoniously on the bed, stepping back to pull off his shirt.

"Get undressed," he commanded tersely, and Alex snorted.

"I will do no such thing," she countered hotly.

"Would you prefer that I do it for you?" he threatened, moving toward her with intent in his eyes. Alex scrambled across the width of the bed, finding the sight of his bare chest annoyingly distracting.

"If you think I would become your whore simply to avoid wedding Pièrre, you are sadly mistaken, sir," she insisted from the other side of the mattress.

Armand rolled his eyes in exasperation and put his hands on his hips. "No one has asked you to become a whore," he stated flatly, and Alex looked at him in outright confusion.

"What, then, am I being asked to do?"

"Simply act the whore."

"I fail to see the difference," she snapped, pushing to her feet on the far side of the bed and placing her hands on her hips, unconsciously mimicking Armand's stance.

"The difference lies in the act itself," he explained patiently, and Alex raised her eyebrows inquiringly. "In whether the act occurs or not."

Alex flushed but she held his gaze. "And will it?"

"Nay, milady," Armand answered firmly.

"Then, pray tell, sir, what is the point?"

"If the act looks to be eminent in such a place as this, then you will be assumed to be a prostitute and hence not worthy of further scrutiny."

Alex turned her back to him, perversely annoyed that Therese's idea made sense. "'Tis ridiculous," she said flatly.

"Had you a better way to escape de Villiers' notice, I would gladly follow it," Armand responded. The sound of men's voices rose from the hall below and Alex turned to him, her eyes filled with panic.

"Get undressed, milady," he repeated softly, and Alex shook her head, feeling inexplicably cornered. She licked her lips nervously and met his gaze steadily.

"Swear to me the act will not be completed," she said in a low voice, only slightly relieved when Armand nodded decisively and without hesitation.

"Willingly do I give you my most solemn vow, milady," he said firmly, and she nodded slowly, some feminine voice deep inside her wishing he had not agreed quite so easily.

"Turn your back," she insisted, a flush staining her cheeks, and Armand grinned with relief even as he turned away. Nimbly, Alex unbraided her hair, shaking out the dark mass over her shoulders. Shoes and stockings fell to the floor, followed by her girdle and kirtle. Alex stopped as she bunched the soft cotton of her chemise in her hands, realizing that she wore nothing else.

"Everything?" she asked in a timid voice.

"What think you?" Armand responded testily, and she sighed, pulling the garment resignedly over her head. Grateful for the relative darkness in the room, she sat nervously on the farthest edge of the mattress from him, unable to move any closer.

Heavy footsteps sounded on the stairs and Armand spun around and dropped to the bed. Urging Alex to the center of the mattress, he rolled her onto her back and slipped between her thighs. Pulling her knees up on either side of his hips without preamble and slipping his arms beneath her, he cradled her against the warmth of his chest.

When Alex instinctively struggled against Armand's familiarity, he glared at her sternly, the sound on the stairs reinforcing his reprimand. "'Twould help if you looked moderately willing," he whispered, his tone deliberately teasing, and Alex flushed, slipping her arms shyly around his neck and taking a deep breath. Had he not given her his word?

The door to the next room hit the wall and Alex's eyes widened in fear as a man's voice rose in anger. Armand winked at her conspiratorially, his warm palm slipping up her neck to cup the back of her head. He bent and possessively took her lips with his, even as his other hand curved around her naked breast.

Alex shivered at the intimacy of his gesture and Armand murmured quiet assurances against her lips, his thumb rhythmically stroking the back of her neck as he tried to soothe her fears.

Alex felt her muscles gradually relax, her breathing slowing as she let Armand's warmth engulf her like a cozy cocoon. He had given her his word and she had already trusted him with her life on more than one occasion. If this was the only way to avoid discovery, the least she could do was help to make their act seem convincing.

Amazed at how safe she felt in Armand's arms, Alex tightened her arms around his neck, tangling her fingers in his hair. Instinctively, her legs tightened around his waist as her body responded, her back arching to force her breasts against the tangle of hair on his chest.

Armand inhaled sharply, his breath tickling her earlobe, his lips burning a path down her throat, his thumb caressing her nipple in slow circles, his touch sure but gentle. Alex gasped at the waves of pleasure emanating from that taut peak, the reverence in Armand's every gesture making her heart sing.

At that moment, the door flew open abruptly and Alex's eyes flew open at the abruptness of the interruption. Armand winked at her quickly before he turned and nonchalantly rested his cheek against hers, the simple gesture shielding her face from whoever stood in the doorway.

"I had understood we would not be disturbed," Armand growled and Alex boldly pressed a kiss of gratitude against his ear.

"My apologies, Chevalier." Pièrre's voice rolled over them smoothly, sending a shiver of revulsion through Alex. Armand tightened his arms around her in silent reassurance, settling his weight more firmly on top of her. He would protect her, Alex realized, the thought melting the last of her rapidly eroding resistance.

"I understand the black stallion in the stables is yours?" Pièrre demanded, his tone icily polite.

"Indeed he is," Armand responded testily, milking his role as the interrupted lover for all it was worth. "Surely the colors on his caparisons would testify to my ownership without this disturbance."

"And so they do, sir, so they do." Pièrre cleared his throat hesitantly. "My interest, frankly, is in the other stallion in the stables. Perhaps you have noticed him, a fine silver steed."

"He is also my beast," Armand growled and Alex held her breath.

"Indeed? He does not sport your colors as the other does. The horse, in fact, wears the colors of the house of Fontaine."

"Does he indeed?" Armand responded in a bored tone. "I was not familiar with the insignia when I acquired him recently, and as the trap seemed in good condition, I did not seek to replace it." He caressed Alex's earlobe lazily with his tongue as if dismissing the conversation and she responded in kind, stroking the back of his neck languidly as she was certain was expected.

Their ruse was working, Alex realized with surprise, easily detecting Pièrre's discomfort at witnessing the intimate scene even from across the room. She could almost see him fidgeting.

Arching her back, Alex stretched and caressed Armand's earlobe slowly with her tongue, smiling against his jaw as his arms tightened convulsively around her, and he muttered something under his breath. In retaliation, Armand pressed the warmth of his lips against her throat, running a row of kisses along her earlobe as if he would devour her whole, prompting Alex to shiver uncontrollably beneath him.

Unwilling to let his challenge pass, Alex boldly hooked the back of his chausses with her big toe, pushing them determinedly down over his buttocks in a smooth caress within plain view of the man at the door.

"Wanton wench," Armand whispered into her ear, and she stifled a giggle with difficulty.

Pièrre cleared his throat and Armand glanced up with a start as if surprised to find him still there. "May I be so forward as to ask where you acquired the horse?" Pièrre asked.

"'Tis of no matter to me," Armand conceded with a disinterested shrug. "An old merchant was selling him when I passed through Venice and his price was fair. My stable is always searching for new breeding stock and he seemed a fine beast."

"A merchant, you say?"

"Yes." Armand frowned in mock concentration. "Maseti or Marsenti or some such Venetian name."

Pièrre sighed with disappointment and Alex smiled in relief against Armand's throat. "May I ask the reason for your curiosity?" Armand asked, his tone almost disinterested as he returned to nibble on Alex's neck.

"I seek a member of the Fontaine family," Pièrre admitted.

"As long as there is no question of the horse's ownership," Armand muttered, still playing the disgruntled knight, and Pièrre shook his head emphatically.

"Nay, sir, I did not mean to insinuate any such thing."

"'Tis just as well," Armand growled. "A fair price for such a beast is still a goodly amount of gold. Would you be finished with your inquiries, then, sir, I would like to return to the business at hand." Armand grinned and squeezed Alex's breast to illustrate his point as she squirmed indignantly beneath him.

Pièrre laughed, his footsteps backing quickly out of the room. "Indeed, sir, sorry I am to have disturbed you with such a trifling matter."

"'Tis no matter," Armand conceded good-naturedly as the door shut behind him.

Alex and Armand froze in place as the footsteps of Pièrre and his men echoed in the hall, stamping down the stairs and fading in intensity. Voices were raised briefly in the kitchen before the back door slammed resoundingly. Alex breathed a shaky sigh of relief as Armand propped himself up on his elbows and listened intently. Their eyes met and they both grinned at the sound of retreating hoofbeats, stifling the urge to laugh at the success of their ruse.

"I shall never believe anything you tell me again," Alex whispered in mock accusation instead. Armand lifted one eyebrow, feigning innocence.

"And you, milady," he murmured, "for all your objections, are shockingly wanton."

"Not as wanton as you might believe," Alex insisted, trying unsuccessfully to extricate herself from Armand's embrace. Her body was betraying her, responding readily to his nearness. "This charade must end immediately," she protested weakly, feeling a telltale flush rise over her cheeks.

"De Villiers might return at any moment," Armand teased, kissing the smooth curve of her jawline. Alex swallowed with difficulty, turning her face away from his as she tried to quell the undeniable desire rising deep inside her. She closed her eyes against it, her nostrils filling with the musky scent of his skin, and felt arousal curl lazily in the depth of her stomach.

Armand watched Alex's response with fascination, unable to believe the evidence before his eyes, some lighthearted jest dying on his lips. His heartbeat quickened as he noted the pulse fluttering unsteadily in her throat, his amazed eyes forced to acknowledge that she seemed to feel the same pull of attraction as he.

Alex licked her lips nervously and Armand felt his gaze drawn to them, intrigued by the sight of her dancing tongue against their rosy fullness. His loins tightened instinctively in response and he bent without thinking to taste her softness again.

Armand's arms tightened around Alex's waist as his mouth closed decisively over hers. His kiss was possessive, his lips demanding, and Alex clung to his neck, her mind whirling, her nerves awash in a sea of sensation. His tongue caressed her lips and she opened her mouth willingly, purring deep in her throat as his tongue invaded her without hesitation. Leaning his weight onto one elbow, he cradled her shoulders, his other hand roaming over her soft skin, caressing her waist and sliding up to cup her breast.

Armand ran the roughened edge of his thumb across the hardened nipple and Alex shuddered in response, watching

with amazement as he lifted his lips from hers and bent to
flick his tongue against the sensitized point. She arched
against him as he suckled her, taking the nipple in his teeth
and teasing it with his tongue to a rock-hard nub. Alex
squirmed, biting his shoulder in her efforts to stay silent.

Armand threw her a mischievous grin, as he lifted himself above her and shifted his attention to her other breast,
his hand cupping the first again and caressing the tightened
peak. Alex trembled from head to toe convulsively and
reached for his shoulders.

"Kiss me," she whispered urgently, and he complied at
his leisure, taking her lips in a sweet embrace while his
thumb continued to tease her nipple. Alex mimicked him
this time, slipping her tongue between his lips explora-
tively, and he groaned with satisfaction. Their tongues
flirted in an erotic dance and Alex wound her hands into the
thickness of his hair, the warm coil of arousal in her belly far
from lazy anymore.

Armand slipped his hand between her thighs without
breaking their kiss, his fingers quickly finding the tiny pearl
hidden there. Alex recoiled at the jolt that ran through her
at his bold touch but he continued undaunted, murmuring
softly under his breath, touching, teasing her ever upward.
Alex exhaled shakily, leaning back and closing her eyes as
she abandoned herself to his caress, instinctively trusting
him.

His fingertips nibbled at her softness, bringing a gasp of
surprise to her lips, coaxing responses from Alex that she
had never imagined possible. She writhed in Armand's
arms, her finger running over the hard muscles of his
shoulders and neck, finding the ridge of a scar on his back,
the neat edge left by the stitches she had made herself in his
shoulder.

And still the heat and tension built within Alex, sending
her tossing and turning, her frustration building to a crescendo, then shattering suddenly as her back arched and
ripples coursed through her tiny frame. Armand crushed her
to him and kissed her fiercely, swallowing the wild cries of
her release.

As Armand rolled to his back, his arms still wound tightly around her, Alex collapsed against the hard wall of his chest, her breathing labored, heart hammering, limbs quivering. He cupped the back of her neck tenderly, his long fingers curling into the tangled mess of her hair, and she leaned her head against his shoulder with a sigh, savoring the warmth of his skin against her cheek, the steady rhythm of his heart beating against her ear, the wiry curls of auburn hair beneath her fingers.

Surely there could be no finer place to slip into dreams, Alex mused as sleep carried her away, closing her eyes as Armand stroked the hair away from her face and pressed a kiss against her forehead.

Alex awoke to find herself alone in bed and the sheets beside her cold. She snuggled down underneath the home-spun coverlet and the scent of her own arousal filled her nostrils, vividly reminding her of the moments she had spent in Armand's arms and bringing a silly grin to her lips.

Love was the most wonderful thing, she admitted happily, hugging herself and rolling onto her back. She marveled at her response to Armand's touch, curling her toes against the coverlet in recollection of the warm tenderness in his eyes, his expression telling her more eloquently than mere words that he cared for her and would not hurt her. How different from Pièrre's assault; how lucky she was to be shown what a rude travesty that act had been.

Alex closed her eyes, picturing her future with Armand, wondering what their children would look like, whether they would take his coloring or hers, how many of them they would have. Fontaine would be rebuilt, she concluded easily, the house restored to its former glory by Armand and her sons. A flush rose in her cheeks in anticipation of countless nights in his arms and the hours of leisurely lovemaking to be spent in creating those proud sons.

Stretching luxuriously, Alex felt her grin subside into a softly satisfied smile as she wondered where Armand had gone. Surely they had many things to talk about now that their feelings for each other were clear.

He must have gone downstairs, she reasoned, perhaps to the garderobe or to have a glass of wine. Slipping out of the warmth of the bed, she quickly donned the shirt she had worn earlier and pulled her surcoat over her shoulders against the chill of the night air.

Peering out into the hall, she judged the hour to be quite late. The house was silent, the lamps in the hall extinguished, the light from the kitchen alone illuminating the open stairs from below.

Frowning with concern, Alex stepped quietly down the hall, the polished wood floor cold on her bare feet. She paused at the top of the stairs to listen carefully, but the house remained eerily silent. Continuing on her way, she stepped carefully down to the first stair, freezing in place as a woman's throaty chuckle wafted through the air to her ears.

Therese.

Alex paused in indecision, not wanting to interrupt an assignation or business transaction. Therese laughed again, her husky voice joined by a deep and very familiar masculine chuckle. Reassured that her presence would not be unwelcome, Alex smiled to herself and trotted quickly down the stairs.

For some reason, she paused at the bottom, glancing toward the light that streamed from the kitchen, the direction from which their voices had come. Armand leaned against a storage chest, his relaxed frame fully visible through the door.

Alex's heart tripped at the sight of him, a bemused smile on his lips, his fingers curved around the stem of a wine chalice, his russet hair still slightly tousled. Therese said something and he smiled tolerantly, taking a sip of wine as she stepped into view, her slim hips swaying suggestively. In a gesture of complete familiarity, Therese linked her hands behind Armand's neck and stretched up to kiss him full on the lips.

Alex froze in place, uncertain how Armand would act, dismayed to see that he did not make any effort to move away. He simply stood there while Therese kissed him leisurely and with great relish, trying first this angle, then that, her hands running over him proprietarily as he stood motionless. A sense of betrayal flooded through Alex's veins, injured pride snapping her spine erect and tilting her chin defiantly upward.

Unable to watch the tender scene unfold any further, Alex turned and dashed up the stairs on silent feet, hurling herself across the bed with a sob as salty tears wound their way down her cheeks.

What a fool she had been! Imagining that there was something important between them, her mind filled with ridiculous daydreams of marriage and children. In Armand's eyes she had clearly been no different from the other women here, despite his assurances to the contrary.

Alex pounded her pillow furiously, despising the male of the species with all her heart and soul. Armand had acted no differently than Pièrre, taking what he wanted and walking away. She rolled to her back, clutching the pillow to her chest as silent sobs racked her frame. One lesson had not been enough for her, she scolded herself, calling herself a fool for trusting a man so easily after Pièrre's betrayal.

Her judgment was not fair, she was forced to acknowledge as her tears slowed. Armand had taken nothing from her that evening. He had simply given her pleasure and she had responded more than willingly to his caresses. Could she really blame him for taking even less than she would have willingly given? Alex conceded the truth grudgingly, a rosy flush stealing over her features even though she was alone.

Perhaps she had misinterpreted the scene below, she reasoned. Armand hadn't put his arms around Therese, nor had he initiated the kiss. And what did she really know about whatever existed between Armand and Therese? They could have been lovers for years for all she knew. Certainly they were more than comfortable in each other's presence. Armand trusted Therese, that much was clear by the fact that he had brought Alex here at all.

Alex kicked her feet absently against the mattress. The evidence was less than condemning, first impressions notwithstanding. She sighed, knowing that she would just have to ask him about it when he came back to bed.

Setting her mind to finding a way of asking about the kiss without sounding like a possessive shrew, Alex pulled the covers up to her chin, and frowned into the darkness in concentration.

Armand sat on the stone back step of the house, sipping his wine as he reflected on the events of the evening. Unbelievable, he conceded, stretching out his legs and crossing his ankles, trying to force himself to think of anything other than Alexandria and the fires she sparked within him.

Therese's resounding disbelief that he could have fallen in love was more than a little unflattering. She had been stunned when he had failed to respond at all to her kiss, calling him a variety of names before calming down and demanding to know what love was like.

Love.

The word filled Armand's mind once again with images of Alex and brought a smile to his lips. Alex angry, Alex laughing, Alex shouting at him; Alex lying beneath him, her eyes wide with wonder; Alex asleep, her dark tresses strewn across the pillow as she smiled a mysterious little smile.

Seeing the desire and love in her eyes, he had known that he could not stay this night, that he must not remain in the same bed with her until they were wed. She was so sweet and giving, so gentle that she tempted his very soul, her impetuous response almost making him forget the vow he had given her only a scant hour before.

Armand frowned thoughtfully in the darkness, uncertain as to how he would manage marriage. Always he came back to the same problem, the financial concern that restrained him from following his heart's desire. There was nothing for him at Avigny, that much was already clear. Throughout the East, he had heard tales of the tourneys north of Paris, and he now gave the idea thorough consideration.

A lucky day or two on the field would provide him with the financial resource that he needed to claim a bride. Perhaps Alex would betroth herself to him in the interim. As his fiancée, 'twould be appropriate for her to stay with his family, he reasoned, a choice that would give him more peace of mind while he traveled. Neither Pièrre de Villiers nor Michel's killer would ever think to look for Alex in Avigny.

Armand took a deep draft of wine and smiled with satisfaction. He had always fought well, and with an incentive like Alex's graceful hand, 'twould be easy to make a good showing in the tournaments.

Hours later, Alex stood at the window watching the sky pinken in the east, heralding the arrival of the dawn. With dry eyes and a chilled heart, she confronted the unavoidable fact that Armand had not returned. Despite her willingness to give him a fair hearing, it seemed clear that her first impression had been correct. Where else could he have been all night if not in Therese's bed?

Knowing that she could not face him again with this ache in her heart, Alex stripped his shirt from her back with one smooth motion. She held the garment for a moment, debating the wisdom of her impulse, then tore it in half with a resounding rip and tossed the two pieces onto the rumpled bed. Inordinately pleased with the gesture, she dressed quickly in her travel-worn clothes and stepped soundlessly out into the hall.

The house was completely silent, and she wondered fleetingly if Pièrre and his men had returned to enjoy the inn's hospitality. If they had, 'twas best that she disappeared now before they awoke.

Alex slipped hastily out the front door and across the deadened grass to the stables, shoving open the door and stepping inside. The scent of hay assailed her as her eyes adjusted to the darkness, gradually enabling her to pick out the forms of the horses as they regarded her with silent interest. She glanced at the trap hanging on the door, breathing a sigh of relief when she saw that none hung there in the de Villierses' signature black and gold.

Sebastien snorted in recognition and Alex stroked his nose affectionately before reaching for his trap. The weight of his saddle stunned her and she dropped it to the floor the first time that she tried to lift it up. Taking a deep breath, she reminded herself sternly that a boy of eight was considered strong enough to squire for a knight. Surely she could lift as much weight as a child.

Concentrating, she tried again and hoisted the saddle successfully onto the stallion's back, but not without considerable effort. The bridle and caparisons were easier to manage and she found a step by the door that gave her enough height to mount.

Sebastien pranced with satisfaction at her slight weight on his back, anxious to run after so many days of rest. Alex trotted him out to the road and checked the location of the rising sun. Pointing the stallion in the most northwesterly direction that the road took, she gave him his rein and he ran like the wind along the dirt road.

The sun was high over the house when Armand awoke, cramped and cold. He rubbed his eyes and stretched, wincing at the tightness the night air had put in his muscles. The nights were getting colder, he thought, acknowledging the bite in the wind that heralded the arrival of winter.

Since Alex was feeling stronger, it really was time that they moved on. He would talk to her this morning about his plans, he resolved cheerfully, bending to pick up the wine chalice where it had fallen. Whistling tunelessly, he strode into the kitchen, winking broadly at the stout woman busily kneading bread, and took the stairs three at a time.

When there was no response to his quiet tap, Armand pushed open the door cautiously, freezing in his footsteps at the sight of the empty bed. Had de Villiers returned? A wave of panic threatened to engulf him before he realized that her surcoat was gone.

She must have gone down to the garderobe, he reasoned, forcing himself to remain calm as he continued into the room. Fear clenched his gut when he noticed the conspicuous absence of any of her clothing. Tossing his own garments aside in a frenzy, he desperately sought some item of hers, but there was nothing left.

Nothing but the shirt he had given her to wear, Armand reflected, picking it up halfheartedly as he dropped to sit on the edge of the bed. The shirt was torn in half, he realized, closing his eyes in dismay at this sign of her apparent anger. Alex had chosen to leave on her own.

But why? A cold weight settled in Armand's stomach as he ran from the room, darting down the stairs and out into the sunlight. He thrust open the stable door, immediately noting Sebastien's absence, and kicked the door resoundingly, swearing loudly in frustration.

She was gone.

Running his fingers through his hair, Armand forced himself to think logically, desperately struggling to ignore the protective instinct inside him that raged now at his failure to ensure his lady's safety. Where could she have gone? Alex must have had some clear destination in mind, he reasoned, recalling the château on the Loire River.

There or her family home, he acknowledged to himself, wherever that might be. Armand frowned, struggling to recall the name de Villiers had mentioned in reference to the caparisons on Michel's horse, but it eluded him. He frowned in concentration, realizing with a shock that he did not know the name of the estate on the Loire, either, pushing away from the wall in frustration.

More than a little disgusted with his inability to trace Alex's path, Armand strode away from the stables in annoyance. How many castles could there be on the Loire River? he wondered, his heart sinking as he admitted that he had never even fully looked at that château two years past.

The lord would have been sworn to the king's service two years ago, of that much he was certain, but the Loire region had a history of allegiance with the Capetian kings. Precious little indeed, he acknowledged to himself, kicking at a clump of faded grass in defeat. He recalled as much as he could of that evening, finding his memory cloudy at best, the main detail he remembered being the vivid blue shade of Alex's eyes.

At the very least, Armand concluded, he could ride west with haste this morning. If the fates smiled on him and Alex had not been long gone, he might even overtake her on the road.

Chapter Eight

Armand gazed down at his father's sleeping form, struggling against the dismay that rose in his heart. His lovely Alex had eluded him, and now this. Baudouin, shrunken and gaunt, taken to his bed this year past. His gaze traveled over his father's sharply delineated cheekbones, his thinned lips and deathly pale skin, tracing the blue veins in the feeble hand lying against the heavy green brocade coverlet. 'Twas just as Guillaume had said.

Baudouin stirred, perhaps sensing his son's watchful presence, his paper-thin eyelids fluttering open as Armand fought back his tears and cleared his throat. When the familiar sharp emerald gaze met his own, Armand breathed a silent sigh of relief, reassured that his father's frailty of body was not echoed by a feebleness of mind.

Baudouin allowed himself the luxury of examining the son he had not expected to see again, his perceptive gaze not missing the new lines of fatigue, the tightness of disappointment around Armand's mouth, the hurt buried in his jade eyes. So the boy had fallen in love and not ridden victorious from the field.

Unaccountably, he was reminded of the haunted look in Armand's eyes the last time he had come home. Impossible 'twas, that the boy should have encountered the same woman again. Impossible, yet he had to acknowledge that the boy was too like him to give his heart twice in such a short span of time. Well did Baudouin know that Fate was a strong mistress.

"So, finally did they send for you," he commented quietly, but Armand shook his head decisively, confusing his father momentarily.

"Nay, no word was sent to me."

Clearly surprised by the declaration, the older man studied his son for a moment, his bright eyes narrowing shrewdly.

"What brings you here, then?" he demanded finally, and Armand shrugged.

"I thought it best," he returned noncommittally, and Baudouin frowned.

"You did not join the Order?"

"I did, but since have left," Armand answered uncomfortably, some last vestige of loyalty to the Templars making him curiously reticent to discuss their failings. His father nodded in apparent understanding, his gaze traveling now around the darkened room, watching the dust motes dance in an errant sliver of sunlight with mock fascination. Armand frowned, sitting down heavily on the side of the bed to draw his father's attention, Baudouin, for his part, favored his son with a look of puzzled inquiry.

"Why do you lie abed?" Armand demanded sharply. "Guillaume claims you have not left this room in a year."

"I am dying," Baudouin shot back defensively, his words sending a pang through Armand's heart.

"Of what?" Armand demanded, refusing to let his father manipulate him. Those bright eyes spoke of living, and he wondered at Baudouin's game.

The older man frowned at his son's audacity and propped himself up on his elbows to argue the point, his action, despite his wince of pain, unwittingly lending credence to Armand's suspicions.

"Of old age I die," he shot back waspishly, his white brows drawing together in annoyance. "Of nameless aches and countless pains and the refusal of this old body to follow my will. Of what else does a tired old warrior die?"

Armand shoved to his feet in annoyance and paced the length of the room. "I know not," he bit out, running his hand through his hair in frustration and glaring at the heavy

drapes concealing the only window in the room. "A healer
I am not," Armand muttered, pulling the tapestries aside
abruptly and squinting at the bright sunlight that suddenly
flooded the room.

So occupied was he that he did not see the flash of mischief in his father's eyes, did not notice the fleeting grin that
stole across the older man's lips before Baudouin carefully
composed his features.

"Nor am I," Baudouin countered in peevish tones, barely
suppressing an urge to chuckle. "Nor is there a competent
healer in these parts, one who knows the old ways and will
not insult my tired body with leeches and such nonsense."

Armand turned slowly, unable to believe his father's
words. "A healer," he repeated carefully, watching Baudouin wrestle with the bed covers in a futile effort to become more comfortable. "You desire a healer?"

"What else would you have a dying man demand?"
Baudouin retorted in annoyance. "And bring me not some
old crone with missing teeth and twisted fingers as Guillaume did. A fair countenance is as conducive to healing as
nimble fingers and a learned mind."

A healer. Armand regarded his father in disbelief, unable to restrain himself from picturing Alex ensconced at
Château D'Avigny, the lilting sound of her laughter in the
hall. De Villiers would not think to search for her here and
he could go north to the tourneys with his mind at ease. He
could surely win enough to respectfully ask for her hand,
and her presence here would give him more than ample opportunity to court her properly.

Baudouin watched him, his expression one of perfect innocence, and Armand wondered briefly how much his father knew, dismissing his speculation as ridiculous. The man
had been here, abed, for more than a year. How could Baudouin possibly know anything about his travels with Alex?

"I will find you such a healer," he vowed softly, and the
old man stifled a chuckle of satisfaction.

Hugues disliked Pièrre de Villiers on sight, though
whether 'twas due to the way the man perched on the edge

of one of the tables in the hall, glancing around himself with disdain, or simply due to his knowledge of the man's deeds, Hugues could not say. The younger man had appeared in the courtyard of Pontesse early one morning just before the Yule, demanding to see the lord of the château. Hugues had needed no prompt to recognize the name of the man who had killed his nephew and abused his niece, some almost forgotten blood lust awakening within him at the sound of the name.

No vengeance was it of his to extract a toll from this villain, though the knowledge rankled Hugues' pride. Alex had asked to hide within the safety of his house and Hugues had agreed to her request, never anticipating that her supposed betrothed would dare to seek her out after his loathsome deeds. Now he stood in the hall below and Hugues knew he must feign ignorance of the man's crimes, Alex being the only possible conduit of the news. Never having been a good liar, Hugues squared his shoulders determinedly as he entered the hall and met the other man's gaze with apparent confusion.

The garb of a gentleman, de Villiers' tunic fell to just below his knees and was cut from a fabulously ornate black-and-gold brocade, the intricate pattern of a pair of fighting lions far more elaborate than was considered tasteful in these troubled days.

The hems and cuffs of the garment were couched with gold embroidery, the plain black tabard that he wore over top giving the eye a welcome relief from the richness of pattern. He wore a full-length black cloak over all, the squirrel pelts that lined it gleaming in the firelight, the jeweled clasp on one shoulder capturing the golden light in its polished stones.

Although he could have been a handsome man, something about the set of de Villiers' face made Hugues instinctively recognize his cruelty and the danger he could pose to an enemy. This was not a man who would easily forget a wrong done to him or would concern himself with following a fair code of conduct, and Hugues felt his ire rising at what Alex had endured at de Villiers' hand.

"Good morning," Hugues greeted the man calmly, and de Villiers stood up.

"Lord Hugues de Pontesse?" the man asked, and Hugues nodded.

"And you are Pièrre de Vil—" Hugues let his voice fade and gestured vaguely with one hand as if he couldn't remember the man's name. The years had taught him the advantage of acting less intelligent than he actually was when first encountering a potential adversary.

"Pièrre de Villiers," the younger man affirmed and Hugues nodded, praying that the jolt of anger he felt at the sound of the name did not show in his eyes.

"I understand, sir, that you administer the Fontaine estate?" de Villiers continued persistently, apparently unaware of the carefully leashed current of violence coursing through the man he faced.

Hugues methodically folded his arms across his chest before he responded. "Indeed I do, and have done so since the untimely death of my sister and her husband." Continuing with his charade, he threw the young man an assessing look. "Are you perhaps interested in purchasing an estate in this area?"

De Villiers snorted. "I should think that I have already done so."

"I beg your pardon?"

"Where is your niece, sir?" de Villiers demanded abruptly. "Alexandria de Fontaine?"

Doing his best to look bewildered at the question, Hugues answered slowly and calmly. "In Venice, she is, to the best of my knowledge, awaiting her brother's return from the Crusades."

"I regret to inform you that she is not," de Villiers asserted firmly.

"How curious," Hugues acknowledged with apparent surprise. "Your news vexes me indeed. Why would the child leave Venice before her brother's return? And where could she have gone?" Hugues dropped into a chair with a sigh, pressing his fingers against his temples as if he were sorely tried by the capricious actions of women.

"My question exactly, sir." De Villiers sat down beside him and lowered his tone as though exchanging a confidence. "News this will be to you, sir, but I have signed a marriage contract with Guilio Masenti, agreeing to the terms under which I would marry your niece." He pulled a rolled document from his tabard, spreading it on the table for Hugues.

"A surprise indeed," Hugues acknowledged, feigning interest in the sheet of parchment. How his fingers itched to snatch the document and toss it into the fire! He controlled himself with an effort, frowning in mock confusion as he tapped the top of the agreement.

"But this document is dated months ago," he pointed out. "The wedding must surely have taken place by now."

"By rights, it should have," the younger man sighed, rolling the parchment and replacing it in his tabard. Hugues gave him a questioning look and de Villiers continued in a low voice. "The lady disappeared several nights before the wedding."

"Ah . . ." Hugues leaned back in his chair, his eyebrows lifting as if he suddenly understood the lay of the land. "The match was not Alexandria's choice," he concluded with a smile, chuckling softly under his breath.

The other man inhaled sharply, his eyes narrowing as he bit out his angry retort. "Not her choice! As if such a thing were pertinent!"

"Indeed," Hugues murmured vaguely. "Pontesse is a long ride from Venice, sir. Must I assume that you seek my niece despite her reluctance to wed?"

"Indeed I do, sir."

"Surely there are other women in Venice, or closer to home, worthy of your attentions?"

"But none, I must point out, who can compare to the fair countenance and character of Alexandria," de Villiers insisted gallantly.

Hugues struggled to conceal a snort of derision, knowing that Alex's countenance would be considered far less fair were she not the only witness of Pièrre's murdering hand.

"You would persist in marrying a woman who chose to run away rather than meet you at the altar?" Hugues asked, forcing himself to remain calm.

De Villiers slapped the document on the table again, unfurling it and jabbing a finger at a sum of money with far too many zeros. "I paid an outlandish price for the woman and I intend to collect the goods for which I paid."

Hugues' eyes popped at the sum. "In advance was this sum paid?" he asked in amazement.

"The gold was owing to me," Pièrre snapped, tapping his gloved fingertips on the table and looking away, his lips drawn to a thin line. "The outstanding debt was forgiven in exchange for the lady's hand."

"Surely Guilio would reconsider your agreement since the girl cannot be found," Hugues countered in a conciliatory tone. "Although I barely know the man, he has always seemed most reasonable." In fact, Hugues' impression of Guilio Masenti was exactly the opposite, but Hugues thought it inopportune to admit such now.

De Villiers laughed, the short dry bark echoing through the room. "The lady was not the only one gone that morning, sir. Guilio also disappeared during the night."

"'Tis indeed sorry news you bring," Hugues commented as he mused over this carefully. Guilio must have found Alex missing and left town in a fright, most assuredly because he could not hope to refund the money to de Villiers. "Perhaps Alexandria travels with him."

"Perhaps," de Villiers conceded offhandedly, leaning toward Hugues with narrowed eyes. "I had understood that the lady lived in your household after the death of her parents."

"Indeed she did, but she has not graced my hall for some two years," Hugues lied as smoothly as he was able.

"And you have had no word from her?"

"None."

"Does this not trouble you?"

"Until this day, I thought Alexandria safely in my sister's home in Venice." Hugues lifted one bushy brow before continuing. "Your news certainly causes me concern."

The two men watched each other silently for a moment, Hugues suddenly afraid that de Villiers knew he was lying.

"So you say." De Villiers stood, sweeping his cloak over his shoulder disdainfully, then leaning back over Hugues for his final shot. "I hope you do not lead me false, Lord Pontesse. The consequences could be most dire, for I assure you that I intend to collect what is mine."

Pièrre flicked an imaginary piece of dust from his cloak, as he continued matter-of-factly. "In the interim and at the very least, sir, my family will expect to be compensated for the insult I have sustained. That would be in addition, of course, to the restoration of the gold owed to me by your brother-in-law."

Rage rose in Hugues' chest at de Villiers' audacity. Beyond the bounds of civility it was to call a man a liar and threaten him in his own house. Hugues rose to his feet, placing his hands on his hips as he savored his height advantage. 'Twould be easy to soundly trounce this foppish young man so filled with his own self-importance.

"A brother-in-law who has conveniently disappeared and cannot confirm your tale," he observed quietly, his voice dangerously low.

De Villiers lifted his brows in apparent surprise. "You would question my word, sir?"

"I would question your intelligence in threatening a lord within his own château," Hugues shot back, his voice now rising in the empty hall. "'Twould seem to me that any man so insulted would be less than inclined to aid you in your quest."

"You admit, then, that you have had word of your niece." The younger man pounced on Hugues' words, anticipation lighting up his face.

"I admit no such thing," Hugues spat, certain that his disgust was clearly etched on his face. "You insult nobility everywhere with your mere existence, boy. Remove yourself from my home."

De Villiers' eyes narrowed with hate, and he clenched his fists as he looked up at Hugues. "Well you may regret those words," he hissed before he turned on his heel, striding through the room, the black hem of his cloak fluttering in his wake. Gervais stepped forward from the shadows, indicating the way back to the courtyard, flicking a meaningful glance over his shoulder to his lord.

Hugues sighed and dropped back into his seat, feeling the full weight of his years. 'Twas clear that the man suspected Alex was being hidden in the castle. He glanced over his shoulder at the few members of his household working in the great hall at this early hour and hoped that he employed no servants who would tell tales to de Villiers for gold.

Hugues could well understand Alex's hatred of de Villiers now; only a fool would be unable to sense the violence running through the man. A fool like Guilio Masenti. He should have insisted on making Justine's marital arrangements instead of letting his sister choose her own spouse. So much could have been avoided had she wed a pleasant French nobleman and raised daisies and children.

His mind wallowing in self-recriminations and accusations, Hugues felt the past come full circle to haunt him again. What was he going to do to protect Alex? She was in more danger in his own home than anywhere else, but he was the last of her kin. Hugues sighed and rubbed his eyes, his heart heavy with the weight of his responsibility as he trudged back up to bed.

"Oh, Hugues, what shall I do?" a wide-eyed Alex greeted him at the top of the stairs, the tears shimmering in those wide pools of blue sending his heart plummeting. Somehow there had to be a way to protect her from Pièrre de Villiers' malicious intent.

"I know not, child," he mumbled helplessly, reaching out and gathering her into a tight hug of reassurance, his frustration growing when Alex broke into tears against his shoulder. "I know not, but some way shall become clear."

Hugues closed his eyes and prayed to whatever gods there were that he spoke aright.

Yule came and went, the icy winds of January and February soon after sending a more than generous sprinkling of

snow to creep around Armand's coif and down into his
boots. Still he and Roarke traveled the length of the Loire,
searching for a healer they might never find in a château
neither might recognize should it loom ahead of them on the
road.

This night, they sought shelter in yet another hall, its
courtyard no more familiar than the last dozen, and the
scent of spring in the air forced Armand to acknowledge
that 'twas time they abandoned the search and headed for
home. Desperately did he hope for the hundredth time that
his lady had safely found shelter among those she loved and
not perished at the hand of some villain or the elements
themselves when she bolted from his side.

Armand was deep in a discussion of the relative merits of
launching an attack against the Muslims holding Jerusalem
when the chatelain announced the Lord Pontesse's arrival
to the great hall. He glanced up at the man with disinterest,
fully intending to return to his conversation, but froze in
surprise, his argument forgotten.

The lord himself was not notable beyond his size and
vaguely leonine appearance. What arrested Armand's attention was the lord's lady, a willowy fair-skinned woman
who strolled gracefully to the head table at her husband's
side. As the chatelain poured his lord's wine, Armand's
mind snapped back to a long-ago evening, the tables around
him dissolving into recollections of wounded knights
sprawled across the stone floor and that same woman
working among those men.

This was the healer who had checked Alex's work, of that
Armand was certain. His heart began to pound in anticipation. Was Alex here? He scanned the company and
caught no glimpse of her, his eyes returning to the head table. The lord of the hall raised his chalice, draining the wine
in one swallow and signaling the beginning of the meal, but
Armand's gaze remained on the lady, watching as she attended her guests' conversation.

"The meat is quite good, my friend," Roarke assured
him, forcing Armand to focus on the meal before him.
Roarke had loaded the trencher the two men would share

with a spicy stew and Armand sampled a chunk of meat with disinterest, his mind alternately verifying details of the hall and leaping ahead to the dizzying thought that Alex was hidden somewhere within these walls.

"'Tis indeed a fine dish," Armand commented lightly, feeling the inanity of the remark but knowing that the serving girl waiting patiently at his elbow expected him to say something. She smiled appreciatively, invitation in her eyes, before she turned away, her hips sashaying provocatively.

"I see I shall have to change my tactics," Roarke muttered dryly, his gaze fixed on the young woman's shapely figure. "Not a flicker of interest had she in my flattery and charm, but one surly word from you and she is ready to meet you in the stables." He rolled his eyes in exasperation and plopped a piece of meat into his mouth.

"'Tis of no import right now," Armand retorted under his breath, dismissing Roarke's reflections with an impatient wave of one hand, a frown etching the space between his brows as he gestured to the healer. "Do you recall this woman at all?" Roarke glanced up in mock annoyance, following Armand's finger with desultory interest before sitting up abruptly in recognition.

"'Tis the healer from that night," he hissed, glancing quickly around the hall as if seeking further confirmation of his conclusion. Armand nodded slowly and settled back, waiting for Roarke to verify his conclusion.

"Yes," Roarke reiterated quietly as he gazed at the room and back at the woman, who was now laughing at some comment the lord had made. "Yes," he repeated more excitedly, "I think you are right. The fireplace, the keystone in the ceiling, the stairs off to that side, it all fits." Roarke turned to face Armand, his face alight with excitement. "This is *it*, this is the hall where we came that night!"

Armand nodded thoughtfully, the sound of his pounding blood filling his ears as he let himself savor the possibility. Alex might be here. Within these walls, within this very hall, mere steps away from him. He folded his hands together, methodically interlacing his fingers, determined not to give any outward sign of his agitation.

Armand scanned the assembled company once again, not surprised to find Alex absent. If she was here, she would almost certainly be hidden from the view of a passing company of knights.

As the meal progressed, Armand's mind filled with questions for which he had no answers. What would he do now? Demand that the woman tell him Alex's whereabouts? It was highly unlikely that she would do so. Could he search the castle after nightfall? Armand almost snorted to himself at the foolhardiness of that thought. Considering the size of the assembled company, he would be more likely to awaken someone than to find a hidden lady. He smiled to himself at the thought of trying to find a reasonable explanation for a midnight visit to the ladies' quarters.

Should he speak to the lord himself and explain his situation? Without knowing Alex's relationship to the household, speaking to the lord could be a risky step. If she was being sheltered by the lady, the lord himself might not know of her presence here. To his own annoyance, Armand found that all his mental planning had never encompassed the possibility that he might guess Alex's whereabouts but find her hidden.

"What should we do?" Roarke whispered, uncannily echoing Armand's own thoughts.

"I know not," Armand growled, the thought of Alex being so close and him unable to even see her filling him with an unbearable feeling of frustration. How could he have been so foolish as to assume that she would be calmly sitting among the company when he found her? Without a doubt, she would have told anyone harboring her that she had been witness to a murder.

The lady cast an offhand glance over the assembled company from her vantage point at the lord's table, Armand's breath catching in his throat as she looked toward the table he occupied. Their eyes met across the room and the lady paused abruptly in her survey, her brows rising ever so slightly in surprised recognition before she suddenly looked away, glancing over the rest of the company with mock interest.

Armand pretended to divert his attention, as well, watching out of the corner of his eye, uncertain whether he had seen or imagined that merest instant of acknowledgment. His heart swelled when moments later, she bent toward the lord, whispering something behind her hand, the lord's eyes quickly scanning the group and settling on Armand before flicking away.

"The lady remembers you," Roarke commented dryly between chews, and Armand smiled wryly to himself in satisfaction, his heart beating a staccato in his chest.

"Indeed, and judging from their response, the lady we seek is also here," he answered quietly, summoning the serving wench and draining the chalice of wine she offered in a single deep draft.

As the meal concluded, Armand made his way nervously toward the head table to see what he could discover. The lord and lady exchanged a quick look when they noted his intent, that furtive move reassuring him but doing nothing to still his inner tremors.

"Good evening, sir," Armand said, inclining his head politely in greeting. "I would thank you for sharing the wealth of your table with my companion and me." The lord smiled and extended one hand in amiable greeting.

"'Twas my pleasure. Welcome to Château Pontesse." Armand clasped the lord's hand and shook it firmly.

"Chevalier Armand D'Avigny, sir," he said simply.

"Lord Hugues de Pontesse," the heavyset man returned, and Armand inclined his head in polite acknowledgment.

"In truth, sir, this is not the first time I have enjoyed the hospitality of your household," he began awkwardly, uncomfortably aware of the lady's violet gaze upon him.

"Indeed?" The lord's question was more of a statement.

"Indeed," Armand affirmed, forcing his voice to remain calm. "Two years ago I was brought here after being injured at Saintes. A young woman assisted me, with the guidance of your lovely wife."

"Ah, yes," the lord commented unhelpfully.

"I was disappointed to note that that woman was no longer among your company," Armand plowed on determinedly, surprised when his words prompted a flash of outright fear in the older man's eyes. 'Twas clear that Hugues de Pontesse was not a skillful liar and Armand feared suddenly for Alex's safety should she be hidden here.

"Naturally, I had hoped to express my gratitude to her. The shoulder has healed thoroughly," he added hastily by way of explanation, watching the relief settle in the lord's eyes. Now was the time to make his proposition. Armand turned immediately to the lord's wife, who had watched the exchange with interest, taking the plunge before he lost his nerve.

"I must confess that my reasons were twofold," Armand explained, stifling his annoyance with the lord for sharply inhaling at his words. Too transparent was he. Did he not understand that Alex's very life was at risk should Michel's murderer learn of her whereabouts? The lady smiled politely, remaining considerably more composed than her husband. "Perhaps you remember my mentioning my father to you," he continued, and the lady nodded, a flicker of interest in her eyes.

"I remember well your father's dancing," she murmured softly, and Armand nodded, his heartbeat accelerating. He could only hope that her sense of responsibility to another of the old faith would prompt her to trust him.

"Indeed, he is no longer able to dance," Armand confessed with a sigh, fixing on the older woman's pale gaze. "And this distresses him deeply. I seek a healer who can assist him and had hoped that your talented apprentice might have completed her training."

"Alex was quite skilled, as you say," the lady confirmed blandly, her bright eyes indicating that she was weighing Armand's words.

"You speak of the lady in the past tense," Armand commented, determined to push a little more. If Alex was not here, these two knew of her location; that much he was willing to wager on. Somehow he had to find her, somehow he had to assist her against the events aligned against her, somehow he had to protect her more thoroughly than this lord seemed able to do. "Has some malady befallen her?"

"We do not know," the woman responded smoothly, her features impassive.

"Her betrothed recently informed us that she left Venice abruptly before their wedding," the lord interjected.

So de Villiers had been here before him. Armand digested the information slowly before he proceeded.

"Has she not come here, then?" he asked, watching the lord's expression close with an almost audible snap.

"Indeed, we have had no news of her," the older man responded with a shrug of his shoulders. Too casual a gesture to be genuine, Armand noted, seeing the tension in the way the lord twisted his fingers together.

"How unfortunate," Armand answered smoothly, seeing that there was no more information to be gained from this discussion. "My father will surely be disappointed." He turned, adding almost offhandedly, "Perhaps if you see the lady, you would give her my regards?"

"Indeed, we shall," the lord assured him primly, and Armand excused himself, feeling their gazes upon his back as he walked away. Would this be the end of it, then? he wondered with a growing sense of futility. That he should find the château where Alexandria was hidden and be barred from seeing her?

Alex paced the confines of her small room restlessly, the sounds of the company gathered below filtering through the heavy wood of the door. Although she appreciated the need to hide her presence in the castle, Alex was heartily sick of the small space.

Yet again she explored the tray of food that Gervais had brought her, still finding the cold piece of meat, cheese and crusty bread unappealing. She poured a glass of wine from the carafe, sipping its rich fruitiness and setting the cup down heavily on the table with dissatisfaction.

Ages indeed, it seemed, had passed since she had arrived home, but in truth, she and Sophie had joined to celebrate the full ripeness of the moon only twice since her return.

PLAY
ONE MILLION
BIG BUCKS
ONE MILLION
AND YOU COULD WIN THE
$1,000,000.00
PLUS JACKPOT!
YOUR *PERSONAL* GAME CARD INSIDE . . .
HARLEQUIN

TWO WAYS TO WIN BIG BUCKS!

1. Uncover 5 $ signs in a row ... BINGO! You're eligible to win the $1,000,000.00 SWEEPSTAKES!

2. Uncover 5 $ signs in a row AND uncover $ signs in all 4 corners ... BINGO! You're also eligible for the $100,000.00 EXTRA BONUS PRIZE!

LUCKY CHARM GAME!

Claim up to 4 FREE books AND a FREE Mystery Gift!

Scratch Here →

HURRY! This jackpot must be claimed!

YES! I have played my Big Bucks game card as instructed. Enter my Big Bucks Prize number in the MILLION DOLLAR Sweepstakes and also enter me for the Extra Bonus Prize. When winners are selected, tell me if I've won. If the Lucky Charm is scratched off, I will also receive everything revealed, as explained on the back of this page.

247 CIH AH3T
(U-H-H-03/93)

NAME _____

ADDRESS _____ APT. ____

CITY _____ STATE _____ ZIP _____

NO PURCHASE OR OBLIGATION NECESSARY TO ENTER SWEEPSTAKES.

© 1993 HARLEQUIN ENTERPRISES LTD.

EXCLUSIVE PRIZE # YB 676157

BIG BUCKS

$

WHY WE GIVE FREE BOOKS AND GIFTS There's no catch! We give away FREE BOOK(S) and a FREE GIFT to interest you in the Harlequin Reader Service®, but you are under no obligation to buy anything...EVER! You may keep your FREE BOOK(S) and gift and return the accompanying statement marked ''cancel.'' If you do not cancel, approximately a month after you receive your free book(s), we'll send you 4 of the newest Harlequin Historical™ novels and bill you just $2.94 each plus 25¢ delivery and applicable sales tax, if any.* You may cancel at any time by dropping us a line or returning any shipment at our expense!

* Terms and prices subject to change without notice. Sales tax applicable in NY.

BUSINESS REPLY MAIL

FIRST CLASS MAIL   PERMIT NO. 717   BUFFALO, NY

POSTAGE WILL BE PAID BY ADDRESSEE

''BIG BUCKS''
MILLION DOLLAR SWEEPSTAKES
3010 WALDEN AVE.
P.O. BOX 1867
BUFFALO, N.Y. 14240-9952

NO POSTAGE
NECESSARY
IF MAILED
IN THE
UNITED STATES

Alex surveyed her simply furnished room critically, enumerating her options in her mind. She could sleep or she could study the books that Hugues had left her. That was the full extent of the possibilities.

Since she wasn't the least bit sleepy, the ledgers of Château Pontesse would have to do. Hugues had insisted that she learn the business of running an estate as she was the last surviving heir to Fontaine. She or her husband would have to assume the duties of her legacy, and Hugues often commented that knights were typically poorly equipped to balance a ledger. Alex knew she was lucky to have been taught the skill to read and write, Hugues undoubtedly believing that her knowledge-thirsty father would have done the same. At times like this she missed Jean's quiet wisdom, his slow smile, his assurance that the forces of good would emerge victorious.

Alex bent and lit the candle on the table to ward off the gathering darkness, resolving that she would need the light to read. With a sigh of resignation, she decided at the very least to slip into a loose and comfortable chemise before beginning her studies.

The gardens were blessedly silent and Armand found his pace slowing to a leisurely stroll as he walked along the white stone paths. The winter sky was flawlessly indigo above him, its darkness marred only by the shimmering pinpoints of distant stars.

He took a deep breath of the crisp night air, savoring its cold snap in his nostrils, the chill spreading through his lungs and making him feel wondrously alive. A thin slice of crescent moon rose over the horizon and he stopped to watch its stately progress, its silver luminescence lighting the slumbering garden like an ethereal sun.

The winding routes of the chipped marble and flagstone paths were curiously emphasized in the moonlight, standing starkly white against the deep blue shadows. Walking slowly, almost reverently, Armand saw not the winter-deadened shrubs that surrounded him but rather the summery visions of them that filled his mind. His breath caught in his throat when he spotted a single small rosebud, its delicate pink shade highlighted by the moon's silver rays.

Thinking his eyes deceived him, he reached out tentatively and touched the bloom, running a finger gently around its softly unfurling petals with wonder. Armand plucked the blossom carefully, methodically removing the thorns from the stem, lifting the tiny bud to his nose. He closed his eyes and inhaled its seductive scent, so much the sweeter for being out of season.

Roses. The scent of the blossom filled Armand's nostrils even as images of Alex crowded his mind. She had always smelled of roses, he realized now, recognizing the delicate perfume of her skin in the bud he held between his fingers. Memories of her assaulted him and he glared up at the facade of the château, frustrated anew that its heavy walls kept her hidden from him.

Light streamed out of a variety of windows and Armand scanned each of them in turn, searching for a familiar figure even as his mind told him of the futility of his action. She was hidden from him as surely as the Grail itself.

When he would have turned away with a sigh of defeat, a window on the second floor was illuminated, the flickering golden light of a newly lit candle calling him like a beacon as the glowing rays silhouetted a slim form.

He watched with a growing sense of anticipation as a woman unbraided her hair, brushing out the waved thickness that fell to her waist. His heart began to pound as she turned, the candlelight catching her face in profile for a moment, and Armand almost shouted with joy at the familiarity of the delicate features revealed.

Alexandria was definitely in residence at Château Pontesse.

Alex pulled a loose shirt over her head and regarded the leather-bound books stacked on her desk with disinterest. Tucking a wayward strand of hair behind her ear, she resolved that she had spent enough time avoiding them. In the same instant that she stepped toward the table, she heard a soft sound of something heavy falling to the floor behind her.

Alex would have glanced over her shoulder but a strong male hand clamped firmly and suddenly over her mouth, effectively silencing her scream. Before she could respond, another arm snaked around her waist and pinned her arms to her sides. Filled with panic, she struggled against her assailant but he only tightened his grip, locking her against the solid wall of his chest and lifting her to the tips of her toes.

"Fool that I was, I thought never to hold you in my arms again, milady."

The achingly familiar voice rumbled in her ear and Alex sagged with relief, knowing full well that Armand's arm locked around her waist was the only thing keeping her from sliding to the floor. The hand that had covered her mouth slipped to her shoulder, and Armand turned her gently within his embrace.

Her breath caught in her throat at the familiar sight of his strong profile, the firm lips now curved into a tender smile, his eyes a smoky green. Alex's mind reeled at the evidence presented, unable to believe that Armand had in fact come to her after all this time.

Needing to touch him, Alex reached up to stroke his cheek, surprising even herself with the simple gesture. The stubble of the day's growth rubbed against her fingertips and she ran her hand back and forth lightly, finding the sensation oddly exciting. She met his eyes hesitantly, her hand stilling against his face as she saw the intense expression reflected in their emerald depths.

Armand captured her hand with his, and lifted her palm to his lips. His gaze never faltering from hers, he planted a kiss firmly against her palm, then another against the inside of her wrist.

Alex's heart hammered in response to his customary caress and she fixed her eyes on his lips, fascinated with the way they moved against her skin. She remembered the gentle pressure of his lips the first time he had saluted her thus, long ago in the courtyard of Pontesse. Easily she recalled the firm imprint of his lips full against hers, the recollection leaving her feeling suddenly dizzy and swaying slightly in the soft candlelight. She closed her eyes, her entire being focused on the tender caress of Armand's lips on her skin, and leaned her head against the solid strength of his shoulder.

Armand tightened his grip around Alex's waist, cradling her against him. Alex took a deep breath, feeling comfortably surrounded by his warmth, safe within the circle of his arms, the uncertainty of the past months dissolving in the security of his embrace.

Tentatively, Alex tipped her chin upward to meet that steady green gaze once again. Her mind savored the memory of the taste of him on her lips and she suddenly felt an overwhelming desire to sample that taste again.

What was it about this man that touched the deepest part of her soul? So little time they had actually spent together, yet Alex felt as if she had always known him. She snuggled closer to his warmth, her soft breasts pressed against the solid expanse of his chest, her lips parting of their own volition in silent invitation.

Armand released her hand to caress her jawline, his warm fingers slipping behind her neck to cup her head and tangle in the silky weight of her hair. He bent his head and touched his lips to hers, pausing to look into her eyes for a moment, the tip of her nose a thumb's width from his. Mutely he repeated the gesture and kissed her with a tender thoroughness, the softness of her lips and breasts beckoning him ever closer.

Alex leaned against him, letting him gather her to him, molding her curves to his angles, her hands finding their way over his shoulders, her fingertips caressing the tightened sinews in the back of his neck. Her heart pounded and the world spun around her, her mind filled with the firmness of his lips, the scent of his skin and the inexplicable smell of roses.

Armand lifted his lips from hers with a ragged sigh and Alex leaned her cheek against his broad chest. He held her close, his fingers stroking her temple, her ear, her jawline in an unceasing and gentle caress as if he too sought to reassure himself of her presence. Alex closed her eyes and desperately tried to steady her breathing. Armand's heartbeat pounded beneath her ear and she smiled at the evidence of his arousal, a response that so closely echoed her own.

"What brings you here, sir?" Alex asked softly, needing to hear some reassurance of his intentions. She gazed up at Armand, convinced that she could lose herself in the warm depths of his eyes. He smiled down at her, the tenderness etched in his features turning her knees to butter.

"I have brought you a present," he whispered huskily, removing a tiny pink rosebud that was tucked into his hauberk and presenting it to her with a flourish.

Wide-eyed with surprise, Alex took the bloom, lifting it to her nose to inhale its delicate scent, caressing with one gentle fingertip the petals bruised when the bud had been crushed between them. Where had he found such a beautiful bud at this time of year? "Thank you," she murmured, and then fell silent, finding no words even remotely appropriate to greet the man she loved after a prolonged separation.

The man she loved? Alex tipped her head back and looked up at Armand to find his gaze still upon her as if he could not believe she stood before him, those green eyes sending a warm wave coursing through every particle of her being. Yes, she loved Armand, she acknowledged, loved him without a shadow of a doubt.

She gazed up at him, noting the russet stubble on his chin that she had felt earlier, the tiny wrinkles at the corners of his eyes, the faded scar just below his ear, and found herself wanting to caress each in turn, to rain kisses of welcome all over his hardened face, for surely there was no other way to greet the man who held her heart in such sweet captivity.

A wry smile tugged at the corner of Armand's mouth as he watched her, and Alex found herself suddenly achingly aware of every point at which their bodies touched within his loose embrace. She took a quivering breath beneath his bright gaze, watching with fascination as he inclined his head toward her, her breath catching in her throat at his evident intent.

Chapter Nine

Suddenly the image of Therese and Armand in a similar position leapt into Alex's mind. How could she have forgotten? This was the man who had left her side to lie immediately with another! She thrust herself away from Armand in an emphatic gesture of denial.

Armand took a step back to steady himself, regarding her with unconcealed surprise, and Alex simmered with anger at his expression. What audacity he had to look surprised at her response!

"How dare you touch me!" she spat vehemently, keeping her voice low so that the women in the next room would not hear.

Armand raised one eyebrow enquiringly. "It seemed to me, milady, that you offered little protest," he commented dryly, mimicking her quiet tones. He flicked a glance to the closed door, then fixed her with a steely look, but Alex paid no heed, giving her anger full rein.

"You dare to come to me again after your deeds?" she demanded.

An expression of complete confusion flitted across Armand's features, fueling Alex's fury still more. Better that he should deny her accusation and defend himself than act as though he did not know what she meant.

"I am not such an innocent as that, sir," she proclaimed haughtily. "I know where you went that night you left my bed."

If she knew he had spent the night on the back steps of Therese's house, why was she so angry? Was it possible that she thought he had left because he found her undesirable? Armand glanced over her slight form appreciatively, stifling his desire with effort as he sought to explain.

"Know you why I went there, milady?" he asked softly, convinced that he would have the matter settled shortly.

Alex repressed the temptation to wipe the smug look of satisfaction from his face. "I should think your reasons would be perfectly obvious!" she spat. "You were pursuing your pleasure, just as every other man in that house of ill repute."

Armand frowned in confusion. Pursuing his pleasure? 'Twas a strange way to refer to his deliberate effort to keep his vow to her. He flicked a look at Alex, acknowledging a niggling doubt that they were talking about the same thing. Determined to get to the root of the matter, he confronted her with a blunt question.

"Where did I go that night, milady?" His voice was low, his tone dangerously even, and Alex doubted the evidence that had confronted her own eyes that night. Was it possible that she had misinterpreted what she had seen? But no. She had witnessed the kiss, had waited all night for his return. He was playing her for a fool.

"I see no reason to discuss this any further," she retorted, turning her back as unbidden tears threatened to spill down her cheeks.

Alex felt Armand come and stand close behind her and she stiffened, knowing that her body would betray her if he touched her. When he spoke, the deep tones of his voice resonated close by her ear and she shivered at the warmth of his breath on her flesh.

"Milady, I fail to understand how my sleeping on the back step should make you so angry." Alex's heart leapt at the unexpected words but she quelled her response sternly, unwilling to believe his assertion.

"Well we both know that you did no such thing," Alex countered flatly, hoping that he would not note the quiver in her voice.

"Then perhaps, milady, you could be so kind as to tell me just what I have done to so infuriate you," Armand bit out in frustration.

Alex whirled around, her anger renewed by his annoyed tone. She jabbed a finger through the air at him as she made her accusation in a low hiss. "With Therese were you that night and well you know it."

Much to her consternation, Armand looked briefly surprised, then threw back his head and laughed. He stopped as abruptly as he had begun, both of them glancing guiltily at the closed door, acutely aware of the women in the next room, as they waited to see whether they were discovered.

The women's chatter continued uninterrupted and they both exhaled slowly with a sigh of relief. Armand chuckled under his breath and turned his full attention back to Alex.

"This truly is the reason for your anger?" he asked, his eyes twinkling as she nodded dumbly. "'Tis true, milady, I shared a glass of wine with our hostess while you slept."

"You shared much more than that," Alex accused, and Armand's eyes slowly grew serious.

"Indeed?" he demanded coldly, arching one brow. "Refresh my memory, if you will, milady."

"There is no need for you to play these games with me," Alex retorted in a low voice that quivered with anger. "I saw you kiss Therese."

Armand ran his fingers through his hair, understanding finally why she was so angry. She had seen Therese kiss him without hearing their conversation and had leapt to conclusions. He forced himself to remain calm, knowing that that was the only way he would convince her of the truth. "Not true, Alex. Therese kissed me."

"Whether you kissed her or she kissed you, 'tis much the same," Alex countered, unable to keep the waspish tone from her voice.

"On the contrary, 'tis vastly different for a kiss to be imposed rather than shared." Armand's eyes twinkled as he advanced upon her, the weight on his heart vastly lightened by her open display of jealousy. "Perhaps I should make my point entirely clear."

"What do you mean?" Alex demanded, her heart pounding in anticipation even as she backed away. Armand reached out and grasped her around the waist, pulling her abruptly against him.

"A demonstration seems in order, milady," Armand whispered, his eyes gleaming devilishly as he lowered his lips to hers. Alex struggled against his embrace, twisting her head from side to side to avoid his mouth. Armand grasped her chin easily in his fingers, holding her captive as he kissed her possessively, teasing her lips with his tongue and his teeth as he tried to coax her response.

Determined to ignore the persuasiveness of his touch, Alex attempted to wriggle free from his arms, but Armand merely braced his legs and leaned back against the wall as he kissed her. His fingers snaked through her hair to cup the back of her head firmly and Alex shivered at the possessiveness of his embrace, secure in the knowledge that although Armand held her powerless in his arms, he would never hurt her.

He was claiming her as his own and she knew it, knowing that submission to this kiss would be fatal. Armand's heart pounded against her fingertips, its unsteady beat eloquently expressing his own vulnerability, making it impossible for Alex to resist any longer. Conceding defeat, she parted her lips with a sigh and reached up to slide her arms around his neck, accepting his love as her own.

At the first sign of her submission Armand lifted his head, abruptly breaking his kiss. "That, milady, was inflicted," he whispered hoarsely, his eyes bright with amusement. "Although ready indeed you seemed to share at the last moment."

Achingly aware that he was teasing her, Alex flushed crimson to the roots of her hair. Mortified, she struggled out of his grip, turning her back to him once again when he released her, desperately fighting her tears.

Armand came and stood behind her as he had before, but this time he rested his hands on her shoulders, his thumbs gently stroking her skin in rhythmic circles. She felt his forehead touch the back of her head, releasing her breath in a shaky sigh as she acknowledged his mute apology. Finding herself unable to concentrate beneath his touch, Alex blurted out the first thought in her mind. "What reason had Therese to kiss you?"

"She wished to prove that I could not have fallen in love," Armand explained softly, and Alex shrank from the import of his words.

Armand was in love with Therese.

"I understand," she said softly, hanging her head and wishing he would leave her alone. How could she have been so blind as to miss something so obvious? 'Twas why Therese had agreed to hide them. Had he not said that he had stopped there on the way to Venice? She could not blame him for wanting to see his lady love again after all that time. A tear of self-pity gathered at the corner of her eye and she sniffled unsteadily. Why did he not simply leave?

Armand watched Alex in surprise. Her response to his declaration of love had certainly not been what he had expected. She seemed upset about it, disappointed almost. He caught the sound of her muffled sniffle and his heart wrenched in two. What on earth was she thinking?

"I understand everything now," Alex reiterated shakily. She turned and reached up to place a tremulous kiss on Armand's hardened cheek, her downcast eyes keeping her from seeing the outright confusion in his. "I would wish you both the best of luck." She folded her arms across her chest and walked to the other side of the room, fully anticipating that Armand would take his leave.

Armand swore violently under his breath, his patience well and truly expired, and Alex glanced over her shoulder in surprise.

"Whatever is in your mind, milady?" he demanded, his voice filled with exasperation. "I tell you of my love for you and you wish me much happiness with another. I must confess that your response is not what I anticipated."

"You love me?" Alex demanded, her voice too small to be heard over the pounding of her heart.

"Indeed I do, milady," Armand asserted firmly, his dark gaze holding hers.

"Not Therese?" she asked, and Armand grinned in relief at the sparkle that appeared in her eyes.

"Only you," he repeated, and she flushed, turning her back to him again.

"I do not believe you," Alex whispered, her own heart calling her a liar.

"Indeed, milady, 'tis true," Armand insisted, his voice low with emotion.

Alex spun around to confront him. "If that be the case, why did you leave me that night?"

Armand's lips twitched as he tried not to smile. "In truth, so I might keep the vow I had made to you."

"Please explain yourself, sir," Alex demanded, and he chuckled outright at her confusion.

"I could not trust myself to keep from touching you." Alex flushed and tried to turn away again, only to hear Armand's solid step and find his arms encircling her again. He turned her around gently, tipping her chin with one finger so that she was forced to meet the intent in his eyes. "I sat on the back step and tried to think of a way that I could respectfully ask for your hand, Alex. When I returned in the morning with my solution, you had gone."

Alex's eyes filled with tears again. "I saw you with Therese and thought that you had gone from my bed to hers."

"Nay, milady," Armand whispered huskily. "Nothing less than respect for your honor could have driven me from your side that night." He touched his lips to hers and Alex arched against him, savoring his gentle kiss, which ended all too soon for her taste.

With an apologetic smile, Armand led her to the only chair in the room, a rough-hewn stool before the fire, seating her as if she were a queen. Taking both her hands in his, he dropped to one knee in front of her. "I love you, Alexandria," he said, his eyes filled with unspoken emotion. "Will you be my bride?"

Alex's eyes filled with tears as she slipped from the stool, her heart threatening to burst with love. "Yes, oh yes," she whispered as she lifted her lips to his. "I would be most honored to be your wife."

With a sigh of satisfaction, Armand kissed her again. Alex snuggled in Armand's lap as their lips parted and he lifted her easily in his arms, perching on the seat she had abandoned to cuddle her close.

"You should not have traveled on your own, regardless of what you thought I had done," he chided her with a gentle shake, surprised once again at the fierce surge of protectiveness in his gut as she clasped her slender arms more securely around his neck.

"Who could guess what sort of wickedness could have befallen you," he scolded, his breath warm against her throat, and Alex went completely still in his arms.

Alex caught her breath, wondering what he would think if he knew what sort of wickedness had befallen her even before she had left Venice. And at whose hand. Should she have told him everything? Should she tell him now?

"Did you have any trouble on the road?" Armand asked, forcing his voice to remain low and calm despite the surge of fear her stillness sent racing through his veins. He stroked her jawline tenderly with the side of his thumb, silently resolving that he would unceremoniously tear anyone from limb to limb who had dared to hurt her.

"None," Alex answered, a warm feeling stealing around her heart at Armand's evident concern. "I stayed off the main road and away from the taverns."

"Clever lady," he congratulated her in a low voice. "The road is no place for a woman alone." His fingers wove into the mass of her hair again and Alex shivered.

"Cold, milady?" Armand asked softly.

Alex shook her head in response as she tilted her chin and reached up to press a kiss against the pulse beating in his throat, rubbing the tip of her nose in the curve beneath his earlobe. She ran her tongue along the underside of his jaw, reveling in the knowledge that Armand was hers and hers alone. Smiling with satisfaction, she heard his breathing change as his hands slipped to encircle her waist securely and he bent to taste her lips again.

Armand's mouth slanted across hers and Alex sighed at the gentle pressure, her own lips parting softly. His tongue stroked the inside of her lips, running along the edge of her teeth, and Alex opened her mouth to its spicy warmth, pleasure coursing languidly along her veins.

Alex reached up and cupped the back of his head, digging her fingers into his thick, curly hair and urging him closer, her own tongue tentatively dueling with his. Armand tore his lips away abruptly, his nostrils flaring, his breath coming in short spurts as he gazed down at her with bright eyes. Alex held tightly on to the strong column of his neck, trying without success to slow her own breathing.

Armand's heart constricted at the passion evident in Alex's expression, the invitation in her deep blue eyes, finding himself achingly aware of the hardened nubs of her taut nipples crushed against his chest.

He realized with a start that she would match him, touch for touch, for as long as he continued with their lovemaking. Her trust was humbling and he found himself relieved that he had stopped as soon as he had, lest she regret their actions later. The women's voices rose again in the solar, seemingly taunting him with their proximity as they laughed at some small pleasantry, and he shifted uncomfortably.

"Perhaps I should take my leave, milady," he whispered with another sidelong glance at the closed door.

"When shall I see you again?" Alex asked, disappointment in her eyes. Armand sighed with dissatisfaction, forcing himself to think of practicalities despite the temptation arrayed before him.

"I do not know," he admitted vexedly, wondering whether the lord would accept his offer, unwilling to falsely buoy Alex's hopes before he knew for certain. He stroked the hair away from her face tenderly and gave her an encouraging smile. "I must make arrangements so that we can be wed."

Alex frowned in confusion. "What kind of arrangements do you mean, milord?"

Armand chuckled and chided her in a soft voice, his heart leaping at her address. "Alex, Alex, well you know that a younger son must earn the right to wed. I had thought to joust in the tourneys in the north this season."

"You could be killed," Alex admonished, sitting up straighter, her eyes filled with concern. Armand grinned as he flicked the end of her nose with the tip of one finger.

"Adequate incentive have I to keep myself alive," he teased, nuzzling her neck affectionately. "And you have patched me up before." Alex flushed at his jest and he sobered as he sought to ease her concern. "Truth be told, I have more experience of warfare than most of the other competitors, milady. Few crusaders came home when I did, fully expecting the king to retaliate in short order."

Alex closed her eyes and leaned against Armand, wondering if she should confide in him now. He apparently did not know that she was sole heiress to Fontaine. Surely he would wonder why she had never mentioned such a thing before. And she did not wish to offend his pride, so sure was he that he could compete well in the tourneys. She sighed with indecision and traced little circles against his hauberk, blinking back the tears that gathered in her eyes.

"'Tis not so long until the autumn," he whispered reassuringly, mistaking the source of her distress as he gathered her closer.

"I fear for your life, milord."

"And I for yours, milady," Armand responded, surprised at the turn her thoughts had taken. Pièrre de Villiers and his marriage contract, the unnamed murderer of Michel, temporarily forgotten, now surged into his mind again and he instinctively tightened his embrace. His heart went cold as he remembered her uncle's poorly veiled lies and he wondered anew how well the Lord Pontesse had convinced de Villiers of Alex's absence.

"Have you a dagger, milord?" Alex asked, her quiet tone and curious request interrupting his line of thought.

"Indeed," Armand answered in confusion, drawing the short blade from his belt at her expectant expression. He watched with interest as she gathered a lock of her hair, gesturing to him to cut it off near the roots.

Smoothing the shorn lock with her hands, she presented the cut ends to him. "Hold this, if you please," Alex directed, and not knowing what else to do, Armand complied, his curiosity growing as she methodically braided the hair into a long and narrow plait.

Braiding the last of the hair with a flourish, Alex wrapped the narrow plait around and around Armand's right wrist and fastened the ends securely, carefully checking that the bracelet was too tight to be easily removed yet loose enough that it would not interfere with his actions.

Her task completed, Alex glanced up at Armand with satisfaction. "'Tis said that such a bracelet will keep a man faithful to the woman of whose hair it is made," Alex explained, an impish gleam in her eye.

"Indeed? You would still doubt my faithfulness, milady?" Armand chuckled, his eyes bright as he tickled her ribs relentlessly. "When last I thought you unattainable, the Templars had a new brother in their ranks." Alex squirmed in his lap beneath his teasing fingers.

She looked pointedly at the closed door, but Armand simply grinned wickedly, tickling her anew until she thought she could hold her giggles no longer. As her lips parted to let the happy sound peal forth, Armand bent swiftly and captured them in a fierce kiss.

When he lifted his head and broke their embrace, Alex noticed that both of them were breathing quickly. She touched her fingertips gently to the pulse throbbing in his throat and he swallowed, his eyes darkening as he looked down at her.

"And what, milady, would I do to have you remember me?" Armand demanded huskily. Alex's own heart leapt to her throat and she studied the expression in his smoky green eyes with wonder, amazed that such a man could love her, amazed at the depth of love that she felt for him. It would be six months, perhaps a year before she saw him again, she realized, her heart chilling with the import of her thoughts.

Overwhelmed by the sadness welling up in her heart, Alex cupped Armand's strong jaw in her hands, reaching forward to kiss one corner of his mouth, then the other. She heard him inhale sharply as his arms closed protectively around her, pulling the soft fullness of her breasts against his hard strength.

Alex pressed ever closer to Armand, feeling a growing inexplicable urgency as Armand watched her intently, his eyes glinting like fiery emeralds in the relative darkness of the room. He was so utterly still that Alex wondered for a brief moment whether he had stopped breathing.

Pulling his head down, she arched against him, reaching up and pressing her lips gently to his. His hands tightened on her waist at her caress, his fingers spreading across her back, and he closed his eyes, exhaling slowly as she pulled away. Alex stroked the hair away from his brow, finding herself unable to keep from touching him, feeling the heat of his gaze on her as she stretched to kiss his earlobe. His nostrils flared as her soft lips made contact and he shuddered, lifting her deliberately away from him and fixing her with a stern glance.

"Milady," he whispered hoarsely, "do you know fully what you do?"

Alex studied his features carefully, savoring his concern. She reached up and pushed away the curl that fell over his forehead, then met his eyes again, the expression she found there sending the love in her heart soaring. Love, she acknowledged with a gentle smile curving her lips. She loved this man with all her heart and she wanted to share that with him.

"You are my betrothed," she answered, her voice a low whisper. "I would have you love me." Alex cupped the back of his head between her hands, parting her lips and pulling him unerringly toward her.

Armand's heart beating a staccato at her words, any hint of gallantry rapidly leaving him in the face of her caresses. He desired Alex more than he had ever desired a woman, the evidence that she felt the same way urging his passion out of control. He knew that he should leave now, before the last vestiges of his self-control abandoned him, recognizing in that same instant that it was already too late. Alex pressed against him and his heart surged with possessive pride that she was his woman, his love, soon to become his wife.

The sweet taste of Alex's lips made Armand's decision easy and he stood up, cradling her in his arms before breaking their embrace. Lowering Alex to her feet, he turned and shrugged out of his tabard, accepting her assistance in removing his heavy hauberk.

In moments, he stood completely naked before her, enjoying the maidenly flush that spread over her cheeks before sweeping her into his arms and depositing her in the middle of the bed. His loins throbbed as he remembered her sweet response to his lovemaking at Therese's home and he forced himself to take things slowly, determined to introduce her to the pleasures of wedded life.

When Alex would have reached to remove her shirt, Armand stopped her, capturing her hands in his and placing them on his shoulders. Cupping her face, he kissed her eyelids gently, his thumbs lazily caressing her earlobes.

Alex kept her eyes closed as his lips met hers, quivering at the sensations aroused by his hands as they traveled lightly over her curves, slowly moving downward to her knees. She let her head fall back as his warm hands slipped beneath her shirt, sliding resolutely over her hips and bracketing her waist beneath the gossamer garment.

Armand ran a row of kisses along her jaw and down her throat, his hands curving over her ribs and slowly nudging upward. Alex sighed as his palms covered her breasts, his thumbs caressing the nipples slowly. His hands continued on their upward path, forcing Alex to lift her arms, the fullness of her shirt caught on his wrists. Armand ducked his head between his hands and laved one breast tenderly as he continued to slowly remove the garment. The cotton covered Alex's face as she leaned back and closed her eyes, the fabric sliding away in a whisper of a caress.

When the shirt fell away, Armand's hands slid slowly back down the length of Alex, his lips moving to her other nipple while his hands caressed the length of her back. He ran his fingertips across the scar on her left shoulder, following the caress with his lips before his fingers continued their exploration, his mouth fastening on her nipple again. Alex lay back across the bed as his warm hands slid over her waist, his strong fingers grasping her pelvis, his thumbs drawing slow circles across the softness of her stomach.

The warmth of Armand's hand moved lower, his fingers tangling in the nest of springy curls, then slipping even lower to caress between her thighs. His other hand slid beneath Alex's shoulder blades, arching her to his questing lips as he stroked her gently, arousing a flurry of sensations much as he had done once before.

Alex writhed in his embrace as he suckled her, the insistent tug of his lips and relentless dance of his fingertips leaving her dizzy. She gasped as Armand's teeth grazed her taut nipple and he moved quickly to silence the sound, his hand slipping from beneath her to cup the back of her head as he bent to kiss her hungrily.

Her mind filling with the need to please her lover as he pleased her, Alex pushed Armand onto his back, her tongue darting between his lips in a frenzy. She rolled on top of him, kissing his eyes, his chin, his throat, his nose, consistently returning to drink of his lips. Wanting to touch him everywhere, she ran her hands across his smooth skin, savoring the warmth of its muscled strength.

Armand groaned in response, his manhood straining against Alex's softness. He clutched her buttocks in both hands and firmly tipped her hips to fit against his, his body tense as he attempted to control his passion.

Alex's fingers slid across his nipples, teasing them to tight peaks as she undulated her hips instinctively against him, reveling in the hardness of his body. Armand inhaled sharply at her simple gesture, any pretense of control gone, and rolled Alex to her back.

His nostrils flared as he bent to kiss her and Alex responded with tongue and lips and hands, her passion unrestrained. Armand held his weight above her, carefully balanced on his elbows, and she marveled at how safe and secure she felt beneath him despite his size. Feeling as though it were the most natural thing in the world to do, Alex parted her thighs and wrapped her legs around Armand's waist, her heart pounding in anticipation of their union.

Armand caught his breath at Alex's gesture, the sweetness of her submission inflaming him still further. His heart swelled with love and possessive pride as he looked down at her, her rosy lips swollen from his kisses, her blue eyes dark and drowsy with passion, her ebony hair strewn beneath them in disarray.

He bent and kissed her tenderly, savoring the way she ardently returned his embrace. He moved his hips as they kissed, gently probing against her to gain entry, then sliding into her warmth unobstructed. Something clicked in the back of his mind, but then the velvety sheath of Alex's soft warmth surrounded him and all conscious thought fled.

Alex lifted her hips to take as much of Armand's length as she could, feeling deliciously cherished in his arms, completely possessed by his love. Armand buried his face in her neck with a sigh as he began to thrust slowly within her. Feeling the passion rise within her once more at his gentle rhythm, Alex rose to meet him, their bodies jutting together in a timeless dance, their tempo increasing as they scaled the heights of their passion, until they reached the peak together and leapt off the precipice.

Armand rolled to his back, cradling Alex in his arms. He certainly hadn't intended for this to happen until they were wed, but matters had gotten out of hand. He could not deny how right her curves felt pressed against him, had not been able to turn the tide of desire once he had known that she wanted him tonight.

He fingered the bracelet she had woven around his wrist with a wry smile, his gaze running warmly over the tousled beauty nestled against his side, her ebony lashes splayed across her cheeks as she dozed softly, her tiny fingers curling into the hair on his chest. There was little doubt in his mind that her charm would work its magic on him. Had he not been chaste these two years past, his mind filled only with visions of her sweet visage?

Staring at the timbered ceiling while she dozed, he knew that he should dress and return to his room over the stables, but he found himself unwilling to leave her side as yet, enjoying the warm sleepy scent of her snuggled beside him. Armand closed his eyes and listened to the soft rhythm of Alex's breathing, his mind filling with images of their lovemaking.

He frowned as he began to doze himself, trying to pinpoint something that kept flitting just out of his reach as he slid into the netherland of sleep. With an effort, he grasped the elusive thought and almost sat bolt upright in the bed.

There had been no barrier to his entry.

Alex's maidenhead was already gone. He glanced down at her as she dozed in his arms, the very picture of innocence, and shook his head in denial. It made no sense.

Images assaulted him of her many invitations, the way she had parted her lips, indeed, parted her thighs for him. Had she not initiated their lovemaking tonight? He tried to tell himself that such thoughts were unjustified, but there was no stopping the question that popped into his head.

Had her response been born of instinct or practice?

Armand took a deep breath to still the pounding of his heart and stared at the top of Alex's head in confusion. She had said she loved him, that she would be his bride. Was it unreasonable for him to expect her to be virginal?

He gritted his teeth as his temper began to rise. He had wanted to be the first man for her, the only man, in a purely possessive way. Jealousy ripped through his chest as he wondered how many men she had had, how many times she had lain so alluring, so sweet and responsive in another man's arms.

Feeling suddenly ill, he rolled abruptly from the bed and pulled on his chausses with jerky movements, his jealousy turning to anger at her deception.

Alex stirred, her eyes opening slowly, then widening in surprise as she saw Armand hastily dressing. Clearly he had intended to leave without awakening her and disappointment welled up in her throat.

"You would leave now, milord?" she asked quietly, and he threw her a fiercely dismissive glance before tugging on his hauberk with sharp movements.

"It would seem that I have overstayed," he answered tightly, and Alex's eyes widened in surprise. Overstayed? His words could have only one meaning. 'Twas clear that he regretted the lovemaking that she had thought so wondrously sweet, so unlike the abuse she had endured from Pièrre. How foolish she had been to expect it to hurt as it had before.

The realization struck her like a brick. It had hurt before and she had bled. Without thinking, Alex shifted on the bed and glanced down at the sheets. No blood. She looked up to find Armand watching her steadily even as he buckled his scabbard around his waist. Now she saw the hostility that lurked in the depths of his blazing eyes, the sharp edge to his abrupt movements.

He was leaving because he knew that she had not been a virgin. Alex felt the heat of a flush rise over her cheeks at his scornful gaze and clumsily gathered the sheets to cover her nakedness, suddenly painfully self-conscious in his presence.

"No pretty story of rape for me, milady?" Armand sneered, and Alex cringed at the sarcasm in his tone.

Hating the harsh sound of his own voice, Armand found himself unable to stop his next words. "'Tis the usual tale for an indiscreet gentlewoman on her wedding night, I am told." Alex dropped her head and he willed her to tell him some such viable tale, realizing with surprise that he cared not whether 'twas the truth or not.

Alex dropped her eyes and chewed her bottom lip in consternation. She could hardly tell him the truth after such a comment. Anger sparked within her at his immediate assumption that she was guilty of some crime without ever giving her the benefit of the doubt. Even when she had seen him kissing Therese, she had waited until morning for his return before running away. If she had not awakened this night, he would have simply disappeared from her life without giving or asking for an explanation.

Her temper flared at the injustice of it all. Clearly he had not been inexperienced before coming to her bed this night, but as a woman she had no right to ask about his past. He had sought his pleasure on many a night while she had been abused on one and he considered her to be in the wrong. She lifted her chin to meet Armand's eyes again, her own sparkling with defiance.

"I have no tale for you, sir," she spat in a low voice. Something flickered in his eyes, but it was gone so quickly that Alex wondered whether she had seen it at all.

"Do you not think I deserve an explanation for your deception?" Armand demanded coldly, and Alex's temper flared anew. Deception indeed! Alex leapt from the bed in anger, wrapping the linens around herself with a savage sweep.

"I would not waste my breath, sir. Only a fool could fail to see that you have already made your own conclusions."

Armand regarded her steadily, some of the anger draining from his features. Although he was less angry, 'twas easy to see that he still believed her to be no better than a common courtesan. The unspoken accusation stung Alex like a whip and she folded her arms across her chest, determined to make him suffer for misjudging her.

"Tell me that I am wrong, milady," Armand insisted quietly, but Alex tossed her head and turned her back to him, ignoring the urgency in his tone.

"I would not give you the satisfaction." She bit the words out, his distrust of her hurting more than she would have believed possible. How could he claim that he loved her, yet hold her character in so little regard?

"Then I will take my leave," Armand said softly. "'Tis clear that earlier I spoke too hastily." The sudden retraction of his proposal stunned Alex but she refused to turn around and face him, biting her lip against the sobs rising in her chest. Armand hesitated but a moment before he paced firmly to the window, the determined sound of his footfalls filling the room, and he was gone through the window as he had come. Only then did Alex allow the tears to spill unchecked down her cheeks.

Chapter Ten

" 'T is a perfect solution, Hugues, would you only consider it," Sophie insisted in an urgent whisper.

" 'Tis no more than foolishness," Hugues reiterated, burrowing his head determinedly back under the covers. Almost dawn it was and still the woman would not let the matter rest. He rolled over to face the wall, groaning when his wife leaned over his shoulder to press her point.

"So pigheaded you are for an intelligent man," she chided gently. Her thick blond braid slipped over his shoulder and Hugues grabbed the end of it, giving it a playful tug.

"So stubborn you are for a dutiful wife," he teased, and caught a glimpse of Sophie's answering smile. "You seem quite determined," he noted quietly, and felt her nod vigorously in the darkness.

"Indeed I am." Sophie's soft voice was firm. Hugues sighed with resignation, knowing that there would be no sleep for him until he heard her out. He rolled to his back, gathering a pleased Sophie up against his side.

"You think she would be safer there than here?" he demanded softly.

"Most certainly."

"But why? Because the child stitched up this knight's shoulder several years past?" Hugues leveled his wife a skeptical look. "You must confess that this is a weak argument."

"But not the only one," Sophie argued, settling in against his shoulder. "You were not here, Hugues. You did not see magic between those two. They were entranced with each other from the moment their eyes first met."

"Sophie, that was years ago. Surely you cannot expect me to believe that alone prompted Avigny's offer?"

"No." Sophie frowned and pursed her lips thoughtfully. "Perhaps he and Alex have seen each other since."

"In Venice and Jerusalem?" Hugues' tone was incredulous.

"Alex was very vague about the knight who assisted her," his wife mused, and Hugues snorted in open disbelief.

"Surely you do not expect me to believe that this knight and he are one and the same?" He shook his head vehemently when Sophie raised her eyebrows and muttered under his breath, "More likely, he is allied with de Villiers."

"No!" Sophie insisted sharply. "He intends no harm to Alex."

"How do you know that?" he demanded, already knowing what her answer would be. Always did they fight thus, seemingly regardless of the issue at hand. If only Sophie's heart wasn't so annoyingly accurate. Hugues fought back a sense that he had already lost this argument and plunged on into the fray. "How can you possibly know his intent?"

"I can feel it," Sophie shot back, her tone defensive. "My heart tells me so. Did you listen to your own, you would know the truth of this."

"You *cannot* send Alex away on the basis of what you feel. You must *know* the facts and make the best possible decision." Hugues felt his wife stiffen beside him and knew that he had said the wrong thing.

"I have made the best possible decision," she argued softly, and he gritted his teeth, fighting for patience.

"You cannot simply send the girl to Avigny. We know nothing about this château. Indeed, we know precious little about this man who calls himself a member of that house."

"He is trustworthy."

"But what of his family? We know nothing of them, not even how many there are, never mind their alliances and interests."

"His father is one of my kind," Sophie insisted quietly, and Hugues looked up at her, momentarily uncomprehending.

"He follows the old ways?" he asked, and Sophie nodded slowly.

"He needs a healer," she added, and Hugues closed his eyes against the darkness, knowing that Sophie would go herself if he refused her request to send Alex.

Hugues sighed, frowning across the room shrouded in shadows. Why not concede the point? Sophie's feelings were notoriously reliable and this path really was more sensible. Almost anywhere would be safer for Alex than Pontesse if de Villiers planned any trouble, and Hugues himself had not been immune tonight to the tall knight's aura of solid reliability. He would take this man into battle with him without a second thought.

Logically, Hugues wished he knew more about Armand d'Avigny and his family, but he forced himself to face the knowledge of his heart. Without a doubt, he knew he could trust the younger man to protect Alex, and that truly was what she needed right now.

Perhaps he had been listening to Sophie for too long.

Hugues sighed, noticing that the darkness was not as complete as it had been moments before. The dawn was coming. Ideally, Alex would be on her way with the two knights before the entire household awoke so fewer souls would witness their departure. May the gods forbid that there was a traitor within his own walls, but 'twould not hurt to be cautious.

"Find some squire's clothes for Alex," he said determinedly as he swung his feet to the floor, a boyish grin curving his lips when Sophie jubilantly threw her arms around his neck from behind. "You can thank me later, woman," he growled with a twinkle in his eye, not ducking nearly quickly enough to evade the pillow his wife swung at his head.

The abandoned pink rosebud taunted Alex as she struggled into the garments that Sophie had inexplicably brought her. Short-tempered from her lack of sleep and the discovery of blood on her thighs, she struggled with the lace in the boy's chausses, refusing to speculate on how different things would be had her monthly bleeding begun a few hours earlier.

Sophie was suspiciously unwilling to divulge any explanation for her strange demands, quickly packing Alex's two kirtles into a saddlebag with her chemise and tossing Alex's dark woolen surcoat over the younger woman's shoulders. She held one finger to her lips and hastened Alex through the ladies' waiting room, disturbing none of the sleeping women as they stealthily made their way to the stairs.

The hall was deserted, as was the corridor to the courtyard, Hugues' bulky form the first Alex saw as he stepped out of the shadows lingering before the stables. He led Argent, a silver charger he had recently acquired. The high-stepping horse was already saddled, and the pack that Sophie carried was quickly added to his trap.

"Your healing skills are needed," Hugues explained under his breath.

"By one of the old faith, name of Baudouin," Sophie added before Alex could say anything, and she nodded mutely, wondering where her aunt and uncle had chosen to send her so abruptly and secretly.

"Good morning," Hugues said, looking over her shoulder, and Alex turned to see two more destriers stepping out from the stables, their proud heads tossing in anticipation of a good run, their red-and-white caparisons lifting in the morning breeze.

"Good morning to you, sir," the young knight who led the first stallion returned, his lips curving into a cocky grin as he saw Alex. She nodded in response to his greeting, painfully aware of his assessing gaze slipping appreciatively over the curves revealed by her snugly fitting boy's garb. Who were these knights? What had they said to convince Hugues of their motives?

The second horse followed closely behind the first, its rider already mounted and sitting tall in the saddle. Alex's eyes lifted to meet Armand's icily condemning ones and her heart stopped cold. He nodded curtly to her and to Hugues and Sophie, flicking an imperious glance to the other knight, who mounted hastily in response. Alex fought a desperate desire to flee rather than ride out in Armand's company, turning awkwardly instead and mounting Argent with Hugues' assistance.

"My father will welcome the aid of your house," Armand said to Hugues as the two men shook hands and Alex struggled to come to terms with her situation. Why did he wish her to accompany them? Who was this Baudouin and would she truly be able to help him?

"Blessed be," Sophie whispered by her side, and Alex spared her aunt a tremulous smile, uncertain of what awaited her at wherever they rode this day.

They turned immediately away from the road, seeking the shelter of the trees as they rode away from Pontesse in the dawning light, the familiar fortress dropping into the distance behind them.

"I regret that we have not had time for proper introductions" came a smooth comment from her left, and Alex glanced up to meet the younger knight's engaging smile.

"'Twas indeed a quick departure," she returned in a low voice, not knowing what else to say.

"Of course, I have had the pleasure of making your acquaintance already," he continued, grinning at the puzzled look his words prompted. "Two years past, I was Armand's squire," he confided, and Alex looked at him with surprise. "Now I am Chevalier Roarke."

"Never would I have recognized you, sir," Alex admitted, only now seeing the features of the boy lurking beneath those of the grown man. "So much have you changed."

"And you, milady, have grown only more lovely, a fact that cannot be hidden by your garb of this day."

"I thank you for your kind words, sir," Alex responded, enjoying Roarke's light gallantry. She flicked a glance at Armand, his back ramrod straight as he rode ahead in stubborn silence. A welcome contrast was Roarke indeed.

"I would ask that you call me Roarke, milady," the younger knight insisted, his tone confidential, and Alex smiled warmly at his words. " 'Tis too long a ride for formalities."

" 'Tis too long a ride for conversation," Armand snapped over his shoulder. "If we are to make Avigny this day, we must dispense with pleasantries and ride harder." With that, he led his horse out of the trees and onto the snow-dusted road.

Roarke raised his eyebrows in silent amazement before dropping behind Alex, who wondered just how far away their destination lay. Tiberias accelerated to a full gallop and she dug her heels to encourage Argent, disappointed that Roarke could not continue to talk to her. Now she was left with only her own thoughts.

And traitorous those thoughts soon proved to be as Alex found her eyes drawn to Armand's proud carriage, understanding his hurt and disappointment. Her lips parted a dozen times to shout the truth at him, but adequate words to explain eluded her. She wondered whether Armand would believe the truth, should she tell him now, and speculated silently on what her stubborn nature had cost her.

When they paused by a stream to give the horses a respite, Alex was despondent and close to tears, fancying that she felt Armand's gaze heavy on her bent head. She glanced up but he was frowning into the distance, his lips pulled to a thin line as he seemingly contemplated the distance left to ride.

They stopped again when the sun was at its peak and Armand offered bread from his saddlebag to his companions, but Alex refused, knowing that she would not be able to choke it down past the lump in her throat. Armand for his part took only a draft of wine, while Roarke, his brow pulled into a frown, ate sparsely and silently considered the other two.

And so the day continued, the miles passing beneath the horses' feet, the sun beating onto Alex's shoulders with its relentless determination to thaw the slumbering earth. Her buttocks ached from the continuous pace, the destriers faltering on the loose stones underfoot as they forded a shallow stream in the fading light, but still Armand urged them forward.

The moon had climbed into the sky, a silver disk high above the silhouetted round keep, when they rode into the courtyard of Avigny. Alex slipped from her saddle in exhaustion, only to find Armand himself catching her weight before her feet touched the ground. She glanced up at the stern set of his features in surprise and he permitted himself a thin smile.

"Relax, milady," he murmured under his breath, "I do not mean to hurt you, even now."

He swung her easily into his arms and Alex flushed, embarrassed that she had doubted his intent for even an instant, but his attention was already diverted. Armand and Roarke exchanged a silent look, Roarke nodding that he would tend to the horses, Armand tossing Alex's saddlebag into her lap and carrying her into the quiet hall on soundless feet. He made his way directly to the stairs and Alex's heart began to pound in trepidation.

"What..." she began in an uncertain whisper, but he shushed her with a quelling glance that brooked no argument and took the stairs two at a time. Had her submission the previous night led him to assume that that intimacy might continue? Nothing could she discern from his face in the darkness, what minimal glimpses she had had revealing only the grim set of determination in his lips.

At the top of the stairs, a hall ran to the right, doors on either side, a wall sconce sputtering fitfully at the far end and casting a dancing orange light over the corridor. Without hesitation, Armand headed for the last door on the left, nudging the wooden mass open with his foot and advancing into the room.

He set Alex on her feet and she caught her belongings before they tumbled to the floor, hugging the saddlebag to her chest against the cold of the room. Armand had already moved away into the darkness and she could hear the rasp of a striking flint on the other side of the room. Clearly Armand knew the room and its contents well, for a mo-

ment later a light flickered in the grate against the far wall
and she spied his silhouette as he dropped to one knee to
build a blaze.

The firelight danced off the stone walls of the room and
Alex looked around with interest, avoiding the sturdy
draped bed in one corner. The small chest, table and pair of
chairs were virtually unadorned, the lack of tapestries on the
walls and absence of color belying a woman's touch. A
man's room this was, without a doubt.

She glanced back to Armand to find him watching her
steadily, his back to the fire so that his face was cloaked in
darkness. What did he expect from her? What should she
say? What should she do?

Alex watched him silently for a moment, her love for him
swelling her heart beyond compare, and she knew that she
could not refuse him should he desire her this night. It
seemed at that moment as if touch alone could dissolve the
barrier between them. Alex took a tentative step toward
Armand, and when he took an answering pace toward her,
her heart leapt in anticipation, but he walked right past her,
pausing on the threshold of the room without turning back.

"None will disturb you here," he said in a low voice, his
long fingers curving around the edge of the wooden door
and flexing experimentally as if he would say more but was
uncertain of the words. The silence stretched uncomfortably between them and Alex tried to think of something to
say, realizing that she should thank him for his consideration. Before she could summon the words, he spoke again.

"Sleep well, milady," he bit out, and was gone, the door
closing behind him resolutely, and leaving Alex to stare at its
featureless expanse.

Alex dressed carefully the next morning, not knowing
what greeting she would receive in the hall below. Nervously surveying her distorted reflection in a small polished
brass mirror she found atop the chest, she adjusted her garments needlessly. Her deep blue kirtle, pale violet veil and
wimple flattered her coloring, though she told herself she

wore it only to make a good first impression on the household.

Enough. She was here to assist Baudouin and Armand had made his own lack of interest in her more than clear. Alex blinked back her tears, replacing the mirror carefully on the chest, taking a deep breath while she looked out the single window. She watched the rain fall softly over a neglected garden beyond the stables for a few moments while she collected herself, then took another deep breath and headed downstairs.

"And who might this be?" an attractive woman demanded archly from the head table as Alex reached the bottom step, sending the glance of every occupant of the hall in the new arrival's direction and launching a flush over Alex's cheeks.

Cursing her lack of composure, Alex lifted her chin, meeting the gaze of the woman, noting the loveliness of her features despite her sneer. A quick scan of the room revealed that neither Armand nor Roarke was present and she took another steadying breath before approaching the head table.

"I am a healer," she explained, "summoned here to tend one named Baudouin."

"Indeed" came the disbelieving comment from the man seated next to the woman, and Alex immediately noted the similarity between this man's features and Armand's. Smaller built he was, with a longer face and a touch of silver in his hair, but his jaw retained that square line, the hair the uncommon russet color. This must be Armand's elder brother.

"Indeed," Alex affirmed, refusing to let the man's sardonic air intimidate her. "Where might I find the gentleman?"

"Back from whence you came," the woman responded, gesturing airily toward the door. "My room, the *lord's* solar, is the first door, my husband's sire rests in the second." A few souls among the company snickered at the woman's emphasis of her role in the household, but Alex did not rise to the bait. The woman fixed Alex with a sharp glance, clearly having expected a retort of some kind, considering the younger woman thoughtfully before she spoke.

"See that you mind your manners, healer," she said finally, her light tone belying the intent in her eyes. "I have little use for your kind."

"I thank you for your assistance," Alex answered with a curt nod, turning smoothly and making her way silently back to the stairs. Such rudeness! To point out her ascendancy over the household to a complete stranger! Alex could not believe that any woman would dare to respond so in public and directly before her husband. And to insult the validity of her healing skills before the company. Alex held up her chin determinedly as she ascended the open stairs, refusing to show any outward reaction to the woman's comments.

"Leave me sleep," Roarke demanded groggily, pushing Armand's hand from his bare shoulder feebly and cocking a glance at his assailant. "I should have guessed 'twould be you at this early hour," he muttered.

Not a morning man, Roarke ran his fingers through his dark blond hair and sat up, scratching his bare chest absently and looking around as if surprised to discover where he had slept.

"I need to borrow your crossbow," Armand insisted, anxious to get on his way before the household awoke.

"And why would you be wanting that?" Roarke demanded suspiciously of his friend.

"Mine is gone and I would hunt this morning."

"Hunt?" That single word brought Roarke awake with a snap and he fixed Armand with bright eyes. "Hunt? Know you not that Guillaume has forbidden any to hunt without him?"

"'Tis no matter." Armand shrugged off the words, wondering what sort of nonsense was this. Was Guillaume truly so uncertain of his authority? Never had his brother liked hunting and Armand would have thought that Guillaume would be glad to be rid of the responsibility of providing for the table. "No one has hunted for weeks for there is not a scrap of meat in the kitchens."

"And the last who hunted without Guillaume was flogged in the bailey until the flesh hung from his back," Roarke shot back.

"Flogged?" Armand demanded incredulously.

"Aye," Roarke confirmed quietly. "'Twas just before you returned from the East."

Armand paced the length of the room and back, scarcely able to believe that his brother had had a man whipped for what amounted to a minor indiscretion. To hunt on the lord's land for the lord's table could hardly be construed as stealing. What did Guillaume seek to prove?

"Truly the man had done nothing else to deserve such treatment?" he asked again, but Roarke shook his head, pulling up his legs to sit cross-legged on the narrow bed.

"'Twas rumored in the hall that he had refused the advances of the Lady Margrethe," Roarke commented tonelessly, flicking a wry glance to his friend, "but I would not expect Guillaume to find such behavior insulting."

"Indeed not," Armand conceded tightly. 'Twas said a woman scorned hath all the fury of hell, but to have a man flogged? 'Twas unthinkable.

Armand pursed his lips thoughtfully, knowing that he alone could challenge Guillaume's foolishness. He would hunt this day and test his brother's confidence in this ridiculous rule.

"'Tis unseemly for a lord's table to be barren of meat," Armand continued softly, meeting Roarke's eyes steadily and cocking one brow. "Will you hunt with me?"

Roarke smothered a smile and shook his head slowly. "Nay," he responded carefully, the words falling slowly from his lips. "I fear he will have me killed this time." With that, he bent to pull his crossbow from under the bed and Armand saw for the first time the barely healed scars crisscrossing his companion's back.

* * *

A gentle tap on the second door in the hall above brought some sound that could have been a call to enter, so Alex tentatively pushed open the wooden door.

"Baudouin?" she asked, blinking for a moment to let her eyes adjust to the darkness within.

"And who else would be sleeping here?" a reedy voice demanded indignantly from the bed. "Is a body to have no peace in this household? First my long-departed son, waking me from a sound sleep to tell me of some healer he has brought, and now a total stranger strolls into my very bedchamber, disturbing my slumber yet again for..." Baudouin halted in midsentence and Alex thought she could pick out his form as he propped himself up on his elbows. "You are the one, are you not?" he demanded sharply.

"Indeed I am," Alex answered, barely stifling a smile. "Is Chevalier Armand your son, then, sir?" she asked tentatively, earning a hearty chuckle from the shadowy figure in the bed.

"Aye, he is. Guillaume and Armand, blood of my blood they are," he declared proudly, pausing for a moment before he mused. "Knighted them both, I did, taught them myself the finer points of battle, the suitable behavior for a knight sworn to honor the king. Not that that one downstairs recalls much of that." This last he muttered under his breath and Alex pretended not to have heard, studying her folded hands with apparent interest as she stood waiting in the doorway. Hard it was to believe that the reticent Armand had sprung from this man's seed.

"Come in then, child," Baudouin summoned her cheerfully, returning to his earlier tone and briskly issuing commands. "Take those drapes from the window that I might have a good look at you. And call someone to stoke up the fire. 'Tis cursed cold in here. No, do not tend it yourself, this keep is more than amply attended. One of your blood should not be bending to such menial tasks." Alex paused on her way to the door in surprise and tossed a questioning glance over her shoulder, drawing a chuckle from the darkness.

" 'Tis not my eyes that are gone, child. Even in this light I can see your lineage asserting itself. Should you expect me to be an idiot, you will be sorely disappointed."

This time 'twas Alex who laughed aloud. "I truly doubt that you will disappoint me, milord," she responded, opening the door and calling for a servant. A young woman scurried up the stairs and Alex requested a fire, the woman hastening away with a nod and murmured "yes, milady."

"Call me Baudouin," the man in the bed insisted. " 'Tis my name and a fine one at that."

"Indeed it is," Alex agreed, tugging open the draperies that cloaked the sole window in the room. She turned back to her would-be patient, surprised to confront a mischievous twinkle in the eyes of a man apparently as broad and tall as Armand. His eyes were as green as his son's, though his hair was snow white, his grin as infectious as a trouble-making child's. Alex found herself returning his warm smile, a question popping from her lips before she could stop it.

"What ails you, Baudouin? You seem as fit as can be."

"Bah." He waved off her question and beckoned her toward him. "Aches and pains that will bore you to tears. Come here and let me see you." Alex did as he bade, sitting on the side of the bed as he indicated, tolerating his scrutiny with difficulty.

"Dark hair, have you?" he demanded finally, alluding to the tresses concealed beneath her veil and wimple. Alex nodded and he nodded slowly himself in recollection. "As did my Elise. Stunning 'tis, spread across white bed linens."

Alex did not know what to say in response to this last comment, feeling the heat of a flush rise over her cheeks. Baudouin chuckled with delight, his eyes twinkling with merriment as he regarded her embarrassment.

"Already do I feel better," he declared, swinging his legs over the side of the bed and waving away Alex's assistance. "No invalid am I to have a woman tend my needs. Send me a squire as befits a man and wait outside. I would enter the hall to break my fast with a pretty woman on my arm, be she healer or no.''

The hall was virtually empty by the time Alex and Baudouin appeared downstairs, the looks of open astonishment on the faces of the servants giving Alex some idea how long it had been since Baudouin had ventured out of his room.

"Good morning, milord," an older woman murmured as she put warm bread and honey on the table, her smile erasing years from her careworn face.

"Blanche!" Baudouin declared with pleasure. "Good morning to you, woman. Good it is indeed to see you again and smell the fine aroma of your bread." He leaned toward Alex and continued in a confidential tone that Blanche could certainly overhear. "Finest baker within a day's ride of Paris, Blanche is." Alex watched a pink flush tinge the older woman's leathery cheeks.

"You are too kind, milord, and as charming a devil as ever you were," she demurred, but Baudouin shook his head definitively.

"Not a bit of it," he declared gallantly, sparing a furtive glance around the room before he leaned toward her to continue. "My dear Blanche, is it possible that you could manage to find me a bit of meat this morning? I must confess I refused my dinner last evening and find myself ravenously hungry."

Blanche looked doubtful for a moment, then gave Baudouin a cheerful smile. "I shall do my best, milord, but you must know that meat has been scarce here of late." Baudouin frowned and pursed his lips, failing utterly in his attempt to mask his frustration. Alex listened attentively, trying to determine what was going on. Could it be true that there was no meat at the lord's table? Such a thing was unheard-of among the nobility.

"Still the boy continues in this foolishness?" Baudouin demanded sharply, offering Alex no clues as to the meaning of their conversation. Blanche nodded unhappily, sparing a furtive glance around the hall before she leaned forward to speak in hushed tones.

"And still he does not ride out himself, milord," she confided. " 'Tis said the peasants fare better than we, for there are so many young rabbits eating their crops that they are forced to snare them."

Baudouin harrumphed with evident dissatisfaction, folding his arms across his chest in open annoyance. "The very peasants eat meat," he snorted derisively, muttering under his breath. "At least Guillaume cannot be accused of abusing the labor."

"I shall see what I can find, milord," Blanche assured Baudouin with a smile, curtsying quickly before turning for the kitchens.

"Tell the cook we have a guest," he called after her, and Blanche responded with a cheery wave. "Perhaps Didier will find us some dainty morsel," Baudouin assured Alex, squeezing her hand encouragingly, his good humor apparently restored, but Alex was not fooled. Of the old school was Baudouin, and he was embarrassed by the lack of bounty at his table. Had she heard aright? Was Guillaume responsible for this turn of events? If so, Alex doubted that she had heard the last of it.

" 'Tis long indeed since I have had honey," she commented politely, seeking to reassure the older man. Baudouin responded immediately, smiling with pride as he tore the bread, releasing a puff of steam and yeasty aroma from the warm loaf as he offered a chunk to Alex.

"I apologize for my manners, child," he said, removing the cap from the crock of golden honey for her. " 'Tis indeed too long since I have sat at the board with a lady." He took the ladle lying alongside, freezing in midgesture before continuing smoothly on. Alex did not miss the spasm of pain that crossed his features and laid a hand on his arm with concern.

"What is it?" she demanded softly, and the older man spared her a rueful grin.

"Sharp eyes you have," he muttered, and Alex smiled, waiting for his explanation. Seeing that she intended to wait

him out, Baudouin sighed in resignation, cradling the right
hand with the left. "A sharp pain 'tis sometimes, other
times a mere ache, here in these two fingers and down to the
wrist." Alex took his hand, probing the muscles with gentle
fingers and noting when the lines tightened around his
mouth. When she paused, he pursed his lips thoughtfully as
if considering whether to tell her more.

"Go on," she urged carefully, and he nodded slowly.

"Sometimes at night," he murmured in a low voice that
Alex had to strain to hear, "sometimes I cannot move my
fingers. Locked they are, half-clenched. 'Tis most distressing," he concluded, with evident discomfort.

Alex massaged his hand carefully for a few moments,
giving him time to recover his composure. "Is the pain
soothed by rubbing?" she asked softly, and he nodded.

"Aye, 'tis."

"Have you had the pain in the other hand?"

"Not yet," he murmured, and Alex saw the source of his
fear.

"But the right is your sword hand?"

"Aye," he confirmed, surprise in his eyes.

"'Tis unlikely to spread beyond your hand," she assured him, drawing a startled look from the older man.

"You know this ailment?" he demanded, and Alex nodded.

"Indeed, it seems to come in later years to hands and feet,
especially to those who have worked hard," she explained-
matter-of-factly. "'Tis common in the hands of spinners
and weavers and in the sword hand of knights who have seen
much battle."

"You can heal this?" Baudouin asked in amazement, but
Alex shook her head.

"Never does it go away completely," she confessed, still
gently massaging his palm. "But I can make a cream that
will ease the frequency of the spasms and the pain itself
when it comes." She glanced up and fixed the older man
with a twinkling eye. "And you can find someone to mas-
sage your hand just so when it needs attention." To her relief, Baudouin grinned devilishly.

"An old one like me? Bah, no woman would have me," he joked, spying Blanche's reemergence from the kitchens with a loaded tray and rising to his feet to applaud her. "Bravo, bravo!" he called in a booming voice. "I knew that Blanche alone could find us some tempting treat this morn."

Expressing his doubts that she would find what she needed there, Baudouin showed Alex the relentlessly overgrown herb garden, sinking to a bench seat with a sigh as he watched her rummage in the beds. He was tired already, she realized, his strength diminished by all his rest. Not wishing to embarrass him, she conceded to herself that sitting in the faintly warm sun for a while would probably do him some good in itself. Almost of spring did it seem today as the sun peeked out from behind the mist.

The garden was tangled with years of dead overgrowth, but surprisingly abundant with new shoots beneath the disarray. Someone had taken a great deal of effort in planting and laying out the beds, Alex mused, glancing back to Baudouin dozing in the sun and wondering if he saw the garden in its former glory, not choked with weeds and decaying growth as it was now.

She found the roots she wanted, pulling an adequate quantity and stuffing them into the single deep pocket in her kirtle, looking about the garden with assessing eyes. Baudouin was not that ill, it appeared, and there would be precious little for her to do here at Avigny. She could remain as Baudouin's companion and make herself useful, restore the garden to its former glory.

And see Armand.

The thought popped into her mind and she shoved it resolutely away. He had been cruel to her, rudely maligning her character when he had no reason to do so. Alex would stay to tend the garden, to make sure the healing herbs prospered in case Baudouin became more ill than he was now. Her decision made, she bent and began pulling weeds from the first bed as Baudouin gently snored behind her.

* * *

Alex was in the kitchens melting the beeswax she had begged to add to Baudouin's ointment when a ragged cheer rose from the courtyard outside the door. She glanced up to see the cook staring out the door in openmouthed amazement, his assistants eagerly gathered behind him, craning their necks in curiosity.

"God in heaven," she heard him murmur, "he's brought a stag."

Turning, the cook rapidly began to shoot orders to his apprentices, sending one to fetch wine, another to sharpen knives, another to find him potatoes, dispatching the dozen or so boys in as many different directions.

"Bless you, sir," he called into the courtyard, dancing a little jig of excitement on the threshold. He glanced up and caught Alex's eye on him and grinned at her across the room. "We shall dine well tonight," the little man assured her, and Alex smiled in response.

Before she could get to her feet to see the object of all this fuss, Armand himself stood framed in the doorway, a large stag thrown over his shoulder, his lips curving in a bemused smile at the cook's enthusiastic welcome. A medley of men and stable hands trailed behind him, congratulating him on the evident weight of the deer, but the cook resolutely shooed them away from the door as Armand shouldered his way into the kitchen.

"A stag," the squat man breathed in amazement, barely keeping himself from jumping up and down on the spot, poking experimentally at the carcass.

"I thought at first not to take it," Armand said with complete solemnity, drawing a surprised glance from the cook. "I know not how good your memory is these days, Didier, and from what I hear it has been long indeed since you had a stag to prepare."

"Oh! You dare to say such a thing to me! Trained for the king's table, I was." The little man puffed up in indignation, finally spying the twinkle in the younger man's eye and relaxing with a grin. "So many wondrous things I can do with venison," he assured him confidently. "Had I a bit of sage and thyme, my meal would surpass anything served at Fontainebleau. Like kings would we dine but for a bit of herb."

He sighed regretfully and gestured toward a wooden table, indicating that Armand should put the dead stag there. "But I will do my best, sir, regardless of the absence of bare essentials."

"Sage, did you say?" Alex asked, rising to her feet and drawing the surprised gaze of both men.

"Indeed, madam. Sage and thyme, perhaps a scallion or two, should I be so lucky."

"I found sage in the garden this morning. 'Twas first growth, young and tender," Alex began, walking toward the door as she talked, intending to head out into the bedraggled garden to pick the herbs in question.

"The garden?" the cook demanded in amazement, interrupting Alex's words in shock, his nose turning up in distaste. "That is no garden but a tangle of weeds. You cannot be sure of what you pick from that space and *I* would not jeopardize the health of the household for a mere frivolity such as sage."

"Nor would I, sir," Alex returned, meeting his doubtful gaze steadily. "But sage there is growing in that garden, and I for one am tempted by what you could do with a bit of sage." He responded immediately to her appeal to his craftsmanship and she couldn't resist the impulse to add, "Undoubtedly, I could find some thyme, as well, for the garden seems to be quite varied beneath the weeds." For an instant, the little man was tempted, but then he shook his head with finality.

"Healing herbs there are," he hissed, clearly afraid to take a chance, "and dyer's plants, poisonous to man one and all." Didier bit his lip and shook his head with evident regret. "I cannot take the risk," he concluded.

Alex sighed with exasperation, any reassurance she might have uttered catching in her throat when Armand spoke suddenly.

"I will eat whatsoever the lady picks," he interjected calmly, and the cook turned to look up at him with surprise.

"But, sir, you cannot," the little man began, falling silent when Armand raised one finger, flicking a level glance at Alex, who dropped her eyes to the floor.

"The lady is a healer and knows her craft well," he stated firmly. "She is here to heal my father's ills, and well you know that I would not entrust his care lightly." Alex looked up to find Armand's emerald gaze still fixed on her, a warmth in his expression that she had not expected to see again. Abruptly, he turned back to the cook, and she wondered if she had imagined his regard. "I would savor the chance to eat like a king," Armand murmured now, and the cook grinned with new confidence.

"And so you shall, sir," he assured Armand, taking Alex by the arm and propelling her toward the door. "Show me this sage, milady, and your palate shall be well rewarded this night."

"Mind you treat the grouse as regally as the stag," Armand added in a droll voice, and the cook spun on his heel, clapping his hands in delight as Armand placed a bulging sack on the table alongside the deer.

"Grouse! How many?"

"Eight," came the reply, and Alex met Armand's eyes again, her heartbeat accelerating at the warm humor there. She smiled tentatively back at him and he raised one eyebrow, his lips curving ever so slightly in response before he turned to leave the kitchen.

"Eight grouse!" The cook squeezed Alex's arm in his excitement, pushing her back toward the gardens again. "We must make haste, there is so much to do and so little time," he fretted.

"Gustave, pluck those birds and skin the deer," he commanded over one shoulder, sending a young boy scurrying before turning back to whisper conspiratorially to Alex. "Did you note any garlic, milady? Mayhap a few early carrots, a little rosemary?"

Chapter Eleven

Armand found himself early in the hall that night, telling himself that it was the promise of Didier's cooking, but knowing in his heart 'twas that mysterious little smile Alex had given him in the kitchen that lent speed to his steps. For the rest of the afternoon, his mind had taunted him with images of her, and he was impatient with the task of tending Tiberias for the first time he could remember.

But now the evening meal was at hand and he had as much right as any to sit alongside Alex and share a trencher of Didier's stew. A number of men at arms and knights had arrived before him, undoubtedly tempted by the tantalizing aroma wafting through the château from the kitchens and twin kegs of wine had been opened at the far side of the room.

Armand was surprised to see his father before the wide hearth that dominated one wall of the hall, engaged in a heated discussion, the weight of a decade seemingly having slipped off his shoulders. Armand smothered a smile and made his way toward his father, acknowledging that Alex had indeed wrought some magic here.

"Armand," Baudouin greeted him jubilantly, beckoning him into the discussion at hand and gesturing to his adversary. "Explain to this poor soul, if you will, why the fall of the Latin Kingdom in the East is inevitable now that Jerusalem is out of our hands."

"'Tis the infidel kingdom that will fall," asserted the other man, surprised when both father and son shook their heads.

"The Muslims fight for their homeland," Armand pointed out calmly, "the Franks for domination in a far land that many here do not endorse."

"We shall crush them still," the other man argued, grinding his fist into his opposite palm. "God himself is on our side and we are destined to win."

"Of that I am no longer so sure," Armand concluded simply.

"I am certain," reiterated the other man, and Baudouin snorted under his breath.

"Empty words unless backed by a blade," he declared dismissively, standing up and draping his arm around his son's shoulders. "Two years did Armand bear the cross in the Holy Land," Baudouin added proudly, "while you, Chrétien, have spent all your days within the walls of Avigny."

With that, he turned away from the hearth and strolled toward the head table, surprising Armand as they matched steps.

"Much better you seem this evening," he commented, watching a long-overdue twinkle of mischief light the old man's eyes.

"Not dead yet, am I," his father noted with a grin. "Took my words to heart, you did, boy, bringing me that fetching little creature to heal my ills. One day she has tended me and already I feel as frisky as a pup."

Armand stifled a ripple of jealousy with an effort, knowing that the old man sought only to tease him. He glanced up but his father was innocently scanning the room, humming a nimble tune under his breath.

"I am pleased that she has helped you," he murmured noncommittally and his father grinned.

"Indeed. And there she is now, such a lovely woman." Baudouin strode away from Armand as Alex appeared at the top of the stairs, offering one hand gallantly as she descended to the hall.

Armand recovered quickly from the shock of seeing her smile so openly to his father, glancing around to find most of the male eyes in the room fixed on Alex's slender figure. Baudouin kissed the back of her hand with a flourish, ushering her toward the head table as Alex flushed slightly under his attentions. Men found seats at the tables throughout the room as Baudouin seated Alex, and Armand headed for the head table himself, hoping to secure a place at Alex's side.

"I beg your pardon" came a frosty voice from the top of the stairs, and Armand looked up to see Margrethe and Guillaume on the top step. An awkward hush fell over the company and Armand met his brother's eyes in sudden understanding. Perhaps Guillaume was right to doubt his authority, for it seemed that Armand was not alone in thinking of Baudouin as lord of Avigny. The company had taken their seats after Baudouin, not bothering to wait for Guillaume.

"Good evening, Guillaume." Baudouin's cheerful voice carried over the crowd and Armand recognized his father's attempt to smooth over a difficult moment. "Do join us."

"Upstarts, one and all," Margrethe sniffed indignantly, accepting her husband's hand and descending to the hall with icy hauteur. Armand waited for the pair to sweep past him, noting that Baudouin had seated Alex to his immediate left. Guillaume sat down beside his father, having seated his wife on his right, but there was still a place remaining on Alex's left. His heart in his mouth, Armand stepped behind the table and was close enough to his goal to breathe of the delicate rose scent that always trailed in Alex's wake when his father's voice rang out unexpectedly.

"Roarke!" he called, freezing Armand's steps with his shout and beckoning to the arriving knight to join the table. "Come here, boy. I would have you sit with Alexandria and me." He turned to Alex with a conciliatory tone. "You have met Roarke, have you not?"

"Indeed I have," Alex returned with what seemed undue enthusiasm to Armand's ears. "He rode with me from Pontesse and was most pleasant company."

Not "us" but "me." Armand gritted his teeth and slipped onto the bench alongside Margrethe with ill humor, ignoring her sidelong glance and nodding curtly in greeting to the knight who took the place on his right.

He overheard Roarke greeting Alex effusively, and writhed at his own stupidity. Justified or not, he had insulted his lady and he did not know what he could do to rectify the situation. As he reached for his goblet to drink the lord's health, the braid Alex had fastened around his wrist pulled free of his sleeve and he glared at the narrow binding, wishing it had not worked its charm so well.

Alex sighed, supposing that it had been too much to hope that Armand might have sat with her at dinner. Truly, he had lingered out on the floor as long as possible to avoid any chance of taking the open seat at her side. She frowned into her chalice as she drank the lord's health, unable to summon any interest in the meal. Roarke made some light comment and she forced a smile, wishing that the time would pass more quickly so she could retreat to her room.

Didier's beaming countenance appeared in the doorway to the kitchen now, a heaping platter of what was unmistakably roast venison cradled in his arms, its rich aroma setting every belly to growling. A round of applause rose from the company and the cook grinned, carrying his burden proudly to the head table. He was followed closely by an entire procession of apprentices, the first with the stuffed grouse, the next with a venison stew, and on and on.

Truly Didier had done himself proud and Baudouin was lavish in his praise, setting even the short stout cook to flushing. Guillaume, Alex noticed, had gone pale, his hands trembling as though he fought for self-control. Armand, in striking contrast, watched the procession dispassionately as if his thoughts were elsewhere.

"I did not hunt this day," Guillaume managed to sputter finally, rising to his feet even as hot color suffused his face. The applause of the company stopped abruptly, Baudouin halting his praise midsentence as all attention focused on Guillaume. Roarke was notably restless, and Alex wondered not for the first time what was the issue here with game.

"I demand to know who killed this stag on my land," Guillaume insisted, staring over the curiously still company with narrowed eyes. Alex's gaze flew to Armand, watching as he leisurely cleared his throat and looked up at his brother.

"I killed the stag, Guillaume," he admitted calmly, and the company gasped at his candor. "As well as the eight grouse," he added, launching a volley of excited whispers across the floor.

"You knew of my edict?" the older brother demanded sharply, and Armand nodded slowly.

"I had heard tell of your ban on hunting," he responded, his own eyes narrowing in assessment of Guillaume's rising rage.

"You deliberately defied my will!" Guillaume shouted, his complexion bloodred, his hands clenched and white-knuckled.

Armand set his jaw and interlaced his fingers atop the table before responding to his brother's accusation. The company seemed to hold their very breath as they awaited his words.

"I provided for this board, which you have not seen fit to do," Armand said softly, and Guillaume glanced quickly away from his brother and back in discomfort. "'Tis your responsibility to hunt the preserve, Guillaume, and well you know it. Avigny's new crops are plagued by foraging animals, their numbers too high because you have not hunted this winter. Do you not wish to hunt, then choose another to do it for you. 'Tis a disgrace to your house to force poor fare upon its residents and endanger its crops."

Alex's mouth almost dropped open in surprise in the instant of silence that followed Armand's unusually long speech, the air fairly crackling between the two brothers before the elder exploded.

"How dare you tell me how to run my estate when you have not even crossed its threshold these two years past?" Guillaume demanded, flinging his hands up into the air.

"How dare you," he sneered, "a mere soldier, advise me on the efficient operation of a château?" Alex saw the frisson of anger ripple through Armand's frame, but his face remained coldly impassive and she wondered if she alone had noticed that Guillaume had struck a nerve.

"How dare you assert your authority so frivolously?" Armand retorted coldly.

"I should have you flogged," Guillaume raged, and Armand characteristically cocked one brow, rising smoothly to his feet.

"As you have flogged other knights and disgraced the honor of this house," he shot back. "Do your worst, brother," Armand challenged, tugging his tunic over his head and tossing it aside, defiantly facing his brother bare-chested.

"No." Alex heard the whispered plea slip from her lips, terrified that Armand might have pushed his brother too far, but none seemed to have heard her. The current of anger between the two men was tangible in the silent hall, the company transfixed by the unfolding drama.

"Enough!" Baudouin shouted finally, rising to his feet, as well, as he pounded the table, his voice echoing clearly through the hall. "He who would strike his own brother over such a trivial matter is not fit to hold a lordship," he declared flatly, drawing an astonished glance from his older son.

"What are you saying, Father?" Guillaume demanded softly, but Baudouin waved him off, his own anger flashing in his eyes.

"Too long have you tested my patience over petty matters," the older man retorted, "and now you push too far. Never should I have let the whipping of any knight within my household pass without comment and now I make my say. Not dead am I yet, and too many times have I regretted my passing the lordship on to you at your wedding to this woman of whom little good can be said. Tomorrow I petition the king to reinstate my rightful position."

The company hesitated for a moment in surprise, then began to cheer at Baudouin's declaration until he held up one hand to silence them, gesturing to the meal at hand. "Save your approval for the king's word. Come, the meat grows cold." He flicked a glance to his younger son, the corner of his mouth pulling in humor.

"You will ride to Paris for me on the morrow?" Baudouin asked more quietly, his words closer to a command than a question, and Armand nodded immediately, drawing a smile from his father.

"Surely your sire taught you to clothe yourself for dinner," he teased in a low voice, and Alex followed the older man's gaze, drinking in the sight of Armand's bare torso.

Armand relaxed his stance at his father's gentle reprimand, a dark flush rising up his throat as he retrieved his tunic and pulled it over his head with jerky movements, sparing Alex a fleeting glimpse of something dark dancing on his wrist. Her heart leapt and she must have gasped aloud, for Armand shot a piercing glance down the table to meet her eyes. Her gaze tripped to his wrist and back, his bemused smile telling her that she had identified the bracelet correctly but giving her no clue as to the source of his amusement.

Margrethe shoved the venison around the trencher with a dissatisfied fingertip. The meat was good but her appetite had abandoned her with Baudouin's declaration of his intent to take back sovereignty of Avigny.

Already Guillaume was shrinking into himself, becoming smaller in her eyes after his public humiliation. A weak man he was, not only in character but soon in role, as well. Any conviction that she had had in making a good match was now well and truly gone. Affairs would no longer be good enough, it seemed, and somehow she would have to find the ways and means to a divorce. Weakness of character she could tolerate in a politically powerful man, a man like that she could bend to her will, but Guillaume had failed to assert his power even over Avigny, let alone extend his influence to the king's court. No future was there in remaining with a man of such limited potential.

Armand, now, was a different story. Possibly she had underestimated the younger Avigny by appreciating only his physical attributes. It now appeared that he had a private code of honor for which he was willing to die. 'Twas said King Louis admired such men to a fault. Margrethe swallowed a very feminine smile and wiped her hands fastidiously on her napkin, sparing a quick glance to a Guillaume lost in his own thoughts before placing her hand unceremoniously on Armand's thigh.

"I must say how pleased I am to see you home again," she purred, and Armand glanced down at her in open surprise. He had thought this matter resolved two years past at the fiasco that had sent him scurrying East, but the slim fingers sliding ever farther up his thigh told him otherwise. He spared her a frown, unwilling to believe that even she would be so bold as to continue this nonsense in Guillaume's presence, but she only smiled a little feline smile and squeezed his leg with slow deliberation.

"I had thought my position clear on this matter," he hissed under his breath, sparing a glance to his inattentive brother.

"Two years of celibacy could change any man's mind," Margrethe returned, tracing little patterns on his chausses with her fingertip.

"Better you than me," the knight to Armand's right snorted under his breath, clearly articulating his opinion of Margrethe's behavior and reminding Armand of what had happened to Roarke. That she had played a major role in that punishment, he had no doubt, and his jaw set with determination to end her little games here and now.

"It has not changed mine," Armand declared flatly, plucking Margrethe's hand from his leg and tossing it unceremoniously back into her own lap. Guillaume did not look up from his introspection, but Armand caught Baudouin's eye over his brother's head and saw his father's lips thin in disapproval. His heart sank as he noted Alex smiling at some pleasantry of Roarke's, completely oblivious of anything he might say or do.

It was almost too much for Armand to bear. His adrenaline was still pumping from that ugly exchange with Guillaume, his father was up to something that he could not guess, Margrethe was back to her role of seductress. This on top of his doubts for his own future and his growing reluctance to frivolously kill or maim other men.

Clearly he could not remain here at Avigny. He had no desire to take up the cross again, to tourney or to hire himself out as a mercenary. The only thing he had wanted in recent days was Alex's company and that was one thing he was unlikely to enjoy again.

After searching so long for Alex and being within a hairbreadth of having her for his wife, 'twas a kind of bitter irony that in one brief exchange he had cast all their carefully laid plans awry, plaguing himself with doubts and severely wounding the lady's pride. Had he misjudged her? he wondered for the thousandth time, recalling the open hurt in her eyes at his sarcasm and berating himself yet again for lashing out indiscriminately.

But a lack of virginity was not an easy issue to dismiss. Crowns were lost over a lady's premarital indiscretions, he knew, and the rift within him gaped wider once again.

To anyone who had known the turmoil within Armand's mind, his response to Margrethe's next move would have been completely explicable, but none of course knew what secrets the taciturn knight held within his heart. Margrethe certainly did not anticipate Armand's response when she leaned confidentially toward him, her exploring fingertips finding their way beneath his tunic to stroke the bare skin of his back as she granted him her most seductive smile.

"Perhaps I could yet change your mind," she murmured in a low timbre of voice calculated to melt his reserves, but instead pushing the limits of his self-control right over the top.

Outrageous it was that this woman should feel beneath his clothes at the dinner table, and Armand's anger erupted unchecked as he leapt to his feet, green eyes flashing furiously.

"For the love of Pan, bed your wife!" he shouted at his brother, his color high. "Otherwise she may bear you a son who is not of your own seed!" With that, Armand turned and stalked from the hall, his fury evident, the abruptly silenced company hastily clearing from his path.

Like the rest, Alex fell mute in surprise at Armand's furious outburst. Guillaume looked openly stunned and Baudouin almost as angry as his younger son. So unlike himself Armand was this night. Alex wondered what could drive him to such extremes. She turned and met the twinkle in Roarke's gray eyes with relief, tentatively matching his smile with her own.

"Poor old Tiberias will have company tonight, I wager," Roarke commented, and Alex smothered a giggle. How she wished that Armand would come to her again, but she knew that that was not to be.

"I suspect that Tiberias is a good listener," she returned lightly. Roarke chuckled politely and she felt his gaze upon her once more, fidgeting uncomfortably beneath his perusal but not knowing how to discourage his attentions. Pleasant enough company, Roarke was, but he did not stir her heart as another did.

"If you will excuse me," Baudouin murmured politely from her right, and Alex nodded to him in surprise, noting the anger still simmering in his green eyes. He forced a smile for her and winked quickly before shoving to his feet and following Armand's path across the hall.

"Well, this has been a busy evening," Roarke said, surveying the spaces in the head table and the discomfort of the assembled company. "Shall we have some music, Guillaume?"

"A fine idea, indeed," Guillaume responded with evident relief, clapping his hands to summon the musicians from their table.

A lutist scrambled from his seat and took a stance at the front of the room, plucking a few strings and breaking into a familiar song. The company quickly joined in, anxious to divert their thoughts from strife to revelry, a few couples taking to the open floor to dance. The music was light and festive, its volume making conversation difficult, and Alex savored the moment alone with her thoughts. What had Armand said to Guillaume? That he should be careful lest his wife bear another's seed? What on earth could he mean?

Did Armand desire Margrethe? The two had merely sat beside each other, barely exchanging a word as far as she had noted. Was his desire for his brother's wife so strong that Armand could not bear to merely sit alongside her? That he must join the Templars and run to the East to avoid discrediting his house?

Alex shot a furtive glance down the table, taking in the pleasing alabaster oval of Margrethe's face, and her heart sank a little closer to her toes. A lovely woman she was indeed, the draping of her kirtle hinting at ample curves beneath, which Alex could not hope to compete against with her own modest bosom and slender hips.

Margrethe slid gracefully to her feet, her every move elegant beyond compare, accepting Guillaume's hand as he led her out onto the floor, the smooth sway of her hips a promise of intimate delights. There was no way she could hope to divert Armand's attention from this splendidly endowed creature and Alex choked on the fact that 'twas her own foolish fault for refusing to answer one question that Armand had had every right to ask.

"Will you dance, milady?" Roarke offered politely, but Alex shook her head.

"I would excuse myself," she demurred, and the young knight pouted briefly in disappointment before gallantly kissing her hand.

"Perhaps I shall see you on the morrow," he said, and Alex summoned a smile.

"Only if you find yourself in the garden," she said, inclining her head politely to Guillaume before leaving the hall.

"A hotheaded man you never were" came a wry comment from the other end of the stables, bringing Armand's head up with a snap. 'Twas his father, predictably, and he got respectfully to his feet, running a hand through his already disheveled hair in frustration.

"True enough," he admitted, not trusting himself to say more, his temper still simmering.

"Hmm," Baudouin responded thoughtfully, advancing into the darkened stables with a measured step and fixing Armand with a piercing look. "What ails you, boy?" he demanded.

Armand snorted at his father's deliberate repetition of the demand he had once made of the older man and their eyes met in acknowledgment of the shared joke.

"Too much, I fear, to be readily resolved," he admitted, and began to pace the length of the stables.

"A few days' absence should cool Margrethe's ardor," Baudouin commented, dropping to sit on the hay with a sigh of relief as he watched his restless son.

"That and the king's approval of your scheme," Armand remarked dryly, drawing a chuckle from the older man.

"Relieved I am that you read that one aright. Trouble she is indeed and you would be wise to stay clear of her plotting."

Armand spared his father a wry grin. "As ever I have endeavored, but to little avail."

"Bah." Baudouin waved off his argument. "Soon she will tire of us all and make for greener pastures, you will see."

"I hope you speak the truth," Armand murmured absently. He continued to pace across the stone floor, feeling his father's eyes on him but not knowing where to begin.

"Margrethe is not the root of it," Baudouin observed quietly, drawing a snort of derision from his younger son. "What will you do now that you have left the Order?" he asked softly, and Armand stopped in the middle of the floor, turning to face his father.

"Truly, I know not what to do," he confessed, flinging out one hand in frustration. "I cannot remain here, Guillaume and I have ensured that, with or without Margrethe's influence, yet I have nowhere to go."

"You had mentioned the tourneys . . ." Baudouin began, but Armand cut him off impatiently.

"I weary of the killing," he retorted, surprised when the older man did not recoil from his comment.

"Tournaments are for sport," his father interjected with a frown, but Armand waved off his objection.

"Well you know that men die or are maimed at every event, regardless of the precautions taken." Armand paused and frowned at the floor. "A man cannot play at making war."

"Hmm." Baudouin considered his words thoughtfully, staring up at the shadowed rafters. "I suppose then that honest mercenary work would be out of the question," he mused, his suggestion earning an angry glare from his son.

"A joke," he explained with a bemused chuckle, gesturing to the length of the floor with one finger. "Pace off the room again, boy. The activity clearly improves your temper." Armand chuckled reluctantly under his breath and did as he was bid.

"You could marry," Baudouin suggested slyly when he reached the far end of the stables, but Armand snorted again.

"And who would have me?" he demanded in annoyance. "An elderly widow to keep me as a lapdog to do her bidding?"

"What about Alexandria?" the old man asked with wide-eyed innocence, and Armand's head came up with a snap.

"Alex?" he repeated huskily, uncertain whether he had seen his father smother a smile. Was it so obvious then that he cared for Alex?

"Yes, yes, Alex, that lovely little healer. Do you not think her fetching indeed?" Undeterred by his son's dumb-founded silence, Baudouin pushed to his feet, slipping one arm over Armand's shoulders and leaning toward the younger man confidentially. "I have been thinking that she and Roarke would make a fine pair," he murmured conspiratorially.

"Roarke?" Armand demanded incredulously, but his father merely wagged one long finger at him.

"Yes, Roarke. You've known the boy for years. You must stop repeating everything I say, Armand, lest people believe you were raised by heathens in the woods and are incapable of civilized conversation. Just think about it—'tis a perfect match. Both are of noble blood, young, and, you must admit, they make a lovely couple..."

"But Roarke is a shameless knave," Armand objected with frustration, still unable to believe that his father intended to make this match. "He beds every woman who will have him."

"Exactly," the old man confirmed, clearly warming to his theme. "'Tis time enough the boy settled down, before he finds himself with the pox, you know, and Alexandria is just the kind of woman to keep a man close to his own hearth. Were I a younger man, I might be tempted to think more selfishly, but she is a lovely little creature and deserves a fine, strong knight to warm her bed."

Armand struggled to keep up with his father's logic against the strident objections of his heart. "Truly I do not know what to think," he admitted, and Baudouin laughed, clapping him on the back enthusiastically and darting toward the door.

"Reflect upon it," he called when he was silhouetted in the open door, and Armand could have sworn the old man was laughing at him. "You will see the wisdom of my plan. I will prepare my missive to the king this night so as not to delay your departure in the morning."

"Yes, Father," Armand answered numbly, now completely unsure as to what he should do. Alex and Roarke? How much would things advance while he was away in Paris?

The sun had barely tinged the sky pink the next morning when Alex awoke and hastened through her toilet, noting with rising excitement that the château remained still. Hoping she might catch Armand before he departed, she trotted down the stairs on silent feet, tiptoeing through the empty hall and abandoned kitchen. In the courtyard she broke into an unladylike run, darting breathlessly into the stables to be greeted by the speculative glances of the curious horses.

Her heart pounding at her audacity, Alex trotted up and down the aisles, absently admiring the extent of Avigny's stables, searching for one great black stallion. Her heart began to slow as she approached the last stall and confronted its emptiness.

Tiberias was not here. She turned away from the vacant stall and saw the trap for the horses of the knights of the house hanging on the opposite wall, her heart sinking when she saw the single barren hook.

Armand was already gone.

Fighting back irrational tears she dragged herself from the stables, wondering what she had intended to say to him. Now he was truly gone and she was alone, in a strange household, without the reassurance of his presence and protection. Though he had not spoken overmuch to her since their arrival in Avigny, she had felt secure just knowing that he was near.

For the first time, she wondered whether Pièrre had traced their path and looked around with new eyes, unsure as to whether Armand had told her tale to any of the others. Indeed, she did not even know if Roarke was aware of the truth of things. Alex wondered how long Armand would be gone, not knowing how far he must ride from here to Paris, tears rising in her eyes at the almost overwhelming feeling of vulnerability that enfolded her in its merciless embrace.

"Early to rise you are, child" came Baudouin's cheerful voice some hours later, and Alex straightened from her weed pulling to grant him a watery smile.

"I thought it best to work here before the sun grew high," she explained tonelessly, fully aware of the older man's speculative gaze sweeping over her, hoping against hope that he would miss the evidence of her earlier tears.

"Indeed," he commented finally, advancing into the garden and taking his place on the marble bench where he had dozed the day before. "I thought perhaps Armand had awakened you before he left this morning."

"Armand?" Alex demanded, her head shooting up in surprise. Did Baudouin think that she was welcoming his son to her bed? Were her feelings that obvious?

"Aye," the older man confirmed, undaunted. "He came to my room to fetch my missive to the king, and although he moves quietly, I thought a healer's sensitive ears might detect his passing." He flicked a glance in her direction and Alex had a fleeting impression that he toyed with her, before she realized that she was blushing and bent to cover her discomfort.

"No, I did not hear him," she replied in what she hoped was an even tone. "'Twas early, you said?"

"Before the very dawn," he confirmed. "Indeed, I wondered if the boy had slept at all."

"'Twas the sun itself that awoke me," Alex lied, her words falling in a rush that did not sound convincing even to her own ears.

"Hmm," Baudouin responded, bending to pull a perky weed wedged between the stones in the walkway. "Three days hence will be the full of the moon," he commented, and Alex flicked a glance in his direction, remembering suddenly Sophie's assertion that Baudouin was one who practiced the old ways.

"Indeed, 'twill be," she answered carefully, letting him see that he had caught her interest.

"Several summers it has been since I danced beneath the moon, Alex," he mused slowly, his green gaze disconcertingly bright. "Will you dance with me, little healer?" he whispered, and Alex smiled in return.

"Indeed I should be delighted to celebrate with you," she said softly, drawing a grin of open pleasure from Baudouin before he sobered again.

"Times were when we all danced. Together. In the open," he reflected. "But now 'tis only the old ones, the healers, the peasants, and we must hide ourselves from prying eyes. The world is not what it was, Alexandria."

"Nor what it will be," she answered, and he looked at her in surprise. Alex smiled and returned to her weeding. "My aunt says that always do times change, my uncle that woe comes to those who do not change with the times."

"Wise words, indeed," Baudouin conceded, frowning into the distance, and Alex knew from his expression that he was thinking of another time, long past.

Chapter Twelve

The sky was clear three nights hence when Alex donned her surcoat before her window, sparing a glance for the ripening golden moon. Already she could spot the bright pinpricks of bonfires burning in the distant hills, signs of others celebrating this night, though she knew a visitor happening along would find each of those fires untended. She sighed and pulled her hood over her loose hair, her thoughts straying yet again to Armand as she turned and faced the meager furnishings of his room.

Three short days had he been gone, more than that since he had spared her a kind word, and how her heart ached with longing. Too many times had she started at the sound of a heavy footfall these past days for her anxiety to go unnoticed, too often had she looked up to find Baudouin's assessing gaze upon her. Too much time had she to herself in tending the garden, her thoughts turning too often to that argument of a mere week ago and her heart bitterly regretting her stubborn response.

At the sound of a gentle tap, Alex slipped across the room, opening the oaken door to reveal Baudouin similarly hooded and cloaked. He held one finger to his lips and offered his elbow, Alex nodding in understanding and matching her silent footsteps to his as they crept cautiously toward the stairs.

They did not breathe a word till the walls of the château were shadowy in the distance, the woods looming ever closer as they ran like children across the newly sprouting grass.

Alex's heart had lightened a hundredfold and she kicked off
her shoes, tucking them in her pocket and loosening her hair
from the confining hood. The cares and worries of the civilized world seemed distant indeed, the new growth beneath her toes and the star-speckled sky above her head
more tangible than any creation of man. Dance tonight, she
would indeed, and celebrate the reawakening of the earth.

"Up here," the older man panted, gesturing toward the
top of a nearby hill, and Alex slowed her pace. She darted
back to Baudouin and grasped his hand, helping him up the
steep incline as he chuckled in good-natured protest.

"No doddering old man am I," he claimed with mock
indignation, and Alex laughed aloud.

"Neither shall I expect you to dance like one," she retorted, and he laughed along with her, pulling her to a stop
as they gained the crest and he paused to catch his breath,
her hand still captured within his larger one. Baudouin
stood silently, looking over the valley spread before him, the
regal château reposing in the darkness, the village of neatly
thatched dwellings beyond, the road rolling out to the horizon in a gentle curve, all clearly visible beneath the
brightness of the moon.

"'Twas my father and his before him who brought unity
and peace to this fief," he said softly, his breathing now
slowed to its normal pace. "Always did the people know
them to be just men, kind and true, as I hope they have
known me to be in my father's stead."

Alex squeezed the older man's hand encouragingly. "But
a few days have passed since we first met and I know you to
be so," she confirmed quietly, earning a quick smile from
her companion.

"My thanks for your kind words, but 'tis the future that
concerns me," Baudouin continued with a reflective frown,
his eyes finding the tall keep of his château. "I take back the
lordship for a few years now, and then what will transpire?
Would that you had the gift of prophecy, my young friend,"
he murmured, and pressed a chaste kiss to Alex's forehead.

Alex stood mute, unable to allay his fears and unwilling
to insult him with some trite comment.

"Come," Baudouin declared a moment later, clearing his throat with an effort and gesturing to a barren patch of ground. "Always have they kept me stocked for a fire on this spot. Let us see what we can find."

To Alex's amazement, an ample supply of wood, tinder and kindling had been assembled near the stones blackened from countless fires set atop them. Baudouin quickly set to work building a blaze while she stood openmouthed, wondering whom he entrusted with the knowledge of his celebration.

"This I must bring myself," he joked as he produced a flint from his pocket and struck a spark, his mischievous wink clear indication that he was enjoying Alex's surprise.

"But who does this for you?" she demanded, recalling how she and Sophie stole logs from the château hearth one at a time for weeks before a celebration, secreting them out to the garden and thence to the hills.

Baudouin shrugged philosophically. "I know not," he admitted, "but always do I thank the fates for their kind assistance and always is the wood replenished." He grinned at Alex. "Mayhap 'tis pixies or little green men of the forest. Surely you were told tales of the green men as a child."

"But of course," Alex responded with sparkling eyes, as the flames leapt skyward between them. "The very woods themselves are alive," she declared gaily, waving her arms toward the forest. "And on this night more than any other!"

"Then let us dance!" Baudouin bellowed, rising to his feet and holding out his hands. "Let us dance until we can do so no longer!" As Alex took his outstretched hands, he raised his voice in an old chant that Alex had learned at Sophie's knee and she raised her voice with his. He swung her around and they danced merrily, singing together, encircling the growing blaze with their steps, the firelight flickering on their laughing faces as they heralded the fullness of the moon and celebrated the mysteries of the earth.

Armand reined in Tiberias as he approached Avigny's gate, unwilling to leave the magical air of the night behind.

There was a special quality in the air this night, a sense of expectation, a joyfulness that was not easily abandoned for a straw pallet above the stables.

Half-afraid to look lest there not be a blaze, he glanced up to the nearby hill his father frequented on such nights, a grin playing across his lips when he spied the leaping flames. Glad Armand was now that he had stocked the firewood as he had of old the night before riding for Paris. Wrong indeed he had been to think his father's dancing days behind him.

On impulse, he urged Tiberias quietly up toward the hill, hoping for a private moment of revelry with Baudouin. Restless he was after the long ride and some feckless dancing might serve him well, calm his jangled nerves that he might sleep this night. Good news he bore for his father, but that could wait until the morrow, the machinations of men seemingly meaningless beneath the endless array of stars embedded in the indigo carpet overhead.

Armand breathed deeply of the country air, cleansing his lungs with relief of Paris and her unbridled filth, wood smoke mingling with the rich smell of the wakening earth in his nostrils. More than the task for his father was behind him, the mysterious parcel with which he had been entrusted in Jerusalem had also been delivered to the Temple in Paris, into the Grand Master's hands. The open avarice that had darted across that man's features had left Armand glad that he had not been tempted to learn the contents of what he carried. A relief it was to leave the Templars to their Byzantine schemes in which one could never tell friend from foe for certain.

He left Tiberias tethered in the woods and walked the last distance on foot so as not to startle his father, the sound of feminine laughter bringing him to a standstill before the edge of the trees. Surely it could not be her. Armand crept forward on silent feet, the sight that met his eyes as he reached the clearing slowing his footsteps as he watched transfixed from the shadows.

'Twas Alex, her dark tresses flowing loose over her shoulders, her delicate feet bare beneath the swirling hem of

her kirtle as she sang and danced with Baudouin as gaily as
a little bird. He watched her hungrily, his longing for her
sharpened to a fever pitch. He must have made some unwilling sound from his hiding place within the trees, for
Baudouin flicked a sharp glance in his direction, turning
back to Alex with his hand over his heart.

"Too much do you ask of this old man," Baudouin protested, greeting Alex's disappointment with an indulgent
smile. "Give me but a moment's rest, child," he urged,
taking her hand and leading her directly toward Armand.
Seeing his father's intent, Armand took a step backward, his
heart pounding so loud that surely she would hear its
clamor.

"'Tis time you tried another partner in my stead," Baudouin added softly, lifting one hand to indicate his son in the
shadows.

Armand's heart stopped in his throat as Alex lifted her
eyes to his, a gasp of surprise falling from the fullness of her
lips. She had not expected to see him, that much was clear,
but would she reject him? He dared not breathe lest that
minute movement break his tenuous hold on her wide-eyed
gaze.

Alex met the deep emerald of Armand's eyes unflinchingly as he stood stock-still, his face impassive, his eyes
burning with some unspoken emotion.

He knew not what to do, she realized, and her heart
swelled with sympathy and love, so unsure was he of her response after his cutting accusations. Alex smiled at him and
watched some of the tension melt from his square jaw, intent filling his eyes now as he stepped forward from the
scrub and doffed his gloves, offering her one work-
roughened hand.

"Shall we dance, milady?" he asked politely, and Alex
nodded mutely, slipping her hand into his beneath Baudouin's bemused eye. That familiar frisson of awareness
tripped along her veins at the touch of Armand's flesh to
hers and she felt herself flush scarlet, knowing he could not
have missed her quiver, so tightly did he clasp her hand.

"I intend you no harm, milady," he murmured beneath his breath, misinterpreting the reason for her shiver of delight, but she did not correct him.

As they approached the fire again, Baudouin lifted his voice in song and Armand spared his father a grin, his deep tones joining those of the older man before Alex lent her own voice to the melody. She flicked a glance upward to find Armand's warm gaze upon her, a smile playing over his lips, and she smiled back, taking his other hand.

He twirled her effortlessly and began to dance around the fire, the rich tones of his voice filling her ears as she took two steps to each one of his. So absorbed were Armand and Alex in each other that they did not notice the third voice no longer singing with them, did not hear the stealthy footfalls of the older man making his way from the clearing.

Faster they whirled until Alex's head spun dizzily and she could no longer match Armand's hectic pace. Undeterred, he swept her into his arms, imprisoning her against his chest, her feet dangling above the ground as still he danced, Alex's singing dissolving into helpless laughter as they frolicked. Armand began to chuckle himself and he spun her still faster, both of his arms locked around her waist as she squealed at his antics. Alex's arms slid around his neck and she laughed up at him, his eyes meeting hers with a jolt of awareness, the smile fading from his face as he stared down at her, his feet slowing abruptly to a halt.

The fire crackled in the sudden stillness, Armand's breath still coming in sharp puffs as they stared into each other's eyes. Unable to resist temptation, Alex curled her fingers into the loose waves at his nape, her hands stroking the corded tension in his neck and Armand groaned deep in his throat, his eyes closing in pleasure as she leaned toward him, helpless to resist.

"Alex," he groaned, and lifted her still closer, bending to taste her lips. Alex sighed beneath his tender embrace, her tears rising unbidden as she realized just how much she had missed his touch. His lips slanted across hers, his tongue gaining easy entry, one hand slipping up her back to grasp a fistful of hair at her nape and imprison her beneath his caress.

Too long had it been since she had tasted his warmth and she matched his ardor, raining kisses across his jaw and eyelids, running her fingers through his hair and touching his flesh everywhere she could reach, knowing she could never get enough.

Armand nibbled on her ears, tracing a path of kisses down the length of her throat that left her breathless, outlining her collarbone with the tip of his tongue. He cradled her buttocks in his broad palms, lifting her ever closer and nudging her kirtle aside to fasten his lips on her straining nipple.

"Alex, Alex, tell me your desire," he murmured against the softness of her skin, his words recalling both of them abruptly to their senses. Armand lifted his head and Alex met his eyes, the doubtful expression she found lurking in those green depths telling her the path his thoughts had taken, and she recoiled in hurt.

Still Armand could not put aside his questions and doubts! Alex shoved away his embracing arms, stinging from his unspoken accusation, tears burning her eyes as she gained her footing and fastened her bodice with shaking hands.

"I have told you my desire." She choked out the words, tears streaming freely down her face as she reached out and jerked at the braid still wound around Armand's wrist. He had the grace to look shamefaced as he stood silently watching her but 'twas not enough to ease her hurt.

"'Tis you who have not decided yours," she hissed, stalking away with unsteady steps as her tears broke anew. Too much it was for him to doubt her integrity now, the truth that she would have given herself to him again tonight doing little to ease the new wounds of her heart.

"Hold up," he called softly from behind her, and Alex stopped but did not turn, refusing to give herself the chance to soften at the sight of his dismay. "I would not have you walk alone," he added in a low voice, and she nodded in silence, folding her arms across her chest against the sobs that threatened to break from her throat.

Armand straightened his tabard impatiently, kicking over the fire and scattering the coals across the cold stones. Too well he could understand Alex's hurt but he could not help the thoughts that crowded his mind. The sight of her very willingness launched such a torrent of possessiveness within him that he could not bear the thought of another man touching her as he did.

When she parted her rosy lips, her blue eyes liquid and unfocused in her passion, he could not help but wonder how many others she had welcomed to her embrace this way. A shallow offering indeed did he make his lady when he could not dismiss these questions solely on the inconsistency of such wanton behavior with her character. He knew his suspicions could not be true, yet there remained the fact of her missing maidenhead and somewhere in his heart he could not help but wonder.

Armand retrieved his gloves and stared at the huddled shadow of Alex's form where she sat now on the side of the hill, her cloak drawn over her shoulders and hair, her slim shoulders still shaking slightly. He frowned, knowing that he alone was responsible for her tears. If only she were not so hungry for his touch, if only she merely tolerated kisses as most women were wont to do. But no, 'twas her passion that he loved, and to change that would be to change Alex herself.

Thoughtfully, Armand strolled down the hill toward her, making enough noise that she would be sure to hear his approach. He squatted down beside her and gazed down upon the château with unseeing eyes as she did, choosing his words with care.

"Would you tell me your tale this night?" he asked softly, determined to try once more to settle things between them. He saw the glance she flicked at him out of the corner of his eye but did not face her, not wanting to appear the judge.

"Would you believe a tale of rape I told you now?" Alex returned quietly, and Armand glanced sidelong in surprise to find her watching him with utmost seriousness. "Would you not think I had contrived a tale you wished most to hear?''

Armand closed his eyes and bowed his head in defeat. Indeed Alex spoke the truth. After the silence between them, could she utter any words that would wholly convince him? Always in some dark corner of his heart would linger a vestige of doubt. He opened his eyes and regarded her again, meeting the question in those azure depths unflinchingly. Surely to have this woman by his side was worth living with a sliver of doubt. Surely he could put such trifles aside.

"You alone must decide," Alex added softly, as if she read his very thoughts. Armand saw compassion in her eyes and knew that she understood his dilemma. He placed one finger beneath her chin and she closed her eyes at his touch, her lips trembling, a tear squeezing free of one corner as he watched.

"I think I am not alone in wishing I could change the past," he whispered, kissing away that errant tear before gently pressing his lips to hers. Alex sobbed deep in her throat and Armand gathered her close, mutely standing and lifting her in his arms, knowing there was only one thing he could say to stop her tears and unable to say it. He strode down the hill with his precious burden, his heart shredding within him at the muffled sound of her crying, calling himself seven kinds of fool as he sought Tiberias.

Baudouin frowned openly the next morning in unrestrained annoyance that none managed to miss. Armand entered the hall in no sweet mood of his own, having had another sleepless night. He noted both his father's stormy countenance and Alex's silence with a sinking heart and knew that he would not escape unscathed.

"I would speak with you," his father growled, and Armand nodded, pulling the king's answering missive from his tunic in apparent explanation.

"I have your response from the king," he said simply, earning another baleful glare from Baudouin. Uncharacteristically, the older man rose immediately from the table without excuse, stalking across the hall and gesturing to Armand to precede him upstairs.

"'Tis not the missive I would discuss and well you know it," he muttered under his breath, and Armand nodded mutely, sparing a glance to Alex before heading up to the solar, his gut wrenching when he spied Roarke cheerfully taking the seat beside her. The other knight made some small joke as if trying to tempt her to eat and Alex granted him a thin smile before Armand turned away and hurried upstairs, knowing that even that wan expression directed at him would set his own heart to singing.

Unbeknownst to either Armand or Baudouin, no sooner had they cleared the top of the stairs than Margrethe excused herself, prettily explaining that she had needlework to tend to, determination in her eyes as she climbed to the solar in the two men's wake.

"What insult have you rendered that child?" Baudouin demanded, his eyes flashing with anger as he confronted his son. "Laughing she was when I entrusted her to your care last night, but she appears this morning at the board with reddened eyes and pale cheeks. Can you not manage a simple dance without distressing the maid?"

Armand sighed and dropped into one of the sturdy chairs before the fire, running his hand through his hair as was his wont. "Apparently I cannot," he admitted in a flat voice, hoping against hope that his father would not lecture him endlessly, for he was loathe to explain his actions to the old man.

"The king approves your plan," he offered in an effort to deflect his father's anger, but Baudouin swept the news aside impatiently.

"Bah, no surprise is that, for he counseled me against giving Guillaume his inheritance before his time. There are more important matters at hand." Baudouin paced the length of the room and back, his hands clenched behind his back.

"More sense had you, I thought," he commented, his temper under control once again. "A fine woman is Alexandria and more than once have I caught your eye upon her. Yet you distress the woman so that she cannot control her tears." He whirled to confront Armand with exasperation. "Have I taught you nothing of these delicate matters?"

Armand sighed and tried to escape the old man's piercing glare.

"Well?" Baudouin demanded, and Armand glanced up reluctantly to meet his father's eyes.

"Alex and I did not meet a mere week ago," he began haltingly, drawing an impatient snort from his father.

"Indeed not," the older man retorted. "She is the same who patched your shoulder. The same whom you have mooned over these days since you returned from the East."

Dumbfounded by his father's certainty, Armand could only nod, wondering how on earth the old man reached his conclusions so surely. Baudouin chuckled at his son's surprise and dropped into the chair opposite.

"Not born yesterday was I," he asserted, wagging one finger at the younger man, "and you I have known from the cradle. I know well what preys upon your mind, boy. You think you cannot honorably ask for her hand."

Armand nodded again in agreement, noting that that was but one of his many concerns regarding Alex. "I have no title or land to offer her," he conceded with a frown of frustration, "only my name and a sword I am curiously loathe to wield these days."

"Bah, you surrender the fight too easily," Baudouin asserted, drawing a choking sound of indignation from his son.

"'Twas you who advised me to forget her two years past," Armand exclaimed in frustration. "'Twas you alone who sat on that bed and explained to me that I could not aspire to a noblewoman's hand!"

Baudouin paused a moment in thoughtful reflection, then waved this objection aside, as well. "'Twas before I saw the prize," he declared, leaning forward to tap his son on one knee. "My father oft said that where the will existed, the way would be found."

'Twas Armand's turn to snort dismissively and push to his feet. "Wishful thinking that is," he argued, feeling the weight of his father's gaze following him across the room, refusing to let any false optimism concerning Alex color his thinking.

"Have you the will to find the way?" Baudouin asked softly, and Armand straightened slowly, shaking his head from side to side.

"I know not," he admitted honestly, closing his eyes against the heated response his words were sure to bring.

"What nonsense is this?" his father demanded, closing the space between them with furious strides. He grabbed Armand's shoulder and summarily spun him around. "'Tis clear you regard the girl highly. What trouble do you make here?"

Armand cleared his throat tentatively. "There is a problem," he began, but his father interrupted him.

"A problem?" he cried in annoyance. "A problem with this lovely child? Surely you do not mean that such a perfect creature dares to have a flaw? Some indiscretion in her past?" Armand winced at how close his father came to the mark, but Baudouin was raging back across the room, hands flung skyward, and took no notice of his discomfort. "Some trait in her character that you find less than pleasing? For the love of Pan, boy," he roared, "did I raise you to have no more sense than this?"

"I believe myself justified," Armand began, but he got no further.

"Hah! Justified!" Baudouin repeated, striding across the room and poking his son methodically in the chest. "Let me tell you of your flaw, boy," he growled, his anger menacing, but Armand did not dare step away. "A flaw you have carried since you were a small child and, unless you change your ways, one you will undoubtedly carry to your grave. Always did you have to see things black-and-white, right and wrong, good and bad. Never was there any middle ground for you, any tolerance for other than the extremes. A dangerous trait indeed, and a high expectation for those around you, a flaw that could cost you dear in the days ahead."

Armand dared not meet his father's eyes lest the old man see the chord of fear he had struck. Should he not find forgiveness in his heart, he would lose Alex, that much he knew, but this belief was proving impossible to conquer. And should he not be able to offer her the fullness of his heart, he truly believed she would be happier without him at her side. Black-or-white, all or nothing, he admitted ruefully, 'twas just as his father declared.

"I name it right, do I not?" Baudouin whispered, turning abruptly to pace back to the fireplace. "You must find some tolerance in your heart, Armand," he concluded softly, and Armand lifted his eyes to the ceiling, blinking back the tears that suddenly blurred his vision.

When he had composed himself, Armand turned back to his father, watching as the old man took his seat by the hearth and removed salve from a jar resting there, rubbing the ointment into the knuckles and back of his right hand with deliberate movements. Baudouin flicked an imperious glance at his son, inclining his head in the direction of the opposing chair, and Armand came to sit before his father. The wind shifted outside and drove a flurry of raindrops against the stone sill, the cold sound sending a shiver down Armand's spine.

"We must discuss Alexandria's fate," the older man began in measured tones, just the mention of Alex's name sending the blood pumping through Armand's veins again. "This ointment she has made me seems worthy of its task and there is ample here for many days." He pursed his lips thoughtfully and Armand caught the barest glimpse of the green eyes beneath those white brows before he continued with eyes downcast. "As her work here appears done, I would send her home."

"No!" The word shot out before Armand could stop it, drawing a surprised look from his father.

"Tolerance is indeed fleet of foot," he commented dryly, but his son shook his head impatiently and leaned earnestly toward his father.

"She cannot return there in safety," Armand declared, his heart in his throat at the thought of sending Alex back to

Pontesse, where she was vulnerable to Pièrre. "In truth, 'tis partly why I brought her here."

"Make you some story to buy yourself more time with her?" Baudouin asked indulgently.

"No, Father, I swear to you 'tis not so," Armand asserted wholeheartedly, and Baudouin sobered at his expression, abandoning his ointment and leaning forward with a frown.

"Tell me what is in the wind," he demanded curtly, and Armand nodded, knowing that he had no choice other than to trust the old man with Alex's secret.

"Know you Pièrre de Villiers?" Armand demanded, and his father made a face.

"A bad seed, that one. A discredit to his father's name," Baudouin muttered under his breath. "But what has he to do with this?"

"An uncle of Alex's wagered her hand in a game of dice against Pièrre in Venice," Armand began, and his father interrupted him with a frown.

"And lost the toss?" Armand nodded and Baudouin shook his head in annoyance. "Always were there rumors that the boy cheated," he mused under his breath, fixing his son with a bright eye. "And she runs from these nuptials as any sensible woman would do?"

Armand nodded and his father made some appreciative sound deep in his throat.

"Rare indeed is a clearheaded woman," he murmured, but Armand interrupted his musings.

"Also does she run from the man who murdered her brother in Venice," he added, drawing a wince from his father. "She witnessed the deed—" he swallowed with difficulty, remembering the wound in her shoulder "—but the killer left her for dead." Baudouin's eyes narrowed assessingly.

"Know you the villain that you might avenge her?" he asked sharply, but Armand shook his head in defeat.

"She would not confide to me his name," he muttered, his gaze flying to the door at some slight sound. "Did you hear something?'' he demanded sharply of his father. ''A scraping at the door?''

Baudouin shook his head and got to his feet, crossing the room and opening the door, staring up and down the deserted corridor. ''Nothing,'' he concluded. '''Twas no more than the storm.'' Armand shook his head, certain that what he had heard had come from inside the château.

''It seems she must remain here for now,'' Baudouin conceded with a frown, making for his desk. ''Who was her uncle, did you say? I will send Roarke with a message that the child is well and suggest that she remain.''

Margrethe took a deep breath, her ire rising anew at the unexpected news that Armand held that tiny healer in such high regard. How dare he grant his heart to a woman other than herself! No place had those tender feelings in her plans for the future, especially now that she knew for certain that Guillaume would not assert any authority at Avigny before the old man's death.

Fortunately, Armand had unwittingly supplied her with a straightforward solution to what irked her and Margrethe smiled in anticipation of the outcome, sorting through her mind for someone in the household she could trust.

Alex picked at her bread with disinterest, spurning the honey that Roarke offered along with his sweet comments, knowing herself to be in as foul a mood as she had ever been. The insistent beat of the rain and rumbling thunder had not lightened her spirits, forcing her to confront the idea of a day spent inside for the first time since her arrival. No needlework had she brought and she was loathe to ask Margrethe for any, intuitively disliking the woman and wanting to have as little contact with her as possible during her stay.

Perhaps she should go home, Alex reflected, chasing a bread crumb around the table with one fingertip, catching a glimpse of a patient hound out of the corner of her eye. She smiled to herself and tossed the beast her piece of bread, watching it disappear in the twinkling of an eye amid more enthusiasm than she could hope to muster.

Certainly Baudouin no longer had need of her, if indeed the white-haired devil had ever needed a healer in the first place. Alex propped her chin in her hand and watched the activity in the hall with disinterest, barely aware of Roarke excusing himself politely. What awaited her at Pontesse should she return there? Had Pièrre made another appearance or had he some inkling that she had left? Alex shuddered at the thought of confronting her betrothed again, her fingers slipping of their own volition to finger the scar that still marred her flesh.

No fair company would she be this day, Alex realized, pushing to her feet and heading to her room. 'Twould be best if she rode out this black mood alone.

"Alexandria!" Baudouin hailed her with a shout as she passed the open door to his room. Alex paused in the doorway, noting both sons clustered around Baudouin's desk.

"Yes, milord?" she answered, feeling her voice no stronger than a mouse's squeak.

"Dare I hope that you can count?" the older man demanded, and Alex nodded in surprise. "Read and write?" he asked, and she nodded again, smiling in response to the grin that broadened over his face. "Ah, no doubt the result of your healing craft," he concluded, and Alex did not correct him. Sophie had taught her to memorize her craft; 'twas Hugues who had taught her to read that she might manage Fontaine's accounts.

"Come here, come here, you marvelous child," he beckoned, and Alex stepped across the threshold. "I have a task that I would set you about."

Alex crossed the room to stand beside Armand as Baudouin indicated, her knees trembling as she hoped fervently once again that he would find it within his heart to accept her as she was.

A high moral code he had, which she admired, but she could not help but wish that she had not fallen short. Standing beside the knight she loved and knowing that she could do nothing else to sway his heart, Alex wished Pièrre de Villiers to an eternity in that hellish place of Christian damnation with a fervor that surprised her.

Alex noted Guillaume's petulant expression as he stood at his father's side, what looked like the account books of the château spread before Baudouin's assessing eye. There seemed precious little writing in the ledger from where Alex stood, leading her to wonder whether Guillaume had maintained the books sufficiently of late.

"Exactly how much gold do you have?" he demanded impatiently and Guillaume shrugged his shoulders.

"I know not," the elder son admitted, flinching from the impact of the fiery gaze his father bestowed upon him.

"Even the Templars tallied their treasury," Armand muttered under his breath, and Alex bit her lip to keep from giggling, though the other two did not note his words.

"You know not!" Baudouin raged. "How many times have I told you that you must keep an accurate count of all you own? Dalliance with your accounts encourages thievery, you foolish boy, for all know that you are ignorant of what you hold!" The older man sat heavily back in his chair, running his hands through his thick white shock of hair. "The two of you will be the very death of me," he muttered, and Alex wondered what transgression Armand was guilty of in the older man's eyes.

"Get the gold and get it now," Baudouin demanded, sending Guillaume scurrying for the door. "You will count it here and now and we will begin these books anew." He sighed theatrically and flicked a speculative glance at his younger son from beneath his brows. "Think you that you can manage to inventory the saddlery? The armory? Bring me a tally of all those weapons of war you so favor?" he demanded sarcastically, and Alex glanced up to see Armand nod respectfully.

"Yes, milord."

"Then, be about your task," Baudouin ordered, turning his attention to Alex, his lips curving in a smile. "Didier thinks well of you, does he not?" he asked, and Alex grinned in response.

" 'Twas the sage, I think," she countered, earning a genuine chuckle from the older man.

"Indeed. I shall need a tally of the buttery, pantry and cellar," he said matter-of-factly and Alex nodded, accepting the parchment and sharpened bit of graphite he offered and hurrying to fulfill her task. Just having something purposeful to do lightened her step and she darted into the hall, almost running full tilt into Armand.

"My pardon!" she exclaimed, but Armand steadied her balance with one hand, grinning at her surprise and offering his hand that she might descend the stairs. Feeling flustered beyond compare, Alex took his hand, the warm smile that he granted her melting her very knees.

"I did not mean to startle you," Armand said in a low voice and she gripped his hand more tightly. "I would apologize for my boorish behavior last night," he added, and Alex could only nod, unable to draw a full breath into her lungs beneath his scrutiny.

She glanced up as they gained the floor and saw Armand draw in a shaky breath himself, the sight of his own awareness of her somehow reassuring. He glanced down at her and she smiled tentatively, his own grin flashing in response though his eyes remained serious.

"My father bids me learn some tolerance," he said in a low voice, his hand holding hers in a punishing grip as his tone dropped to a husky whisper. "And with all my heart, milady, I shall try."

Alex watched the tears fill his eyes and impulsively stretched up on tiptoe, pressing a kiss against his hardened cheek, her own vision blurring anew.

"I trust you will find the way, milord," she whispered, wishing that she could help him with his struggle, knowing she could do naught but wait. Armand tucked her hand into his elbow, leading her to the kitchens without another word.

Chapter Thirteen

Hoofbeats in the courtyard awakened Armand from a fitful doze, the sound bringing him to his feet. He rubbed his eyes blearily and peered out his narrow window, surprised to see Émil from the stables atop a swift horse on the cobbles below. Even more intriguing, Margrethe stood beside the young stable hand, apparently issuing him instructions and pressing a missive into his hands.

Armand withdrew into the protective shadows of his room, wondering what Margrethe was doing. The boy nodded and brought his steed around, spurring him on to the gate while Margrethe watched, her lips curling with satisfaction. She spun on her heel and Armand fell back against the wall, unable to shake an uneasy sense that he had witnessed something important.

Did Margrethe think to petition the king for Guillaume's reinstatement? Surely the time to present her case to the king would have been when he himself rode to Paris. The decision had been made now and the king was unlikely to change his mind.

But if Margrethe did not petition the king, to whom had she sent a missive? Correspondence to a friend, perhaps? But why the clandestine nature of her envoy's departure? And why use Émil, reliable enough for a boy, but not comparable to any one of the knights of the household whom she could easily have sent? Armand frowned into the darkness, fighting his feeling that his sister-in-law was making mischief of some unknown persuasion.

* * *

As she rose the next morning, Alex hugged herself with delight, Armand's warm attention of the previous day convincing her that time alone stood between the two of them. A matter of days it was, she was sure, before he settled things in his mind and asked for her hand again.

She jumped out of bed and danced jubilantly around the room, recalling each instance she had found his speculative green gaze upon her. A marvelous day it was indeed and she tore open the shutters, leaning out the window and inhaling the clean scent of the springlike air.

A tap at the door brought her head up with a snap, her eyes widening with surprise as one of the serving women tucked her head around the door.

"Are you clothed, milady?" she asked softly, and Alex nodded, pulling her surcoat over her sheer chemise without knowing what to expect. The woman smiled encouragingly, throwing open the door and ushering in two stable hands carting a large tub. A procession of women with kettles of hot water followed and Alex smiled with delighted anticipation of a steaming bath. Quite by accident had she expressed her longing for a bath yesterday when she had come across the tub in the pantry, not thinking Armand had even noted her chance comment, and now she hugged his thoughtfulness to herself.

"Milord Baudouin suggested that you might appreciate this," the woman said by way of explanation.

"Indeed, yes," Alex breathed. "I would thank him for his kindness." And to Armand for passing the news to his father lest he arouse the household's suspicions by summoning the bath for her himself. The fire was rekindled on the hearth by nimble hands, the tub placed before the blaze and filled with hot and cold water until Alex declared the mix just right.

No small feat was it to assemble this bath in the privacy of her room and Alex thanked each who had helped as they left the room, barely able to contain her pleasure. The woman who had first tapped on the door was the last to leave, fumbling in the folds of her kirtle as she came before

Alex. Her color rose as she produced a remnant of something pink and offered it to Alex on her outstretched palm. 'Twas soap and scented for a lady proper. Alex took the small bar, lifting it to her nostrils and finding the familiar scent of roses tickling her nose. The serving woman blushed deeper and dropped her gaze to her hands, her embarrassment clear in her hesitating speech.

"'Twas confided in me that you favored the scent of rose," she mumbled, and Alex flushed in turn, knowing that this could have come from only one source.

"Thank you kindly," she said with heartfelt appreciation, impulsively squeezing the other woman's hands in hers.

Never had she savored a bath more, Alex realized as she descended to the hall, her skin scrubbed pink, her hair shining wet beneath her veil. Roses filled her nostrils, the scent rising from every part of her body and prompting her heart to sing. She met Baudouin's questioning eye and sailed a sparkling smile of appreciation in his direction, her gaze sliding quickly to his son sitting alongside. Armand stifled a grin himself, his eyes flicking back to watch Alex as she approached the head table. Days, she thought to herself dismissively, 'twould be mere hours before he claimed her for his own.

Armand stood as she reached the table and she took his proffered hand, sliding into the seat beside him without comment, determined to speed along his decision. Alex thought she heard Armand inhale sharply but she ignored him, waiting until he sat again before she leaned against him to greet Baudouin, knowing full well that the curve of her breast pressed against Armand's arm.

"Good morning, sir," she said cheerfully, and the older man flashed her a smile.

"Good morning yourself, child. You are looking happy today."

"Indeed. I must thank you for the bath. 'Twas wonderful," Alex enthused. Baudouin looked momentarily blank, his gaze flying to his younger son, surprised to find him fidgeting, the color rising on his neck. His eyes met Alex's again and they exchanged a mischievous wink before she turned her attention back to Armand.

"Armand, 'twas marvelous. They even brought me scent!" Alex exclaimed, baring her wrist and holding it beneath his nose. She saw Armand catch a whiff of her perfume and grit his teeth, shooting her a murderous look.

"Indeed you are fortunate," he bit out, and Baudouin chuckled behind his hand, feigning a coughing fit when his son turned a furious eye upon him.

"Let me smell," the older man demanded, rolling his eyes appreciatively as he sniffed Alex's wrist. "Ahh, roses. A haunting scent for a lady, think you not, Armand?"

With a muffled oath, Armand shoved to his feet, leaving Alex and Baudouin chuckling together, his ears burning red as he stomped from the hall.

"Already have you claimed his heart, child," Baudouin murmured encouragingly under his breath. "The boy has only to realize 'tis gone." They sat in silence for a moment, then the older man cleared his throat, fixing his attention on Alex again.

"Who taught you to make sums as you did yesterday?" he asked directly, and Alex flushed beneath his perusal.

"My uncle," she answered simply, suddenly taking great care with applying the honey to her bread.

"He must have much leisure time to teach such a skill to a girl," Baudouin mused, and Alex flicked a sidelong glance in his direction.

"He thought I might find it useful," she confessed, realizing instantly that she had said exactly the wrong thing.

"Useful?" Baudouin shot back, his brow furrowing into a frown.

"Useful for herbal potions and such," Alex returned inanely, unable to think of anything else quickly and ruing how easily she had revealed her true circumstance. The only reason to teach a woman sums was so that she could manage an estate, and Baudouin, she was certain, was fully aware of that.

* * *

Armand stomped out to the stables, saddling Tiberias with jerky movements as he fought for self-control. The woman would drive him fair mad with desire! Deliberately had she pressed herself against him, certain he was of it, and still could he feel the impression of that swelling breast against his arm.

How he had longed to kiss her breathless, there, before them all, and he had not a doubt that she knew it well. Still she taunted him, presenting the softness of her wrist directly beneath his nose, tempting him to toss her over his shoulder, carry her back to his bed and spend the whole of the day making sweet love to her. As if his mind of late had been able to summon thoughts of anything else.

And his father! Armand swung into the saddle with ease, spurring Tiberias too hard toward the gate, much to the beast's disgust. No effort had the old man made to cover his surprise and now Alex surely knew that he held her in such regard that he could think of naught but what would please her.

'Twas true enough, Armand knew, but he would not wish to mislead her by his gestures should he be unable in the end to offer her his heart in full. For the question of tolerance harried him still and he rode Tiberias hard in a futile attempt to escape his relentless thoughts.

No sign did Alex see of Armand again that day and she began to regret her forwardness, thinking she had pressed him too far too soon. The next day when he made no appearance at the board, she knew without a doubt that he was avoiding her and her heart grew heavy again. Even Baudouin could summon only a thin smile of encouragement for her when she rose from the table to go upstairs, and her steps faltered as she crossed the hall.

'Twas on the third day of Armand's absence that Guillaume rode out of the courtyard, ostensibly to hunt, but in truth he sought only his younger brother.

"What know you of tolerance?" Armand demanded as he stood on the riverbank confronting his faithful steed. Tiberias fixed his master with an indulgent eye before bending to drink of the quick running water. Armand chuckled to himself and scooped up a few smooth stones, skipping them across the shallow stream. "Aye, tolerance for me you have aplenty," he murmured, watching the last stone settle into the water before he turned back to the beast.

"You and I, we understand each other, we both know the same rules," he asserted, flinging out his arms in frustration. "But women! Ah, who knows what rules they play by? Never does a man know what they truly think." Armand shoved his fingers through his hair, noticing for the first time the stubble of beard that had grown on his chin and fixing Tiberias with a knowing grin.

"Again do I test your tolerance, my friend," he concluded softly, reaching for the steed's reins. "Come, I have kept you from your warm stall long enough and for no better reason than my own selfishness."

In the woods a young stag darted across the path ahead and Armand pulled Tiberias up short, stunned to see his brother in hot pursuit, crossbow in hand. As he watched, Guillaume raised the bow and let the arrow fly, crowing with victory when the shot hit home.

"Well done," Armand cried, and Guillaume's head shot up, a proud grin transfiguring his visage.

"Long indeed has it been since I plied a bow," he commented, swinging down from his steed and retrieving the fallen deer from the woods. Armand rode alongside, dismounting to help his brother lift the carcass to his horse's back and tie it behind the saddle.

"I thought you did not hunt," he commented dryly, and his brother grinned.

"That was some foolishness of Margrethe's," Guillaume said dismissively. "And I was fool enough to follow her advice."

"But why?"

Guillaume frowned down at the muddy ground for a moment before lifting his gaze to meet Armand's. "She had this idea that I must prove myself in control of the estate in the old man's stead. That to let things continue as they had been did not make the transition clear to those around us."

Armand nodded, understanding a little better but still skeptical. "But to forbid hunting?" he asked doubtfully, and Guillaume grinned apologetically.

"Margrethe has little appetite for meat so I suppose it seemed an easy sacrifice for her," he answered with a shrug. "An error of judgment she made perhaps, but I would not cast her love aside for such a trifle."

Armand raised his eyebrows, unwilling to be the one to cast further light on Margrethe's trifles. "You love her, then?" he asked instead, earning a vigorous nod from his brother.

"Aye," Guillaume admitted, climbing back into his saddle with ease. "Not perfect is she, but neither am I and so am in no position to hold her faults to light."

Armand nodded slowly at the wisdom in his brother's words, lost in thought until Guillaume spoke his name.

"Armand, would you ride for home now?" his brother demanded, and Armand threw him a wide smile.

"Indeed," he declared, swinging up into Tiberias' saddle. "And the swifter the better," he said, knowing he had much to do this night.

"To the gates then!" Guillaume cried and spurred his horse, the two men racing out of the woods toward the distant château in echo of their childhood games.

Dark it was by the time they reached the hall, Didier stunned by the arrival of yet another stag in the kitchens as he busily enumerated his culinary options. Flushed with a growing sense of camaraderie, the two brothers entered the hall together, laughing and joking, only to find the meal completed.

Armand glanced up the shadowy stairs toward Alex's room with trepidation, gratefully accepting an offered chalice of wine. One to bolster his spirit was all he needed, he told himself, half-convinced that Alex would turn him away after his prolonged absence. The lutist struck a tune and Armand quaffed the contents of his goblet in one swallow, the red wine that instantly refilled his cup looking good, as well.

Who knew how much time had passed when Armand next looked around the hall, or indeed how many goblets of wine he had drained, but he and Guillaume were the only ones remaining who could still raise their voices in song. Not tunefully perhaps, but they were conscious, which was more than could be claimed for their fellows. Guillaume staggered to the garderobe and back, Armand watching his brother's difficulties in negotiating around a sleeping dog with a chuckle.

"Woho!" Guillaume taunted giddily, spying his brother's grin. "Think you more steady than I?" Armand struggled to his feet, laughing aloud when the room cavorted merrily around him and slumping back against the table. Guillaume convulsed into helpless laughter and the two chortled until tears ran down their cheeks.

"Mayhap together we can manage the stairs," Guillaume suggested, and Armand nodded, crossing the room unsteadily. Guillaume threw one arm around his brother's shoulder when he grew close and Armand grasped Guillaume's waist, the two ambling toward the stairs rumbling the unrecognizable vestige of some song.

"Hold up!" Guillaume objected some minutes later when they had managed to climb half of the stairs. He fixed Armand with an unsteady eye and poked him in the chest. "No longer do you sleep up here."

Armand nodded, closing his eyes for a moment in the hope that the room might stop swirling. "I must talk to Alex," he murmured confidentially and Guillaume nodded enthusiastically in turn.

"Alex!" he exclaimed, rolling his eyes in appreciation. "A fair wench, she is," he managed, but Armand only nodded, the two turning back to attempt the next step.

"Do you know," Guillaume began a moment later when they had gained the step, his breathing labored and his speech slurred. "Do you know that a man might claim whatever he finds in his own bed?"

Armand fixed his brother with a doubtful eye.

"'Tis true," Guillaume insisted, and Armand turned to see his brother's eyes wide with innocence. "'Tis the king's own law." He burped fruitily and nodded assertively, a lecherous gleam in his eye. "Well do I plan to claim what is in my bed this night." He chortled, and Armand chuckled along with him.

"Margrethe!" Guillaume bellowed drunkenly up the stairs, and the two brothers fell against the wall with his effort.

"Alexandria!" Armand hollered in turn, convulsing in laughter and sending his brother into a fit of helpless giggles.

"In your bed she is," Guillaume whispered in evident delight, the promise of what waited above sending them both lumbering up the remaining stairs. Armand leaned against the wall with relief as they gained the landing, chuckling as Guillaume tapped gently on the door opposite.

"Awaken, my love!" he cooed unsteadily at the closed portal, losing his balance when the door was abruptly opened from within. Guillaume gasped in surprise, falling into a stupor at his wife's feet.

"What drunken mess is this?" Margrethe demanded, prodding Guillaume's motionless body with one delicate toe. Armand roared with laughter, finding the complete failure of his brother's amorous intent unspeakably hilarious, clinging weakly to the wall in an effort to remain upright despite his guffaws. Margrethe turned her attention to Armand, running a speculative eye over him and summoning an inviting smile.

"Would you join me in his stead?" she murmured seductively, but Armand held up both hands, shaking his head in adamant denial.

"Oh, no," he declared, edging his way farther down the wall with tentative steps. "The woman that holds my heart will I have this night or none at all," he asserted, gripping the wall with one hand as he struggled to put one foot before the other.

"Indeed, more than my heart does she hold," Armand muttered to himself, "for have I not been chaste since laying my eyes upon her?" He staggered unsteadily as he made progress toward the last door in the corridor, chuckling as he recalled Guillaume's assertion. "Far be it for me to flout the king's own law," he mumbled, raising his voice to a bellow once again. "Alexandria!"

Alex had leapt to her feet when first she had heard Armand shout her name, thinking him hurt until the drunken laughter she heard convinced her that 'twas not his voice and that she best not reveal herself.

She stood then in the middle of the room, unwilling to go back to bed, as the drunken men grew ever closer. What should she do? Surely Baudouin and Guillaume would hear the ruckus and turn the vagabonds away, but apparently they did not, for the sounds of one man's progress grew ever louder.

Alex jumped when her name was bellowed a second time, seemingly from right outside the door, no doubt in her mind this time that 'twas Armand who called. Filled with relief, she raced across the room and tugged open the door to find him on her very threshold. Disheveled and unshaved, his clothes torn and dirty, a lopsided grin on his face, he was indeed a sight for sore eyes.

"Armand!" Alex gasped, launching herself into his arms and raining kisses all over his bewhiskered face. He stumbled unsteadily back against the opposite wall at her onslaught, nuzzling her neck affectionately as he gained his footing, and she caught a whiff of some foul brew.

"Drunk you are!" she accused, and he grinned happily down at her, seemingly undisturbed by the swat she leveled at his shoulder.

"Aye, drunk with love," Armand asserted, planting a firm buss on Alex's cheek and squeezing her in a bruisingly tight embrace. She struggled free of him without much difficulty, shaking an admonishing finger beneath his nose.

"A base knave you are indeed to come to me in the middle of the night in this state," she scolded, her heart softening at the confusion in his eyes at her response.

"But, Alex," he murmured with difficulty, "I come only to claim what is in my bed."

"How dare you!" Alex shouted, landing a solid kick to his knee and pummeling his chest with her fists. As he had done once before, Armand gathered her wrists together in one hand without sustaining much damage and cradled her up against his chest.

"Do not misunderstand me," he crooned in her ear as she fought her tears. "I would have you be my lady and us exchange our vows."

Alex looked up at Armand in surprise, distrusting the tender light in his eyes because of his state. "Drunk you are and know not what you say," she reiterated coldly, but he shook his head slowly in denial.

"This I knew before I lifted a cup to my lips," he claimed, apparently having gained some sobriety by her assault. "And I am not so drunk to not know my own mind."

With that, Armand scooped Alex up into his arms and strode into the room, making a slightly weaving path for the bed. Alex held her breath, certain that he would stumble, yet unwilling to break his concentration by raising her voice in complaint. Armand gained the bedside with a heartfelt sigh of relief, his knees buckling underneath him, sending him sprawling back across the mattress Alex still clutched to his chest.

"Think you still that I am drunk?" he demanded playfully as she squirmed against him, a twinkle in his emerald eyes that Alex should by now have learned to distrust.

"Aye, I do!" she shot back defiantly, and Armand rolled her beneath him in one smooth move, his breath in her ear sending her squirming anew. His free hand curved to match the swell of her breast and Alex shivered at his tender touch, knowing herself lost once again.

"I shall have to convince you otherwise," he murmured into her ear, and Alex sighed, winding her arms around his neck in submission.

"Armand!" The sharp word brought the lovers upright with a start, Alex clutching her sheer chemise to her chest as she spied Baudouin framed in the doorway. Armand groaned at the sudden movement and rolled to his back, his head in his hands, freeing Alex to scramble to her feet and struggle into her surcoat as Baudouin advanced angrily into the room.

"Never have I seen such unfitting behavior in a knight I have trained!" he stormed, but when he would have made for the bed, Alex laid a restraining hand on his arm.

"He is drunk and knows not what he does," she explained shakily. " 'Tis after all his room that I occupy. No doubt he grew confused."

Baudouin looked at Alex skeptically, not missing the trembling of her hands or the flush staining her cheeks.

"There seemed little enough confusion in what I saw," he commented dryly, "but perhaps 'tis as you say." They turned of one accord to Armand, only to find him gently snoring.

"He seems in no position to threaten your virtue further this night," Baudouin added with a rueful smile. "Perhaps between us we can rid him of his clothes."

Some minutes later, Armand snored contentedly in only his chausses, his arm flung out across the bed. Baudouin turned to Alex again. "You may use my chamber, if you wish," he offered, but she shook her head.

"I suspect he may be ill before the night is through," she murmured, and the older man grinned at the thought.

"No doubt your healing skills are best applied here." He chuckled, patting Alex's shoulder before heading for the door. "No envy have I for your task, child. If I remember aright, the boy is an unwilling patient." Alex smiled in agreement and Baudouin was gone, leaving her alone with the soundly sleeping Armand.

Had he spoken the truth when he asked her to exchange vows? Or was he merely deep in his cups and unaware of what he said? She watched him sleep for a few moments, suddenly beginning to feel the toll that the tension of the past few days had taken on her. Now she could admit to herself that she had been worried about Armand, but she would never dare to tell him so.

Alex stifled a yawn, her gaze running over his stubbled jaw, the uncompromising line of his lips, trailing down to his broad shoulders and his outflung arm. Her tired mind fancifully imagined that he invited her to his side with that sprawling arm and she considered the idea for only a moment before tossing aside her surcoat and curling up against his shoulder. Armand shifted slightly in his sleep, drawing the coverlet over them both, his arm flexing to curve possessively around Alex's waist and hold her fast against his side.

Armand sat up with a jolt, wincing at the din that erupted between his ears at the sudden movement. Desperately, he tried to disentangle himself from the bed covers, his hand falling on a trim ankle and thence to a familiar sleeping face.

Alex! Armand rolled his eyes in exasperation, certain he had stupidly done something else to insult her but unable to spare the time right now to reflect upon it. He lifted her legs out of his way, gritting his teeth when he unexpectedly caught a glimpse of her smooth bare buttocks. Undoubtedly, he had gone too far. He lurched to his feet and fairly ran across the room, spewing the contents of his stomach into the pail left to clean the ashes from the hearth.

Feeling somewhat appeased, Armand dropped onto a low stool, running his hands through his hair and across the fairly decisive growth on his chin. He spared a glance to Alex and realized he could remember nothing of the night before.

Things did not look good. Well enough did he recall his acceptance of her as she was and his intent to tell her so last night, the cup of wine that he accepted to strengthen his step and no more after that. Had he jeopardized everything he hoped to gain by some drunken bumbling? Armand busied himself with starting a fire in the grate while his stomach rolled in aggravation. 'Twas chilly this morning and Alex might appreciate the blaze.

And there was no way that he could casually climb back into bed beside her without knowing what had transpired.

Alex's fingers ran across the sheets in search of Armand's solid warmth, frowning with disappointment when she found the space empty. Had he gone already then, without even a kiss to awaken her? Sounds of activity in the room behind her sparked hope anew and Alex rolled to her other side to find Armand's wary gaze upon her.

"You look terrible," she commented, noting the unusual pallor of his skin and the shadows beneath his eyes. He grinned self-consciously and gestured toward the soot pail.

"And feel much the same," he confessed. "'Twas not the sun that woke me this morn." Armand met Alex's eyes again with evident embarrassment. "I apologize for any insult I made last night," he said, and Alex got abruptly to her feet.

"Do you not remember, then?" she demanded, her heart sinking when he shook his head slowly.

"I remember nothing after that first cup of wine," Armand admitted, dropping to sit on a stool before the hearth, his frustration clear in his tone. "I know I came to ask for your hand—" he pounded his fist into his open palm "—and now I have only offended you the more."

Alex gasped at his words, her hands lifting to her lips, but Armand did not notice, rising to his feet to pace the length of the room in annoyance. "Why can I do nothing right in your presence?" he demanded angrily. "What is it about you that so muddles my thoughts that I cannot act in a reasonable manner?" Unable to restrain her glee any longer, Alex giggled.

"Do not expect so much from yourself," she teased as he looked at her in surprise. "'Twas endearing when you said you had come to claim what was in your bed." Armand flushed crimson in mortification at her words, turning to face the window.

"This I said to you?" he demanded in amazement, and Alex laughed aloud.

"That and much more," she insisted, sneaking up behind him and slipping her arms around his waist. "There was some talk of exchanging vows but I thought you were merely deep in your cups." He twisted around in her embrace, tipping up her chin with one finger.

"I did not insult you," Armand said softly, and Alex could feel the rumble of his voice in his chest. She shook her head slowly, watching with wonder as his smile grew to light his eyes. "And what did you say?" he murmured, bending to touch his forehead to hers.

"I had not the chance," she retorted pertly, giggling when he growled playfully and tickled her ribs.

"Truly you tease me, woman," he whispered against her throat, his teeth nibbling gently on the soft flesh there while Alex squirmed in delight.

"Nay, I do not," she claimed, pushing her hand against his chest. "Ever the knave, you fell asleep before I could answer." Armand laughed and scooped her up into his arms, whirling her effortlessly around.

"Then answer me now," he demanded. "Will you be my bride?" Suddenly the teasing light in his eyes dulled and Alex knew the spinning had not been well received by his stomach. Armand bent over and she scrambled out of his arms, helping him to the slop pail and shaking her head in mock disapproval.

"Ever do you avoid my answer," she complained when the spasms had passed and he was leaning weakly against the wall, trying to catch his breath. "Now I shall leave you wait," she threatened, crossing the room to slip her kirtle over her head and lace it hastily.

"Witch," Armand teased weakly, his attention caught when Alex tossed her surcoat over her shoulders. "Where do you go at this hour?" he asked with a frown, and Alex trotted back across the room to his side. She smoothed the damp hair back from his brow and pressed a kiss against his forehead.

"Get yourself back to bed," she advised quietly. "I go only to the garden for some herbs to ease your ills."

"Do not tarry," Armand muttered as he made his way across the room. He dropped his weight to the bed and fixed Alex with a concerned look. "I would keep you close until you wear my ring."

Alex chuckled and tapped him smartly on the nose. "You, sir, leap to conclusions. I have yet to give you my answer," she maintained archly, drawing an amused grin from her companion.

"Already have you told me of your heart's desire, Alex," he murmured in that low voice she could not resist. "And now I have told you mine." He reached up and cupped her face with gentle hands, his thumb sliding softly back and forth across her lips. "You will wear my ring, Alexandria, as I will wear yours, I swear it to you now."

Tears rose in Alex's eyes and she leaned toward Armand, her heart swelling with her love for him and the promise that their future held. He buried his face against her throat, rolling to his back and cradling her against his chest protectively.

"Ah, woman," he whispered into her ear. "Find me something to rinse my mouth that I might kiss you fully." Alex laughed and propped her elbows against his chest as she stared down at him assessingly.

"A troubled stomach, a foul mouth," she enumerated, ticking off one finger with each claim. "A pounding between the ears?" she asked, and he nodded ruefully. "Anything else?" Armand shook his head and Alex sighed with feigned exasperation.

"A sorry mess you are indeed, Armand d'Avigny," she teased, "and I shall have to consider taking such a sad excuse for a man to my side." Armand's eyes glimmered and he rolled Alex abruptly beneath him, tickling her ribs until she begged breathlessly for mercy.

"Be quick," he advised with a wicked grin when she stood moments later adjusting her tousled kirtle. "I am in sore need of a maiden's healing kiss." Alex smiled and bussed Armand's scratchy cheek, expertly capturing the hand that trailed toward her bosom.

"You should be sleeping," Alex admonished, grinning at his heavy sigh of resignation and stepping quickly to the door. "I shall be but a minute," she whispered over her shoulder, her heart warming at Armand's indulgent smile, her feet gaining wings at the love she saw glowing in his emerald eyes.

The household was quiet as Alex flew down the stairs with silent steps. No doubt there would be others looking for her assistance this morn, she thought with a wry smile, tiptoeing through the kitchen and out into the walled garden.

A sprig of this, a handful of that. Alex's nimble fingers pinched off pieces of the young plants, the bundle of herbs she clasped in her hand growing minutely with every step. She heard horses in the courtyard behind her and men's voices raised in greeting but thought nothing of it, sparing only a glance up to the window of her chamber with the guilty knowledge that she lingered too long. Hopefully Armand had fallen back asleep and would not be annoyed with her. She pinched off one last twig and spun on her heel, freezing in place as she confronted three knights in the garden gate.

Their dark helmets concealed their faces and Alex saw that they wore full battle garb as if they expected a fight, some tremor of fear launching deep inside her when they took a step toward her in unison. Too late she noted the black and gold of their garb and uttered a strangled cry of recognition. She took a step backward, releasing the herbs from her grasp as the men lunged toward her of one accord.

Alex tried to scream but a fourth knight had sidled up behind her, his presence declared when he clapped a strong hand over her mouth, muffling her cries with a heavy cloth. A cloyingly sweet smell rose to Alex's nostrils and she named the sedative in her mind, tears rising in her eyes as she fought desperately against its power, knowing all the while that her struggles were futile.

The four knights nodded mutely to one another when the woman slipped bonelessly to the ground, the one of broadest stature tossing her limp form easily over his shoulder at a gesture from the smallest and leading the way back to their waiting steeds.

"A fine fool you made of yourself last night." Baudouin's chastising voice brought Armand back to consciousness with a start, his eyes immediately scanning the chamber for Alex. "Gone she is, as any sensible woman would be," his father declared smugly, dropping to the stool before the hearth.

Armand frowned at Baudouin for an instant, then saw that the fire had burned down to mere coals. He was on his feet in the blink of an eye, striding to the window and looking down at the garden. It was empty, a small pile of greenery abandoned in the middle of one of the paths. Armand swore under his breath and turned blazing eyes on his father.

"Have you seen her this morning?" he demanded sharply, swearing again when Baudouin shook his head calmly.

"With all honesty, I do not believe she was as angry as perhaps she ought to have been," the old man remarked mildly, but Armand only reached for his shirt.

"Nay, she was not," he shot back to his father's surprise, struggling into the uncooperative garment. "Something is amiss. I have known it since I awoke this morning," he muttered in self-recrimination, and Baudouin got to his feet with a frown.

"But what . . . ?" the older man barely began before his son interrupted him unceremoniously.

"'Twas before the sun had fully risen that she ran down to the garden for a few herbs to ease my malaise," Armand practically shouted. "A moment, no more, yet she has not returned, the sun nearly at zenith and a pile of leaves abandoned on the path." He found his shoes beneath the bed and shrugged into his tabard, striding out of the room and into the hall, his father behind him. "The air is too still," he muttered as he gained the corridor. "I like it not."

"Calm yourself," Baudouin advised reassuringly, but Armand did not slacken his pace, scooping up the cloak he had abandoned the night before and sweeping through the hall with long strides. "She could be anywhere, boy," the older man argued. "In the kitchens, perhaps."

"See you her here?" Armand demanded curtly as they crossed the kitchen threshold, Didier looking up from his work with surprise. "Or there in the garden? Or behind us in the hall?"

"Nay, I do not." Baudouin shook his head slowly, the conviction seeping out of his voice as he trailed behind his impassioned son.

"Have you seen the Lady Alexandria this morn?" Armand demanded of the stable hands when he reached the courtyard, the lot of them shaking their heads in denial. "Any others arriving or departing at an early hour?" Again the stable hands shook their heads in evident confusion.

"I saw her," piped up a tiny voice from behind the men, one of the older grooms making an impatient silencing gesture.

"The boy is full of tall tales," he explained apologetically. "None there are who still believe him here." Armand frowned thoughtfully for a moment, then beckoned with one finger.

"Let the boy speak," he demanded, summoning the lad forward. No more than seven summers had the boy seen, his brown eyes wide with surprise as he faced Armand, the tall knight frowning with hands on hips, but the lad did not flinch before his anger.

"I would know what you saw." Armand spoke slowly, his eyes fixed upon the boy as if he would will the truth from his lips. Anger ran unchecked through his veins that some evil had befallen Alex while he slept and he stifled an urge to shake the boy's story loose. Armand saw the child hesitate for an instant and knew that he could not gain the entire story while he glared furiously at him.

"Yes, sir." The boy nodded, but before he could say more, Armand squatted down before him, taking a deep calming breath before he spoke.

"Would you be a squire?" he asked softly, and the boy nodded enthusiastically, his face pulling into a wide grin. Armand breathed a sigh of relief. Now the fullness of the tale would be his.

"And then a knight," the lad confided with assurance, and the knight before him smothered a smile.

"I have need of a trusty squire," Armand explained in a low voice, placing one hand on the child's shoulder companionably, "but a squire must always tell the truth with no embellishment or delay. Would you be capable of such a task?" The boy's chest puffed out with pride and he nodded vigorously.

"Indeed I am, sir," he asserted, and Armand granted him a crooked smile.

"Tell me then what you saw this morn."

"'Twas early and I saw the lady in the garden," the boy began, his tone earnest in his desire to please his lord's son, his gaze flicking between Armand and Baudouin. "Picking things she was, as she does."

"Indeed she does." Armand nodded to urge him on and the boy pointed to the gates.

"Then four knights came to the gate, rode right through they did, without stopping." The boy paused, taking a deep breath and frowning in recollection. "Directly they went into the garden and the lady fell asleep right in front of them. 'Twas so strange, then one picked her up and they rode off again with nary a word."

Armand nodded, the boy's words sending a chill through his heart. He felt his father's stillness behind him and knew the old man feared for Alex's welfare, as well.

"What were their colors?" he demanded softly, watching the boy carefully to see that he told the truth.

"Sable and or," the lad responded promptly, and Armand's heart sank to his toes. Black and gold. He pushed abruptly to his feet in annoyance that his sense of disquiet should be so ominously fulfilled and offered the boy his hand.

"I believe you speak the truth," he said firmly, shaking the lad's hand without ceremony. "Go now to my rooms,

fetch my hauberk, my blade, my helmet, coif and gloves.''
The boy grinned with delight until Armand raised one
threatening brow, then he was off, whooping with joy as he
ran through the stables and pounded up the stairs to the
room Armand had been using.

"Saddle Tiberias for me," he commanded, and the
groom nodded immediately, sending stable hands scurrying in preparation for the knight's departure. "And see to
the gatekeeper's welfare," he shouted after them, turning to
meet his father's thoughtful frown.

"Probably dead," Baudouin said flatly with unusual
terseness, and his son nodded in agreement.

"Tell me exactly where is the Château Villiers," Armand
demanded with cold determination, his intent burning in his
eyes.

Chapter Fourteen

Alex awoke groggily to find well-trodden dirt filling her vision, the sound of hoofbeats and her awkward discomfort telling her that she had been tossed over the saddle of a horse. She tried to part her lips to scream and realized that she had been thoroughly gagged. She struggled to right herself, only to feel the rough rope bite tighter into her wrists where her hands were bound tightly behind her back.

A deep laugh rang out overhead followed by a heavy hand landing on her buttocks, the blow sending the pommel of the saddle grinding mercilessly into her hip. Alex moved her feet experimentally and was not surprised to find them tied, as well, her last few moments of consciousness coming back to her in a sudden rush.

"The wench awakes," the man above her cried, giving her buttocks a healthy squeeze that set Alex wriggling in indignation. As if to be kidnapped and trussed up like a boar were not enough, she was to be fondled, as well.

A harsh voice commanded a halt from somewhere behind her and Alex shivered, knowing that things could only get worse. The horses slowed to a standstill and Alex's heart began pounding in time to a pair of approaching footsteps, each deliberate pace crunching the gravel underfoot. Cruel fingers grasped her jaw, tipping her chin skyward to meet the self-satisfied smile of Pièrre de Villiers.

"Well met, *chérie*," he greeted cavalierly, gesturing to his man to dismount. "All of you, away for a moment," he commanded sharply, his eyes narrowing as he looked at Alex once more. " 'Tis time the lady and I came to terms.''

Alex's riding companion dismounted, grabbing her by the hips and swinging her down with a grunt. Taking a quick look at her jailer, Alex was surprised to find him as tall as Armand and thicker through the midsection. Her gaze flew to his eyes, barely visible in the shadows cast by his helmet, and she stifled a shiver at their coldness. No mercy could she expect at this one's hands, nor did she trust him not to hurt her.

Armand, Armand, she cried in her mind, hoping against hope that he had seen her abduction from the window even though she knew not what he could do singlehandedly against four opponents. At Pièrre's direction, the hulking knight lifted Alex by the waist and planted her against a tree, pushing her weight backward with one broad hand and leering at her as he knew Pièrre's attention momentarily diverted.

Alex's heart picked up its pace and she closed her eyes in desperation. What would become of her? Was she doomed to be the plaything of Pièrre and his knights for the rest of her days? Somehow, someday, there would have to come some small possibility of escape.

"Enough," Pièrre snapped impatiently, and the knight gave her a final pinch before he stepped away, ambling across the small clearing to join his fellows. Alex saw with dismay that the others were as heavy as the first, every one leveling assessing eyes her way.

"We must discuss our arrangement," Pièrre began, and Alex struggled pointedly against the gag, intimating that she could discuss nothing in this state. Pièrre chuckled dryly, flicking one gloved finger against her cheek. "Not yet, *chérie*. First you will hear me out and then you may have your say." He trailed that fingertip down the side of her neck, his hot gaze following its path. Alex stiffened in indignation beneath his touch.

She made some unintelligible protest behind her gag, but Pièrre only smiled and continued undeterred. Casually, he propped his elbow against the tree above Alex's head and leaned his weight toward her, his breath fanning her cheek as his hand continued to wander. Alex averted her face as best she could, tears of helplessness clouding her vision and a trembling assailing her as she was forced to endure his intimate caresses. How could she bear this?

"A bargain was made and a contract signed," Pièrre whispered, "and soon we shall enjoy the fruits of our betrothal." Alex leveled a glare of loathing at her captor but he only smiled, his hand sliding up to close around her throat. Alex's eyes widened in fear and he chuckled, his eyes narrowing as he stared down at her. "Remember, my love, that you draw breath by my will alone, and my mind is apt to change without warning."

So he would threaten her with her own demise. Alex's chin lifted a notch and she met his eyes with defiance, doubting that a premature death was any worse a fate than years beneath Pièrre de Villiers' hand. He evidently read her thoughts, for any vestige of a charming manner fled, his lips contorting in a sneer.

"So you care nothing for your own existence," he hissed. "How very noble you are, *chérie,* but doubtless there are those close to your heart whose passing you would regret. Friends I have with the Inquisition—surely you are familiar with their august endeavors to rid the countryside of witches." Pièrre smiled and took a few paces away as if deep in thought, glancing slyly over his shoulder as Alex awaited his next words with baited breath.

"To be accused is to be guilty, as you may know, and burning at the stake the fate of the condemned." He folded his arms across his chest and frowned at the darkening sky overhead. "Terribly fond of herbalists are they," he mused finally, "and I cannot help but think of your dear aunt." Pièrre spun on his heel and confronted Alex with a malicious gleam in his eye. "Sophie de Pontesse, is she not?"

"No!" Alex shouted behind her gag, lunging toward her captor with hate in her eyes. He laughed easily, stepping quickly forward to grasp her as her weight toppled unsteadily.

"Listen to me well, Alexandria," Pièrre said in a low voice, gripping her shoulders tightly and compelling her to meet the intent in his eyes. "Do not fool yourself that I would not do this thing to punish your disobedience to me. My wife you will be, and the union will be a willing one to the eyes of those around us. Is my meaning clear to you?"

What choice had she? Already had this man murdered Michel and tried to kill her. Alex had no doubt that even should Sophie's fate be tossed to the notorious inquisitors, she would still not escape retribution herself at Pièrre's hand. She flicked a glance at the knights watching their discussion and the man before her smiled a wickedly confident smile.

"Right you are to fear their caresses, *chérie*," he murmured, drawing Alex's frightened gaze to his own. "No scruples would I have in sharing a wench of whom I had tired. Should you dare to run from me, you will not escape."

A tear slid down Alex's cheek in recognition of the very neat trap Pièrre had laid for her; seemingly he had blocked every possible path. Mutely, reluctantly, Alex nodded her head, her shoulders drooping beneath his merciless grip. Pièrre smiled with practiced charm and patted her cheek with satisfaction.

"Now then, to the matters at hand," he said briskly. "The hour grows late, the distance to travel yet far. I would stop this night at a tavern just ahead and you, *chérie,* may consider it the first test of your obedience to me."

He pulled his dagger from his belt and unceremoniously cut away her gag, Alex barely noticing that the tip of the blade nicked her cheek as she spit the foul cloth into the dirt with relief. Before she could take a breath, Pièrre pressed her roughly back against the tree. The knife flashed in his hand and she gasped, but he merely cut the rope that bound her hands, bending to do the same to her feet. Alex rubbed her bruised wrists with relief, freezing when he straightened and glared at her anew.

"Cleanse and tidy yourself, woman," Pièrre spat in derision. "You are not fit to take the table." He turned and paced away in annoyance, pointing to his knights. "Watch her!" he shouted imperially, not bothering to see whether they did so as he disappeared across the clearing. Alex sank back against the tree and gulped the fresh air gratefully, her body limp and exhausted from her ordeal, hating that Pièrre's surety of her compliance was so completely justified.

Armand gritted his teeth in frustration as Tiberias' breakneck pace put the miles behind them and still no sign of Alex and her captors appeared on the road ahead. As he rounded every curve, he held his breath, hoping to catch a glimpse of them on the horizon, but nothing had he seen. Now the moon climbed into the sky and the countryside fell silent. 'Twas as if the very earth had opened and swallowed them up and he began to pray fervently that Château Villiers was indeed their destination.

The footfalls of the great destrier were beginning to falter, though Armand knew the stallion would run as long as he was bidden to do so. The time was ripe to stop and take some measure of relief. Bright lights appeared to one side of the road ahead, outside a small tavern. Armand slowed Tiberias to a walk and approached with caution, wondering whether he should stop at so frequented an establishment or make his camp in the woods to secrete his passing.

The caparisons of the first steed he laid eyes on decided the matter, de Villiers' signature black and gold spread over the haunches of a black beast harnessed in the tavern's small adjoining courtyard. Without another thought, Armand led Tiberias around back, tethering him beside a rain barrel and slipping from his back. He closed his eyes while the horse drank, standing silently in the shadows while he struggled to control his temper, knowing he could not enter the tavern with blood lust in his eyes.

Armand strolled around the building, pulling open the heavy oaken door with slow deliberation, the smoke and smell of the company within assaulting his senses. 'Twas darker inside than out and his eyes took a moment to adjust after he doffed his helmet, his gaze finding the portly keeper and gesturing that he would have an ale. Sipping the foul brew, he perched on the edge of a sturdy table. Dismissing the invitation of an amply endowed wench with a thin smile, he surveyed the crowd of merrymakers.

The wood smoke that stung his eyes combined with the congestion to make his survey doubly difficult. Peasants rubbed elbows with traveling friars, the lot of them rank with the odor of their labors. A sharp-faced old man by the fire tried to hawk pieces of what he claimed was the true cross to his skeptical companions. Women with gaping kirtles dipped in and out of the men, their lips rouged and gazes bold. A cheer erupted from the dice game in the corner and Armand watched with disinterest as coins changed hands.

The woman who had propositioned him earlier sauntered by again and this time Armand drew a coin from his glove and beckoned to her.

"Changed your mind, have you?" she demanded, looking askance at the coin between his fingers. "More than that 'twill cost you," she added but Armand shook his head firmly.

"I thought perhaps you might have seen the other knights," he began, surprised when she nipped the coin from his grip and dropped it between her breasts.

"In the back corner, they are," she said, pointing off to the far end of the *salle*. "And a less festive lot you could never hope to see." She smiled at Armand seductively as he got to his feet, pressing herself against him. "You look to be a discriminating gentleman," she wheedled, batting her generous lashes. "Could you not convince them to partake of the wealth of the house?"

"I shall do my best," Armand assured her solemnly, earning himself a damp kiss that he deflected to his cheek. Reminding himself to remain calm, he detached the woman from his side, shouldering his way through the crowd in the direction she had indicated.

When he was close enough to the corner to look over the heads of those before him, Armand paused to take in the scene. Another fire blazed in a second hearth at this end of the room, a man and woman seated at the table before it. The man draped in black and gold Armand recognized easily from their exchange at Therese's establishment.

The woman was less easy to identify. Though she was as tiny as Alex, her hood was drawn against the gaze of strangers and her shoulders drooped dejectedly beneath her surcoat. Armand's heart stopped in recognition of the blue garment, his blood running cold when the woman reached for a piece of bread and he saw the angry rope burn scarring her delicate wrist.

"Alexandria!" he roared, his rage erupting anew at the evidence of her abuse, his sword clearing its scabbard in the twinkling of an eye. Alex's head shot up at his call, her terrified eyes searching for his form in the darkness until they met his gaze and held. Too late did Armand see the warning in her eyes, too late did he recall the boy's words that there had been four knights, and he swore at his own impulsiveness as someone kicked out the lights.

"Not again!" wailed the keeper from afar as Armand caught sight of a shadow overturning the table where Alex had sat and felt the crowd clear away before him in the wake of the breaking crockery.

One knight. Armand could hear him breathing and tightened his grip on his blade, willing the shadowy outline that he could now discern to advance still farther. The heavyset knight came closer to swing his blade but Armand parried and struck in a flash, separating the man's head from his shoulders in one fell swoop. The sound of the man's corpse hitting the floor was unmistakable and he thought he heard Alex gasp from the corner.

"One!" he bellowed to reassure her fears, all senses bent on discerning the next attack against him, some survival instinct prodding him with the news that the odds stood sorely stacked against him. No choice had he now but to see the battle out, Armand thought as he spotted the flash of a rising blade, burying his own where he expected the knight's midsection might be.

A groan rewarded his guess, but Armand was struggling against pain himself as the man's falling weight buried an upheld sword in his shoulder. He fought to rise anew, feeling the blood run freely from the gash, but someone hit his head from behind, sending him staggering to his knees.

He could still get out alive, he realized suddenly, his thoughts spinning in wild speculation. There might yet be a better opportunity to free Alex and it might be well to have de Villiers think him dead. Armand closed his eyes and emitted what he hoped was a heartfelt groan, letting his weight slip unencumbered to the cold stone floor.

"All over 'tis!" came the jubilant cry of the one who had attacked him from behind, and Armand schooled his features carefully, hoping he could pass further scrutiny when the light was restored.

"I would have him dead for this insult," Pièrre snarled, and Armand held his breath, hearing the striking of a flint. The golden glow of a lamp filtered through his eyelids and he felt the crushing presence of the crowd surrounding him. A murmur of voices rose as fingers poked and prodded him experimentally. He heard a woman stifling her tears and knew it to be Alex, his heart wrenching that he could do nothing to reassure her.

"Dead he seems indeed," Pièrre mused, idly kicking Armand's boot. "But I would be certain of the fact. Dismember him," he commanded icily, and Armand's blood stopped in his veins in shock, numbness seizing his mind at the barbarian command.

"No!" Alex screamed as though in a distant dream, and he felt her slight weight flung atop him, her tears bathing his face as she touched him tenderly. Her anguish ran over Armand in waves and he marveled that he had been such a fool as to doubt the fullness of her heart.

"Have you not already taken his life?" she cried, her voice desperate, the soft ends of her hair sweeping across Armand's cheek as she turned to plead with Pièrre.

The surrounding crowd fell silent as they expectantly awaited the lord's decision. Alex's fingertips absently caressed the edge of Armand's jaw, her healer's touch tracing the jagged line of broken rings in his hauberk and finding the gash inside.

"'Twill be as the lady desires," Pièrre decided finally, the crowd erupting in excited whispers, and Armand almost wept with relief. Alex sagged against him, her tears falling anew on his whiskered chin. She bent to press a kiss to his cheek and the scent of roses filled his lungs, his heart strengthening with new resolve to emerge victorious from this fight.

"Au revoir," Alex whispered in his ear, and Armand panicked at her words, his eyes rolling beneath his lids as he fought to keep his eyes closed.

Until we meet again! Did she know that he yet lived? Would she unwittingly slip and lose the day? A fool he had been to think that he could deceive a healer. But no, he felt her crumple towards him and knew her sorrow could not be feigned, her sobs breaking as she buried her face against his throat.

"Enough" came Pièrre's harsh voice, Alex gasping audibly as she was jerked to her feet.

"No taste have I for resting here. We will ride now," Pièrre ordered. Armand heard a jingle of coins being dropped onto a table and the murmured negotiations with the keeper before another few pieces of silver joined the rest. "Dispose of them both," Pièrre continued, disdainfully shoving Armand with his foot as he strolled past.

The *salle* broke into excited chatter as the door fell closed behind the departing knights, the keeper dispatching a boy to the cellars for another keg of ale as his patrons swarmed to ease their thirst. Someone bent over Armand in curiosity but he paid them no mind, straining his ears for the sound of hoofbeats outside as Pirre's party passed the door, the horses accelerating to a gallop as they raced down the road to Villiers.

No sooner had the hoofbeats faded in the distance than Armand sat up abruptly, almost stopping the heart of the woman crouched before him. Intent on picking his pockets, no doubt. He granted her a wicked grin, sheathing his sword and leaping to his feet in one smooth move, savoring the numb shock that settled over her features as she sat back on the floor openmouthed.

Armand tossed a coin to the keeper as he scooped up his helmet, darting out the door amid amazed silence. Round the corner he was in an instant and climbing into Tiberias' saddle, a heartfelt apology murmured under his breath to the tired beast as he spurred him on. With distaste, he noted the clouds obscuring the moon and felt the first drops of rain slip down the back of his hauberk.

The incessant downpour was both a blessing and a curse, shrouding Armand from the men he trailed but similarly obliterating all signs of the horses' passage ahead of him.

Armand knew Château Villiers was somewhere to the southeast of Avigny, but his father's directions had been vague, and in this foul weather he had not the time to make a wrong turn. Always did he strive to keep Pièrre's party just barely within sight, yet remain steadfastly out of theirs, the beat of the rain hopefully concealing Tiberias' footfalls.

And what of Alex? Did Pièrre abuse her now? Armand's mind willingly summoned the image of the red marks on her wrists that he had glimpsed in the tavern and he wondered if she had been bound again or simply drugged as she had undoubtedly been this morning. He ground his teeth as his imagination supplied a wide range of abuse she could suffer, his fingers gripping the reins tightly as he fought to control his desire for revenge. Wrong 'twas to handle a gentlewoman thus, a willful rejection of all to which a knight pledged troth, and Armand longed to extract a toll from Pièrre for his transgressions.

Too easily had he fallen back to sleep this morn despite his sense that something was amiss. He should have accompanied Alex to the garden, Armand berated himself, knowing that she would never have tolerated such overprotection within the walls of his father's keep. Still, he blamed himself, for without a doubt he could have prevented her abduction had he been close at hand.

But how had Pièrre found Alex? The question plagued Armand as he rode ever onward in the incessant rain. 'Twas as if Pièrre had not known of her whereabouts until recently, the strength of purpose he showed in his attack intimating that he had ridden straight out on learning she was at Avigny.

Armand frowned to himself in the darkness, recalling that 'twas four days past that he had confided in his father. Baudouin? Impossible. The old man was half in love with Alex himself.

Abruptly he recalled the sound he thought he had heard in the corridor. Someone had eavesdropped on their conversation. Someone who had betrayed his family's trust to Pièrre de Villiers. Who among his father's house would do such a thing? Armand could think of none with such malicious intent, save...

Margrethe's image appeared in his mind and he considered the thought briefly before discarding the possibility. Surely even her dissatisfaction with her lot could not extend to this. And what possible reason had Margrethe to see Alex dismissed from Avigny? His lips thinned to a harsh line, his eyes growing cold as he vowed to himself that when all was over, he would find the identity of the one who had betrayed his lady.

The faintest hint of sun lightened the overcast sky ahead when the walls of a château became visible through the morning mist. Fog rose from the wet fields surrounding the castle walls, a number of peasants already out and working the muddy earth.

Armand dropped back discreetly from the knights preceding him, leading the exhausted Tiberias into the shelter of the surrounding forest as Pièrre paused at the gate ahead. Armand squinted into the distance, noting that the fourth horse ran riderless, barely detecting a huddled form riding in front of Pièrre before two knights closed rank behind their lord. His heart went out to Alex, certain she felt alone and abandoned.

The echo of the other man's shout carried faintly over the greening fields to Armand's ears, the gate laboriously rising in response. Pièrre impatiently urged the horses onward before the iron grid was secured and disappeared into the darkness within.

Armand ran a speculative gaze over the well-maintained keep as he dismounted and pulled off his helmet, his heart sinking at the task before him. The square tower rose tall from the bailey, the walls surrounding it high and smooth, the moat encircling the whole wide and dark. His experienced eye picked out the carefully concealed sentries pacing the perimeter walls, and he folded his arms across his chest at their sheer numbers.

Well made and well defended was Château Villiers, he was forced to concede, frustrated that Alex should at once be so close and so far. A frown of annoyance puckered his brow as he turned his attention to his exhausted steed, still keeping one eye on the distant château.

A light flickered from a window high in the keep and Armand memorized its location, certain that this was where Alex had just been taken. He frowned at the château again, wondering how he would manage to reach her without detection.

Armand sighed, recognizing that his exhaustion did little to improve his thinking. Nothing could he do before nightfall and hopefully some plan would reveal itself to him before then. Right now, he had to get some sleep while he had the chance so his wits might be quick when he needed them.

Château Villiers was bustling when they arrived, but Alex did not even bother to look about at her surroundings. As they rode during the night, she had wept silently in the darkness, mourning Armand's demise. Unlike him, 'twas, to draw his blade impetuously, so cautious had he always been to know the full truth before he acted. 'Twas his love for her that had betrayed him, she was sure, for she had seen the evidence of it in his own eyes before he fell, wondering then how she could ever have doubted his heart.

Was it truly Pièrre's intent to slay everyone she loved? How her heart had chilled at the very thought of Armand's body being dishonored as Pièrre had demanded. No mercy had Pièrre in his heart, 'twas clear, and Alex heaved a ragged sigh, confronting the possibility that he had granted her request only to justify some further abuse.

For the blink of an eye, when she whispered in Armand's ear, Alex had foolishly thought he yet lived, but she knew that her wishful thinking had played a cruel trick upon her senses. So motionless Armand had been, his complexion pale, his body not even flinching when Pièrre hooked a boot beneath his ribs in disgust. And the blood. Alex bit her trembling lip and clutched her shaking hands together as she sought some semblance of control.

For with Armand's death, any hope for the future was extinguished like a flame in the open wind. No longer did she care about anything.

Pièrre hauled Alex down from the saddle and she followed his order without complaint, every fiber of her being aching with an exhaustion that she knew sleep would not assuage. Eyes downcast, she stood mutely before him until he shoved her toward the portal, pinning her hands together behind her back as he urged her on.

Alex paid no attention to the twists and turns of the corridor, to the interest of the servants that they brushed past, to the furnishings of rooms that opened to the left or right, keeping her head down and plodding forward as Pièrre dictated. They reached a staircase and Alex climbed numerous stairs interspersed with landings that she refused to bother counting. Soon enough would she grow familiar with her prison.

Pièrre pulled her to a stop before a solid wood door, drawing a ring of keys from his cloak with his free hand and shoving Alex forward angrily into the small space revealed. She stumbled as he released her hands, catching her balance on a tall chest, pushing her tangled hair from her eyes as she turned to watch him.

"All night have you sobbed," he shouted, his eyes flashing as he advanced on her anew. Alex cringed against the chest and Pièrre grabbed a fistful of her hair, pulling her face to within a finger's width of his. "Too easily did your whoremonger die," he hissed, and Alex gasped at his words.

"I was not his whore," she spat back, shocked that Pièrre could make something so magical sound so base.

"Liar!" he shouted and slapped her face, releasing her hair to stride angrily across the room. Alex's hands flew to her burning cheek and she watched Pièrre bear down on her again, uncertain of what he would do.

"Think you that I do not remember his face?" he demanded vehemently, jabbing his finger viciously at Alex's chest. " 'Twas you and no other writhing beneath him at that brothel." Pièrre struck Alex with the back of his hand as he spat out this last, the force of his blow sending her flying backward, the resounding crack of her head hitting the heavy wooden chest the last she heard before all went black.

The aches in her joints and muscles made themselves known as Alex awoke slowly, the throbbing in her head declaring itself with ferocious intensity. Tentatively, she felt the back of her head, her exploring fingers finding a lump that was tender to the touch. She winced and forced her eyes open, surprised at her lushly unfamiliar surroundings.

The chamber contained few pieces of furniture, the bed that she occupied, the chest that had dealt her the lump, a table and chair beside the fireplace, but each item was finely crafted of excellent materials. The oriental woods, the inlays of ivory, the gracious curves all spoke of a wealth beyond Alex's experience, the silks and brocades draping the bed finer than any she had seen in the markets in Venice.

Soft silk caressed her skin and Alex realized that the clothes she had worn were gone, replaced by a gossamer shift that floated all the way down to her knees, its edges trimmed in ornate lace.

Alex propped herself up on her elbows in amazement, the whole of the splendid room swirling around her until she closed her eyes against the nausea. Slowly the recollection of what had transpired filtered into her mind and she felt her tears rise anew, an emblem of a rampant lion in the draperies confirming that she had not dreamed the horrific events. She curled up against the silk-tasseled pillows and summoned Armand's image to her mind, sobbing softly to herself amid the finery.

Armand shrugged out of his hauberk and mail chausses, all the while keeping a watchful eye on the comings and goings at the gate of the château. He winced at the glimpse he managed of the damage to his left shoulder, tying a wad of cloth from shoulder to underarm, round and round, hoping that his makeshift binding would do. He fingered the lump on the back of his head and acknowledged himself a virtual invalid, stubbornly quelling any doubts that he would be able to free Alex unassisted.

Already the sun sank toward the tops of the trees and he knew the gate would not remain open much longer. This would be his last chance to get inside the castle before the morning and he dared not imagine what would befall Alex during the night.

Tiberias nickered as Armand stowed his mail, shrugging into simple woolen chausses and tunic before turning the worn lining of his surcoat to the outside and tossing it over his shoulders.

"Aye, Tiberias," he murmured in agreement, setting his sword aside with an effort, "I have little love of this path myself but 'tis unlikely they would let me pass otherwise."

Determined not to enter the fortress completely unarmed, Armand concealed his dagger at his waist before bending to smear dirt on his face and hands. With one final check that his belongings and Tiberias were well hidden, Armand patted the stallion reassuringly on his nose. He crept through the undergrowth back to a bend in the road so that none might note where he emerged and began to stride along the dusty way to the château, thanking the fates that he had not had the opportunity to remove his whiskers these last days.

An elderly man struggled toward the gate with a pair of kegs and Armand offered his assistance, tossing one heavy keg up onto his shoulders while the relieved tenant rolled the other onward. Armand flexed his shoulders, finding the most comfortable way to carry his burden, knowing that his passage through the gate was now assured.

And just in time, he thought, tossing a glance over his shoulder at the sinking sun and urging the old man forward. They would surely be among the last admitted within the walls this night.

The savory smell of stewed meat brought Alex back to her senses again and she opened her eyes to find her pain much diminished and the room cloaked in murky darkness. Her stomach growled and she sat up carefully, noting that someone had left a burning oil lamp on the table, its light bathing the meal laid out for her in a golden glow. A fire crackled in the hearth and she swung her feet to the floor, surprised to find the stone comfortably warm.

Alex rose and made her way slowly to the heavy wooden door with its ornately curved iron hinges, tugging futilely against it. Locked or barred, she acknowledged. And to what end? Would Pièrre truly force the nuptials to proceed as he had threatened? Or, convinced of Alex's promiscuity, would he toss her heartlessly to his minions? It mattered not, she realized, folding her arms resolutely across her chest to protect the barren emptiness where her heart should be. No greater hurt could Pièrre inflict upon her than the callous murder of two she loved, and a small cold kernel of determination began to form in her mind.

Indeed, she had nothing to lose at this point, nothing to gain, no respite to hope for, no certainty that her path would grow easier as the days passed. Too long had Pièrre escaped the reckoning for his crime against her house, too sharply did she ache to quickly forget Armand's death.

Alex straightened and paced the length of the room. Why should she not avenge these deaths herself? Should she succeed and end Pièrre's evil existence, she could hold her head with dignity that her name stood avenged; should she fail, she would undoubtedly die in the attempt and end her own misery as Pièrre's captive.

Wandering to the single narrow window, Alex closed her eyes at the sight of the dizzying drop, expelling her breath with a heavy sigh. She would not let Michel and Armand's passing come to naught.

Alex's stomach grumbled again and she eyed the still-steaming bowl of stew with a frown. At the very least, she would need strength for whatever lay ahead. Unable to deny her gnawing hunger, Alex tasted the meat and found it both hot and deliciously seasoned, sipped the wine and savored its rich, fruity taste.

Chapter Fifteen

"God's blood, step more lively or the gate will close in your very face," the gatekeeper taunted the last of the peasants filing into the fortress.

Armand was dirty and tired from the brisk walk under the weight of the old man's keg. Stones from the road had embedded in the bottoms of his shoes and gravel dust raised by passing wagons caught in his teeth. He passed the gatekeeper and breathed a silent sigh of relief.

He was inside. And Alex was here somewhere.

The old man Armand accompanied stumbled on the threshold behind him, not for the first time losing his balance and dropping to one knee, his face contorted in a grimace of pain.

Apparently oblivious to the old tenant's plight, the gatekeeper began to crank down the gate, the elderly man's agonized gaze flying upward to the slowly descending spikes.

He struggled to rise, his aged limbs betraying him while the gate creaked lower, his gnarled hands shaking as he mutely panicked.

Armand's heart stopped in his throat. Without a thought, he dropped the keg he carried and in two swift steps was beside the older man, helping him to his feet and propelling him forward with one hand, gathering the stray keg with the other, practically carrying the wizened figure over the threshold.

Barely had they stepped inside the walls than the gate was dropped with a resounding thud. The old man clutched Armand's arm in silent gratitude as he wheezed unsteadily, but before he could recover himself the gatekeeper joined them.

"God's blood, we all love a hero," the gatekeeper sneered, his pocked face distorting into a parody of a grin as he confronted both peasants before him.

The gatekeeper fixed a steely eye on him and Armand barely remembered his place in time, dropping his gaze to his toes instead of staring steadily back.

"I know you not," the gatekeeper observed, and Armand called himself a variety of uncomplimentary names for getting himself into this predicament.

"Name yourself," the man demanded, and Armand clenched his teeth, knowing his accent would betray his class, if not his identity.

"I said, name yourself," the gatekeeper roared when no answer was forthcoming. Armand felt the heat of a flush rising over his skin and the assessing eyes of the surrounding peasants land on him. He would have to answer and the consequences be damned. He opened his mouth to speak but the old man at his side interrupted him with a throaty cough.

"My sister's boy," the tenant stated hoarsely, his reedy voice filled with assurance as he patted Armand on the arm. "Good strong boy to help me with the lord's wine," he continued, gesturing to the two kegs at their feet.

"I would know his name," the other man growled, and the old vassal nodded quickly.

"Yes, yes, 'tis Beauregard, may the good Lord bless my sister's soul for giving the lad such a name."

"Can he not speak for himself?"

"No, no." The old man leaned forward to whisper conspiratorially, "Plain simple he is, but strong as an ox." He continued then in a louder voice, apparently destined for Armand's ears. "Yes, fine strong boy. Fetch the wine, Beauregard. I expect the lord is thirsty."

"Hmm." The gatekeeper pondered the old man's story and Armand felt those probing eyes sweep over him, holding his breath while he awaited the man's verdict.

"What's this?" the gatekeeper demanded suddenly, darting forward to tug at Armand's surcoat, revealing the red wool that he had carefully turned to the inside. Armand groaned inwardly, certain that he would find himself outside those forbidding walls momentarily.

"'Tis red," the man remarked in astonishment, raising amazed eyes to Armand's dirty face before looking to the old man. "How came he to afford this dye?" he demanded sharply. "No peasant's garb is this."

"Indeed not." The old man chuckled softly under his breath, fixing the gatekeeper with an indulgent eye. "Strong as an ox, I said, and so said the lord whose wagon the boy lifted out of the mud. Cold 'twas, and the lord gave him his cloak in gratitude."

The gatekeeper's eyes narrowed craftily and he darted a glance at Armand before he spoke. "He cannot wear this garb in the château," he hissed, and Armand stiffened for an instant before realizing the man's intent. Smoothly, he slid the garment from his shoulders and offered it to the gatekeeper.

"A trade, he says," the old man whispered, nodding happily when the gatekeeper removed his own heavy brown cloak. Well-worn it was and shabbily made, its hem caked with mud and grime, but Armand donned it willingly, not yet believing that this would be the only price he was doomed to pay.

The gatekeeper pulled Armand's cloak over his shoulders, his chest puffed with pride as he turned and admired the rich color, his scowl breaking into an unfamiliar sneer that could have been a smile.

"Get thee from my post," he commanded with a regal wave, turning again and again to admire himself in his new finery. Armand immediately stooped and picked up the two kegs, gratefully following the old man's hasty steps toward the confusion of the inner bailey.

The sound of footsteps brought Alex's head up with a snap from where she dozed on the bed, her eyes widening as the tumblers in the lock rolled.

Two maids stepped into the room, their arms piled high with feminine finery. One called back over her shoulder and a man responded with an unintelligible grunt, pulling the door shut behind the girls, and the tumblers rolled again, the metallic sound echoing in Alex's heart.

"Milady," the two girls chorused in unison, dropping into elegant curtsies before her. Not knowing what else to do, Alex indicated that they could rise and one promptly burst into giggles. The second shot her a disapproving glance and stepped forward to speak.

"Lady Josephine has sent us to help you dress for the ceremony," she explained in a wispy voice.

"I do not understand," Alex admitted in confusion.

"Surely you know that you are to wed Monsieur Pièrre this night?" the second maid demanded softly, and Alex felt the color drain from her face. 'Twould be Pièrre rather than his men, she realized, not knowing even now which alternative she had dreaded the most.

"I would thank you," Armand murmured to the old man once the wine had been delivered, drawing a sharp glance from his wizened companion.

"Wise you were not to speak," the vassal commented dryly. "Your accent is most strong."

Armand smiled ruefully at that, rummaging in his pocket for a gold coin and offering it to the other man. The old man looked up at him in surprise.

"For your assistance," he explained, but the older man shook his head.

"'Twas the only way I could repay your aid at the gate," he insisted, waving Armand off indulgently.

"Get you about your business, Beauregard, whatever it might be," he added with a grin. "No time have you for talking to an old man like me."

Alex paced the confines of her chamber impatiently, hoping against hope that her insistence that she meet Pièrre before the ceremony was heeded. A kirtle of the finest golden silk fluttered around her ankles as she paced restlessly, the brocade tunic overtop resplendent with embroidered black lions. The sheerest whisper of a veil covered her hair and throat with a soft ochre glow, the surcoat tossed over her shoulders heavy with the emblems of Pièrre's house.

Alex was oblivious to her finery, thinking only of her plan for vengeance. No blade had she, but she must find a way to fulfill her plan, the passing of the nuptials equating with failure in her mind. Already the moon mounted in the sky, each passing hour more solidly sealing her doom. The lock tumblers rolled once more and Alex caught her breath in her throat, her gaze fixed on the opening door.

Pièrre stood framed in the doorway as he surveyed her with a secretive smile, his smug expression feeding her carefully controlled anger. Alex noticed immediately the jeweled dagger hanging from his belt, her mind racing as it sought some way to gain the weapon. Pièrre's gaze went immediately to her cheek, a frown darkening his brow at the colorful bruise evidencing his abuse.

"Could you not contrive to cover that blemish?" he demanded sharply, and Alex straightened slowly, struggling to keep her gaze from falling again to the blade she so desired.

"'Twas a badge of your regard for me, I thought," she returned sweetly, and Pièrre's eyes narrowed in suspicion as he tried to discern her game.

"Test me not, Alexandria," he hissed under his breath, reaching out to take her hand.

"Think you that I will willingly exchange vows with you despite all that you have done?" Alex gritted out the words, unable to keep her fury in check any longer, spitting on his outstretched hand in her anger.

"Confidence have I that you are a clever woman and will see the wisdom of fulfilling my demands," Pièrre mused, reaching out to caress her cheek, but Alex jerked her head away. Undaunted, he grasped her jaw determinedly with cruel fingers and forced her back against the wall, running one fingertip across the fullness of her bottom lip.

"Always must you force your women?" Alex demanded venomously, her words setting Pièrre's eyes ablaze. Fearing he would hit her again, she moved quickly, instinctively, biting the finger that rested on her lip.

Pièrre growled, swearing vehemently as he slapped Alex across the face. The room echoed with the resounding crack of the blow and Alex gasped, her tongue instantly tasting blood.

"My tooth!" she cried, bending forward in apparent agony, her hands clutched to her face, thinking only of the dagger in Pièrre's belt. Come closer! she screamed at him in her mind, willing him to fall for her ruse.

"Do not dare to bleed on your wedding garments!" he shouted furiously, rushing to her side and bending over her huddled form. As soon as he came close, Alex moved with lightning speed, savoring the surprise in Pièrre's eyes when she abruptly jabbed the dagger against the soft flesh beneath his chin.

"The worm turns," she whispered softly, and watched the terror settle in his eyes.

Armand stretched to his full height, grasping the window ledge above with outstretched fingers and slowly pulling himself upward. He refused to acknowledge the warm trickle of blood from his wounded shoulder, refused to look down and see the height he had already scaled, focusing his attention instead on the ledge that he grasped now. His fingers gripped the stone, the hard edges of the sill cutting into his fingers as he scrambled to gain a footing on the narrow sill.

Far below the bailey was filled with sounds of merry-making, the flickering light of a bonfire casting eerie shadows onto the wall around him. So far, Armand could only assume that none had glanced up to the keep, for there had been no outcry of discovery of his presence as he hung like some great spider on the wall. He supposed he had the festivities of the night to thank for that small mercy and wondered absently what the inhabitants of Villiers celebrated this night.

Cold sweat rolled down his back as he gained the sill, slowly and carefully standing upright and leaning against the wall of the keep for balance. Armand rested his face against the cold stone and wondered how many walls he was destined to climb for Alex.

A narrow ledge ran around the keep at this height and he shuffled slowly toward the corner of the building. A sentry paced the length of the curtain wall far below and Armand held his breath until the man had passed before moving completely around the corner and out of the light cast by the celebration below.

Light poured from the window on his left where the light had blazed early that morning, the window of the room where he assumed Alex had been taken. Now, perched on a narrow windowsill dizzyingly far above the earth, Armand was assailed by doubt. She could be in any one of a thousand other places in the expansive château. Armand leaned his forehead against the cold stone, momentarily lost in indecision.

No. His heart told him that she was here. Armand took a deep breath, forcing himself to remain calm while he took the last step, his fingers gripping the stone wall until he gained his footing. Voices rose from the room inside and he strained his ears to listen, struggling to silence his labored breathing as he recognized both voices.

Pièrre's threats carried easily to Armand's ears, sending a chill to his heart at the blackness of the man's intent.

Leaning his weight carefully into the wall, Armand ventured to peek around the edge of the window and steal a glance into the room, just in time to see Alex spit on her captor's hand, her eyes snapping with anger.

Determined to learn from his lesson of so few hours past, Armand scanned the opulent room as he checked for guards or knights. Crouching like a cat on the broad sill of the window opening, his presence veiled by the dark shadows, Armand considered his options with a grimace.

"Miserable bitch!" Pièrre shouted in response to something Alex had done, the sight of his raised hand sending Armand hurtling into the room, his feet hitting the floor as the blow landed.

"My tooth!" Alex screamed, and Pièrre was beside her with some muffled threat regarding her garments, when Alex straightened and pressed a dagger against the man's throat.

Armand backed into the shadows, seeing no need to reveal his presence as yet, his heart glowing with pride at Alex's audacity.

"No need is there for bloodshed," Pièrre argued pitifully, backing away slowly from his assailant.

"No concern had you for sparing blood last night," she spat back, poking the dagger more vehemently at his throat and drawing a thin trickle of blood. Pièrre's eyes widened in fear and he held up his hands, his words falling in a rush as he sought to sway her mind.

"A misunderstanding," he claimed with a pleading tone that almost brought an audible snort of derision from Armand. "'Twas a misunderstanding, no more."

"A misunderstanding!" Alex shouted, her fury well and truly fueled as she backed him into a wall. "'Twas no doubt a similar misunderstanding that left my brother drowning in his own blood!"

"He lost the battle," Pièrre hissed, earning himself another jab of the knife.

"No battle was that," Alex spat, "but an ambush, pure and simple. No blade did he draw, no noble death did he die when you slit his throat from behind and left him to die. And for what purpose?" she demanded on the verge of hysteria, her words horrifying Armand at the cruelty she had witnessed. "That he might dare to tell of your assault on me?"

"No assault was that," Pièrre shot back, his eyes narrowing as he argued despite the insistent prick of the blade. "Well we both know that you enjoyed the ride."

"'Twas no doubt why you held the blade to my throat!" Alex claimed shakily. "You raped me," she whispered tearfully, choking back a sob that wrenched Armand's heart. "Be man enough to admit the truth in my presence at least."

The words summoned an image in Armand's mind of Alex stumbling into that tavern in Venice, battered, bruised and pale from loss of blood. This man had done that to her and left her to die along with her brother. Anger rolled in Armand's chest and he knew that he could not leave Pièrre any opportunity to see another day.

"Man enough I be to take you again!" Pièrre cried, taking advantage of Alex's tears to lunge for the knife. Armand darted out from the shadows but the two had tumbled to the floor, an incoherent jumble of entwined black and gold as they rolled across the room, struggling for control of the blade.

"Mine!" Alex suddenly shouted jubilantly, rolling atop Pièrre with the blade glinting in her hand. Kill him, Armand commanded in his mind, but Alex stared down at the man lying helplessly on the floor, the dagger beginning to tremble ever so slightly in her hand.

Armand realized what ailed her. A healer she was, not a warrior, to inflict death on another against everything she knew.

Barely had the thought struck him than he leapt across the room to finish the gruesome task, but too late. Pièrre had seen the hesitation in Alex's eyes and lunged for the knife himself, grabbing the blade and rolling Alex beneath him, his arm rising as Alex stared up at him unflinchingly, seemingly daring him to strike the fatal blow.

"Move!" Armand roared, launching his weight toward the other man. Alex rolled obediently away, abandoning in the very nick of time the spot where the men tumbled heavily to the floor.

"Armand." Alex barely breathed his name, stunned at his appearance, her mind unable to accept the evidence before her eyes.

The men tumbled end over end until Armand slammed the smaller man's head against the wall, taking advantage of Pièrre's brief stupor to rise to his feet. His foot landed heavily on Pièrre's wrist and the jeweled dagger fell from his opponent's grip with a tinkle. Armand kicked the blade across the floor as Pièrre struggled to his feet, his fist sending the smaller man reeling back against the wall.

"How many times has he struck you?" Armand demanded, his eyes blazing like emerald lightning when he glanced sharply at Alex, and she shook her head in an attempt to collect her scattered thoughts.

"Twice," she said, and frowned in recollection. "Thrice," she corrected, then shrugged her shoulders in confusion. "I cannot exactly recall."

"Such tales do not speak well of your comport among the ladies, de Villiers," Armand muttered, his mouth thinned to a grim line as he dealt two more telling blows to the man standing unsteadily before him. Pièrre fell weakly to his knees, mumbling incoherently for mercy from his cold-eyed assailant. Armand pulled his dagger from his belt with deliberation, turning the blade before Pièrre that it might catch the light.

"Rape and murder did you charge, as well, milady?" he demanded softly, and Alex nodded mutely, slipping to her feet and leaning against the wall. Not a doubt was there in her mind that Michel's murder would shortly be avenged by the hand of her love.

But now Armand hesitated, as well, and a malicious light appeared suddenly in Pièrre's eyes. Alex stepped forward with a cry of warning but 'twas too late.

"Guards!" Pièrre shouted at the top of his lungs. "The wench is yours!"

The unmistakable rumble of footsteps rose from the hall below and Pièrre smiled a slow vindictive smile. Armand swore as the tumblers rolled in the lock and Pièrre chuckled to himself in satisfaction.

"'Tis true, the wench must be held down," he murmured confidentially to Armand, clearly certain that the larger knight could not deal the telling blow. "I will be sure you have the chance to watch."

The door began to swing open but Armand was oblivious to it, an enraged roar erupting from him as he slashed Pièrre's throat. The guards drew back in surprise at the sight of Pièrre sliding to the floor. Armand swore again as

Pièrre's men shouted to one another and erupted into the room. Without hesitation, he grabbed Alex's hand, ushering her unceremoniously toward the window. Sparing not a word, he caught her up against his chest and stepped off the edge of the sill into nothingness.

Alex would have screamed but his mouth was on hers, hungrily plundering her sweetness. She wound her arms around his neck, pulling herself ever closer to him, loving him all the more for the decision he had made. Better to plunge to their death together than be forced to watch each other's torture.

The water in the moat was cold and foul smelling against Alex's skin as she plunged into its depths. She surfaced with a gasp of surprise, Armand barely sparing her a mischievous grin before hauling her toward the opposite bank.

"You knew," she sputtered and he chuckled as they gained the shallows, locking one arm around her waist to propel her forward more quickly.

"Milady, after all this effort to win your hand, think you that I would so casually toss you to your death?" he demanded in mock indignation, stealing a brief kiss before a shout rang out from the window far above.

Immediately, an arrow buried itself in the ground to their left and a man launched himself from the window in their wake. Armand pulled Alex bodily to her feet, but the weight of her sodden wedding finery dropped her to her knees again before she could manage another step. Swearing in frustration, she tore at the heavy tunic. Another arrow planted itself a bit closer than the last and her heart began to pound in fear.

"The cloth is too heavy," she gasped, shrugging off the surcoat with its hated emblems and desperately fighting against the kirtle's lacing. Armand wasted no time with such frivolities, bending to scoop Alex into his arms and breaking into a run as the château stirred to life behind them.

"You cannot do this!" Alex protested, but Armand tossed her an angry glare.

"Indeed I can and will, milady," he shot back. She spied the dark stain on his shoulder and regarded him with horror.

"Your shoulder! 'Tis too much for you," she argued, but when she would have continued, Armand curtly interrupted.

"Hold your tongue, woman. Well you know this is not the time for discussion."

Taking offense at his tone, Alex folded her arms across her chest and set her lips in annoyance, determined to do no more and no less than he bade her from this point forward. Armand sighed theatrically and she spared a glance upward, fancying that she caught a glimmer of amusement in his eyes.

"Years you have to chastise me for my manners this night, Alex," he murmured. "Kindly busy yourself and watch my back."

Armand's breathing became more labored as they neared the perimeter of the forest, his wound taking its toll of his strength despite his claim to the contrary. The moon cast its long shadow on the field and Alex watched as torches appeared along the high curtain wall, their flames throwing light across the cold moat and into the fields behind them. Cries rose from the sentinels as Armand was spotted and Alex clutched his shoulder, the unmistakable sound of horses and their trap making her quake in fear.

"They mean to hunt us down!" she whispered in horror, and Armand's lips drew into a thin line.

"Surely you expected no less?" he demanded between labored breaths. "'Twas their lord we left dead on the floor."

"But his cruelty," Alex began, her voice faltering. "Surely they would be relieved to be free of him." Armand fixed her with a steadily skeptical glance before he spoke.

"But duty-bound they be, milady," he reminded her softly, his words doing little to settle her fears. Now she heard the gate creaking as it was raised, the impatient prancing of the saddled horses from the bailey far behind, the moving shadows of men pursuing them on foot visible in the fields.

Armand made his way unerringly to a tethered and well-rested Tiberias, tossing the saddle hastily on the steed's back and Alex shortly thereafter. He threw her his armor and sword, swinging up into the saddle behind her and pressing his spurs to the beast's hide. Even as he fumbled with the buckle of his sword belt, he urged Tiberias homeward at full gallop.

"Astride," Armand commanded Alex curtly, and she struggled against her garments until he stood in his stirrups and lifted her bodily into place. His arms wrapped around her waist and he gripped the pommel with both hands, giving Tiberias full rein to run like the wind.

Barely had they gained the road than the echo of hoof-beats closed behind them, arrows shrieking through the air on either side of them and falling ineffectually into the dirt. Armand swore under his breath and hunkered down over Alex, gathering her beneath him protectively and digging his heels into Tiberias' flanks. His weight made it difficult for Alex to breathe as he pressed her down into the saddle, but she dared not protest, knowing that they were making a run for their very lives.

Tiberias too seemed to recognize the fullness of their peril, the great beast running as Alex had never seen a steed run before. His strong legs seemed to swallow up the road before them, his breath exhaling noisily and steaming the air as the muscles beneath her bunched and strained. Gradually, the other horses fell behind, their hoofbeats fading ever farther into the distance, the arrows no longer showering around Armand's shoulders.

Still Tiberias raced forward, his pace slowing imperceptibly as he settled into a steady gallop along an apparently familiar road. The pursuing party dropped out of earshot and Alex lifted her head, studying the peacefully moonlit countryside around her. Armand did not speak or move and she nudged him in the ribs, amused that his protectiveness continued unabated in the absence of assault.

"It seems we have left them behind, milord," she murmured, but Armand did not respond. Alex wriggled beneath his weight uncomfortably, her heart stopping cold when his hand slid from her lap, his arm dangling limply toward the ground.

No! It could not be! She clutched at his weight as he tipped precariously in the saddle behind her, struggling to keep him balanced atop the galloping destrier.

Alex twisted in the saddle, her searching fingers finding their way over Armand's shoulder. She froze as her fingertips encountered the shaft of an arrow, her blood running cold when she found no trace of the arrowhead protruding from the smooth muscles.

Armand's head lolled on her shoulder and Alex slapped his cheeks to no avail, her panic rising with every passing moment. Now she noticed his pallor and the faint white bracketing around his lips. Grasping at his hand, she found the telltale blue tinge of his nails beneath the grime.

The arrow had been poisoned.

Alex stared at the unfamiliar countryside with new eyes, her heart pounding in her fear. Where would she go? What could she do? She needed herbs, water and mostly time, for any treatment needed to be administered quickly if 'twere to be effective. The road wound endlessly onward, seemingly devoid of habitation, and she considered stopping Tiberias in his tracks, running the risk that Pièrre's men continued their pursuit.

'Twas Armand himself that made the decision for her, his weight toppling backward unsteadily and Alex unable to stop his fall. She slipped to the ground, catching his shoulders in time, praising the fates for making his foot catch in the stirrup. Now she stood beside the panting Tiberias in the middle of the road, a poisoned knight precariously balanced on her already aching shoulders, and considered what to do.

She tried to ease Armand back to lie across the length of the saddle, but she had not the strength to lift him from her shoulders, and indeed her very knees were threatening collapse beneath his weight. For the first time in her life, Alex cursed her small stature, her hands drawing into tight fists of frustration. No power had she to tend Armand's wound in this position and she considered for a moment what damage would be wrought should she let him tumble to the ground.

The growing sound of racing hoofbeats from the road brought her head up with a snap, but nothing could she do to avoid the approaching riders in her current predicament. Alex's hands shook and she dared not look as the riders crested the small rise ahead, a shout rising from their midst as she was sighted. Tiberias nickered calmly and she cursed his interest in other steeds, burying a kiss in Armand's ear as she admitted her failure to complete their escape.

"Who rides there?" cried a man's voice when the riders slowed before her, and Alex's eyes widened in recognition.

"Guillaume?" she whispered beneath her breath.

"Identify yourself before the knights of Avigny, lest you suffer the consequences of your trespass," the knight continued, his tone more threatening, and Alex fairly wept.

"Guillaume, 'tis you," she cried with relief, standing away from Tiberias that she might be seen. "Armand has been poisoned, you must help me."

"Tell us what to do," Roarke said sharply from behind her, his hands reaching to take Armand's weight from her shoulders.

"The poison must come out," Alex said quickly, her hands pulling at Armand's tunic as Guillaume and two other knights lowered his inert form from the stallion's back. A fur-lined mantle was cast on the ground and Armand deposited there, his back torn bare, Guillaume's dagger in Alex's hand before she could demand it. With one sure stroke she freed the offending arrowhead, tossing it aside and bending to suck at the wound, desperately hoping that she could remove enough poison at this late moment to make a difference.

When Alex straightened to spit, Roarke bent to take her place, drawing venom and blood from the wound while she took a breath.

"What do you need?" Guillaume demanded softly from Alex's side, and she met the uncertainty lurking in his eyes with her own.

"Hot water," she answered, watching the knights spell one another at cleaning the wound, "time and the good wishes of Dame Fortune." So little could she do to counteract the unknown poison. Either 'twould claim Armand's life despite her efforts or he would be strong enough to overpower its claim.

"We make camp here!" Guillaume shouted to his men. "Post sentries and build a fire. 'Tis hot water the lady needs and quickly!" That said, he leaned forward to cover Alex's hand silently with his own as if he would ease her sorrow. Alex tried to summon an encouraging smile for him, but her tears rose instead and he squeezed her hand in reassurance.

"Stronger than you know, he is," he murmured, and Alex bit her lip, closing her eyes against her tears. When the knight crouched over Armand straightened to spit and take a breath, Guillaume bent in his turn to draw venom from his brother's flesh.

By the time the water was ready, the blood was running clear from the angry red welt on Armand's back, but still Alex applied the poultices, hoping to draw more poison from the wound. Armand's breathing was shallow, his color pallid, but still he breathed, and most poisons she knew did their damage swiftly.

The knights rolled him over carefully for her and she tended the ugly gash in his shoulder, pausing in her work to study his face as his head lay in her lap. Would that she had Sophie's skills, Alex thought to herself, brushing the russet waves back from Armand's brow tenderly. So little knowledge had she of poisons.

"How fares he?" demanded Roarke quietly from her side, and Alex looked up at him, noting the concern in his gray eyes.

"I know not," she admitted helplessly, running her fingertips over the stitches she had just made and shaking her head. "Precious little do I know of poison and its ways."

Alex surveyed Armand, sadly stroking his cheek. "Would that Sophie were here," she murmured beneath her breath.

"Sophie de Pontesse?" Roarke demanded sharply, reminding Alex abruptly of his presence at her side. She nodded mutely, surprised when the young knight rose immediately to his feet.

"Guillaume!" he shouted, bringing Armand's brother running to their side, his eyes wide with fear.

"What has happened?" he demanded, clearly fearing the worst, but Roarke laid a reassuring hand on his arm.

"The Lady Alexandria recommends a healer skilled in treating poisons. I would ride to Pontesse to fetch her."

"More than a day's ride each way, 'tis," Alex protested, her heart pounding at the prospect of having Sophie's skill at hand. "She might come too late."

"'Tis well worth the risk," Guillaume decided curtly, clapping Roarke on the shoulder. "Ride safely and meet us at Avigny as soon as you are able."

Over the next week, Armand's wounds sealed closed and he did not die, nor did he awaken, much to Alex's growing despair. They had returned to Château d'Avigny the next evening, having ridden all day at a slow pace, Baudouin's face drawing in pain at the sight of his unconscious son.

Sophie and Hugues had ridden into the courtyard at breakneck pace before the sun reached its zenith the following day, Sophie abandoning her steed in the courtyard and running into the hall in search of her patient. Herbs possessing magical powers she had brought, but Alex was not fooled by her aunt's false bravado before Guillaume, the two women's eyes meeting in silent acknowledgment of the truth.

Never might Armand awake and well Alex knew it. Time 'twould take, should he be destined to recover, and nothing else save some measure of luck, and there was nothing either healer could do to turn the tide.

Margrethe had been gone from the household when Alex returned from Villiers, and nary a word was said about her departure. Guillaume's lips thinned with displeasure when any slipped to mention his wife's name and Alex wondered at what transgression the other woman had made to raise his ire. Happier indeed did the elder brother seem without his wife at his side, much to Alex's surprise, Baudouin and he seeming more at ease with each other's company.

'Twas the fourth day of Armand's undisturbed slumber that Sophie insisted everyone talk to him as if he listened in truth.

"Tales have I heard that this can make a difference," she asserted with a small frown between her blond brows as they all assembled in Armand's chamber to watch the regular rise and fall of his chest. "That such talk can call the lost soul back from its wanderings."

Hugues had studied the floor in apparent understanding that his wife was at a loss. Guillaume frowned skeptically; Roarke raised his brows in surprise. Baudouin had sighed with resignation while Alex stood mute, flicking a glance to Sophie before stepping forward and sitting on the edge of his son's bed.

"Sorely did I miss your hand at the chase this day," the old man began slowly, his voice gaining strength as he warmed to his tale. "Remember you that little clearing near the river where we snared hares when you boys were young? A boar there was this morn, rooting at the earth, and such a mean beast I have never seen in all my days." Baudouin had glanced up to meet Sophie's encouraging smile before turning back to his son as the others had filed out of the room.

The fullness of seven days and nights had passed and still Armand did not stir, Alex's heart weakening in her conviction that he would yet awaken. The sky was dark outside the window as she took her turn to speak with him, as always the last of the day, the spring sounds of birds and bullfrogs carrying to her ears in a muted melody.

Last night she had fallen asleep here and she recalled the absence of any response to her cuddled against Armand's side, his arm remaining limp against the cover instead of curling protectively around her. Now she touched his hand tenderly, having not the heart to fool herself any longer that he listened while she spoke.

So far for naught they had come, Alex reflected, her fingertip tracing a meandering path up Armand's arm as she edged ever closer to his warmth. Despair filled her heart that he had been stolen from her side yet again, his silent form before her ensuring that he could not walk through the door unexpectedly and ease her loneliness. Alex sighed and pushed his shirt aside, checking the healing of his shoulder with absent professionalism. Would that the rest had healed so easily.

She laid her head on Armand's chest, lifting his limp hand to her waist as if he held her there, the steady rhythm of his heartbeat filling her ears as it pounded beneath her. Still his skin carried that dusky masculine scent and she closed her eyes against the barrage of memories, curling up her legs like a little cat, her fingers caressing the pelt of auburn hair that covered his chest.

"I cannot speak to you of Fontaine this night," she whispered softly, once again playing the charade as one heavy tear dropped on Armand's flesh. "No tales of the Loire rumbling by the verdant hills, no arching plane trees stretching to meet each other and cast the road in dappled shadows." Another tear fell and Alex's hands balled into fists of frustration as she felt the oncoming storm.

"No stories have I for you of the château we would build there," she murmured, "its proud keep on the ashes of the old, its pennants snapping in the breeze, its towers smooth and tall. And of russet-haired sons to carry forth the line of your father and mine, I cannot even bear to dream this night." Alex's tears fell now in such rapid succession that she could not count them, her blurred gaze falling to the dark braid encircling Armand's opposite wrist where it lay against the bedclothes.

"Your faithfulness I did desire," she whispered, her tears gathering with renewed vigor, "but never, never at this price." Unable to speak anymore, Alex fell against Armand's chest, her torrent of tears running unabated, her sobs shaking her slender form.

* * *

Armand heard Alex's weeping as though from afar, his mind a blur of dark tunnels and shadowy corridors that he had wandered endlessly in search of light. Her sobs carried to him through the caverns and he sought her there, struggling to find her that he might somehow reassure her. Did she not know that she held his very heart? That he could be entrusted with hers? He fought anew against the darkness that shrouded his vision, the fog lifting slowly from before his eyes.

He became aware of a dampness on his chest and then a slight weight cradled there. The scent of roses filled his nostrils and long tendrils of hair tickled his flesh. He flexed one hand experimentally, surprised to find a pleasing curve fitted beneath it.

"Hush," Armand whispered hoarsely when he found his voice, but Alex's tears flowed unceasingly. He opened his eyes tentatively to find the twilight sky had invaded the room, casting shadows and silhouettes of furnishings and the lady on his chest in shades of indigo.

He lifted his other hand and found her tiny fingers clutching the bracelet she had placed there, extricating her hand carefully that he might slide his own in the soft tangle of her loose hair. Armand closed his eyes and inhaled deeply of Alex's sweet scent, savoring the soft press of her against his side, his arms tightening protectively around her.

"Hush, milady," he murmured again, and her tear-streaked face tipped up suddenly, those brimming azure eyes flying to his, dark lashes wet, rosy lips swollen.

"Armand," she breathed in wonder, seemingly unwilling to believe what she saw, and he lifted one hand to stroke the hair away from her face, his thumb sliding across her smooth cheek to stroke away one last tear.

"Armand," Alex whispered again, and her tears began to flow anew as he hugged her close and rolled her happily to her back.

"Always are you crying, milady," he teased, cupping the side of her face as Alex smiled at him through the shimmer of her tears. "Truly you shall drown us both before the nuptials, should you not cease,'' he murmured, bending to accept the soft invitation of her lips. Armand smiled against her kiss when Alex sighed with contentment and wound her arms around his neck, opening her mouth and inviting him ever closer.

Epilogue

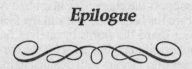

Alex sat on the stone bench in the garden behind the kitchens at Pontesse where she had frolicked as a child, listening to the sounds of merrymaking drift out from the hall. She caught the aroma of cooked meat on the night air and her stomach rolled restlessly, making its objections to her fasting abundantly clear.

Leaning her head back, she watched thin clouds flit across the full moon. By this time tomorrow, 'twill all be over, she thought to herself, trepidation stealing around her heart once more.

Alex sighed and tapped her toes absently against the flagstones as she gazed at the moon, allowing fatigue to slip through her body. A long day it had been, up at dawn to continue preparations for the nuptials and the feast to follow, the party from Avigny arriving just as the sun set. Alex fingered one of the clove pinks entwined with the gold links of her girdle, knowing that tomorrow she would cast aside these tiny betrothal flowers to take her wedding vows.

Not for the first time in recent days, Alex wondered about Armand's feelings, wondered that he had not claimed love for her since that distant night here in her rooms when they had parted so angrily. Maidenly doubts assailed her, nerves no doubt, but she could not help but wish he had told her of his feelings before Baudouin and Hugues announced the contract they had made. Well she remembered Armand's surprise to hear that she was an heiress and too easily did his agreement to wed come, barren of sweet confessions as it was, for her comfort.

Was it possible that he cared for her as he had once said he did?

Such a thought was intoxicating and Alex could easily spin a tale to support the claim, so gallant had Armand always been to care for her needs. But still the fact remained that she had not heard the words themselves fall from his lips of late, the thought making her scuff the toe of her delicate pink slipper into the dirt with dissatisfaction.

Truly Armand had seemed pleased to see her today, she consoled herself, his bright gaze searching her out from among the welcoming party in the courtyard, the warm smile he sent her way melting her knees like butter in the sun. Barely a moment had passed that he had not been attentive at her side, making teasing comments beneath his breath for her amusement, pressing her hand affectionately, his warm green eyes seeming to follow her every move with fascination.

'Twas true that as sole heir to Fontaine she was very eligible, but the thought that he might be marrying her for that alone rankled her pride. Would all between them diminish to dry ashes once the nuptials were performed? Alex sighed and looked around the garden impatiently, resigning herself to the fact that she would probably never know what dwelt within Armand's heart. Was it not enough for her that she was marrying the man she loved?

Footsteps sounded on the path and Alex glanced up, recognizing Armand's silhouette as he strolled toward her. Almost as if she had summoned him by her thoughts, she reflected, watching him approach with a pounding heart. He stopped in front of her and looked up at the moon, its silvery rays playing over his profile as she watched.

"I thought that I might find you here," he said quietly.

"In truth, I could not stand to smell the food any longer," Alex admitted with a rueful smile. Armand chuckled and looked down to meet her eyes as he spoke.

"'Tis a kind of torture, I think, to test your conviction in what you would do," he jested. The smile slipped from Alex's lips at his words and she dropped her gaze to her hands.

"How convinced are you?" she asked quietly, the question that occupied her mind dropping from her lips before she could stop it. Silence fell between them and Alex felt Armand's eyes on her but she refused to look up.

"There is not a doubt in my mind," he answered finally, his voice unusually low. When she did not respond, he sat down beside her, reaching to take her hand in his. Alex looked up at him, surprised to see the solemn expression in his eyes. He watched her carefully for a moment, studying her features as if to memorize them, his thumb stroking the back of her hand all the while.

"Does it not strike you as odd, milady, how many times the paths of our lives have crossed?" Armand asked softly, and Alex shook her head mutely in response, her brow puckering into a frown. Here, Jerusalem, Venice, then here again, 'twould seem indeed to be against the odds.

"Do you think it coincidence?" she asked hesitantly, watching Armand shake his head emphatically.

"Nay, milady, 'tis stronger than that." His eyes met hers again, darkening to a compelling emerald shade as he spoke. "From the first moment I saw you, Alexandria, you touched my heart as no woman has done before or since. I knew that night that you were the only woman who would ever hold me willingly by her side."

Alex's heartbeat accelerated at his words even as she recognized the truth in what he said. Truly no other man had even piqued her interest, let alone touched her very soul as Armand had from that first night. It did indeed seem that something was destined to be between them.

"And each time we part, we are driven back together again," she whispered, acknowledging the truth. She saw a flash of white as Armand smiled in the darkness.

"Indeed we are, milady." He stroked her hand absently as the silence grew between them, a comfortable silence of companionship and contentment. Alex edged closer to him, leaning her head on his shoulder as she watched his fingers, a quiet swell of happiness settling around her, a certitude that he did indeed hold tender feelings for her.

"I owe you an apology," Armand said a few moments later, reaching to tip her chin so that their eyes met again. "Sorry I am that I spoke so harshly to you when we were intimate. I had no right to condemn you out of hand."

Alex felt herself flushing under the warmth of his scrutiny, surprised to find her words faltering in her throat. "I should have told you," she managed to say, and Armand chuckled, flicking the end of her nose affectionately.

"As I recall, I was less than encouraging," he said, his eyes twinkling. "And the timing of my anger less than ideal."

"True enough," Alex acknowledged with a grin. "You did not seem in the mood for confidences." Armand laughed outright and scooped Alex up effortlessly, depositing her squarely in his lap, his expression sobering as his arms stole around her waist.

"I love you, Alexandria," he whispered with utmost seriousness, his gaze running over her features as though he marveled that she was here before him. Alex's heart tripped a staccato at his words and she reached up to touch his face in wonder.

"I love you, milord," she responded shakily. "I think I always have."

Armand nodded mutely at her words and his voice was husky when he finally spoke. "'Tis as if we were looking for one another all of our lives."

Alex's eyes glazed with unshed tears and she buried her face in his throat. "How many times I wished I had not left Pontesse," she whispered huskily, and Armand's arms tightened around her. "We might have courted and wed like civilized souls, instead of the madness of these two years past."

"You have indeed led a merry chase, milady," he teased, and she smiled mistily at his jest. Armand took her chin firmly between his finger and thumb, forcing Alex to meet the steady gaze of his eyes.

"There is naught to regret, Alex," he assured her solemnly. "Perhaps our love is stronger for the trials we have endured."

The words came from his heart and Alex reached to touch his cheek with gentle fingers, feeling the prickly day's growth of his beard beneath her fingertips.

"I expect you are right, milord," she agreed, startled anew by the power of the love thrumming through her.

Armand grinned at her crookedly and cleared his throat. "There is something I would ask you," he began, settling her weight more comfortably in his lap as Alex threw him an enquiring look. "That night in the tavern, you knew not that I was alive?"

"No," Alex whispered, her heart clouding at the memory of the anguish that had swept over her, but Armand gathered her close and gave her a little shake.

"Think not of that," he bade her sternly. "I would know what your words meant." Alex looked up at him in confusion, unable to recall what she had whispered in his ear. *"Au revoir,"* Armand supplied, and she felt a flush rising over her cheeks.

"'Tis nothing really," she said, trying to dismiss his question, "some folly of Sophie's." Alex flicked a glance to Armand to see that she had not deflected his interest, his one brow arching in silent query.

"An old story 'tis," she explained softly, "that when we die, our souls are reborn in new form and that always do we find the ones we love." Alex shrugged in embarrassment and cleared her throat delicately. "Some romantic foolishness 'tis, no more than that."

"No foolishness could make such sense," Armand whispered to her huskily, and she met his eyes tentatively, surprised by the ardor that burned in those green depths. "Should I be so fortunate to live again, be assured, milady, that I will seek you out." With that murmured promise, he bent and tasted her lips, sending the world spinning about her.

* * *

Armand's assertion rang through Alex's mind as she walked toward the chapel the next morning, the crowd of well-wishers gathered around them falling away as she met the steady green of his eyes. For all eternity would their souls be bound together.

Armand stood at the doorway of the chapel watching her approach, his hands folded in front of him as he waited, the sunlight burnishing his hair to bright copper. Alex acknowledged inwardly how splendidly the deep green tunic complemented his coloring, the breadth of his shoulders evident beneath the draping of his ochre mantle.

Baudouin stood slightly behind his son, the older man's stance and build clearly indicating the blood bond between them. Armand's father wore the signature red and white of his house, his long tunic rich with embroidered leopards, the snowy whiteness of his thick hair contrasting sharply with the red of his cloak. Behind Baudouin stood Guillaume, the shortest of the three, the sprinkling of silver already etching the auburn hair at his temples.

Hugues squeezed Alex's fingertips as they reached the steps to the chapel and she glanced up at him, surprised to see a glaze of tears in her uncle's blue eyes. He cleared his throat in discomfort and Alex reached up to press a kiss of silent gratitude against his cheek, stepping before him to similarly embrace Sophie. So much had they done for her and Michel these many years, never could she forget or repay their kindness.

Nibbling nervously on her bottom lip, Alex inadvertently met Armand's eyes again and he smiled, the warmth she saw there easily dismissing the fluttering around her heart.

The priest appeared from inside the church; a plump and balding little man, he moved with fastidious precision, fixing both Alex and Armand with a piercing stare before he nodded curtly. He accepted the rings from Hugues, laying the two circles of gold flat in the palm of his left hand as he bestowed his blessing upon them. Hugues squeezed Alex's fingers reassuringly as the priest asked for the common consent, his voice ringing with conviction as he gave his approval in concert with Baudouin.

"Then let him come who is to give away the bride," the priest intoned, glancing down to Alex as Hugues led her up the last of the steps toward Armand.

"Let him take her by the right hand," the priest continued, "and let him give her to the man as his lawful wife, with her hand covered if she is a maid, with her hand uncovered if she is a widow."

Hugues obediently covered Alex's hand as he passed her to Armand. A tingle rippled down Alex's spine at her first contact with those warm fingers and she flushed, glancing up again to meet the intensity of her betrothed's gaze. Armand took the smaller ring from the priest's outstretched hand, slipping the plain gold band onto Alex's right index finger.

"In the name of the Father," he said, moving the ring to her middle finger, "the Son—" he moved the ring to her third finger "—and the Holy Ghost—" he removed the band again and set it on the ring finger of Alex's left hand "—I take this woman for my wife."

Alex glanced up to meet his eyes, catching her breath at the love evident in Armand's expression as he made his vow, his voice carrying clearly over the assembly.

"With this ring I thee wed, with this gold I thee honor, and with this dowry I thee endow."

Alex lifted the other ring from the priest's palm with unsteady fingers, her words gaining strength as she repeated the vow, placing the ring on three successive fingers of Armand's right hand before placing it on his left hand. She met his eyes as she made her oath, returning his smile as the last words fell from her lips. Armand grasped Alex's hands in his own and leaned forward, pressing a gentle kiss against her forehead.

The priest stepped back, beckoning to Sophie and Hugues to first congratulate the happy couple. Alex slipped her hand through Armand's elbow, her heart tripping with excitement as family gathered around them and voices rose in hearty encouragement.

It was done, she thought, glancing sideways from beneath her lashes to her husband's profile. As if sensing her
eyes on him, he turned to take her elbow and lead her to the
feast laid in the hall.

The wedding banquet was a boisterous affair, the afternoon passing quickly as endless courses of the meal were
served. Wine flowed like water, the voices of the guests
gradually rising in volume, a few happy souls bursting
spontaneously into song in accompaniment of the min-
strels.

One part of the hall had been left clear of tables and some
people danced between courses, Baudouin insisting on
turning an ankle with Alex. He was a surprisingly good
partner and she enjoyed herself thoroughly before they
made their way, breathless and laughing, back to the head
table, her new father-in-law but one of many who claimed
her hand.

The hall darkened gradually as the sun dropped below the
horizon and Alex suddenly found herself surrounded by a
group of giggling women intent on escorting her upstairs.
Alex went along with them good-naturedly, ignoring Armand's chuckle, laughing herself when she glanced back
from the stairs to see him rapidly being surrounding by men
determined to share their sage advice.

Amidst much giggling and fuss, the women helped Alex
out of her crimson kirtle, scrubbing her back in the rose-
scented bath that had been prepared, rubbing creams on her
skin, brushing out her hair. One produced a sheer pink
confection of a night garment that fluttered delicately
around Alex's knees, the fabric concealing little of her nakedness, much to the horrified delight of the women. After
a good deal of teasing and twittering, the women finally
made their departure, their soft laughter fading in the solar
as Alex was left to her own devices.

This room was filled with memories for Alex, it being the
chamber she had occupied for years at Pontesse. The window facing over the gardens drew a smile of recollection to
her lips and she wandered around the small space, touching

this and that, poking at the fire blazing on the hearth, happy anticipation in her future warming her heart.

Finally, she heard footsteps and laughter approaching the room, smiling to herself at the drunken sound of Armand's escorting party. With a start, Alex remembered that the gown she wore was less than modest, a quick glance around the room revealing that her other clothing had been efficiently removed. Alex gasped and dove toward the bed, flinging back the covers and huddling in the darkest corner of the heavily draped piece of furniture just as the door flew open.

A group of men spilled into the room and Alex pulled the covers nervously up to her chin, noting with relief that the men seemed content to badger Armand. He laughed along with them good-naturedly, gradually ushering each and every one back into the hall, closing the heavy door firmly and leaning against it with a sigh. He ran his fingers through his hair and dropped the latch, glancing around the room with interest.

"Milady?" he asked quietly, and Alex sighed with relief, knowing that none of the men had been able to see her from the doorway.

"I am here, milord," she responded, and Armand's eyes flew to hers as he smiled.

"I thought myself alone for a moment, you are so quiet," he teased, moving to the fireplace and holding out his hands to its warmth. As if he sensed her nervousness, Armand half turned away from Alex as he talked conversationally.

"My father has been asking pointed questions about the running of your household," he said after a moment's pause, and Alex sat up with interest, pulling up her knees and folding her arms over them.

"I think he is hinting for an invitation to Fontaine," he added in a confidential tone.

"But 'tis no more than rubble as yet," she exclaimed, and Armand threw her a grin over his shoulder.

"Ah, but my father fancies himself a mason at heart," he commented, his eyes twinkling with mischief. "What think you of having him underfoot throughout the construction?''

Alex gasped, her surprise promptly turning to laughter. ''Surely you jest,'' she insisted, but Armand shook his head, strolling toward her as he unfastened his girdle nonchalantly and laid it aside.

''Meaningless 'twas to explain to him I meant to have you to myself for a time,'' Armand mused thoughtfully. He pulled his tunic over his head and Alex caught her breath at the sight of his bare chest, her heart pounding when he threw her a mischievous grin.

''Once Hugues convinced him that you had learned the 'proper' way to candy elecampane, I thought the day was lost.'' Armand sat casually on the side of the bed, unfastening his garters and removing his hose. He flicked her a confidential look and commented, ''Always did he say that Margrethe made the sweet too hard for his teeth, a sign of her poor breeding asserting itself.''

''He would not!'' Alex laughed and Armand shrugged.

''Well, not before Guillaume, he did not dare,'' he conceded, focusing his attention on his second stocking.

''What happened to her?'' Alex demanded abruptly, drawing Armand's surprised gaze.

''Margrethe?'' he demanded, and she nodded, his brow pulling into an answering frown. ''She left,'' Armand said simply, turning his back to Alex as he stood to remove his chausses.

''That I know, but I would have you tell me why,'' she demanded, but he shook his head.

'' 'Tis of no importance.''

'' 'Tis of great importance should you wish to share my bed this night,'' Alex shot back, grinning when Armand glanced over his shoulder with surprise. His eyes twinkled as he saw her smile and he dove across the bed, splendid in his nudity, and cupped her chin in one hand.

''I shall change your mind,'' he whispered mischievously, and Alex barely had a chance to giggle before his lips closed purposefully over hers.

Alex was warmed from head to toe when Armand pulled away to take a breath, his eyes smoky with intent. She shivered in delight beneath his gaze but did not soften her own demanding regard, Armand shaking his head with a chuckle as he conceded defeat.

"'Twas she who summoned de Villiers," he said quietly, studying her carefully for any tremor of fear. "Guillaume had word from the stable hand she dispatched and cast her from the house, insisting that he would gain a divorce."

"That can be done?" Alex asked wide-eyed, no fear darkening her mind at mention of Pièrre's name. Dead he was and powerless to hurt her again.

"In your case, 'tis impossible," Armand whispered, nuzzling her earlobe with his teeth. Alex chuckled and pushed him away, drawing down the bed linens that covered her and watching Armand's eyes widen with satisfaction. He reached out and reverently cupped one of her breasts with his hand, rubbing his thumb across the nipple that was clearly visible through the gown, his nostrils flaring as the peak hardened and strained against his palm.

"And what did your father say of this?" she prompted breathlessly when he did not continue. Armand met her eyes with confusion for an instant before clearing his throat, his gaze drawn back to the rosy nipple as he continued to stroke it.

"Well deserved but too long in the execution, I believe were his words," he concluded huskily, reaching suddenly to grasp Alex around the waist and slide her effortlessly beneath him. Watching his eyes darken to jade, she parted her lips as she wound her arms around his neck, purring with satisfaction as he gently touched his mouth to hers.

Armand gave her no more than a taste of him before his lips moved to her jawline, tracing a path of kisses to her earlobe. His breath in her ear made Alex shiver and he chuckled at her response, tightening his arms around her as his lips moved leisurely down the side of her neck. Alex sighed and closed her eyes, savoring the languid warmth spreading in her stomach, her fingers lightly caressing the corded strength of her husband's neck and shoulders. Husband, she repeated to herself and smiled in the darkness.

Radiant sunlight filled the solar when Armand awoke and he turned instantly to the woman snuggled in his arms, the silky tendrils of her hair cast across his torso like a net holding him captive at her side. Her left hand lay across his chest, the gold band he had placed there glinting in the sunlight, and his heart surged with possessive pride.

His wife. Stunning she had been the day before, resplendent in crimson as she crossed the bailey with delicate steps, the brilliant color of both his house and marital vows. How its richness had heightened her own coloring as she stood before him in the sunlight, her lips more darkly red, her eyes more vividly blue, the flush on her cheeks a fetching pink.

Armand stroked the hair away from her cheek with a tender finger as images of their lovemaking filled his mind and he marveled at how securely this tiny creature held fast his heart. Alex stirred at his touch, burrowing more determinedly into his shoulder, settling there with a sigh, and he tightened his arms around her protectively, leaning back against the pillows with a contented smile.

The silence of the château testified to the earliness of the hour, the warm golden light of another fine April day filtering through the window. Armand frowned at the recollection of something he had intended to do the night before. Pressing a kiss against his wife's hair, he carefully extricated himself from Alex's embrace without waking her and slipped from the bed, striding to his folded clothes to quickly find his dagger.

Returning to the bed, he pulled back the covers, coaxing Alex to roll out of the hollow delved by his warmth. She murmured unintelligibly to herself, her chemise pulling up to her waist, and Armand admired the luscious curve of her hips for a brief moment.

With a shake of his head, he turned his attention back to his task, sliding the sharp blade of the dagger across the plumpness of his left thumb and holding his hand out over the bed. Half a dozen drops of blood stained the white linen before he slipped the wounded digit into his mouth to stanch the bleeding, pleased with himself for anticipating the last shame Pièrre de Villiers could bring against Alex.

Putting his blade away, Armand hurried back across the chilly floor to the warmth of the bed again, pulling Alex back against his shoulder. He stroked a fingertip leisurely across the fullness of her bottom lip and she murmured his name sleepily. The soft sound set his heart racing and he bent his head, gently kissing her lips. Alex responded instantly, her hands slipping around his neck to pull him closer, her lips parting beneath his own.

For all eternity this woman will be mine, Armand thought to himself in wonder, cupping the side of her face tenderly as he rolled her smoothly beneath him.

Forever was going to be very good indeed.

* * * * *

Following the success of WITH THIS RING and
TO HAVE AND TO HOLD, Harlequin brings you

JUST MARRIED

SANDRA CANFIELD
MURIEL JENSEN
ELISE TITLE
REBECCA WINTERS

just in time for the 1993 wedding season!

Written by four of Harlequin's most popular authors, this
four-story collection celebrates the joy, excitement and
adjustment that comes with being "just married."

You won't want to miss this spring tradition, whether
you're just married or not!

**AVAILABLE IN APRIL WHEREVER HARLEQUIN
BOOKS ARE SOLD**

Harlequin® Historical

We hope you enjoyed your introduction to our March Madness authors and that you will keep an eye out for their next titles from Harlequin Historicals.

Castaway by Laurel Ames—A British shipowner gets more than he bargained for when he becomes "heir-apparent" of a large and zany family.

Fly Away Home by Mary McBride—The story of a half-breed Apache and the Eastern-bred woman who proves to him that their love can conquer all.

Silver and Steel by Susan Amarillas—The western expansion of America's railroads serves as the backdrop for this tale of star-crossed lovers who can't escape their destiny.

The Unicorn Bride by Claire Delacroix—A young woman finds herself married to an enigmatic nobleman veiled in secrets and legends in this French Medieval setting.

Four stories that you won't want to miss. Look for them wherever Harlequin Historicals are available.

HHMMAD

OFFICIAL RULES • MILLION DOLLAR BIG BUCKS SWEEPSTAKES
NO PURCHASE OR OBLIGATION NECESSARY TO ENTER

To enter, follow the directions published. **ALTERNATE MEANS OF ENTRY:** Hand print your name and address on a 3″×5″ card and mail to either: Harlequin "Big Bucks," 3010 Walden Ave., P.O. Box 1867, Buffalo, NY 14269-1867, or Harlequin "Big Bucks," P.O. Box 609, Fort Erie, Ontario L2A 5X3, and we will assign your Sweepstakes numbers. (Limit: one entry per envelope.) For eligibility, entries must be received no later than March 31, 1994. No responsibility is assumed for lost, late or misdirected entries.

Upon receipt of entry, Sweepstakes numbers will be assigned. To determine winners, Sweepstakes numbers will be compared against a list of randomly preselected prizewinning numbers. In the event all prizes are not claimed via the return of prizewinning numbers, random drawings will be held from among all other entries received to award unclaimed prizes.

Prizewinners will be determined no later than May 30, 1994. Selection of winning numbers and random drawings are under the supervision of D.L. Blair, Inc., an independent judging organization, whose decisions are final. One prize to a family or organization. No substitution will be made for any prize, except as offered. Taxes and duties on all prizes are the sole responsibility of winners. Winners will be notified by mail. Chances of winning are determined by the number of entries distributed and received.

Sweepstakes open to persons 18 years of age or older, except employees and immediate family members of Torstar Corporation, D.L. Blair, Inc., their affiliates, subsidiaries and all other agencies, entities and persons connected with the use, marketing or conduct of this Sweepstakes. All applicable laws and regulations apply. Sweepstakes offer void wherever prohibited by law. Any litigation within the province of Quebec respecting the conduct and awarding of a prize in this Sweepstakes must be submitted to the Régies des Loteries et Courses du Quebec. In order to win a prize, residents of Canada will be required to correctly answer a time-limited arithmetical skill-testing question. Values of all prizes are in U.S. currency.

Winners of major prizes will be obligated to sign and return an affidavit of eligibility and release of liability within 30 days of notification. In the event of non-compliance within this time period, prize may be awarded to an alternate winner. Any prize or prize notification returned as undeliverable will result in the awarding of that prize to an alternate winner. By acceptance of their prize, winners consent to use of their names, photographs or other likenesses for purposes of advertising, trade and promotion on behalf of Torstar Corporation without further compensation, unless prohibited by law.

This Sweepstakes is presented by Torstar Corporation, its subsidiaries and affiliates in conjunction with book, merchandise and/or product offerings. Prizes are as follows: Grand Prize—$1,000,000 (payable at $33,333.33 a year for 30 years). First through Sixth Prizes may be presented in different creative executions, each with the following approximate values: First Prize—$35,000; Second Prize—$10,000; 2 Third Prizes—$5,000 each; 5 Fourth Prizes—$1,000 each; 10 Fifth Prizes—$250 each; 1,000 Sixth Prizes—$100 each. Prizewinners will have the opportunity of selecting any prize offered for that level. A travel-prize option, if offered and selected by winner, must be completed within 12 months of selection and is subject to hotel and flight accommodations availability. Torstar Corporation may present this Sweepstakes utilizing names other than Million Dollar Sweepstakes. For a current list of all prize options offered within prize levels and all names the Sweepstakes may utilize, send a self-addressed, stamped envelope (WA residents need not affix return postage) to: Million Dollar Sweepstakes Prize Options/Names, P.O. Box 4710, Blair, NE 68009.

The Extra Bonus Prize will be awarded in a random drawing to be conducted no later than May 30, 1994 from among all entries received. To qualify, entries must be received by March 31, 1994 and comply with published directions. No purchase necessary. For complete rules, send a self-addressed, stamped envelope (WA residents need not affix return postage) to: Extra Bonus Prize Rules, P.O. Box 4600, Blair, NE 68009.

For a list of prizewinners (available after July 31, 1994) send a separate, stamped, self-addressed envelope to: Million Dollar Sweepstakes Winners, P.O. Box 4728, Blair, NE 68009.

SWP-H393